THRIVE

THE GUARDIAN PROTECTION SERIES, BOOK TWO

ALY MARTINEZ

THRIVE
Copyright © 2018 Aly Martinez

ISBN-13:978-1979437721
ISBN-10:1979437726

THRIVE is a work of fiction. All names, characters, places, and occurrences are the product of the author's imagination. Any resemblance to any persons, living or dead, events, or locations is purely coincidental.

Cover Designer: Hang Le
Photography: Wander Aguiar
Editing: Mickey Reed
Proofreader: Julie Deaton
Formatting: Stacey Blake

THRIVE

PROLOGUE

Lark

The day I lost her...

"**A**DMIT IT! YOU PLANTED THAT AMMUNITION IN MY WALL locker," I accused, stepping up until Kurt and I were nose to nose.

"Stop it. Both of you!" Mira cried, her voice trembling as she attempted—and failed—to shove her way between us.

His lips lifted into a slow smile. "I don't know what you're talking about."

Oh, but he did. And the moment my platoon sergeant had found them, I'd wished he'd shot me with those bullets instead.

It was no secret that rules and I didn't get along. I'd been in and out of trouble from the time I was ten. I'd cleaned my act up for the most part, but I was far from the star soldier on post. I'd earned my way onto the radar of every member in my chain of command in one way or another. So, with a history like mine, when a two-hundred-round SAW drum had come up missing, my room was one of the first they had searched. I'd thought nothing of it. I'd had nothing to hide. But lo and behold, there it was, sealing my fate as a *former* member of the U.S. Army.

"You couldn't stand that I was getting my shit together," I snarled. "I was finally soaring and you couldn't handle it."

He laughed. "You think I give one flying fuck what you do? You could fall off a bridge tomorrow and it wouldn't faze me. Hell, I might be willing to give you the final shove. But make no mistake about it: You will be falling off that bridge without my woman."

My body locked up tight, and out of the corner of my eye, I saw Mira's do the same.

He bumped his chest with mine. "Yeah, that's right, motherfucker. I know you have your eyes on my girl. You poor, pitiful bastard. You really thought you could take her from me."

I didn't *think* I could take her. I *had* taken her. Numerous times. And, right then, I wasn't leaving until I'd taken her from him permanently.

Yeah. I knew the rules. Technically, you weren't supposed to fall in love with your best friend's girl. But, if we're talking technicalities, he wasn't supposed to be cheating on her every time his dick got hard, either.

He treated her like shit. And, for reasons I would never understand, she took it as if she had no idea how much better she could do. Not even when I was standing right in front of her.

I'd be lying if I didn't admit that a part of me reveled in the nights I saw him sneaking off with whatever girl he was sleeping with at the time. Because I'd spend those nights sitting by the phone, waiting for her call so I could pick up the pieces of the most amazing woman I'd ever met.

"I don't have to *take* her," I spat into his face. "She always *comes* willingly."

It was a dick thing to say, especially with her standing right there, but I was sick of being the only one who lived in silence.

Every story has two sides.

But, in our case, it had three.

Countless nights, I'd spent hours on the phone with Mira, learning all about Kurt through her eyes. And, by all accounts, he was a selfish prick who didn't even try to hide his cheating ways—but she loved him.

Countless days, I'd spent hours with Kurt at work, learning all about Mira through his eyes. And, by all accounts, she was a jealous, overbearing bitch who wouldn't get off his ass about some bullshit—but he loved her.

And, during every single minute between those exchanges, I tried to figure out a way to make her mine without losing the only family I had left—because I loved them both.

Kurt Benton and I had grown up in the same small town of Driverton, Illinois, albeit in very different income brackets. His was upper class. Mine was somewhere around the poverty line, depending on how often my dad's gout had acted up that year. We'd met in sixth grade, when the school district had decided to mix things up by bussing some of the poor kids to the public school across town. Kurt was the big-mouthed king of campus who wanted the entire world to bow at his feet, and I was just a kid from the wrong side of the tracks who stirred up shit because it was the only way I knew to make people pay attention to me.

The two of us were a match made in hell. But, somehow, it worked. Kurt kept me from getting into too much trouble, and I kept him in enough to keep him from being bored. The Bentons eventually adopted me. Well, not literally, but his mom took to making me lunch every day and his dad started driving me to and from school. Throughout high school, I spent more time at the Bentons' house than I did my own, which was probably the only reason I didn't end up in jail.

When we graduated, Kurt had the whole world in front of him, while my options were limited to follow in my father's footsteps and get a job at the chicken plant or join the Army. It was an easy choice—for me anyway.

Kurt's parents lost their mind when he told them that he hadn't gotten into a single college he'd applied to. Secretly, I knew that was because he hadn't applied to *any*, but I sure as shit didn't mention that to the Bentons.

We went to Basic Training together, struggled through Ranger School together, and got assigned to the same battalion together. Up until then, the farthest we'd been apart was when he'd been sent to Charlie Company while I was two barracks over in Alpha Co.

We were as tight as two people could get.

Or had been.

Before Mira.

If only I'd found her first. We all could have been spared.

Kurt had met Mira York one fated night after he'd gone solo "dumpster diving." This was what he'd not so affectionately called hitting the shithole bar next to the low-income housing on the other side of town. He loved to prey on the broken ones. The ones who were eager for a way out and acted like they'd seen Jesus because he'd pulled up in a fancy truck, throwing his parents' fifties around like pennies.

Yeah. Okay. He was an asshole. I'd known it even back then, but he was all I'd had. And, because of that, he was all I couldn't afford to lose.

It's crazy how one person out of the billions on this planet can change the entire trajectory of your life. But that was exactly what had happened the day Kurt walked into my room in the barracks with Mira on his arm. She was young, nineteen to our twenty-three, but she had this way about her that was so damn cool. She was gorgeous, but she was also funny and down to earth. She made it feel like I was hanging out with one of the guys, but she looked like my wildest fantasy.

However, she was Kurt's. Off-limits. And I never would have crossed that line.

Until the line got so blurred it became unrecognizable.

The three of us started hanging out—a lot. Sometimes the other guys from our squad came with us. Sometimes she brought her friends and tried her hand at setting me up. None of those girls worked out. They always had one major flaw I couldn't get over.

They weren't Mira.

It didn't take long before she and I started hanging out on our own. She didn't have a car, so I'd occasionally give her a ride home from her job waitressing at the bar when Kurt had CQ or Staff Duty. And then it became more common, like dinner and drinks, when his company went out for weeklong field exercises. It wasn't a secret that we were close. The two of us had more in common than either of us had with Kurt.

We were cut from the same cloth. Laughed at the same jokes. Dreamed of one day rolling in a pile of cash.

We used to drive out to the woods, drop the tailgate, stare up at the stars, and discuss how we'd spend the imaginary millions we were going to make one day.

Our relationship was innocent—at first.

And then it wasn't.

One day, while Kurt was in the shower, she found pictures of him with another woman. She brought them straight to me and demanded answers as if I could control the man's dick. Yeah, I'd known he wasn't exactly the most faithful guy in the past, but it had never mattered to me before. I was his friend, not his keeper.

I subtly told her to leave him.

The following day, I not so subtly told him to leave her.

They both ignored me—until the next time.

And, with Kurt, there was always a next time. It got to the point that I didn't even feel bad for wanting her the way I did.

I kissed her one night while we were throwing back beers at our spot in the woods. She slapped me. I lied and told her I was drunk. Considering I'd had one beer, she didn't buy it, but she let it go.

Two weeks later, same place, more beer, heat lightning flashing all around us, *she* kissed *me*.

"In another life, we would have been soul mates," she murmured against my lips.

I wasn't sure why we'd have to wait for another life. We had a perfectly good one in front of us. But, as she moved her hands under my shirt, I didn't bother asking questions.

After that night, we didn't discuss it. We didn't label it. We just kept going back to that place where only the trees and the thunder witnessed our betrayal.

I fell in love with Mira York in the back of that truck, one stolen kiss at a time.

The only problem was: She kept going back to him.

And nothing changed between them.

They'd get into a fight. He'd go downtown trolling. She'd inevitably find out. She'd call me crying. I'd go pick her up. It'd start with us talking and laughing. It'd end with her soft, naked body pressed to mine. The next day, Kurt would tell me all about his night, explaining in great detail how he'd gotten the claw marks on his back. I'd smile and pretend that I cared. And then, the following weekend, when they'd show up at the bar, arm in arm, stealing kisses while I stole side-glances, I'd silently wonder how long I'd have to wait until we could start the process all over again.

For six months, I swore the next time would be different.

For six months, I swore to myself I'd take her from him once and for all.

For six months, I was a coward, too afraid to risk losing my best friend, even if it meant gaining her.

Until the night when I'd had enough.

In the span of twenty-four hours, the whole world had rained down on my shoulders. The only identity I'd ever had to be proud of had been snatched away from me. And, like most things in my life, Kurt was responsible.

So, with nothing left to lose, I'd gotten drunk, driven to the apartment they shared, and dumped what felt like an eternity of lies and deceit at the feet of my former best friend.

Mira once again tried to push between us.

A sinister grin grew on his lips as he cocked his head to the side. "You already fucked her?"

I swayed away from him, the effects of the alcohol in my system finally burning through the adrenaline. "More times than I can count."

"What the hell, Jeremy!" Mira yelled, shoving hard on my shoulder.

I kept my gaze leveled on Kurt. His shoulders tensed, but his grin never faltered, not even as his fist soared through the air and landed square on my jaw.

I vaguely remembered Mira screaming as I stumbled back and landed on my ass. The pain in my face didn't register amongst the clusterfuck going on in my head.

"Kurt, stop!" she yelled.

His lean body followed me to the ground, and his fist once again smashed against my face.

I had him in size, always had, but the bottle of Jack I'd downed on my way to their apartment gave him the edge.

"You son of a bitch. I should have left your ass in the trailer park where you belong."

I rolled to the side, flipping him off me. "You think you got us here?" I slammed my hand into his mouth, splitting his lip. "*I* got us here." I straddled him, pinning him to the ground with my weight, and pounded down on him again. "You'd still be jerking your dick in your parents' basement if it weren't for me."

He tried to defend himself, but I was too far gone to let anything slow me.

Kurt Benton had everything I'd always wanted in life.

Yet he'd stolen away the little I'd had left.

My hands flew through the air, connecting punch after punch, driven by a blinding rage even as his body fell limp.

It was like an out-of-body experience. The day before, I would have murdered a man if he'd so much as looked at Kurt wrong.

But there I was, releasing the fury of the unfair universe on his face.

"Jeremy, please!" Mira cried, pulling on my arm. She dropped to her knees and moved into my line of sight. "Just look at me."

My drunken eyes shifted on command.

Even with tears streaming down her face, she was easily the most beautiful woman I would ever see. She was tall and thin, but her large breasts and round ass had more than enough curves to keep a man busy for the rest of his life. And, every day for the last six months, I'd hoped that man would be me. Her long, dark hair hung over her shoulders, and I knew all too well the way it felt when it brushed my chest as she curled in close.

But, with Mira, it was all about her eyes. She had these big, innocent, brown eyes that drew you in and held you captive. They were surrounded by thick, black lashes that could seduce you with a single blink. It was the most amazing combination of sweet and sexy that made men lose their fucking minds.

And God knew she'd made me lose mine.

"Get off him!" she pleaded. Her hand shook as she lifted it to her mouth, her gaze drifting to Kurt's bloody and battered face. "Oh, God."

I swallowed hard, my chest heaving and my heart racing, but there wasn't an ounce of guilt to be found.

Pushing off his unconscious body, I struggled to keep the adrenaline shakes out of my legs as I stood. "Come with me."

She scoffed, tears rolling down her cheeks as she backed away. "Are you insane?"

"Yes." I took another step toward her. "Mira, please. Let's go, baby."

She shook her head. "Go home, Jeremy."

I barked a humorless laugh. "I don't have a home anymore. All I have left is you."

Her eyes nervously flashed down to Kurt before she choked out, "What are you talking about?"

I slapped a hand over my heart. "Me. You. We can finally be together."

She blinked, her whole beautiful face transforming with confusion. "What?"

"Come with me. We'll go to the mountains and start a life. Leave him and all this other bullshit behind. Let him suffer for a change."

Dawning hit her eyes. "So *he* can suffer," she repeated. "Because you think he put that ammunition in your wall locker?"

I stepped forward. "I don't fucking think, Mira. I know he did. He found out about us, and he set me up. He's taken everything from me. I'll be damned if I'm going to let him keep you."

"Keep me?" she whispered. Pressing her lips together, she stared up at me, her dark-brown eyes filling with tears. "Riddle me this, Jeremy. If today hadn't happened, would you be standing here right now? Asking me to come with you? Telling Kurt exactly how easily I *come*? How you've fucked me more times than you can count?"

With two long strides, I closed the distance between us. Her body flashed stiff when I curled my hand around the back of her neck. "No, but—"

And then I lost her.

"Then no!" she exploded. "You'll have to forgive me for not rushing inside to pack my bag with an offer like that."

"Oh, because his offer is better?" I shot back. "Fancy apartment. Fancy clothes. Fancy car. Forget about the fact that he's out cheating on you every weekend. You've finally found your first-class ticket out of town, huh?"

Her glare became murderous. "That is not fair!"

I swung my arm out to the side, anger radiating through me with every slam of my heart against my ribs. "Then get in my fucking truck, Mira. Show me I'm wrong."

She barked a laugh, tears rolling from her eyes. "Are you seriously standing there, calling me a gold digger, and then asking me to come with you in order to prove I'm not? Wow." She shook her head, pausing to use her shoulders to dry her eyes. "Every girl's dream."

Guilt corroded my insides. "Mira, baby, I didn't mean it like that."

She rolled her shoulders back and lifted her chin high. "I don't give a fuck how you meant it. You don't know me as well as you think." She walked over to Kurt and kneeled beside him. "Goodbye, Jeremy."

"Mira," I whispered, my chest constricting until I could barely breathe.

"Leave!" she screamed. Cradling Kurt's head, she settled on the ground until it was in her lap. "Make your own life. Do something great with it. But stay out of ours."

"Mir—"

"Go!" she roared, her voice echoing off the surrounding buildings.

My stomach knotted, and I stood there, blinking at her. My heart screamed for me to drag her into my arms and force her to come with me and live the rest of her natural life by my side—where she belonged.

But it was my mind that told me she was right to choose him. I had nothing to offer her. Kurt had made sure of that.

But, damn it, nobody in the world could love her like I would.

It just wasn't enough.

"Mira," I pleaded one last time.

She looked up at me, but she didn't utter a word.

Her silence was the loudest answer of all.

Numb, and not because of the alcohol, I walked back to my truck. My head pounded and my gut churned, but it was the hollow ache in my chest that I knew was going to be permanent that hurt the most.

CHAPTER ONE

Mira

Seventeen years later...

"DOES THE RENT COVER ANY UTILITIES?" I ASKED, WALKING around the small apartment. Given the shit-tastic exterior, I wasn't expecting much from the inside. But it was surprisingly clean and in our price range, and it didn't have a naked man passed out in the breezeway like the last complex we'd looked at.

Doug, the middle-aged man with a comb-over that would make the Trump family proud, leaned his elbow on the bar dividing the small living room from the smaller kitchen. "Are you planning to illegally splice cable off Terry in 3D?"

I twisted my lips. "Absolutely not."

He righted himself, shoved his hands into his pockets, and strolled in my direction. "Then no. It doesn't include any utilities."

I shifted my pink Gucci bag to my other arm. It was one of the few possessions I'd managed to sneak out before the Feds had seized everything three years earlier. Before then, I'd had a house with a walk-in closet three times the size of that apartment full of designer labels. Now, the only labels in my clothes were from places that doubled as grocery stores. But I couldn't complain. I was happier than I had been in years. Hell, maybe ever.

Okay, not necessarily *ever*. There had been a few years there before everything had fallen apart.

"We'll take it!" Whitney shouted as she walked inside.

I spun to face her. "But we haven't looked at the bedrooms yet."

She leaned around me and asked Doug, "Are there four walls, a door, a ceiling, and a floor in the bedrooms?"

He quirked an eyebrow. "Last I checked."

She swung her gaze back to mine and smiled. "Then, like I said, we'll take it."

There was no arguing with Whitney. And let's be honest, it was the nicest thing we'd seen all week.

Doug shifted his gaze to mine. "Should I draw up the lease?"

"Uhh…" My chest tightened and my stomach wrenched.

There was no reason to be scared. This move was a good thing. Whit and I had been saving every penny we'd had for over a year to get out of the one-step-above-a-crack-house we were currently sharing with two other women, both of whom were strippers. Not that there was anything wrong with stripping. It was honest work. But Sherri and Tammy should have hung up their thongs and pasties about twenty years and seven pounds of cocaine earlier. But I had to give it to 'em. They always paid their rent on time, and on more than one occasion, one of them had covered my portion until payday.

But, even with as sweet as they were, Whit and I wanted more.

A new apartment was just the first step in finding that. We were getting new jobs and new friends, and we had vowed to get new hair-styles—though I was starting to reconsider my promise to go blond. It was a new phase in our lives, filled with endless possibilities. Or so I told myself every morning when I'd wake up alone and in a panic.

I'd never been good with change. If it had been up to me, I'd probably still have been in Alabama, regardless how much I'd wanted to escape. Fear was like that. It paralyzed me to the point that even my smallest hopes and dreams seemed out of reach. But, for three years, I'd been doing everything in my power to ignore the dark part of my brain that so often sabotaged me.

It was time for a change. Up to that point, I had little to show for my life. I was a thirty-six-year-old divorcée with no kids, no education, no house, an old-as-sin Toyota Camry that had already been roughly old as sin when I'd bought it, a job as a bartender in a hole-in-the-wall bar in Chicago. Oh, and a Gucci purse I had smuggled out of my house one week after my husband had been arrested.

Yeah…it was *definitely* time for a change.

I flashed Whitney a tight smile. "Bitsy would love this place."

"Bitsy? I thought it was just the two of you?" Doug asked.

"It's her dog," Whitney replied. Her long, raven hair brushed her back as she walked to the window to peer out at the slab of crumbling concrete they had advertised as a patio.

"Oh, no way. Dogs are *not* allowed."

"What?" we exclaimed in unison.

"Nope. No way. No how," Doug replied. "No pets allowed. That includes dogs, cats, birds, hamsters, gerbils, guinea pigs, regular pigs, chickens, goats, or really farm animals of any kind—"

Whitney's eyebrows shot up. "Farm animals?"

He shrugged. "You would be surprised by what people try to get away with. But make no mistake about it: This is a one hundred percent pet-free zone."

Whitney's gaze slid to mine, worry carved in her delicate features. "Not even a teeny-tiny Chihuahua?"

"Especially not a teeny-tiny Chihuahua. Nobody wants to hear one of those damn things yipping all hours of the night."

"But the ad said pets were negotiable with a deposit," I interjected.

He rolled his eyes and waved me off. "Pets *are* negotiable. Fish. You can have a fish." He started past me to the front door, but then he suddenly stopped. "*One* fish. Don't get crazy and act like you are building the Illinois aquarium. One fish. In a bowl. Nothing more."

"Come on. Please. I promise she's a good dog." I folded my hands in prayer, purposefully pressing my boobs together in a way no man could miss.

His gaze didn't even drop. God, I was getting old.

"The only good dog in a rental property is no dog." He hitched his thumb to the door. "Let's go. No sense standing here, arguing about a dog. I've got another, *pet-free* couple interested anyway. You might have better luck across town at Harrington Village. I think they allow cats."

I drew in a deep breath and closed my eyes. I couldn't do this to Whitney. Not because of Bitsy.

Whitney Sloan was an amazing woman and an even better friend. We'd met two years earlier when we'd been working at a night club in downtown Chicago. She was a go-go dancer, and I was a bartender forced to prance around in a barely there skirt and tube top. It was exactly as glamorous as it sounded, and my stint there was short-lived. But Whitney was the one person I refused to leave behind. She was only twenty-one at the time, but in a lot of ways, I looked up to her. She was young, but she was passionate about doing something big with her life. And she didn't take the cop-out like I had when I had been her age. She didn't need to ride anyone else's train out of town. She simply pulled up her big-girl panties and worked her ass off to put herself through college. She was currently in her last year, and she needed this apartment more than I did.

The house we were currently sharing was loud, and with four of us in the little over a thousand-square-foot space, someone was always coming or going. She worked long hours at the club and spent longer hours studying for classes. She needed a home where she could relax and focus on her schoolwork so she could graduate and succeed. And, in some weird way, I needed her to succeed to prove to myself that it was possible for people like us—even if it was too late for me.

And, for this reason alone, I said, "We'll take it."

Her eyes grew wide, and her face paled. "Mira, no. We can keep looking."

"You know we aren't going to find anything better in our price range," I replied.

"But what about Bitsy?" she whispered.

Bitsy was my entire life. All three pounds of her. She was a black-and-white Chihuahua that could fit curled up in both of my palms.

I'd adopted her the day my divorce was finalized. Back then, I could barely afford to feed myself, much less pay for a dog, but when I'd seen her tiny little face on Craigslist, I had known I had to have her. I had been mourning the loss of a life I'd created for myself—I'd deserved a damn dog if I'd wanted one.

I shot her a pained smile and choked out, "We'll find her a good home."

Doug swung his head between us.

Whitney gasped. "I can't let you do that."

I walked over and took her hand in mine. "Honey, don't worry about me. Okay? You need this place. We've been looking for a long time and this is the first place I've seen you excited about. Bitsy will be fine. We'll talk to Sheila next door about keeping her. You know she loves that dog."

She stared at me for a beat and then threw her arms around my neck. "Oh, Mira. Thank you so much. I'll make it up to you. I promise."

I smoothed her curly, black locks down and tucked her face into the curve of my neck, murmuring, "I know you will."

Doug leaned back inside the door. "So, is that a yes?"

I released my best friend and nodded. "It's a yes. We'll take it."

He clapped his hands. "Perfect. I'll go draw up the lease." He threw his arms wide and waved them around the room. "Welcome home, ladies."

Home. I didn't know what that word meant anymore. I'd realized over a decade earlier that *home* wasn't a location, but rather a state of mind. I'd had a lot of houses. Big ones. Small ones. Expensive ones. Ones that should have been condemned. But never, not in any of them, had I found a sense of belonging. It was always just a place to rest my head. This would be no different.

Once the door had clicked behind him, Whitney looked at me and smiled. "I can't believe we actually found a place."

I nodded, sweeping my gaze through the small space while mentally arranging the limited amount of furniture we owned. "It's actually pretty nice too. I think we'll like it here."

She hooked her arm through mine. "No. It's definitely not nice, Mira. It's *okay*. And we will both live here *temporarily*. I don't want you getting too comfortable and setting down roots in a place like this. You have bigger and better things on the horizon. I can feel it."

I laughed. "You're sweet. But I'm thirty-six. The only thing on the horizon is mixing fiber into my morning oatmeal."

She sauntered to the kitchen and started inspecting all the drawers. "Fine, but you aren't mixing your fiber into your oatmeal in this apartment. You're going to do it in a nice house. With a nice man. And a nice life."

I'd had that once. Way back when. Okay, at least I'd had the nice house part. The rest was up for debate. But I'd made that life for myself. I'd chosen it. I had no right to wallow in self-pity for the way everything had turned out.

"You want to start moving our stuff over this weekend?" I asked.

Her eyes lit. "Hell yeah. I don't care if we have to sleep on the floor and snuggle for warmth until we can borrow Glenn's truck. I want out of that damn place."

"Glenn?" I drawled with mock horror. "What happened to sexy dimple guy?"

She sighed. "Don't get me started on Dimples. He didn't even know my name before he declared I was his woman and shall forevermore bow down at his feet."

I gave her a side-eye. "Bow down at his feet?"

She met my side-eye with her own. "Okay, he might not have said those exact words, but a man is in my life two weeks, demands I quit my job, and tries to make me move into the other side of his duplex? Trust me—bowing down at his feet was only one weekend away."

I laughed. "He was right, ya know?"

Her mouth fell open. "And he never even met you but he somehow got my best girl on his side too? Oh, hell no. He had to go. I don't care how pretty he is."

"Apparently, you do care how pretty he is, because every single time we talk about him, you end it with, 'I don't care how pretty he is.'"

She glared, but it packed no heat. She knew I was right.

Changing the subject, she propped her hip against the counter and grinned at me. "By the way, that was a nice touch about giving Bitsy away to Sheila. I almost believed you until I remembered we don't know anyone named Sheila."

I laughed. "That man has lost his damn mind if he thinks I'm getting rid of Bit-Bit. I would get rid of you before I gave that dog away."

"Hey!" she laughed.

"He won't even know she's here. We can sneak her inside in the Gucci. But, if he does find out, I'll figure something out. I don't want you to stress about it, okay?"

She offered me a warm smile. "Okay. I promise."

"Come on. Let's look at the bathrooms."

"Ohhh." She threw her head back and moaned. "Say it again."

My grin stretched wide. "Bathroomsssssss."

"Oh my God. This is better than foreplay," she breathed. "No more getting ready while you're in the shower or peeing while you brush your teeth."

"Oh, please. Don't act like you won't be sneaking in to use my shampoo."

She crossed her arms over her chest, but her smile grew. "Not any more often than you'll be sneaking into mine to use my curling iron."

"Touché." I laughed and hooked my thumb toward the hall. "Come on."

She stared at me, her lips forming a thin line. "You sure you're okay with this? This place…" She motioned around the living room. "It's really going to cut into your bar fund."

"I know. But I've got time. Besides. I still haven't heard back from the bank. Who knows. I might get the loan."

I'd been jumping through a million hoops for the last month while applying for a small-business loan. I had a ton of experience running my own place from when Kurt and I had been married, but funding one was a different story altogether.

She walked over and looped her arm with mine. "I feel good

things in our future, Mir. This apartment. Your bar. Me finishing school. And it's only going to get better for us."

I swallowed hard and pulled her in for a side squeeze. I didn't necessarily agree with her.

But, then again, it wasn't like it could get worse.

CHAPTER TWO

Lark

Three months before I lost her...

"**Y**OU'RE CRAZY AS HELL," I LAUGHED, CRUSHING AN EMPTY BEER can before throwing it into the almost empty Styrofoam cooler.

"Tell me you wouldn't want a hot tub in your bedroom?" she asked, her mouth split into a hypnotizing smile.

I'd been under her spell for so long that I never wanted to wake up.

But I would.

In a few hours, when I was forced to drive her home and watch her walk to the front door, unsure of when or if I'd ever get her back.

Being on the wrong side of a love triangle was slippery like that.

Ignoring the ache in my chest, I shot her a grin, popped another beer open, and passed it her way. "Hot tub belongs on the back deck overlooking the mountains, not tucked away in a bedroom."

She arched her thin, brown eyebrow and stared down at the beer. "Why do you always do that?"

"Do what?" I asked.

"Pass it to me for the first sip."

I rested my elbows on my legs, which were dangling over the tailgate of my pickup, and cut my gaze to the woods. "No reason."

"Bullshit," she laughed.

As she reached across me to take the beer, her breasts brushed *against my arm.*

My shoulders locked up tight. There wasn't much of Mira's body I hadn't touched. I'd kissed, licked, and memorized her every curve. But I'd never instigated it. Not since the first time.

I was always a more-than-willing participant, but I needed her to make the first move and choose what was going to happen between us that night.

Or, more accurately, I needed her to choose me.

And, right then, as she inched over until our thighs were touching and looped her arm with mine, that was exactly what she had done.

In that moment, Kurt wasn't between us.

On the back of that truck, Mira was mine.

A small smile played at my lips as I looked up at her.

Her long, dark hair fell into her face as she rested her head on my shoulder and snuggled in close.

"You drink too slow. And you dump it out when it gets too warm," I said, sweeping her hair over her shoulder so I could see her better. "If we share one, you always have a cold beer and I don't have to watch you water the pine needles with my hard-earned cash."

Her eyes twinkled in the moonlight as she took a sip and then passed it back. "Fair enough, but why do you always give me the first sip?"

I shrugged.

"Be careful. I might confuse you for a gentleman, Jeremy Lark. Next thing you know, you're going to be opening car doors for me and shit."

I chuckled and allowed my gaze to flick down to her breasts. "Trust me. I'm no gentleman, Mira."

It was a partial lie. Because, while I wasn't exactly a gentleman yet, for Mira, I would have become a fucking unicorn if that was what she'd wanted me to be.

She peered up at me, all humor vanishing from her eyes. "I call bullshit again."

"Oh yeah? Well, how about this for a gentleman?" I reclined into the bed of the truck, resting the beer on my chest and my head on a

rolled-up T-shirt, but there was nothing relaxed about the knot in my stomach. The truth always made me nervous. Mira knew everything about me—except for how much I loved her. The rejection was too much for a guy like me to risk. "I give you the first sip because, when I started doing it, I wanted you more than I've wanted anything in my life. And that one damn sip was the only way I could taste you." Nervously, I glanced at her from the corner of my eye.

Her infectious smile faded and surprise lit her face.

I took a sip before setting the beer on the tire well we so often used as an end table. "It's habit now, I guess."

Suddenly, she threw a leg over my hips and straddled me. Folding forward, she palmed either side of my face and pressed a deep, closed-mouth kiss to my lips.

I gripped her hips and sucked in, desperate to inhale her, to absorb her, to make myself a part of her the way I knew she would always be a part of me.

"You can taste me whenever you want, Jeremy," she murmured against my lips.

But she was so fucking wrong. "Whenever I wanted" meant every minute of every day.

Not the secret moments we had in the woods.

Not the late-night phone calls.

Not the stolen kisses when no one was looking.

I wanted Mira York all day, every day, for the rest of my life.

I'd dared to dream that, one day, I'd have that.

Though the stabbing pains in my chest told me otherwise.

"Unfortunately, that's not the way this works, baby," I whispered.

Her eyes flashed dim, and she cut them off into the distance. "No. I guess it's not."

"But I got you right now, don't I?" I murmured, rolling my hips so my cock pressed into her core.

She gasped.

Moving my hand to her chin, I turned her head back to face me. "So dip that sexy mouth of yours down here and give me a sample before

I forget what you taste like."

She kissed me deep and slow until there wasn't a chance in hell I'd ever be able to forget her.

Even when I would need to.

When she pulled away, she planted her hands on my chest and stared down at me as though she were waiting for a response.

I had no answers. I didn't even know the question.

Desperate to keep my overflowing emotions locked away, I went for a subject change. "A hot tub in your bedroom is a terrible idea."

Sniffling for reasons I couldn't fathom, she replied, "You can't get naked on the deck, dummy."

I smirked and slid my hands up her sides, allowing my thumbs to glide over the curve of her breasts. "I can. Even the mountains deserve a good show every now and again."

She giggled. "So, we're living in the mountains, huh?"

That pain in my chest spread like a wildfire over my body. Her words pierced through me, allowing an avalanche of hope to douse reality.

We.

Stunned, I stared at her, the moon lighting her from the back, her dark hair cascading over her shoulders.

I had no words. At least none I could tell her.

I love you.

Leave him.

Be with me.

When I failed to say anything, she snagged the beer and took a pull. "I didn't mean to insinuate… I'm sorry." Passing it my way, she avoided my gaze and asked, "What mountains?"

The beer never made it to my lips. I moved quick, setting it down and rolling her all at the same time. She laughed as I gently laid her down and settled my hips between her legs, careful not to give her too much of my weight.

And then, just before I kissed her, I told Mira York the most honest thing I would ever say to her.

"Any of them."

Present day…

"Motherfucker!" I grumbled as I dove across the hood of a Prius parked on the curb.

My fingertips skimmed the back of his black Polo shirt as he darted out of my reach.

"Go left! I'll cut him off at the back of the building!" Johnson yelled, storming past me, his black-tattooed arms pumping at his sides as he disappeared around the corner.

The sound of feet thundering against concrete behind me made me whirl around in time to see Jude's blond, chin-length hair flapping in the breeze.

"You get him?" he asked as he slowed to a stop in front of me and offered me a hand.

I clasped it and pulled myself up. "Does it look like I got him, Fabio?" I brushed the dirt off my navy slacks. Those damn things had cost me a mint, and the price tag hadn't been off them for a full three hours. If there was one thread out of place, I was going to nail that punk to the wall.

"No, it looks like all buck-fifty of him put you on your ass," he smarted back.

"That little shit is fast."

Jude chuckled. "Or your old ass is getting slow."

"My old ass?" I repeated, incredulous. I was a big guy at six three, two sixty, but Jude was tall as all hell and I had to crane my head back to glare at him.

He grinned and shoved a hand into the pocket of his perfectly pressed slacks. "Retirement's just around the corner."

I scoffed and slapped my hard chest. "Fool, you didn't look this good at twenty-one. Talk to me when you turn forty. I'll still be running circles around you."

As one of the oldest members of Guardian Protection Agency, I heard this bullshit a lot. I didn't take it to heart. Trust me. When it came to bullshit, I gave as good as I got.

I pushed up onto my toes and narrowed my eyes on his forehead. "Is that a receding hairline coming in?" It wasn't. The man had a mane.

"What?" he barked, lifting his hand to pat the top of his hair as if he could catch the strands before they fell out.

I shook my head and laughed, muttering, "Dumbass."

He twisted his lips and jutted his chin to the back of the building. "You think we should go help catch him?"

"Nah." I pointed to the front door of Murphy's bar, which was only a few feet away, and then down the block to where Guardian's southern beast known as Alex Pearson was standing at the other corner of the building. "Johnson'll smoke him out eventually. All points of exit are covered."

Jude nodded and ran a hand under his hair, where thick scars covered the back of his skull. We all knew how he'd gotten them, but we didn't talk about those. Not even to give him shit. It wasn't fun if the jokes actually shredded the guy.

"How's Rhion?" I asked.

His lips twitched almost imperceptibly. They did that any time anyone mentioned his girl. He loved that woman something fierce, which was good because Rhion Park had been a part of Guardian long before Jude. There wasn't a man in the entire agency who wouldn't destroy him if he even thought of hurting that crazy woman.

"She's good. Working on a new book." He paused and fisted his hands on his hips. "She is going to lose her shit when we haul Apollo in like this."

My eyebrows drew together. "Leo didn't talk to her first?"

"Nope. And, I'll be honest, I'm not sure I agree with this, either." He shrugged. "But he's the boss. So here I am."

"So here we *all* are," I corrected. "This isn't on you. Leo didn't talk to her first. She finds out about this, you make sure *she* talks to *him* first."

Jude shook his head and folded his arms over his chest. "How'd court go this morning?"

I groaned. "It went about as well as a court date with your ex-wife who wants to double her child support can go."

"Ouch."

"It was a crock of shit. But I try to keep her happy. For the girls. That 'happy wife, happy life' shit doesn't end because you get a divorce."

"I feel you. Val isn't even mine and I swear I spend more money keeping April happy just so I can keep visitation than I would if I were paying child support."

I laughed. "You put a ring on Rhion, money wouldn't be an issue. Word is she's loaded."

His eyes flashed dark. "Is that why you married Melissa? Word is her family has *plenty* of money too."

"Nope. I married Melissa because I thought she was sweet, had her head on straight, gave it to me good between the sheets, and we were both getting older, so we agreed to start a family ASAP. Three years later, we divorced because she was *not* sweet anymore, her head was so fucking crooked it was a wonder she could walk straight, she started manipulating me before she gave it to me good between the sheets, and I was thirty-nine with two little girls to look out for. But Rhion is *not* Melissa. The two of you have been together for over a year with no signs of slowing down. There a reason you're holding out?"

He raked a hand through the top of his hair. "Jesus Christ. When did we become sorority sisters?"

"I'm just stating the facts. With a woman like that, you don't solidify what you got, another older and wiser man might come along and try to slip his way in there."

His chin jerked to the side. "Are you fucking kidding me here?"

I grinned wolfishly. "I'm just sayin'… My girls love her. And the other day, when she came into the office in those heels—"

His body turned rock solid, and it was a miracle of epic proportions that I managed to keep my laughter locked down.

"Do not finish that fucking thought," he growled.

I lifted my hands in surrender, but my smile grew. "All right. All right. But don't say I didn't warn you."

He jabbed a finger in my direction. "You stay the hell away from my woman, asshole."

It was too easy to fuck with Jude. Sometimes I honestly felt bad about it. This was *not* one of those times.

"Okay. Okay." I took a step away. "But for real. You two got plans tonight? Because I was thinking maybe she and I—"

He lunged toward me, and I was laughing so hard that I barely got out of his reach in time.

All humor was forgotten when the door to the bar suddenly flew open and Apollo Park dashed out.

"Shit!" he yelled as he saw me. He spun and bolted in the other direction only to come to a screeching halt when he saw Alex. "Fuck!"

He threw both of his palms up to stop our advances. But the sooner we dragged his ass back to Leo, the sooner we could get some lunch. I was starving. And bored.

"Stay back!" he ordered, his gaze frantically flicking between the three of us.

"Don't fight it, my man. This is not going to end well for you," I called.

He turned his wild eyes on his soon-to-be brother-in-law and pleaded, "Jude, come on. You know this is fucked up."

"I know you're an idiot for blowing off Leo...*again.*" Jude prowled closer. "He gave you plenty of opportunities to plant your ass in his office. Now, he's sent us to plant it there for you."

"I own a bar! I'm not fucking working for Guardian," he snapped.

"See, you should have thought about that before you told Leo you would."

"It was one job!"

Silently, I crept closer while Jude had his attention. Alex was doing the same, moving with a stealth invisibility no man his size should be able to possess.

"One job you did *not* complete," Jude replied, stepping up onto the sidewalk.

"Stop moving!" Apollo yelled without ever taking his gaze off Jude. "And make them back off!"

Alex and I pulled up short, and I started to think maybe Leo was onto something with this kid. What he lacked in brains, he definitely had in sixth sense.

However, that sixth sense did not take my patience into account.

"Oh, for fuck's sake," I grumbled, bolting toward him.

Less than a second before I got my hands on him, Johnson came barreling out the bar door, a world of pissed-off energy vibrating off him. "You," he growled, stabbing a finger toward Apollo.

Swear to God, I thought Apollo had turned into a ghost. He spun so fast that I was barely able to register his movements.

Being the closest, I tried to grab him, but my efforts were rendered useless.

He slid in behind me and fisted the back of my button-down. "Okay! I'll come. Just keep him away from me."

Once upon a time, Johnson had worked as a bodyguard for Rhion and Apollo's father. He'd always been good to Rhion, so I thought it was improbable that he was going to behead Apollo on the sidewalk in broad daylight. Though, with that said, Aidan Johnson could be a scary motherfucker when he wanted to be. From his dark hair, even darker eyes, the tattoos running down his neck and arms, the gauges in his ears, and the recent addition of a beard, the whole package screamed *don't fuck with me*. It appeared Apollo had gotten the message loud and clear.

I considered questioning what the hell he could have possibly done to piss Johnson off that badly in the five minutes since he'd disappeared around the building, but honestly, I didn't give a fuck.

Twisting around, I grabbed Apollo by the bicep and gave him a rough shove toward the Guardian office across the street. "All right. Party's over, kids. Let's deliver the package to the boss man and then get some grub. Who's in the mood for Mexican?"

Johnson continued to glare.

Jude rubbed the back of his head, obviously nervous about hauling his girlfriend's little brother in.

Alex nodded. The man was always up for food.

And I smiled. All in a day's work.

CHAPTER THREE

Mira

Six weeks before I lost him…

"HE DOESN'T EVEN SAY BLESS YOU," I CONFESSED TO THE STARS, the sound of classic country playing on the radio in the background.

"What?"

"When I sneeze, he doesn't say bless you."

"Yeah," Jeremy drawled. "He's always been more of a *gesundheit* kind of guy."

I pushed up onto my elbows as a bolt of heat lightning illuminated the sky. "No. He doesn't say anything *when I sneeze.*"

His lips tipped up, but he never gave me his gaze. "I'm not sure that's his worst quality, Mir."

I rolled my eyes. Given that Kurt was out God only knew where, it definitely wasn't, but it still pissed me off to no end. "I mean, what kind of person hears someone else sneeze and doesn't say bless you? It's, like, the rudest thing you could possibly do."

He turned, planted his elbow on our T-shirt pillow, and propped his head in his hand. "How in the hell is that the rudest thing he could possibly do?"

"It means he doesn't care! It means he doesn't even pay attention enough to hear a sneeze. It's a common courtesy. Everyone knows that.

I could sneeze in a crowded movie theater and someone would say bless you. But not Kurt. It's like he doesn't give a rat's ass about anyone but himself."

He licked his lips, and a strange shadow sifted through his features. "Maybe he doesn't."

I inched toward him until my front was pressed against his side and kissed the underside of his jaw.

Resting his hand in the curve of my hip, he gave me a firm squeeze.

"He cares," I defended.

I lied to myself about stuff like that a lot. It was easier than facing the facts. The truth was: Kurt wasn't the one I wanted to care.

I loved Jeremy Lark. I'd fallen for him fast and hard over conversations about mansions with swimming pools and expensive sports cars neither of us would ever be able to afford. We laughed and counted quarters to buy beer because both of our paychecks were usually gone the same day we got them. I knew in great detail how he'd spend a million dollars, and he knew the exact design of my custom closet that would house my vast collection of heels and designer handbags. But, short of winning the lottery, neither of us was ever going to have that. However, money wasn't everything. There was a lot to be said for a man who would treat you well. I just couldn't find one of those, either.

I'd heard too many stories from Kurt to believe that Jeremy would ever view me as anything but a woman to keep him entertained. He and Kurt were two of the same. They were gorgeous and they knew it. Neither of them had ever had a girlfriend they hadn't cheated on.

Boy, did I know how to pick a man—or, in this case, men.

Over the last few months, it had become clear that, even if Kurt wasn't in the picture, Jeremy and I had no future together. But that didn't mean I didn't love him in the present.

Gliding a hand up his strong shoulders, I pulled him closer and brushed my nose with his. "Enough about Kurt. Kiss me."

His eyes sparked, and his hand drifted to my ass. And then his mouth came to mine with the intoxicating flavors of desperation and need that would forever remind me of Jeremy Lark.

Only it was my need.

And my desperation.

His lips moved to my neck as he forced me to my back and rolled on top of me.

Moaning, I arched off the hard bed of his truck, pressing my breasts into his chest.

"Bless you," he murmured, his hand moving under my shirt, where he palmed my breast.

I giggled softly. "I didn't sneeze."

He peppered kisses down my chest. "No, but I'm sure I'll miss a few while I'm in the field next week."

My heart cracked. I told myself that it was because he was being sweet, but I knew that it was because I was going to miss him like hell when he was gone.

And he wasn't even mine to miss.

"Mmm," I hummed, not trusting my voice.

"And I'm sure I've missed a few this month when I wasn't around. Clearly, I should make up for being so rude. Can't have my girl's sneezes going unblessed."

My girl.

I smiled despite the way my nose started stinging.

"Of course not," I murmured, threading a hand into the short, auburn hairs on the top of his head, and closed my eyes, pretending we never had to leave those woods.

"Bless you," he whispered against my stomach.

"Bless you," he whispered as he popped the button on my jeans open.

"Bless you," he whispered as he kissed my inner thigh.

"Yes," I hissed as he sealed his mouth over my core.

Jeremy Lark had been wrong though.

God hadn't blessed me.

Not that night.

And certainly not six weeks later, when I lost him forever.

Present day...

I was lounging in my bed when I heard Whitney turn the shower on in the bathroom. The pipes in that old house screamed, jarring my teeth.

"Sorry!" she yelled. She said that every single time she turned the water on as if she had made the noise herself.

I didn't have to yell when I replied, "It's okay." The walls in that house were paper-thin. I swear I could hear her plucking her eyebrows sometimes.

Snuggling deeper into my bed, I pulled a snoozing Bitsy onto my chest. She burrowed between my boobs—her favorite place to sleep—and then let out an adorable puppy sigh.

"I know, sweet girl. It's been quite a day," I whispered, pulling the blanket up to cover us both.

We'd been busy preparing for the move. Surprisingly enough, Sherri and Tammy had been super supportive when Whitney and I had told them that we'd found a place. They'd even bought a celebratory twelve-pack and pitched in to help us pack for a few hours before they'd had to leave for the club.

Three beers later, I had a nice little buzz and a room full of boxes. I should have been able to fall asleep with no problems. But, as it so often did, my mind refused to shut down. Anxiety was awesome like that.

Staring at the ceiling, I tried to focus on the positives of this move.

The extra space.

The peace and quiet.

The fresh start.

The additional rent.

The higher utility bills.

The prospect of never being able to open the bar.

The reality that I might be stuck in this life forever.

"Fuck," I groaned, sitting up in bed, and grabbed my phone off the nightstand.

With dread churning in my stomach, I stared at that little, blue icon with the white F, and before I could stop myself, I clicked on it. I shouldn't have been on there. It wasn't going to help me find sleep. Facebook was a drug. And I was an addict. So much so that I only allowed myself to check it once a month because, regardless of how harmless I told myself it was, it'd always leave me hung over the next day.

Eyes swollen from crying.

Body aching with regret.

Heart heavy with reality.

It was torture. But, like a masochist, I kept going back for more.

I scrolled through various political rants, viral cooking videos, and pictures of happy families on my newsfeed until…

"Jesus," I breathed.

He didn't post much. So my once-a-month visits usually only garnered me a few pictures and maybe a shared article about the military. But they were always enough to send me reeling.

Jeremy Lark had been gorgeous in his twenties, but he'd grown into a beautiful man. His lean muscles now held more bulk, and his once boyish face was now made up of sharp angles and a chiseled jaw. He still had a thick head of dark hair with red highlights, and he kept it clipped short much like he had in the military. His hazel eyes still sparkled with mischief, but they were somehow more guarded than those of the carefree boy I'd once known.

In some ways, he was exactly the same.

Yet completely different.

He was wearing a black T-shirt with the words Guardian Protection Agency stretched over his muscular chest. His lips were split in a glowing smile, showing off his straight, white teeth. Well, all except that one on the top right that turned in just the tiniest bit. I knew that one well. I used to stare at it when he'd be lost in laughter. And, with the two of us, that happened a lot.

He was sitting on the redbrick front steps of a large, two-story home. It was gorgeous, with perfectly manicured flowerbeds and a huge covered porch that all but demanded rocking chairs. It wasn't in the mountains the way he'd always dreamed about, but it was still perfect.

His strong arms were hooked around identical little girls. They were nearing four, and their red ringlets now hung over their shoulders. Amelia was on his left. She had the most adorable crooked smile. It was the only discernible difference between her and her twin sister, Sophie.

I'd never forget the day I'd logged in and found a picture of him with a very pregnant woman. They'd both been smiling at the camera, and I knew Jeremy—or at least I had—and his was genuine. Not at all like the ones I'd aimed at Kurt so often over the years. Jeremy's large hand had been resting on her extremely swollen belly, his other arm slung around her shoulders. Before that moment, I'd never in my life experienced the simultaneous feelings of elation and agony.

I'd been happy for him. I'd learned from the caption that her name was Melissa, and even the jealousy I had no right to feel wouldn't let me deny that she was stunning. Long, red hair flowed in waves, and her green eyes were bright with life. From her tasteful jewelry to her manicured fingernails, all the way down to her designer heels, she was a classic beauty. Just like he'd deserved.

Numerous times when we had been younger, he'd told me that he'd wanted kids—a family he could call his own.

And that day, well over a decade after I'd been a coward and sent him away, I'd stared down at my phone with tears leaking from my eyes and a huge smile on my face, knowing he was finally getting what he'd always wanted.

Even if I wasn't.

At least one of us deserved to be happy. And, as I'd learned so many years earlier, it wasn't going to be me.

I jumped when my door suddenly cracked open. Bitsy flew to her feet and started barking only to quiet when Whitney walked inside.

"You okay?" she asked, concern crinkling her forehead.

I shimmied up in bed. "Yeah. Why? You?"

She frowned. "I heard you crying when I got out of the shower."

I quickly lifted my hands to my face, and sure enough, there were tears streaming down my cheeks. I pointed to my phone. "Damn animal rescue videos. They get me every time."

She tightened her towel around her and then propped her shoulder against the doorjamb. "You worried about the move?"

"No," I semi-lied.

Her frown deepened. "You thinking about Kurt?"

"What? Dear God, no!"

Though that was another semi-lie because I could never think about Jeremy without thinking about Kurt.

Sighing, she walked over to my bed and scooped up Bitsy for a snuggle. Without making eye contact, she said, "It'd be okay if you were, ya know. You two were married a really long time. And I know things didn't go quite as you planned when you got a divorce, but I'm sure you have to miss him sometimes."

Things had never gone as planned with Kurt. Not when we'd started dating. Not when he'd started cheating on me. Not when I'd started cheating on him. Not when he'd gotten Jeremy kicked out of the Army. Not when we'd gotten married. Not when he'd started using steroids. Not when *he* had gotten kicked out of the Army. Not when he'd started *selling* steroids. And especially not when he'd gotten arrested and sentenced to twenty years in a federal penitentiary. Hell, our divorce might have been the only thing that had ever gone as planned. It had been coming since approximately twenty minutes after we'd met.

I set my phone on the nightstand and then folded my hands over my stomach. "Whit, honey. I'm not thinking about Kurt. And I'm definitely not missing him."

"But if you were…"

"I'm not!" I snapped, guilt immediately icing my frustration. "I'm sorry. I'm just…tired."

She offered me a sad smile and then deposited Bitsy on the foot of the bed. "Okay. Then I'll let you get some sleep. But stop stressing about the move. And no more animal rescue videos."

I chuckled. I was thirteen years her senior and she was still taking care of me.

"Yes, Mommy."

She winked and headed for the door. "All right. Lights out. We've got a big day tomorrow."

She was right, and if I picked my phone back up, who knew how long it would be before I found any rest, more than likely with tears soaking my pillow.

"Night, Whit."

She smiled warmly. "Night, Mir."

CHAPTER FOUR

Mira

Five days before I lost him…

"I HOPE THIS HURTS," I HISSED, HOLDING A COLD BEER TO JEREMY'S swollen eye.

"Get off me." He snatched the can from my hand and jumped off the tailgate.

I looked to Kurt, who was standing in a pressed baby-blue dress shirt, dark washed jeans, and trendy boots that cost more than the entirety of my wardrobe. His short, blond hair was perfectly styled, gel and all, not a strand out of place.

Yet, he'd told me that he was going to sleep before hanging up on me earlier. I swear it was like he picked fights so he could have an excuse to go downtown without me.

"He needs to ice that," I gritted out through clenched teeth.

He kept his gaze leveled on Jeremy. "No, what he needs is a new brain."

"Oh, fuck off," Jeremy snapped, popping the beer open before throwing it back for a long draw.

Kurt's jaw tensed as he marched over and grabbed it from his hand mid-sip. "Christ, you really are an idiot. You can't chug a fucking beer in the middle of the gas station parking lot. Are you trying to get arrested tonight?"

Kurt dumped the beer on the ground and tossed the empty into the back of Jeremy's truck. A pang of guilt hit me when it clanged against our fully stocked cooler. Jeremy and I had been planning to head out into the woods. But, when he'd arrived to pick me up, I had been in the middle of an all-out brawl with my mom's new boyfriend. They weren't common. But they definitely weren't unusual. The guys knew that Ron was a nasty drunk, but I'd downplayed how rough it really got. He was yet another reason I needed to get the hell out of there. But I needed time to figure out a plan first. However, thanks to Jeremy's beating the shit out of him and then my mom kicking me out, it was now time I did not have.

After I'd dragged him to his truck, we'd driven to the gas station, where I'd used the payphone to call Kurt's cell. I hadn't known what else to do. I was worried about sending Jeremy back to post with two swollen eyes, a busted lip, and a split eyebrow. He already had two strikes against him. To hear Kurt tell it, Jeremy's chain of command was looking for a reason to chapter him out of the Army. I couldn't be responsible for that.

Jeremy got into Kurt's face. "No. I was trying to do your fucking job."

Kurt jolted, the muscles in his neck straining as his back bowed. "Excuse me."

Aaaaand that was my cue.

I hopped off the tailgate and squeezed between them. "Stop. People are watching."

Jeremy leaned around me. "Yeah, I said it. Your fucking job. She's been showing up with bruises for weeks. And you haven't done one goddamn thing about it. For fuck's sake, she had a size-twelve boot mark on her back last week!"

Kurt's eyes narrowed. "And how the hell would you know about that?"

Uh oh.

I opened my mouth for what I hoped would be a sharp response, but nothing came out. For a woman who was sneaking around behind my boyfriend's back, I was shit for a liar.

Thankfully, Jeremy was not.

He laughed. "Because it looked like a fucking shoe advertisement hanging out of her tank top at dinner last weekend. And you did dick about it."

Kurt grew angry, but I mildly relaxed.

Turning to face Jeremy, in order to keep the guilt on my face hidden from Kurt, I said, "Because I told him not to. The same damn way I told you not to do anything stupid, either. Yet here we are!"

Jeremy laughed again. "Right. Next time, I'll sit back and drink a beer while I wait for that piece of shit to knock you unconscious." He pointedly glanced to my busted lip. "Would that be better for you?"

"Yeah. It really would. Because at least then I wouldn't be homeless."

"And probably not alive, either!"

I rolled my eyes. "Could you possibly be a little more dramatic here? He slapped me." And dragged me out of my room by my hair. But, luckily Jeremy had missed that.

He planted his hands on his hips. "Oh, I'm being dramatic now? Well, heads up, Mir. If that man ever lifts a hand in your direction again, it's going to be a whole new level of dramatics. The kind where he ends up in a body bag."

My attitude momentarily slipped as my chest started doing some seriously warm things. Jeremy was hotheaded about pretty much everything, but when it came to me...he was so far over the top that he wasn't even visible on the horizon anymore.

I loved it—almost as much as I hated it.

It was sweet, and it made me feel important.

But it was also reckless and irresponsible. Two words that might as well have been the definition of Jeremy Lark.

I shook my head, focusing on the issue at hand. "Awesome. He's in a body bag, and you're in jail. Really great plan, Jer."

"You got a better idea? I'm all ears, Mir." He stressed my nickname like an insult.

"Um, how about we don't get me kicked out of my house when I have nowhere to fucking go?"

He scoffed. "Nowhere is still a hell of a lot better than staying there *and dealing with him hitting you."*

"No, it's not!" I yelled. "Damn it, Jeremy. You have no idea what the hell you're talking about."

"Oh, I don't?" he whispered ominously.

He did. More than anyone. But that didn't change the fact that his temper had once again put me in a seriously bad situation.

I pushed up onto my toes and yelled, "I have twelve dollars in the bank! Twelve! No car, and now, I have no one to take me to and from work, which means, by tomorrow, I'm going to have zero dollars for the foreseeable future."

He twisted his lips. "Don't be stupid. You know I'll pick you up from work."

I threw my hands out to my sides and let them slap on my thighs on the way down. "Oh, goodie! I'll be sure to pick the bridge closest to your barracks to live under. Ya know, to make it convenient for you."

What little I could see of his swelling eyes flashed dark. "You don't have to have an attitude here."

"Are you kidding me? An attitude is all I can afford to have right now!"

He groaned, the fight momentarily leaving him. He reached out and gave my hip a squeeze. "Just get off my ass and let me think for a minute. I'll figure it out, okay?"

I sighed. I wanted to believe him. But short of letting me live in his truck—which he probably would have done if I'd asked—he had no way to fix this.

"I'll figure it out," Kurt stated definitively.

Jeremy and I jumped in surprise. It should have been the blinking neon light of reasons why Jeremy and I belonged together. Kurt had been standing right there and we'd both gotten so wrapped up in each other that we'd forgotten about him altogether.

Jeremy's hand instantly fell away from my hip.

I spun to face my boyfriend. "You don't have to—"

His face was hard, but he slung his arm around my shoulders and pulled me into his side. His words were for me, but he pointedly kept his gaze locked on his best friend. "I'll call my parents and borrow some money for the first and last on an apartment. I'm sure Sgt. Richardson will grant me permission for off-post housing." He glanced down at me and smiled. "We can move in together. I pay the bills, you do all the housework." He dipped low and kissed my temple, where he finished with, "Naked."

Pain consumed me as I watched Jeremy's handsome face remain heartbreakingly emotionless. He didn't care if I moved in with Kurt. And that slashed through me like the sharpest blade.

"No. I can't ask you to do that," I whispered to Kurt.

Jeremy shifted his weight between his feet but remained utterly silent.

Kurt cocked his head. "Don't be ridiculous. You're mine. *I'll take care of you. Besides, Jeremy's right. I should have done something about Ron before now. We're all really lucky he was there tonight." He tipped his chin to the cooler in the back of Jeremy's truck. "Especially since he told me he was staying in tonight."*

Oh, fuck. Oh, fuck. Oh, fuuuuuuck.

My stomach knotted, and my throat closed.

But, once again, Jeremy came to the rescue. Really, it should have worried me how good he was at lying.

He smiled. "She called and asked if I'd drive her to the barracks to surprise you." He took a step closer and lowered his voice as if I weren't standing right fucking there. "I convinced her drinking a couple beers with me was a better idea."

He was so full of it. We'd been heading to our place in the woods after my big fight with Kurt. And, since Kurt wasn't in a pair of pajamas but rather his favorite downtown club attire, it was safe to say we'd all been up to no good that night.

Only Jeremy had been there for me.

And Kurt had been looking for someone else.

Stepping out of Kurt's arms, I blurted, "Actually, that's not why I called Jeremy tonight."

"Mira. Don't," Jeremy breathed.

"Don't what?" Kurt asked, swinging his head between us.

Mentally, I weighed the pros and cons of telling Kurt the truth, of finally hurting him and forcing him away once and for all. This whole charade was exhausting.

Right then, I could have ended it all.

The betrayal and the pain.

But there was always one thing that kept me from telling Kurt.

My stomach soured as I peeked up at Jeremy through my lashes. The panic on his face cut me to the quick.

I wasn't the only one who didn't want Kurt to find out.

No matter how sweet, kind, and protective he seemed, I was Jeremy Lark's dirtiest secret of all.

"I tried calling you tonight. You didn't answer. So I thought maybe you were—"

"I went out for a drink with Ken. I figured you were still mad at me, so I didn't bother to call. I'm sorry."

Lies. Our universal language.

As long as we were all telling them, a few more wouldn't hurt.

"If you were serious about us moving in together, I'd love that."

He smiled. "Of course. You know I'll always take care of you."

Unfortunately, I did know that.

And a few minutes later, as I walked away, my hand folded in his, with Jeremy watching me go without a single objection, I told myself the biggest lie of all.

I am better off with Kurt.

Present day...

The sound of the screen door slamming at four a.m. was nothing out of the ordinary. It was rare that the girls actually came home at night rather than finding a man for the evening. But, if they did, I knew I'd hear it. I'd warned Sherri and Tammy at least seven hundred times that I was going to take the damn thing off the hinges if they didn't remember to manually guide it shut instead of letting it slap closed behind them. Did they listen? Hell no.

I made a mental note to follow through on that threat first thing in the morning—well, later in the morning. Maybe after I'd actually opened my eyes. Those thoughts died and a sleepy smile curled my lips when I remembered we'd be out of there before I could even find the screwdriver.

With all stressors momentarily forgotten, I started to doze off again. Then my bedroom door suddenly flew open.

"Mira!" Whitney cried in a terrified tone that hit me like a freight train.

I bolted straight up in bed, but it took a second for my eyes to adjust. Lifting my hand, I tried to block out the light flooding into the room, but all I could make out were their silhouettes.

Their—as in two people.

One of which was definitely a man, and his hand was attached to the back of Whitney's hair.

My pulse skyrocketed, and a blast of adrenaline tore through my system.

"Whit!" I yelled, throwing the covers back and going for the baseball bat I kept under the bed.

My mother used to say, "Men think a woman is the most vulnerable in the bed on her back. Show 'em you aren't." It was the best—and possibly the only—thing she'd ever taught me.

I lifted the bat high and planted my feet shoulder-width apart before demanding, "Let her go."

A deep, somewhat familiar voice filled with humor asked, "Is that a fucking bat?"

"I don't know. I'll ask your skull fragments in about thirty seconds."

He barked a laugh. "Jesus, woman. You always were a fucking nut."

I tilted my head to the side, my brain working overtime to place his voice. Then it finally hit me. "Jonah?"

Jonah Sheehan was Kurt's best friend for the majority of our marriage. He was a good guy. Nice enough. A little too cocky, and therefore obnoxious, but Kurt thought he was a riot. He was elbow-deep in the wonderful world of steroids with my ex-husband—using, buying, and eventually selling.

"The one and only," he sing-songed.

My shoulders sagged. "Christ, Jonah. You scared the hell out of me." Slowly lowering the bat, I sighed. "What are you doing here?" I twisted the switch for the lamp on my nightstand.

And then my entire life changed.

The first thing I saw was Whitney standing there, tears streaming down her cheeks, her eyes wide with panic.

Confused, I slid my gaze to Jonah. I hadn't seen him in over three years, and the man standing in front of me was a shadow of the one who had sat at my bar.

Gone were the pyramids of muscles that had covered his tall frame. Pale skin sagged under his eyes, and what had once been an attractive smattering of freckles across his cheeks was now covered by blotches and open sores. He looked at least twenty years older.

But that wasn't why I gasped.

His hand wasn't in Whitney's hair.

His gun was.

I stumbled back a step, my mind unable to make heads or tails of what the hell was happening, but I lifted the bat again. "You need to let her go, Jonah."

He smiled, revealing a headful of yellow and brown teeth. "Oh, no. This one is coming with me." He shoved Whitney hard, sending her stumbling out the door, and only then did I notice the other man.

"No!" I yelled, racing forward, momentarily letting my guard down long enough for Jonah to grab the end of the bat and snatch it from my hands.

Hooking his arm around my throat, he pulled me against his chest and pressed the metal tip of his gun to my temple. "Shut up!"

"Let me fucking go." Kicking and clawing, I fought against him.

But, while he wasn't the same mountain of muscle, he had no problem overpowering me. "Whitney!" I yelled when the screen door slammed shut.

My heart felt like it was going to beat out of my chest, and my mind swirled. It all felt like a dream. But, when I heard her scream from the driveway, I knew there would be no waking up.

I froze, terror ricocheting inside me. "W-where are you taking her?"

"She'll be fine as long as you listen closely and do what I say."

I cried out when he painfully forced my head to my shoulder with his gun.

"Is that a yes?"

"What do you want?" I snarled.

"First, you need to chill the hell out."

"You have a fucking gun aimed at my head, Jonah. It's safe to assume I'm not going to chill out."

He tightened his arm around my neck. "Then stop fucking fighting me."

The last thing I wanted to do was give up. If he was going to kill me, I wasn't going out of this world quietly. But, then again, this wasn't just about me anymore. Whitney was involved.

With a deep breath, I willed my heart to slow and dropped my hands.

"Good," he praised. "Now, listen up. Kurt needs a favor."

Bile rose in my throat as I craned my head back to stare at him. I hadn't spoken to my ex-husband in over three years.

Kurt had been shit for a husband. And, come to think of it, shit for a boyfriend and shit for a fiancé too. But, even after everything that had happened between Kurt and me over the years, I'd never doubted that, in his own twisted way, he loved me. He would have lost his mind if he thought someone was hurting me.

"Funny, because I'm thinking Kurt would put a bullet in *your* head before he allowed you to put your hands on me," I seethed.

He chuckled, his putrid breath breezing over my face as he

whispered, "Who do you think got me the gun, Mira?"

The hairs on the back of my neck stood on end, and my stomach tied into a million knots. "He's still in prison," I choked out.

He smiled sardonically. "Doesn't mean he's stopped working."

Make that two million knots.

"What does he want?" I whimpered.

He roughly shoved me to the bed, and Bitsy jumped on top of me when I landed beside her.

After tucking the gun in the back of his pants, he walked to the door and kicked a huge rectangle duffel bag into the room. It was all but bursting at the seams.

"W-what is that?" I breathed, scrambling across the bed while holding Bitsy close to my chest.

"Seven hundred thousand dollars. And I can't spend a fucking penny of it without the Feds crawling up my ass."

I pursed my lips. "Okay?"

He lifted the gun and aimed it at me. "I need you to clean it."

I looked down at the bag. Back up at Jonah. Then back down at the bag. Then back up at him. "Like in the washing machine?"

It was his turn to look down at the bag. Back up at me. Then back down to the bag. Then back up at me. "Not in the fucking washing machine! *Clean it*! Pay your taxes and then get it back to me."

I shook my head. "I don't know how to do that."

"I do not have the patience for your bullshit, Mira."

I blinked.

He blinked back.

I blinked again.

He planted his hand on his hip and blinked harder.

I threw my hands up in the air. "I have no idea what you are talking about!"

He tipped his head to the side and smirked. "Word is you're opening another Sip and Sud."

"So?"

"So, I'll repeat, clean my fucking money!"

I ground my teeth. "Okay, again, *I'll* repeat, like in a fucking washing machine?"

He sulked over to the bed and sat on the corner. My whole body went on alert as he reached out and picked up Bitsy.

"Put her down. Now," I demanded.

He stroked his dirty fingernails down her neck. "Not usually a fan of little dogs, but I gotta admit this one is right cute." He lifted her up into his line of sight and asked in a ridiculous baby voice, "What do you say? You want to come home with Uncle Jonah for a little while?"

My heart stopped, but a fire ignited inside me. I lunged toward him, blood roaring in my ears, murder coursing through my veins. But he moved, which sent me crashing to the floor.

After snatching the gun from the back of his pants, he leveled it on me, all of this done with Bitsy still tucked into the curve of his arm.

With a heaving chest, I threw my hands up in surrender. "Okay. Okay. Just stop."

He jutted his head toward the bag. "Clean it."

"I can't," I cried, climbing back to my feet. Folding my hands together in prayer, I took a step toward him. "I swear to God, Jonah. I don't know how."

"That's not what Kurt said."

"Then Kurt lied!"

He scoffed and stroked Bitsy on the head, using that baby voice again to say, "Your mama is a crazy-ass bitch who is about to get a bullet in her head if she doesn't stop trying to bullshit me."

My back shot straight as he lifted his eyes to mine.

"You got three days to figure it out."

My stomach dropped, panic exploding within me. "Three days? What the hell can you possibly expect me to do with seven hundred thousand dollars in that time? I'm at least six months away from opening the Sip and Sud. I don't even have a loan for the building yet. But, honestly, even if I did, I don't know the first thing about laundering money. I ran a business, Jonah. A *legal* business. Any of the rest of that shit was Kurt."

"So you're telling me a fucking bar inside a laundromat made you hundreds of thousands of dollars each year?"

"Well, not *one* of them. I had three before they were seized. Sure, everything was in Kurt's name." I rested my hand over my heart, pride swelling inside me. "But those were my babies."

I hadn't exactly had pie-in-the-sky expectations when I'd opened the first Sip and Sud, but after refusing to allow Kurt to beg more money off his parents, the old laundromat was the only location we could afford. I'd worked my ass off to get that place in any kind of shape to open the doors. I'd figured we'd get some cash flow and I could open something bigger, preferably without washers and dryers playing the bassline to the music.

However, the Sip and Sud exploded. Over half of our revenue came from the laundry side. At first, I hired a few of the local college girls to come in and wash, dry, and fold customers' laundry in bikinis. I charged a mint by the pound for that service, and while they waited and watched, I charged another mint for drinks. As to be expected, our clientele was mostly men—bachelors and married alike. But, when the novelty wore off and they realized no one was getting naked, business became so slow that it almost died. That is until I realized I was catering to the wrong audience. Switching things up, I hired a group of off-season *male* athletes from the local college to wash, dry, and fold shirtless. That was when things went nuts. Women poured through our doors in flocks. Which, in turn, brought the men back in flocks.

Soon, the Sip and Sud was providing two-thirds of our income without Kurt's illegal shit involved. Money we both could have lived on very comfortably if he had just stopped with the drugs.

But it was Kurt. He didn't need the money. He needed the thrill of the game.

He'd played me more times than I'd ever be able to count.

And, as I stared up at Jonah, who was standing in my apartment and holding my dog after he'd kidnapped my best friend in the wee hours of the morning, it seemed like, once again, Kurt had dragged me in as his pawn.

Christ. Why did that hurt? Oh, right. Because I was getting my life back on track. I was terrified, doubting myself at every turn, but damn it, I was doing it.

Or at least I had been.

Defeat rolled my shoulders. "I can't do it."

"You're a smart girl, Mira. Figure it out."

Tears sprang from my eyes as he headed for the door, Bitsy still in his arms, Whitney God only knew where.

"Wait, please," I begged.

"Tony is gonna stay with you to make sure you don't do anything stupid," he called over his shoulder. "You figure out a plan. I'll figure out how long I can give you to execute said plan. But, until that happens, your girl stays with me."

I rushed after him and tugged on the back of his shirt. "Please, Jonah. Don't do this. Just leave them here. I'll make it happen. I promise."

But his legs never stopped moving.

Frantic, I followed him to the front door, where a young kid with long, blond hair and a face full of tattoos—yes, his actual face—was glaring at me.

"Get her off me," Jonah ordered.

Tony's arm hit me hard around the stomach, knocking the breath out of me as he lifted me off my feet.

"No!" I screamed, but there was no air in my lungs to carry the sound.

"Three days," Jonah declared as Tony dragged me toward my bedroom.

Gasping for air, I did my best to fight, but it only made Tony's grip tighten painfully.

"Jonah!" I managed to choke out, tears streaming off my chin. "You can't do this!"

He snapped and Tony suddenly stopped. "Oh, Mira," he breathed. "This was not the reaction Kurt was hoping for." Slowly, he prowled over to me, an evil smile pulling at his lips, and brushed the hair off my neck.

I wrenched my eyes shut and turned my head away from his tender gesture.

"It would be good for you to remember how well Kurt took care of you before he got locked away. I don't think he's going to be so nice if you turn your back on him now." With his thumb and forefinger on my chin, he turned my head. "Eyes open," he demanded.

My chest ached, and I was sick with dread and betrayal. Kurt hadn't been nice to me. Kurt had been a nightmare to deal with. He'd ruined my life time and time again. This was just one more reminder that I was never out of his reach.

I found the strength to flutter my lids open at Jonah's order.

He was standing only inches away. Tony's arms were still wrapped around me, rendering me unable to escape.

"Mirabell," he whispered, and I flinched at Kurt's silly nickname for me. I'd hated it then, and I hated it even more now. "I will only say this once. You call the cops and your girl is dead. Do you understand?"

His threat slayed me from all angles. I'd known that day would come. Kurt had been out of my life for over three years, but he'd never let me go.

I'd been wrong when I'd thought I was the pawn in Kurt's game.

I was the fucking queen—whether I wanted to be or not.

Slowly and filled with threat, Jonah repeated, "Do you understand?"

I did. Loud and clear. So I nodded, but I felt like I was dying.

He tapped my nose. "Smart girl. Three days."

"Three days," I repeated on a broken sob.

And then he was gone, just like every hope I'd had for the future.

Tony released me when the door shut behind Jonah, and it was all I could do to keep my knees from buckling. From my fingertips to my toes, I was numb as I heard a car roar away, Whitney inside, and there was not one damn thing I could do to help her.

"I suggest you get to work," Tony said, tucking a gun into his waistband before collapsing onto my couch and propping his biker-boot-clad feet on the coffee table.

A coffee table I'd bought at a garage sale the Saturday after Kurt had been sentenced. I hadn't had much money to celebrate that day, but something inside me had told me that that damn coffee table was the start of a new life. It was the first thing I had ever owned that was completely mine. Not Kurt's and not something the government could take away.

I'd bought that forty-dollar coffee table with money I'd made.

On my own. The legal way. Free and clear of Kurt and any sludge he could rain over me.

It had taken me thirty-three years of life to finally own a fucking coffee table.

And there it was, two boots covered in Kurt's filth resting on it.

I couldn't clean that money. Not even if I'd wanted to. But I could make sure Kurt lost his very last game with me serving as his queen.

I stumbled to my room, careful not to trip over the seven hundred thousand dollars that had literally been dropped at my feet, and sank down to my bed.

"Oh, God," I choked out, slapping a hand over my mouth, far too many years' worth of tears finally escaping.

Calling the cops was risky while Jonah had Whitney. But short of a miracle, I had no way to help her without getting the police involved.

Reaching out to my nightstand, I retrieved my phone. My hands were shaking so violently that I was barely able to click the home button. The bright light on the screen illuminated the dark room. And then I froze, chills pebbling my skin and a blast of hope igniting my system.

The answer was staring back at me.

In a tight, black Guardian Protection Agency T-shirt.

CHAPTER FIVE

Lark

"How much do you love me?" I asked while holding my phone in front of me as I walked through the underground parking garage of Guardian Protection Agency.

Sophie laughed, edging her sister out of the screen as she exclaimed, "Infinity!"

"Dat's what I was gonna say!" Amelia yelled, shoving at her sister.

Sophie was all of twelve minutes older, but she had taken the role of big sister extremely seriously. She loved getting under Amelia's skin. And there was one thing you could always count on: Amelia was going to give her one hell of a reaction.

"I said it first," Sophie said with a mischievous grin, fanning Amelia's flames.

"Dat's not fair!"

"Too bad!"

My girls loved each other, but they also fought like a pack of rabid dogs. I had no doubt a hair-pulling brawl was going to ensue, and when the phone fell, leaving me staring up at the ceiling, I got the feeling it already had.

"Ow!" they both screamed.

"Girls!" I scolded, but it was a worthless effort. The brawl carried on without me.

"Daddy!" one of them yelled, but without seeing them, I was

hard-pressed to tell you which one.

Hell, without the aid of their favorite pajamas when they'd answered my FaceTime call, I couldn't have told you which one was which on looks alone. The two of them were as identical as twins came. Since birth, they'd been the same height and weight, without so much as a birthmark to distinguish the difference. Thankfully, they'd gotten to the age where they would tell me if I got it wrong, but when they got old enough to pull the old switch-a-roo game on their dad, I'd be fucked.

But, then again, I had gorgeous twin daughters with fiery-red hair and an attitude to match. When they got older, I'd be fucked regardless.

"You two. Stop. Now," I growled, swiping my keycard at the sensor beside the elevator. The door opened and I stepped inside. After stabbing my finger on the number four, I pressed my back into the northeast corner in order to keep my signal on the ride up. I'd learned that little secret months earlier, after we'd started these morning video chats.

After my divorce, I'd struggled with not having the kids around all the time. Melissa and I hadn't worked out, but the day I'd driven away in a moving truck, my girls waving goodbye from the porch, I'd realized why so many couples stayed together for their kids. I had known why I was leaving Mel, even if I'd refused to admit it, but my babies shouldn't have been a part of that. And, for that reason alone, I put up with whatever shit my ex-wife wanted to throw my way.

And that shit had been plentiful for the first year we'd been separated. Recently, since she'd started dating again, it had become more manageable. But, even when we were at each other's throats, the girls were *not* involved. We both went out of our way to ensure that.

Melissa and I had a unique relationship. We'd been divorced for going on two years, but we still had dinner as a family every Wednesday night. She'd pick the restaurant. I'd pick up the check. And, for that hour or so, we were still a family. We didn't bicker or argue about the past. We usually didn't even do the whole "how was your day?" thing. Those dinners weren't about Jeremy and Melissa. We talked about preschool and nannies, funny things the girls had said, and things we needed to work on with them.

Melissa was my ex for a reason, but when it came to those dinners, we were all business. I respected the hell out of her for giving that to me—to them. Now, that's not to say she didn't call and light into my ass about some bullshit or another every couple of weeks. But, at those dinners, our shit was secondary. We were parents. Nothing more. Nothing less.

My little girl's green eyes, which matched her mother's, once again appeared on the screen, only this time, there were tears dripping from the corners.

"Sophie scratched me!" she wailed, lifting her arm to show the tiniest red mark I'd ever seen, but for a four-year-old diva, it was clearly life threatening.

"Amelia scratched me first!" Sophie defended, her tear-filled eyes reappearing too, her arm lifted high as exhibit B.

Shaking my head, I mustered my scariest dad voice and snapped, "Enough!"

They both startled and the argument fell silent.

It served them right. I was no pushover—or so I told myself. They would probably tell a different story. And theirs would be more accurate. Because, as soon as their round faces crumbled and their crocodile tears became genuine, I buckled.

"Hey, hey, hey. It's okay. I'm sorry. Daddy didn't mean to yell." Without looking up from my phone, I stepped off the elevator, the cool Chicago air whipping all around me, and headed straight for the door at the end of the breezeway.

The building that housed Guardian Protection Agency was made up of privately owned, luxury apartments with a few offices mixed in. I couldn't imagine how much one of those things cost. It had to have been a small fortune, considering that each floor was only one residence and roughly four thousand square feet. Money wasn't an issue for me anymore, but it was safe to assume that, short of selling a kidney to a dying heiress, my name would never on be on the deed to a place like that.

The girls were still crying when I scanned my keycard at the door to Guardian and walked inside.

The warm floral scents of whatever fru-fru reed diffuser Leo's wife, Sarah, had put out that week invaded my nose. It was nice, but I'd be choking on it by lunch.

"What did you do to my sweet girls!" Rhion accused, appearing at my side, pressing up to her tiptoes to get a peek at the phone.

"Sophie scratched Amelia. It left a mark. So Amelia scratched Sophie. I yelled at them to stop fighting and then the world ended. Friday morning business as usual."

She smiled up at me. "You want me to talk them through the apocalypse while you go get some breakfast? The muffins are almost gone."

Have I mentioned that Rhion was a godsend?

As a bodyguard, I had anything but a regular schedule. After my divorce, Leo had done his best to give me every other weekend off so I could spend time with the girls, but the final verdict came down to who my client was and what their needs were. The first time I'd gotten called in on my weekend off, Rhion had been kind enough to volunteer to keep the girls for me. They loved her, and despite the fact that they had come home in full makeup and a feathered boa that later shed all over my house, I loved her too. She lived on the floor below Guardian, so dropping them off and picking them up was convenient as hell. Rhion didn't have to keep them often, but because I was a single father, it took a huge weight off my shoulders to know I had someone I could trust.

I grinned and then aimed the camera down at Rhion. "Hey, look who I found!"

"Hey, girlies," Rhion cooed, her tattooed arms and chest showing from beneath her pale-pink tank top as she took the phone from my hands.

"Love you!" I called, but they had already forgotten about me.

"Why are you gals crying?" Rhion asked. "Oh, Amelia, that night-gown is beautiful. Is it new?"

I gave her shoulder a squeeze and mouthed a silent, "Thank you."

She winked and then shooed me toward the food. I did not need to be told twice. I was starving, and regardless of how much food Rhion brought for the team each Friday, there was never enough.

After squeezing through the crowd of guys surrounding the large oak table like a flock of hungry vultures guarding their prey, I lifted the lid on the first pastry box and not surprisingly found it empty.

"Shit," I mumbled, moving to the next one only to find it empty too.

"Here," Devon said from the other end of the table, sliding a box my way. "There's one left."

"Thank fuck," I replied, opening it to reveal a lone chocolate chip banana muffin. It wasn't my favorite flavor. However, as long as it was followed by the word muffin, I was good.

Rhion's Friday morning breakfasts were the only time I allowed myself to eat sweets, and I'd be damned if I was wasting that on a Danish or one of those tart things. A bear claw or apple fritter, maybe. But, if it had real fruit on it, I was out.

With his hands in his pockets, Devon meandered toward me, sporting a white smile that was nearly blinding in contrast to his olive skin. "You almost missed it," he said, stopping in front of me. "I thought Alex and I were going to come to blows when I pulled that off to the side. Ethan used a donut to distract him."

Devon was a good dude. We'd been tight for some years. Once a bodyguard to the stars in LA, he'd joined the agency after some serious shit had gone down with one of his longtime celebrity clients. He didn't talk about it much, and we were all too fond of our front teeth to ask. But, considering that said client was superstar Levee Williams, singer-songwriter and every man's walking, talking wet dream, and that Devon had gone on a three-day bender that had almost gotten him fired when news broke that she had gotten married, it wasn't hard to connect the dots.

"We got donuts?" I asked around a mouthful of muffin.

"We *had* donuts. Those went about five seconds after she sat 'em down."

"Damn," I mumbled before going back to work on my banana-flavored slice of heaven.

He inched closer and dropped his voice low. "You talk to Leo yet?"

"About what?"

He ran a hand through his short, dark hair and flashed his gaze around the room. "Apollo's refusing to track for him."

My hand froze with the last piece of muffin halfway to my mouth. "Still?"

His lips thinned and his brown eyes lifted to Rhion, who was sitting on one of the overstuffed leather couches while she chatted with my girls. "She's been in there with them all morning. Leo won't let him leave. Apollo won't cave. Jude and Johnson have been trying to talk sense into him, but that is one stubborn motherfucker."

"See, that's the problem. They need to stop trying to talk sense into him and *beat* the sense into him. Leo lied for Apollo. That shit comes at a price. Where I come from, you don't pay your debts, you end up unconscious."

Devon barked a laugh. "Oh yeah? Where you come from?" He crossed his arms over his chest. "Please. Tell me more about southwest Illinois in the eighteen hundreds."

"Whadda ya know? An old man joke." I balled the muffin wrapper up and tossed it into the empty pastry box. "Aren't you Mr. Originality today?"

He smirked. "It's funny because it's true."

I patted him hard on the shoulder. "Well, son. Let me know when your testicles drop and I'll be happy to sit down with you and explain how to use that two-inch stub between your legs."

He laughed loudly.

Sarah's voice from across the room cut off any further insults. "Lark! You got a call on line one."

I twisted my lips and yelled back, "Who is it?"

"Do I look like your secretary?"

I opened my mouth, but Leo strolled into the room, a file folder in his hand.

"You want to keep your balls, you won't answer that." He put two fingers between his lips and wolf-whistled to catch everyone's attention. Loud scrapes of the heavy chairs against the wood floors echoed through the room as the guys started taking their seats around the table. "Go take it in my office. See if you can talk to Apollo when you're done."

I scoffed. "With my mouth or my fists?"

He swayed his head from side to side in consideration. "Surprise me."

My grin spread wide.

After pulling a manila file from his folder, he passed it my way. "You're off this weekend so you can spend time with the girls, but I've got you on an overnight job on Sunday."

"Good deal," I replied, taking my assignment from his hand. Casually flipping through the pages, I blindly made my way down the hall to his office.

"Fuck you!" Apollo shouted when I opened the door.

"Don't worry, my man. The feeling is mutual," I smarted.

He sank down into a chair and kicked his legs out in front of him. "Sorry. I thought you were Leo."

I waved him off. "Nah. Don't apologize. He gave me permission to beat your ass old-school interrogation-style. We're square."

He shot back to his feet. "What?"

Chuckling, I tipped my chin to Johnson and Jude, who were scowling behind him. "Can you keep him quiet for a minute? I gotta take a call."

"I am not a prisoner here!" he shouted, turning in a circle before stopping on Johnson. "This is illegal. I swear to God I'm going to get an attorney and—"

Jude's hand came down on his shoulder. "Shut up, sit down, and stop acting like a spoiled little shit."

I figured this task was impossible considering that Apollo *was* a spoiled little shit. He was also one of the best trackers I'd ever met. For years, he had been able to keep tabs on his sister and evade our every effort to locate him. And he'd done this right under our noses, appearing only long enough to taunt us before he was off again. A year ago, he'd been a huge pain in all of our asses. Now... Well, that was still the case.

Laughing to myself, I moved around Leo's desk and picked his phone up. After shooting a pointed glare at Apollo, I lifted the receiver to my ear and clipped, "Lark."

And that was exact moment Earth fell out of orbit.

Or maybe we'd fallen through a wormhole.

Or a portal into the past.

Because, with one word, I was transported back in time.

"Jeremy?" she said.

It had been no less than a million years since I'd allowed that woman to have any kind of control over me. The last time she'd spoken to me was when she'd screamed at me to go. But no distance I'd put between us had allowed me any freedom.

When a man hits rock bottom, one of two things happens:

He withers.

Or he thrives.

After I'd been kicked out of the Army, I'd had nothing. No job. No money. No home. No family. No best friend, and I wasn't talking about Kurt. Though she'd taken him too.

It was just me, a broken heart, and a fucking beat-up truck filled with so many memories of her that it was a wonder I hadn't set the damn thing on fire.

Withering had never sounded so good.

With a dishonorable discharge on my record, I moved back to Driverton, where the only light at the end of the tunnel was a *dead end* sign.

I tried drowning myself in the bottom of a bottle, but despite my best efforts, I kept waking up. Same ache in my stomach. Same emptiness in my chest. Same picture of her burned into my memories.

Bitter. Broken. Lost.

Occasionally, I'd try losing myself in other women, but most never got their shirts off before I was done with them.

They weren't her.

And, because of that, I wasn't Jeremy.

For over a year, I withered, succeeding at nothing more than failing.

Then one day, after I'd woken up on the couch at a buddy's house, with four dollars to my name, surrounded by a bunch of idiots, none of whom I truly liked and all of whom would die in that small town before they ever grew the balls to leave, I realized that, if didn't pull my head out of my ass and stop pining over a girl who'd never given a damn about me, I was going to die right along with them.

I was twenty-four with the world at my fingertips. Sitting still while the future faded into the past wasn't hurting anyone but me.

So fucking what she'd chosen him?

She'd done that.

She'd done it to me. She'd done it to us. And she'd done it to herself.

Mira had always been weak. Nervous. Scared to take a damn chance on anything, including herself. When we'd been together, I'd thought I'd seen a pillar of strength hidden beneath the surface, but in the end, she proved she was nothing more than one of Kurt's sheep following him blindly for no other reason than the promise of greener pastures. Sure, he could buy her a nice car, maybe a nice house. But she, too, would be forced to wake up one day, realizing he'd led her in circles, having wasted her entire life. And, when she did wake up, I wanted to be so far out of her reach that she'd never be able to tangle me in her webs again.

Part of that thought process was out of spite. But, more than that, it was self-preservation.

She'd told me to go.

I couldn't risk that she'd ever ask me to come back.

After that day, I packed up, moved to Chicago, and allowed the bitterness brewing inside me to fuel my fire rather than be the acid that ate me away from the inside out.

Fuck her.

Fuck Kurt.

Fuck the whole damn world.

I could do bigger and better things than she could ever dream of.

Life didn't begin or end with Mira. The dreams we'd discussed late at night in the back of that truck still existed without her. Mira was extraneous. Just as I'd always been to her.

And what do you know?

Once I got pissed off enough to let her go, I thrived.

I worked my ass off. And, in the end, I got it all.

Good job. Better money. Huge home. Gorgeous family. Loyal friends.

Every-fucking-thing.

So yeah, seventeen years later when she called my job out of the blue, her sexy voice whispering my name across the line, calling me *Jeremy* like she had any right to utter those syllables, I had but one response.

I hung up.

CHAPTER SIX

Mira

"**F**UCK," I BREATHED, STARING DOWN AT MY PHONE.
Call ended.

I wanted to throw up. I'd been pacing a hole in the floor of my bedroom while waiting for the clock to strike eight a.m., which, according to a quick Google search, was when Guardian Protection opened. It was nerve-racking, strolling into the past like that. As I'd sat on hold, the sound of elevator music playing in the background, I'd almost hung up.

But then I remembered Whitney. And stupid fucking Jonah Sheehan.

"Damn it!" I yelled, kicking the bag of money.

Suddenly, my bedroom door swung open, and Tony appeared, holding a glass of orange juice.

My orange juice.

My six-dollar-a-quart, pulp-free, the-only-thing-I-splurged-on, orange juice.

Son of a bitch!

"Everything okay?" he asked.

I ground my teeth, fighting the urge to find my bat and then utilize it on his head. "Yep. Just making some phone calls. I think I've got a lead."

His eyebrows perked. "Already?"

"Old friend." I smiled. "Who knows—maybe we'll both be out of here by tonight." *And you'll be in police custody, but ya know. Whatever. Semantics.*

He narrowed his eyes. "Jonah's not going to be happy if you bring in some bitch who runs her mouth."

My attitude slipped as I snapped, "*He's* an old friend of Kurt's, so I'm not thinking Jonah is going to say shit." *Hopefully because he's dead from a blunt force trauma to the groin.* I tossed him a sugary-sweet smile, and after a few beats, his scrutinizing gaze flicked away.

He lifted the glass of orange juice to his lips, and I vowed right then and there that, regardless of what happened, Jonah only had 699,994 dollars because he was paying to replace my damn orange juice.

"Then get back to it," Tony grumbled, pulling the door shut behind him.

My shoulders sagged, but the hurricane still blew inside me. I'd dodged a bullet, but I was still before the firing squad.

Jeremy had every right to hang up on me. It'd hurt like hell, but I was desperate enough that I couldn't allow myself to acknowledge it. I could be embarrassed and riddled with guilt *after* Whitney was safe.

I hit redial and put the phone back to my ear. As the ringing droned on unanswered, my chest tightened until I feared it was going to break.

This was it. My only hope. And he hated me.

"Guardian Protection Agency," a woman said with the slightest Southern accent that matched my own.

"Hi, uh… May I please speak to Jeremy Lark?"

"Oh, honey. He didn't pick up? I'm sorry—"

"He did. But, um…" I nervously brushed the ends of my hair over my lips. "I think we accidentally got disconnected."

"Okay. Let me grab him again. Hang on for a second."

I sucked in a deep breath, trying to calm my frazzled nerves. I'd had a gun to my head, but somehow, talking to Jeremy was scarier.

As I paced my room, waiting for him to answer, a million

scenarios danced through my thoughts. In most of them, he hung up on me again. In one, he apologized, stating that it really had been an accident. But, no matter how far I allowed my mind to drift, never once did *my Jeremy* answer that phone. That was the impossible.

Too many years had passed. Too many things had changed. What if he didn't even remember me?

After walking over to the full-length mirror on the back of my bedroom door, I realized that the woman staring back at me wasn't the Mira he had known. For the better—and the worse.

Time had taken its toll. I'd aged well at least physically; my hair was still thick and healthy. I'd gained a few pounds, but luckily, they had made themselves at home in areas like my butt and boobs. And, while gravity hadn't exactly been my friend, it wasn't my enemy, either. Men still noticed me. I felt their gazes when I was at work at the bar. More than a few phone numbers scrawled onto cocktail napkins got slipped my way. But I knew too well that the advantages of beauty were limited to the beauty of the world around you. And, since the last time I'd seen Jeremy Lark, I'd lived an ugly existence.

When his voice finally filtered across the line, a part of me died. I was bringing that filth to the most beautiful thing I'd ever had.

"Do *not* call back," he snarled in greeting.

"Please don't hang up," I rushed out, tears welling in my eyes. "I'm in trouble."

The line went silent and I had to pull it away from my ear to see if he'd hung up.

He hadn't.

With hope washing over me, I dropped my voice to a whisper. "Listen, there's a man in my house, so I don't have time to explain it all, but someone broke in last night and kidnapped my best friend. I know you do personal protection and...I... Well, I have seven hundred thousand dollars I can pay you to find her."

Christ. Saying it out loud sounded ludicrous.

But it was the truth.

And that was all I had left.

Nerves rolling in my stomach, I sank down on the corner of my bed, praying for a miracle.

That miracle remained painfully silent.

"Jeremy," I whispered, my anxiety climbing. "*Please*. I need help."

"Then I suggest you call the cops," he rumbled.

A wave of relief crashed over me. At least he was talking.

"I can't. At least not yet. God only knows what Jonah would do to Whitney." A lump lodged in my throat. "I'm sorry, okay? I know I shouldn't be calling you. But I don't know what else to do." I screwed my eyes shut and pinched the bridge of my nose. "I'm not asking for a favor. This is strictly professional. The seven hundred thousand dollars is in cash. Though I'm not exactly sure it's legal—"

"Shut up!" he boomed.

My back shot straight, and my heart jumped into my throat. "Jer—"

"Do not fucking call my job and dump this shit on me. I don't want to know why you won't call the cops. I don't want to know why someone broke into your house and kidnapped your best friend. And I sure as fuck don't want to know why you have seven hundred thousand dollars in cash that may or may not be legal. Hang up the phone and never dial this number again. I am not involved in whatever-the-fuck bullshit you have going on in your life right now. And, most importantly, I am not involved in your life *at all*."

Every word felt like an arrow searing through me. He was right; I couldn't deny that. But…

"I don't know who else to call!" I whisper-yelled, watching the door for any sign of Tony.

"Your husband!" he yelled so loudly that I had to pull the phone away from my ear.

It had been a lifetime since we'd spoken, but at the mention of Kurt, the hurt and betrayal in his voice were as prominent as they'd been the day he'd walked away.

But, for me, Kurt was nothing more than the spark that lit my fuse. He'd cost me too many years of my life.

Not anymore.

Jumping to my feet, I seethed, "Kurt is the one who sent them to find me! Four hours ago, a man held a gun to my head—a gun my *ex-husband* somehow supplied him with, despite the fact that he is currently in prison. They took my roommate and my fucking dog, Jeremy. My goddamn *dog!*" I sucked in as much air as my lungs could hold and carried on. "Right now, there is a different *armed man* sitting in my living room, drinking my fucking organic orange juice, ready to put a bullet in my head if I don't figure out how to clean seven hundred thousand dollars in drug money for my aforementioned *ex-husband*. So, yeah…it is safe to assume Kurt doesn't give one single fuck about me." I laughed without humor, the reality of it all shredding me. "I am *not* asking for a favor. I'm asking to *pay you* for your protection services in order to get a terrified twenty-three-year-old girl—an *innocent* girl—somewhere safe so that they cannot hurt her when I call the police, turn Jonah in, and then bask in the world of ugliness that my piece-of-shit ex-husband rained down *on me*." By the time I finished, my chest was heaving and my heart was racing, but the fire burning inside me roared stronger than ever.

I was mad. So fucking mad.

But not at Jeremy.

Hell, maybe not even at Kurt.

Yes, he'd played me more times than I could count. But it had taken almost fourteen years of my life before I'd finally grown the balls to get rid of him forever.

That was the hardest part. Knowing that there was no one to blame for my current predicament except myself.

And, not surprisingly, there was no one left to come to my rescue.

It was time to save myself. But that wasn't what I was doing… I was dumping my garbage on someone else. Holding that phone in my hand, begging for Jeremy's help, made me no better than Kurt.

Jeremy had a good life. One he'd made for himself out of nothing. He had a job that, while I wasn't sure what his position entailed, I assumed accepting known drug money wasn't going to win him any accolades. And then there were his kids… They depended on him. Yet there I was, asking him to risk it all. For me—the woman who had never chosen him.

My shoulders shook as realization dug its claws in. It was over. My last hope had been nothing more than an oasis born from desperation.

"I'm sorry. I shouldn't have called," I blurted.

But I was a coward, because even though I realized what a fool I'd been in making that call, I didn't hang up. With trembling hands, I held the phone at my ear, listening to him breathe while pleading with the universe that he'd tell me to wait.

Mira. That's all he'd have to say.

But it never came.

He didn't hang up though. That's not the way Jeremy and I worked.

Seventeen years earlier, I had been the one who had let him go.

This time would be no different.

CHAPTER SEVEN

Lark

"SON OF A FUCKING BITCH!" I SENT THE PHONE SAILING ACROSS Leo's office. The cord caught, yanking the base and a large stack of papers off the side.

Jude, Johnson, and Apollo jumped out of the way, but I was too busy plotting someone's death to pay them any attention.

I wasn't sure whose death it was going to be yet. My ever-spinning roulette wheel of emotions hadn't yet landed on my victim. There was a solid chance that it was going to be Kurt, but I hadn't ruled out Mira—or, hell, even myself.

"Lark, man. You...okay?" Jude asked cautiously.

"Motherfucking dandy," I sneered, raking a rough hand through my hair.

Fucking Mira.

"Care to tell me what the hell is going on?" Johnson growled, prowling toward me.

"Nothing."

"Didn't sound like nothing."

I pinched the bridge of my nose. "Well, it was. And I'd appreciate you fucking dropping it."

He stopped in front of me, uncomfortably close, and planted his hands on his hips. "Try again. And, this time, explain the cops, kidnapping, and seven hundred thousand dollars."

Outstanding.

I considered Johnson a friend, and a good one at that. But, as twenty-five-percent owner at Guardian Protection, he was also my boss. I did not need him getting all up in my business.

Shit! How the hell had Mira fucking York become my business again?

My answer came as her voice echoed in my ears. *"Please. I'm in trouble."*

Indecision warred inside me.

On one side of the battle lines was a petty little man, pissed off and angry for all the bullshit she had pulled on him back in the day. That man didn't want to care that she was in trouble. Served her right. That part of me was dying to tell her to fuck off like I'd planned out in my head on the rare occasions I'd allowed myself to think about her over the years.

But, on the other side, there was the man I had become—the father of two daughters—who had just heard that a woman I cared about—even in the past—was being held at gunpoint.

For some asinine reason, I had been the man she'd chosen to call for help. And I'd let her hang up without so much as finding out where she was. All because I was so torn that I couldn't form a goddamn sentence.

I hated that woman.

But it was Mira.

Not even seventeen years was enough to keep my heart from reacting to the sound of her voice. However, it hadn't reacted with thoughts of roses and long-lost loves. It had been an explosion of pain in my chest and a sharp stabbing in my gut.

Time changed people. God knew I was a different person. But, for the life of me, I couldn't figure out how she could have gotten herself into a situation that involved drugs, guns, and kidnapping. Mira had always been good to the core. It was one of the things I had loved most about her. She'd kept me on the straight and narrow. Hell, the first time I'd taken her to our spot in the woods, I'd had to blindfold her so she couldn't see the *no trespassing* signs.

And now…

Kurt.

His moral compass had always resembled more of a watch without batteries. But this mountain of bullshit was a stretch even for him. Then again, she'd said that he was in prison. Surprising. But not shocking.

For the first year as I'd withered, I'd done my best to secretly keep up with Kurt and Mira. Thanks to a few friends back at battalion, I had known they'd gotten engaged and then later married. But, after the day I'd decided to turn my life around, I'd never looked back again.

Until now.

"Fucking hell," I groaned.

Johnson cocked his head to the side and eyed me warily. "Melissa in some kind of trouble?"

My head popped up. "That wasn't her."

Jude closed in on me. "Then who was it?"

Wasn't that the million-dollar question?

Mira was a stranger to me.

I knew her name. I knew her past. I'd once known her heart.

And, because of that, I knew I was about to make the biggest mistake of my entire life.

The decision had been made the minute she'd dialed my number. And I fucking hated her for it. Mainly because, regardless how much I hated her, she knew me well enough to know I'd do it anyway.

One call. One word. And I was back at her mercy.

Seventeen years and the strings that had bound us together still held strong, no matter how hard I'd tried to break them.

"I need a favor," I said, sweeping my gaze through the room.

Johnson's response was immediate. "Anything."

Jude's was a little more cautious. "You gonna tell us what that favor is first?"

"No. I need it from him," I said, turning my attention to Apollo.

I could only imagine how murderous I must have looked, because before I started in his direction, he was already scrambling away.

"Mira York," I stated.

Nervously, he flashed his gaze to Johnson. "Wh-what?"

"Mira Renee York. Maybe Benton." The name felt like acid on my tongue, but I powered through. "Last I heard, she was back in Driverton, but it might be Chicago."

"I don't—"

"Find her!"

"It doesn't work that way," he argued. "I can't just magically produce a person because you give me their name. I need—"

"Eleven eighty-seven South Euclid, Chicago, Illinois," Johnson announced.

My heart stopped as I spun to look at him.

He pointed to the computer screen. "Google. She recently applied for a business license."

I sucked in a deep breath, nerves radiating over my entire body. Was I really going to do this? Willingly wade into Kurt's bullshit?

What the fuck was wrong with me?

"I'm in trouble."

Yep. Those three words were all it took. I was out of that office before I could talk myself out of it.

"Whoa, whoa, whoa," Johnson said, catching my arm as I marched down the hall. "Where the hell do you think you're going?"

I stared at him defiantly. "Don't do this. I gotta go."

His dark gaze drilled into me. "Then tell me who she is and what the hell is going on before you fly off halfcocked, getting yourself into a situation where I gotta buy a suit to be your pallbearer."

My jaw ticked as I ground my teeth. "Just some girl I used to know."

"Just some girl, huh?" Johnson smarted. "That why you look like you're about to rip out of your skin, fashion it into a noose, and hang someone with it?"

"Let me go," I growled.

"Then tell me the story before I'm forced to start guessing like this is a goddamn game of charades."

So it appeared keeping Johnson out of my business wasn't going to be as easy as I'd hoped. But maybe that wasn't a bad thing. He was a big enough dick to give it to me straight. And, given the fact that I was currently considering storming the door at eleven eighty-seven South Euclid, where there was an armed man holding a woman hostage, I figured now was as good of a time as any to gain some perspective.

I yanked my arm from his grasp. "Fine. She was a girl I used to date. Or fuck." *Or love like the world was ending.* "Or whatever. A couple of guys broke into her apartment, put a gun to her head, kidnapped her best friend, and dumped a fuck-ton of cash on her. Her ex-husband, who is coincidentally my ex–best friend, is in lockup. And, despite the fact that the last time I saw her was an eternity ago after she fucking destroyed me, she still called me for help because there is an armed man parked on her couch, drinking her organic orange juice. Now, if you will kindly crawl out of my ass, I'm planning to go get her until I can figure out what to do about the rest of that bullshit."

"Huh," Johnson scoffed, scrubbing his beard with his palm. "Not quite what I was expecting. But okay. Give me ten to gather up a few of the boys and I'll meet you in the car."

"No. I go at this alone."

He roared with laughter liked I'd told a joke, complete with bending over and resting his hands on his thighs.

"For fuck's sake," I snapped, glowering as he lifted a finger in the air while trying to catch his breath.

When he finally sobered, he shot me a smile and a wink. "As I was saying…" Grabbing the front of my shirt, he spun, slamming me hard against the wall. My breath left on a rush, and pain exploded in my lungs. "Okay. Maybe I didn't make this clear." He stabbed a finger against my pec. "You will *not* go at this alone. You think it's important enough to run into the line of fire over some woman you haven't seen in years, then you are going to do it smart. You're taking Devon. He's sharp and will watch your six while you're off thinking with your dick. *And* you're taking Alex because he's big enough to drag both of your asses out in case you boys discover that you are not in fact capable of dodging bullets like Keanu Reeves. *And* you're taking me because… well, I like a good show."

The idea of having backup made me feel a hell of a lot better. But, in the same breath, that relief turned toxic. It was one thing to deal with Mira's shit on my own, but dragging the guys into it too?

I clenched my teeth tighter. "No."

He chuckled. "Too fucking bad. We're already involved. Despite how big this office is, you forget it's really fucking small." He grinned and then yelled into my face, "Come on out, boys!"

Devon and Alex appeared at the mouth of the hall, shit-eating grins covering both of their faces. Clearly, they had been eavesdropping like a bunch of fucking women. And just when I thought it couldn't get worse…

Now, everyone was involved in Mira's bullshit.

Johnson pushed off me and straightened his tight, black T-shirt. "Suit up, gentlemen. Lark's got a wild hair to play Casanova today."

I rolled my eyes. Going after Mira had nothing to do with romance.

But, then again, I wasn't sure what it did have to do with.

And, given the speed of my pulse and the heavy weight in my stomach, I was afraid to find out.

CHAPTER EIGHT

Mira

I AWOKE TO THE SLAM OF THE SCREEN DOOR. MY EYES WERE SWOLLEN and thick with exhaustion. I wasn't sure how long I'd been asleep—or when I'd drifted off. Last thing I'd remembered was staring up at the ceiling as tears trailed into my ears, hosting a pity party for one, and trying to figure out how my life had gone so wrong.

After swinging my legs over the side of the bed, I patted the empty spot where Bitsy would so often sit, staring up at me with her cute little bug eyes while I got ready. Bile clawed up the back of my throat, and guilt slashed through me. And then there was Whitney. I allowed myself a second to imagine her sitting at the rickety table in the kitchen, eating a bowl of cereal, a textbook laid out in front of her.

I smiled at the thought and it forced a fresh tear to slide down my cheek.

I'd failed them both.

With shaking hands, I covered my mouth as if I could physically hold in the sob that so violently ricocheted inside me. Breaking down again wouldn't solve anything. Then again, I had no clue what would.

Suddenly, the blast of a gunshot tore through the room. I wasn't exactly an expert on firearms, but there was no mistaking the sound. It was so loud that I instinctively covered my ears and ducked my head. A myriad of men's voices erupted in the other room. I prayed that it was the police and not more of Jonah's guys.

Much to my disappointment, when the door to my room flew open, there were no uniformed officers on the other side. That would have been too easy. Instead, a monster of a man came storming inside. A thick, black beard covered his face, and his eyes were so dark I could see the malevolence swirling within them.

Christ, I'd have taken Jonah, Tony, and every other man they could brainwash into their army of idiots over this guy.

Scrambling across the bed to get as far away from him as I could, I threw my hands out in front of me. "It's in the closet. The money... I..."

But he didn't slow. His every step was heavy with purpose, and each one carried him closer...to me?

Fear consumed me as my back hit the wall. "No!" I screamed.

"Relax," he grumbled, planting a knee to the bed and extending two long, tattooed arms toward me.

Yeah. Like that was going to happen.

I turned my head, squeezing my eyes shut, frantically trying to disappear as I chanted a dozen variations of, "Please, don't."

I waited for him to grab me. To drag me away like Jonah had done to Whitney. Or worse...

But, as I sat there, cowering in the corner, my knees tucked to my chest, my trembling hands lifted in surrender, God finally granted me a miracle.

"Get away from her," was ordered from somewhere in the distance, but I didn't dare open my eyes to see who it was.

My confusion intensified when the bed shifted and I felt the bearded man's presence move away.

And then I swear the entire world tipped on its axis.

"Mira," he rasped.

That single solitary word shook the Earth, or maybe that was just the sob that tore from my throat. I could have lived a million years and there never would have been another sound that beautiful. Tears hit the backs of my lids as hope soared inside me.

It had been seventeen years since I'd heard him say my name, yet

I'd played it in my head so many times that it still seemed familiar. Every consonant and vowel fluttered across my skin like the softest feather. And, as my lids flew open, I found him standing in my doorway, his hazel eyes boring into me with the weight of the world, I knew I'd never see something so beautiful again, either.

He was leaning on the doorjamb, one arm across his chest, holding the opposite shoulder, his face more gorgeous than even in my dreams. And I wasn't too proud to admit I'd dreamed about him a lot.

"Jeremy," I breathed.

It was the wrong thing to say. Because the gorgeous man standing in front of me disappeared. His whole body jerked as if I'd slapped him, and his jaw turned to stone.

But I couldn't stop staring.

"Wh-what are you doing here?" I stammered.

"I have no fucking idea," he replied.

I'd never told him where I was. He'd had to have looked me up... Oh. My. God.

My hopes spiked to an all-time high, butterflies swarming in my stomach. Until I remembered the promise I'd made to him of seven hundred thousand dollars.

Money. Always fucking money.

The promise of it.

The pursuit of it.

The use of it.

Money had ruined my entire life. Why would this be any different?

My throat got tight as disappointment ravaged me. "The cash is in the closet."

His jaw ticked as he cut his gaze to the closet door.

When he didn't move, I decided maybe he wanted the information on how to find Whitney. And, while I didn't trust my voice, I needed him to leave sooner rather than later so I could have an emotional meltdown in private. "Her name is Whitney Sloan, and the man who took her is Jonah Sheehan. He used to be Kurt's—"

"Get her out of here," he barked.

My body jolted. "I'm sorry. What?"

He ignored me. "Take her to the office."

I'd been in such a trance that I belatedly noticed that the brute who had originally stormed in was still looming terrifyingly close. He seemed to be with Jeremy, so I decided to give him the benefit of the doubt.

"Did you get shot in the head, dumbass?" Scary Guy rumbled.

Jeremy's face got tight. "I said—"

"Yeah, I fucking heard you. But that shit is not going to happen. You need to get to a hospital, and you show up with a GSW, questions are going to be asked. Questions that you do *not* have answers to without throwing your woman under the bus."

"She's not my fucking woman," Jeremy shot back so fast that it was insulting.

However, I was still focused on the rest of his statement. Maybe it was shock. Or maybe I couldn't keep up with the broken-sentence man-code, but they weren't making sense.

"GSW?" I asked.

They both ignored me.

Scary Guy planted his hands on his hips. "Oh, really? That man's face in the other room says otherwise."

Oh, damn. Tony.

I leaned to the side and peered around Jeremy. Tony was lying facedown on the floor. His hands had been zip-tied behind his back, his legs turned up and connected to his wrists. Two huge men were standing around him, their thick arms crossed as they casually talked to each other, utterly unfazed.

As I righted myself on the bed, I allowed my gaze to sweep over Jeremy. Jesus, I really wished I'd changed into something other than jeans and an oversized long-sleeve T-shirt. I was seriously underdressed.

He was every bit as handsome as he had been in those Facebook pictures I'd tortured myself with over the years. Navy slacks and a pale-blue button-down stretched over his tall, muscular frame made him look like he should have been on his way to a boardroom rather than standing in my bedroom. His dark-auburn hair was clipped shorter on the sides than it was on the top, styled away from his face, not a gray in sight. Okay…so maybe he was even more beautiful than he had been in those pictures, mainly because he was there in the flesh rather than an image on the screen of my phone.

"That asshole is lucky he's breathing," Jeremy declared.

It made me a terrible person, but the idea of Jeremy exacting any kind of revenge in my honor did some seriously warm things inside me. My lips twitched, and I felt my cheeks heat.

And that's when I saw it. Dark red pooled on his shirt at his left shoulder.

"Oh my God! You're hurt." I exploded off the bed and raced toward him.

He quickly sidestepped me. "Don't fucking touch me!"

I froze, his scathing rejection blistering my heart. "I…I wasn't going to. It's just…" I flicked my gaze to Scary Guy, who was ten times scarier than before as he scowled at Jeremy. "You're…bleeding a lot."

"It just grazed me. I'll be fine," Jeremy mumbled.

Scary Guy laughed. "Well, would you look at that. He's a fucking doctor now too."

Jeremy's lips thinned as if he were barely keeping his patience in check. "Get her out of here. I'll deal with the rest of this shit."

"Perfect. We'll just leave you to it, then." Scary Guy casually walked over to him and slapped his shoulder. It would have been a friendly gesture if, ya know, he hadn't been shot.

"Motherfucker!" Jeremy boomed before folding over in pain.

"Hey!" I wedged myself between them and planted a hand in Scary Guy's chest. So, one could say, putting my hands on him wasn't my smartest move, but I was already committed, so I gave him a shove that didn't move him at all. "What the hell is wrong with you?" I accused. "He's hurt."

I swear to God it was like I was invisible with these two.

Scary Guy leaned over me and whispered to Jeremy, "Your ass is not the only one on the line here. Shut the fuck up. And let's make some magic happen. Yeah?"

If looks could kill, he would have been in an unrecognizable heap of flesh and muscle for the glare Jeremy aimed at him.

But their standoff didn't last long. Scary Guy suddenly lowered his menacing gaze on me.

I startled and stumbled back a step into Jeremy's rock-hard chest. He jumped away from me as if I were a leper. I pretended that it didn't hurt. But, truth be told, it killed.

"Mira, babe. Call nine-one-one," Scary Guy said in a tone so soft and so gentle that I had no idea how a man who looked like he did was capable of producing it.

"I can't. Not until we get Whitney. Jonah said he'd kill her."

"If we don't report this and gunshots get called in by your neighbors, we're all going to be fucked, and that includes your friend." He patted my arm seriously gently and seriously sweetly. "Call the cops. Tell them the truth about everything that happened this morning. Maybe leave out the part where you got the fantastically ridiculous idea to offer Lark seven hundred thousand dollars instead of calling them in the first place." His face got warm. "I promise you your friend is a hell of a lot better off with the CPD out looking for her than a team of bodyguards. Kidnapping and ransom is not our specialty, babe. Call the cops. Tell them Guardian Protection took on your case a couple months ago, after you heard your ex was going to try to drag you into his crap. We showed up today since you didn't check in last night, apprehended the intruder, but not before Lark got shot."

"I didn't get shot! It's a scratch," Jeremy defended.

Scary Guy rolled his eyes, and if my life hadn't been in the middle of falling apart, I would have laughed.

"Make the call," he ordered.

"But I've never paid Guardian. What if they look into my bank records?"

"You don't have to pay when your man is part of the team." He grinned, clearly proud of himself.

Jeremy *clearly* felt otherwise. "No fucking way! We're old friends. Nothing more. I took it on as a favor."

Well, at least he thought we were friends. I could live with that.

I smiled with gratitude, hope once again singing in my veins.

That is, until, he gave me a quick head-to-toe and said, "If I'm going to lie, at least make it something believable."

Woooooow!

I mean…he'd come for me. And I was pretty damn desperate for help, but insults? Seriously?

I couldn't even pretend that it didn't hurt.

Nor could I pretend that it didn't piss me the hell off.

I spun to face him, all hope flatlining. "Was that really necessary?"

He loomed closer and glowered down at me. "Is it necessary that I'm here at all?"

I pushed up onto my toes and got in his face. "No, it's not! If you recall, I *never* asked *you* to come *here*. And I sure as hell didn't ask you to come in on what is quite possibly the worst day of my entire life, slinging insults. I asked you to save my friend, who I would like to point out is still out there, alone, and probably terrified." I drew in a deep breath and attempted to calm down but quickly decided that it wasn't happening. "I'm sorry. I don't mean to sound ungrateful—"

"Well, you fucking do!" he snarled, ominously stepping forward, forcing me to back away. "I'm standing here, bleeding, after driving half an hour to save your ass after not seeing or hearing from you for the better part of two decades. You'll have to excuse—"

"Not excused!" I screamed, my face vibrating with anger. Sure, he'd only made one rude comment. And he had technically taken a bullet for me, so he probably deserved a free pass. But, for fuck's sake, a woman could only take so much. "You think I *wanted* to call you?" This time, *I* took the step forward and *he* was forced to back away. (Leprosy had its perks.) "I would have rather swallowed a rusty sword while walking back to Alabama in shoes made of broken glass—"

He stepped forward. I backed away.

"It's not too late, Mir."

I stepped forward. He backed away.

"Clearly, I made a mistake."

He stepped forward. I backed away.

"Ya think? What part of this clusterfuck gave it away?"

I stepped forward. He backed away.

"You're an asshole!"

"Says the bitch screaming in my face." He stepped forward.

I did *not* back away.

I blinked. A lot. Predominantly because tears were welling in my eyes and I was desperately trying to keep them hidden. But also because I couldn't believe that this was the same Jeremy Lark I'd known all those years ago.

"Who are you?" I whispered.

For the briefest of seconds, his face flashed soft, but he quickly covered it and dealt his final blow. "No one to you."

Turning, he walked away without another glance.

I was stunned, aching from head to toe, inside and out, heart and soul.

"Mira," Scary Guy murmured, stepping in front of me and giving my arm a reassuring squeeze.

"Well, that was pleasant," I smarted, craning my head back to give him my gaze.

He smiled and, holy shit, it was anything but scary. It was actually quite…beautiful.

"Oh, wow," I breathed.

His knowing smile grew, lighting his dark eyes and brightening his whole demeanor. "Mira. Nine-one-one."

"Right," I replied, but I didn't move.

He chuckled and shook his head. "*Now*, babe."

My feet didn't want to move, and not because Scary Guy was suddenly Sexy Guy, but rather because it meant I'd finally have to snap myself out of my Jeremy Lark–induced fog and deal with my problems.

With a hollow sensation in my chest and a vortex of regret

spiraling inside me, I pulled up my big-girl panties, picked my phone up, and made the call.

After that, everything became a blur.

Sexy Guy, who informed me that his name was Aidan Johnson, stayed close as I made the call. He even took the phone from my hand when I dissolved into a puddle of tears while recounting the part when Jonah had taken Whitney. He'd finished talking to the dispatcher with his arm hooked around my neck, my face buried in his chest. It was a sweet sentiment, but I was beyond the point where comfort from a stranger would do me any good.

And, minutes later, as I watched Jeremy Lark being loaded into an ambulance, something he was not happy about, an injury I had caused him in his shoulder, his furious gaze locked on mine, I knew with an absolute certainty that I was past the point where comfort from *anyone* could do me any good.

CHAPTER NINE

Lark

I'D WALKED OUT OF THE HOSPITAL WITH A GLORIFIED BAND-AID, A script for antibiotics, and headful of fucked-up information about my ex-best friend. Leo's brother-in-law, Caleb Jones, a detective at the Chicago PD had met me at the hospital. It seemed Kurt Benton didn't just get around when it came to women. From the way Caleb had made it sound, Kurt had his finger in shit all over the map. By all accounts, it seemed Mira was innocent, and it enraged me to think of Kurt dragging her into that. However, I wasn't the least bit surprised to hear she'd still been married to him the day he'd gotten locked away. Mira had never been strong enough to leave him. And knowing that that hadn't changed pissed me off more than anything else.

Fucking Mira.

When we'd arrived at her house that morning, the truck had barely come to a stop before I was out the door. With every step closer, my heart had thundered louder. It'd had little to do with the fact that she'd told me there was an armed man inside and everything to do with the hum in my veins from knowing she was so fucking close.

I hated that I'd felt that way.

I loathed that my heart still felt a connection with her.

And I despised that my mind hadn't been strong enough to sever that connection years earlier.

One fucking phone call and I was a dumbass, out of control,

twenty-something all over again.

I should have waited for the rest of the guys. I should have been more cautious. I sure as hell should *not* have nearly torn that fucking screen door off the hinges as I'd tried to get inside.

Lucky bastard had gotten one shot off before I'd reached him. After that, I'd had to be dragged off him. The pain in my shoulder was sharp, but the hardest hit came from the realization that it could have been *her* body had she not called me.

Or, worse, had I been too much of a prick not to have gone after her.

And, when I saw her cowering on that bed, scared out of her wits, I didn't give a single fuck that she was dodging Johnson's hands and he was trying to help. I wanted to murder him all the same.

That feeling did not die when I saw him hugging her with a familiarity he had no right to have. Johnson was a stubborn bastard who needed a lesson in personal space. Back in the day, I'd laughed when Jude had gotten possessive with Johnson over Rhion in the beginning of their relationship. It'd made no sense. The guy dated *men* for the most part. But I was well aware he had more than once taken a woman to his bed, and it was that knowledge that had felt like nails on a chalkboard inside my skull when Mira was staring up at him all breathy and dreamy-eyed like she'd seen Adonis himself.

The human psyche was a crazy beast. I could physically feel the hate brewing inside me when it came to Mira York. How that somehow flared with jealousy was beyond me.

That wasn't true. Any man with a dick would have felt the same way.

Despite what I'd said, Mira was still fucking gorgeous. Maybe more so than she had been as a girl. She'd filled out. Those natural curves she'd always possessed had deepened and softened. Her hair was shorter now, ending just above the swell of her full breasts. But her eyes—they were exactly the same.

Which, for me, might as well have been the kiss of death. Those eyes had always been my undoing. They'd assaulted the backs of my eyelids long after I'd sworn her off.

Seventeen fucking years and I couldn't escape that woman. Yeah, I'd moved on with my life. Got married. Made babies. Set up a family. But, with one single glance into those deep-brown eyes, I knew I'd never truly forgotten her. I'd buried her memories deep. So deep that I'd been able to convince myself that they no longer existed.

But, as I marched into Guardian after I'd been released from the hospital what felt like eight hundred years later, I knew those feelings still burned hot.

And I knew there was not one goddamn thing I wasn't going to do to finally extinguish them forever.

"Where is she?" I growled, stopping in the doorway of Leo's office.

"How ya feeling?" he asked, never tearing his gaze off his computer screen.

It sounded genuine, but I was all too aware that it was only a pleasantry before he laid into my ass. Given the fact that Johnson wasn't sitting across from him with his feet propped up on the desk as they shot the breeze, it was safe to assume that Leo had already dished out a ration of shit to him for going with me.

"Where. Is. She?" I repeated.

He turned to face me and arched an incredulous eyebrow. A smirk pulled at one side of his mouth as he said, "Interesting. I heard you were all fucked up over this woman…but this. This is impressive."

"I'm not all fucked up. I don't even know her."

"That's not what the sworn affidavit the cops had me sign earlier stated." He rocked back in his chair and steepled his fingers under his chin. "You know. I'm getting real sick and tired of lying on behalf of my men when they don't seem to have the courtesy to give me a heads-up before flying off on a kamikaze mission. First Apollo, now you? I gotta say, Lark, you're the only level-headed man I got. I did *not* expect this bullshit from you."

Funny. When I'd woken up that morning, I hadn't expected it, either.

Yet there I stood.

"Can we possibly have the father-son I'm-so-disappointed-in-you chat in the morning? I've had a hell of a day."

"Tomorrow? No. You're suspended."

My body locked up tight and I winced when pain stabbed in my shoulder. "Come again?"

He rose to his feet and planted his knuckles on his desk. "No pay for two weeks. Same goes for Johnson."

"What the fuck, Leo! You can't do that."

"I can. And I did. You're lucky I didn't suspend Devon and Alex too. What you four did today... For fuck's sake, you all could have been killed."

"What the hell are you talking about? You send us out with clients every goddamn day where our sole job is to put ourselves in harm's way. Oh, but suddenly, it matters that Mira wasn't a paying client?" I stabbed my hand into my back pocket and retrieved my wallet before slapping it down on his desk. "By all means, let me cover the men's time."

"You better watch yourself before I skip the suspension and go straight to the pink slip."

I didn't think he'd fire me. This was literally the first time he and I had ever crossed each other, but I valued my job enough to bring it down a notch.

"I'll take the suspension, but don't punish Johnson. He knew I was going with or without him. He was trying to watch my back."

Leo laughed. "Full disclosure: It was Johnson's idea to suspend you without pay. It was mine to extend that punishment to him as well."

I blew out a ragged breath. "Of course it was."

He moved around his desk and perched on the corner, crossing his legs at the ankle and kicking them out in front of him. "Look, I don't know what's going on with you and that woman. Honestly, I've never heard of her before today. But, if you felt the need to go all Incredible Hulk and charge the gates of Hell over her, I'm going to give you the benefit of the doubt and assume that it was for a good reason. But I will say this… You aren't one of the boys living carefree. You got two kids who depend on you. Something happens to you, that changes their lives. You better make damn sure Mira's worth the risks."

"She's not," I replied immediately. I could almost taste the bitterness in my tone.

His brow furrowed. "Then that makes today exponentially more stupid."

He wasn't wrong. I hadn't been thinking. Not about my girls. Not about my life. Not the safety of the men who had come with me.

Nothing but Mira.

I couldn't afford to make that mistake twice.

"I'm gonna take her home and be done with it."

"You sure that's a good idea? Word is she's got a shitstorm swirling around her."

I shrugged…and it fucking hurt. "I don't care what she's got swirling. That is not my war. She was in trouble. I got her out of it. End of story."

"All right," he chirped, clapping his hands and rising to his feet.

But this was Leo. All right never meant all right. It actually sounded a whole lot like he'd called bullshit.

"I'm serious. I've done my job. The rest is on her."

"Okay." He grinned and walked back around his desk.

"Leo, I'm serious. This thing with her—"

"Lark, I'm not arguing with you here. You say it's over. It's over." He grabbed a folder off his desk and flipped it open. "Oh, by the way, Johnson took her home with him."

My chest got tight, and before I could stop it, "What the fuck?" flew from my mouth.

Leo glanced up, the biggest smile I'd ever seen the man wear splitting his face. "That a problem?"

I glared.

If possible, his smile got bigger. "I haven't seen Johnson interested in a woman in a long time."

"Don't do that."

"What?" He laughed.

"It's not gonna work. He wants her, he can have her."

He sank down into his chair. "Oh, good. Because he offered to let her stay with him until things settled down."

"He doesn't even know her!" Yeah. I couldn't stop that, either.

He intertwined his fingers and rested them on his stomach. Still. Fucking. Grinning. "But, according to you, you don't know her, either." He partitioned his mouth off as if we weren't the only two people in the room and said, "But it sounds like somebody is trying to get to know her. If you know what I mean."

"Oh, fuck off, Leo."

He laughed again. "Just look at it this way. At least it wasn't Braydon. With Johnson, you got a fifty-fifty chance that she won't be naked when you pick her up."

He was prodding me. More than likely, Devon and Alex had gotten back to the office running their mouths, filling his head with shit they did not understand. A man almost gets shot while blindly flying into a house to save a woman who was in danger and suddenly the country's premier protection firm turns into a goddamn episode of *Love Connection*.

But the worst part about the shit he was spewing? It was working.

Turning on a toe, I marched out of his office. Destination unknown.

Okay, fine. That was a lie. Explanation unknown was more like it. I didn't know what excuse I was going to use or how I was going to spin it, but I was going to Johnson's place to find her.

"Oh, come on, Lark. Be a good sport!" Leo yelled, his footsteps following after me. "She'd be good for Johnson. I might finally get godchildren."

I winced, but it wasn't from pain—at least not in my shoulder. I felt like a maniac, shifting back and forth between emotions so fast that it was a wonder I didn't have whiplash. But I couldn't stop myself. That woman got under my skin.

"You go anywhere near Johnson's house, you're fired," Leo called behind me.

I froze, a new rage bubbling inside me. "Stay out of this, Leo."

"I tried to," he said, sauntering around me. His smile was gone, and his face had become hard. He pointed to my shoulder. "But you brought this to me the moment you decided to walk out that door this morning. You handled that shit *your way* and look where it got you. Now, we're handling the rest of it *my way*."

"And your way is getting godchildren out of the situation?"

"No. My way is not hanging her ass out to dry. Cops still can't find her friend, and you're talking about dumping her back at her house after she turned seven hundred thousand dollars over to the authorities? Jesus, Lark, she'd be as good as dead."

"What the fuck do you expect me to do?" I huffed, raking a hand through my hair.

He laughed without humor. "The thing you were trying to do this morning when you went after her in the first place. And the thing you were about to do before I stopped you from racing over to Johnson's house and more than likely having your second near-death experience of the day."

"I don't know what that is!" I roared. And, for the first time since I'd gotten that phone call, I realized it was the God's honest truth.

I didn't know what to do. I didn't know how to feel. I didn't know how to react. I'd never once considered a scenario when she'd reenter my life.

I did hate her.

But I'd also loved her. Once.

Nothing made sense anymore.

I mean…were people even allowed to be angry about something from so long ago? We'd been kids, and I was holding the choices she'd made against her like it had happened yesterday. What the hell did that say about me? But I knew… It said that I was a dick.

I allowed my head to fall back between my shoulders and stared up at the ceiling. "This woman… She fucks with my head."

He chuckled. "This is not a newsflash."

Blowing out a ragged breath, I looked at him. "I'm sorry. For all of it."

He shrugged. "I guess it made the day interesting enough. Though I could have gone without Melissa calling and laying into me after she'd heard you'd been shot."

It was my turn to laugh. "Yeah. She gave me an earful too, until she found out it was just a nick. Then she got mad and gave me another earful for scaring her and *not* being shot."

"Damned if you do…"

I extended a hand his way. "Damned if I don't."

He took my hand and pulled me in for a quick back pat.

When he stepped away, he crossed his arms over his chest and cocked his head to the side. "So, what are you going to do about Mira?"

"Well…" I scratched the back of my head. "I guess I'm gonna call Johnson and—"

"She's downstairs with Rhion." He winked. "Johnson flew out of here like a bat out of hell when I suspended him."

My mouth gaped open. "You son of a bitch."

He barked a laugh. "I'd like to apologize, but it got me more answers than you were ever going to give me."

"And what answers were those? Because I gotta be honest here. I'm clueless."

He shrugged. "Actually, you being clueless was one of the best answers I got. Never seen you off-kilter, Lark. And I'm not looking forward to seeing it again. The group of men I got, one of you is always on your period. I guess it was finally your turn." He tipped his chin toward the front door. "Go. Get out of here. Figure out whatever the hell is or isn't going on with you and this woman. I'll let you know if I hear anything about her friend. I called in a few favors. I'm hoping they'll help."

"What kind of favors?"

He smiled and backed toward the hall. "The kind you don't talk about unless you're calling 'em in." He winked. "Let me know if you need anything." He paused. "Well, anything besides a paycheck."

"Hilarious," I deadpanned as he disappeared down the hall toward his office.

Sucking in a deep breath, I made my way out the door and to the elevator.

I had no idea what I was going to say to her. Or what I was planning to do. And, as I exited the elevator and stood outside Rhion's front door, that confusion only got stronger.

She was in there. After all those years, Mira York was only one door away.

I knocked and waited, equally hoping Rhion wouldn't answer while also wishing she would hurry up before I lost my nerve.

Finally the door swung open and Jude was standing on the other side, a knowing smirk pulling at his lips.

"Christ, not you too," I grumbled, planting a hand in the center of his chest to push past him.

"I wish I could have been there," he said, his voice full of humor. "Even getting bullets shot at you had to be better than babysitting Apollo all day."

"I wouldn't be so sure about that," I said, scanning Rhion's huge, open living room and kitchen. Mira was nowhere in sight.

"Devon said it was quite a show."

"Devon's got a big fucking mouth." I brought my gaze back to Jude. "Where's Mira?"

He pointed down the hall. "Ocean room."

Rhion Park was a special snowflake in a lot of ways, one of them being that, when she'd first bought that apartment, she'd hired a contractor to build her a room that simulated being at the beach. From the sound of the waves crashing, scents of the salty water, all the way to lighting to mimic the sun, it was a true experience. And it didn't surprise me one bit that it was where Mira had chosen to hang out.

Back in the day, we'd driven to the gulf once. It had been one of our typical late nights in the woods when she'd told me how much she'd loved the beach as a kid. Kurt had been in the field and my company was on a ninety-minute recall, but there wasn't much I wouldn't have done to make her happy. So, with a cooler stocked with beer and pop, a couple of gas station sandwiches, and a never-ending supply of laughs, we left for Destin, Florida. For over four hours, we'd driven, the windows rolled down, country music blaring, her head in my lap, her bare feet hanging out the window. And, for every single minute of those four hours, nothing else had existed except the two of us.

In all the years since she'd been gone, I hadn't been able to go back to the beach without thinking of that night spent under the stars, our feet in the sand, her snoozing in my arms as the sun rose on the horizon. I was never the same after that night. It was only a taste of how good life could have been if we had been together, but it made me an addict.

And I'd been in withdrawal for too long.

"You want me to get her?" Jude asked, snapping me out of the past.

The loss was staggering.

I shook my head. "Nah. I'll...get her." Only I didn't move. I just stood there, staring down the hall, silently debating if the emotions spiraling inside me were that of excitement or dread. And then I wondered if maybe those two things were one and the same when it came to her.

But one thing was clear.

She was there.

Only a few yards away.

And I'd never been more terrified of someone in my entire life.

CHAPTER TEN

Mira

I WAS BEYOND EXHAUSTED. MY HEAD ACHED, AND MY EYES WERE painfully swollen from crying. The adrenaline had worn off, leaving me spent, but my frazzled mind refused me any rest. The cops had asked me a million questions, most of which I had been able to answer honestly. A few were half-truths, like the ones about Jeremy and me being old friends.

There was no word on Whitney.

Or Bitsy.

And, as time passed, I began to fear there never would be.

"Are we talking about the same Jeremy Lark?" Rhion asked, toying with a large diamond hanging at the base of her neck.

We were sitting crosslegged on a king-sized bed in her guest room, the sound of the waves crashing all around us. If I hadn't been in the middle of the worst day of my life, I would have been jealous of that ocean room. It was the coolest thing I'd ever seen. From the sound and the smells, it was just like being on a beach without the gritty sand and suffocating heat.

I smiled weakly. "Yep. He got into the security guard's face and told him that he was Garth Brooks's little brother."

Her eyes flashed wide. "Did you get into the concert?"

"Good God, no. We were lucky we didn't get arrested. I've never run so fast in my life."

She fell over laughing, and I smiled, watching her.

Rhion reminded me a lot of Whitney. Well, minus the apartment that might as well have been a mansion and the closet full of Jimmy Choos. But she had Whitney's kind heart and infectious smile. And, because of that, everything she said had made my chest ache.

And, Jesus, the woman could talk. So, in the six hours since Johnson had dropped me off with her and her boyfriend, Jude, my heart had hurt a lot.

I glanced to the clock on the white, antiqued nightstand. It was getting late and I still hadn't heard anything about Jeremy. A beautiful, dark-haired man, who looked like he might or might not be Hispanic, named Leo James had assured me Jeremy was fine and would be by for me later. But, due to our little showdown in my bedroom, I didn't completely believe him. Nor was I sure if my heart could withstand going toe-to-toe with Jeremy again.

I just wanted to go home and forget the last twenty-four hours of my life. I wanted Whitney to come into my room and wake me up be-cause I was having a nightmare. I wanted Bitsy to curl into my chest, safe and sound, reminding me that I was safe and sound too. I wanted my house, my bed, my life, no matter how shitty it was. It was mine.

My chin quivered, and my nose started to sting. I couldn't imag-ine I had any tears left to cry, but it seemed I had an endless supply.

"Hey," Rhion breathed, rising to her knees and crawling toward me. She pulled me into a hug, one of many that evening. "Don't cry."

"I'm sorry." I covered my mouth, but I couldn't make it stop. "It's just... I'm a little overwhelmed."

"I don't blame you at all. You've had a crazy day."

Okay, so I'd talked a lot in those six hours, too.

I sniffled. "It's been a crazy life."

"That too," she whispered.

"I feel like—"

"Hey," he called from the door.

That same hope that was quickly becoming my biggest enemy ex-panded inside me almost as quickly as my stomach sank.

He'd come for me. *Again.*

Only I knew he wasn't the same Jeremy I so desperately needed him to be this time.

"Jesus, Lark! Don't sneak up on people like that," Rhion scolded.

"The waves were on. I didn't think you'd hear a knock," he replied, and it stole the breath from my lungs.

It was kind—teasing, even—and reminiscent of a man I'd once known. But that was only because his words were aimed at someone else. That man would be gone the minute I turned around.

With a sharp inhale, I steeled myself for more insults.

More anger.

More resentment.

More hurt.

But I could have built an iron fortress around myself and Jeremy Lark could have leveled it with a single word.

"Mira," he whispered.

Yep. That was the word.

Squaring my shoulders, I braced for the worst.

And, as I turned to look at him, I knew that was exactly what I'd gotten.

Because he looked so much like my Jeremy that it ripped my heart from my chest.

He was wearing the same navy slacks, but a plain, white T-shirt now hugged his broad chest and thick biceps. A delectable five-o'clock shadow covered his jaw, and soft, concerned eyes topped off the entire beautiful package.

I could do nothing but blink at him.

My mouth dry.

My throat tight.

My pulse racing.

And he did nothing but blink back.

His face gentle.

His body taut.

His breathing labored.

"Well, um…" Rhion said awkwardly, standing up. "I'll give you two a minute. Let me know if you need anything, Mira."

I never tore my gaze off him as she moved toward the door.

Before leaving, she patted him on the chest. "I'm glad to see you're okay. But be nice or I promise you won't be when you leave."

His gaze flicked down to hers, warming immediately. "Noted," he replied with an honest-to-God smile. It felt like salt to the gaping wound in my chest.

She nodded and then walked out the door, closing it behind her.

When his gaze came back to mine, his smile had disappeared but his face remained soft.

"You okay?" he asked as he meandered to the bed.

My stomach dipped with the bed as he sat only a few feet away from me, my folded legs acting as a physical barrier between us. Lord knew we had enough emotional ones.

I shimmied back a few inches to gain some space. "Yeah. You?"

He turned, casually crooking one long leg between us on the bed, the other hanging over the side. "I'm fine. Nothing but a scratch."

"That's…good. Right?"

Yes. That's what I said to him. The man who had come to my aid and gotten shot, or nearly shot, in the process—I *asked* him if this was a good thing.

I pressed my lips together and pretended not to be mortified.

He glanced up at me, his eyes dancing with humor. "Yeah, Mira. That's a good thing."

"Yeah. I know… I didn't mean to insinuate that it—"

"Relax." He lifted a hand, and it looked like he was going to pat my leg, but it froze in midair.

I stared at it, nerves rolling in my stomach, waiting to see what he was going to do.

Were we old friends who could offer each other such casual affections?

Or were we archenemies sworn to hate each other for the rest of our days?

Clearing his throat, he lowered his hand to rest it on his ankle and became enthralled with his shoes. "So, I think this is the part where I apologize for being a dick, but I honestly don't know what to say. Any chance you'd be willing to let it slide, seeing as I got shot and all?" Without lifting his head, he glanced up at me, one side of his mouth twitching adorably.

A surge of relief blasted through me.

I half laughed, half sobbed. "What happened to it being a scratch?"

He lifted his head, that playful smile now pulling at both sides of his mouth. "That was before I needed to utilize the guilt card."

I laughed, the levity relaxing me even further. "Fair enough," I whispered.

His forehead crinkled as if he were in pain, but just as quickly, he grinned and stood up. "Okay. Now that we got that out of the way, we need to talk about the next few days." He gripped the back of his neck—his bicep flexing deliciously, not that I was staring or anything—and looked at me expectantly.

"The next few days?" I repeated, my voice rising to a squeak.

"I need a couple days to figure out the best plan of action long term. But, in the meantime, you'll crash at my place. We'll swing by tomorrow and pick up some of your things. I could call one of the…"

He kept talking. I was sure of it. However, my mind was stuck on the fact that he had declared that I'd be *crashing at his place.*

It was a ludicrous statement. Last I'd checked, Hell had not frozen over, nor were pigs flying. And, while I hadn't been outside in several hours, when Johnson had driven me over, I'd not seen the first sign of zombies or the beginnings of the apocalypse. So yeah…it was safe to say I would not be going anywhere near Jeremy Lark's house.

I leaned forward and cupped a hand to my ear. "I'm sorry. What? Whose place?"

He looked at me. Cool as a cucumber. Poor thing didn't even appear to know he was having a stroke. "My place."

"Your place," I repeated.

"My place," he confirmed by repeating my repeat.

I stared at him.

He arched an eyebrow and stared back. "You got a problem with that?"

Closing my eyes, I tipped my face to the ceiling and performed some quick multiplication in my head before looking back to him. "Oh...about sixty-one hundred of them. No...wait. Sixty-two hundred."

He blinked. And then blinked again, his eyebrows drawing closer each time. "I have no idea what you're talking about."

"I can't *crash at your place.*" I tossed him a pair of air quotes. "We haven't seen each other in seventeen years!" Yes. I was yelling. No. I had no idea why. But it seemed absolutely warranted at the time. Unable to sit for a minute longer, I pushed to my feet and began to pace a circle.

He chuckled, but it wasn't in humor. "See, this morning, I'd have agreed with you. But then I got this phone call telling me you were in shit so deep you were drowning in it." He shrugged. "Maybe I misunderstood, but I *distinctly* remember you asking for my help."

"Yes! Help in getting Whitney back. Not help in relocating my life!"

"Not asking you to move in, Mir. Not even asking you to unpack a bag." He leaned forward and whispered, "Sure as hell not asking you to relocate your life. But you do gotta sleep under my roof for a few days until the cops find your girl and get Jonah's ass behind bars. After that, you and all your sixty-one or sixty-two hundred problems are free to go wherever you'd like."

If I had been feeling rational, I would have seen that he was trying to do me a favor. Well...*another* favor. But I was *not* being rational. I was tired mentally and physically, drained emotionally, and all around done with the day.

"There is no way I'm going home with you! Have you lost your mind?"

His face lit in understanding. "Ahhhh...okay. So this is the part where you have the snit fit." He shifted on the bed, making a show of getting more comfortable. "Sorry. It's been a while. I wasn't prepared." He crossed his thick arms over his chest and made a shooing motion with four fingers while holding his bicep. "Carry on. I didn't mean to interrupt."

I pinned him with a glare. "I don't have snit fits, Jeremy."

"Mira, you have snit fits when the seasons change. And, though it's been quite a while since we last spoke, considering that we've had three conversations today, this being one the third, and you've had a snit fit every single time, I'm of the mind that some things don't change."

"You have no idea what you're talking about."

He lifted a finger in the air. "Organic orange juice." He lifted another finger. "Swallowing rusty swords and shoes made of broken glass." He lifted a third finger. "I'll let you know when you get to the good part of this one."

Shit. Maybe I did have snit fits. But definitely not when the seasons changed. Illinois winters were the worst. "I've been under an exorbitant amount of stress today. You cannot call this a snit fit."

"Well, not yet. You haven't really gotten started. Though you are an overachiever. I didn't know it was possible to have a snit fit about having a snit fit."

"I'm not having a snit fit!" I yelled loud enough for it to rattle the window.

And that's when Jeremy lost it too.

"Then shut up!" he yelled back. "Jesus, woman. What the hell is wrong with you?" He stood up and prowled over to me.

Defiantly, I stared up into his hazel eyes. I told myself to stand my ground and refuse to back down. But, as he loomed over me, his strong shoulders rounded forward, his trim waist bent bringing his upper body impossibly close, caging me in, the louder voice in my head told me to run as far and as fast as I could.

Because I didn't actually want to move at all.

My fingers tingled to reach for him. To rest my hands on his abs and curl into his side, stealing a fragment of the comfort he'd always offered freely when we were younger.

Jeremy Lark's hugs had been life altering. They were like this warm blanket that enveloped me and shielded me from the elements. They didn't fix anything. The world still existed outside his arms, but whether they lasted seconds or minutes, those hugs were the one thing that made the rest of my life manageable.

I'd been wasting away without them.

My heart raced as I peeked up at him through my lashes. He was staring down at me, fury brewing in his eyes. But, even when narrowed in anger, they held a certain comfort.

I'd stared into those eyes too many times to ever be scared.

Lost in lust.

Lost in laughter.

Lost in…love.

I'd have given anything for his eyes to light, his pouty lips to split into a smile, and his perfect mouth to whisper that everything was going to be all right.

But it wasn't all right.

And he wasn't mine to touch.

Not now. And not ever again.

"Back up," I whispered, tears pricking the backs of my eyes.

"You can't go home," he seethed.

I closed my eyes and sucked in a sharp breath in an effort to get myself under control. It backfired, because he was so close that his masculine scent filled my senses.

It was different than the way I remembered him smelling. More understated and subtle. Like soap rather than cologne. But it was no less intoxicating.

And heartbreaking.

"Mira, look at me," he snapped.

My eyes fluttered open.

"You *can't* go home. If you have somewhere else you'd like to go to wait this thing out, fine. Tell me where and I'll see what I can do about getting one of the guys to keep an eye on you. Trust me—I don't like the idea of you staying with me, either. But the alternative is you getting killed."

Ignoring the ache in my chest, I forced my legs to carry me away from him. It was only a few steps, but it might as well have been miles for the distance it put between us. "I have an apartment. Near the college. Whitney and I were supposed to be moving today anyway. I'll be safe there."

"Johnson Googled you," he stated as if it should have been a revelation.

I twisted my lips. "Okay?"

"That's how we found you. If you know enough about a person, it doesn't take much to track them down."

"Yeah, but this is a new place. Trust me. It'll be fine. Just drop me off and I'll be out of your life forever."

He scoffed. "Funny, I thought you were out of my life years ago. And yet here you are."

My whole body jerked as if I could dodge his jab, but it hit me square in the stomach. It shouldn't have hurt the way it did. He was speaking the truth, which was probably why it was so painful.

Slapping on a little sarcasm for defense, I replied, "And you seem *thrilled* about it. So, yeah. I'm thinking it's best if I let you off the hook now and we go about our separate ways."

His eyes flashed wide as if I'd dealt a verbal blow of my own. "I'm not *on* your fucking hook, Mira."

I swallowed hard. "That's…that's not what I meant. I just thought—"

He planted his hands on his hips. "That you'd get yourself killed? Because that's exactly what's going to happen if you go at this shit alone."

"I'm not trying to go at anything, Jeremy! That's the whole point in going home. You, Rhion, Johnson, Leo… Everyone was great to me today. I will never be able to repay all of you. And I'm not going to sit here and allow that debt to grow."

"I don't know how you can repay people, either, but I assure you dying is *not* it."

"So I'll lay low. He won't be able to find me."

"Jesus, you are so fucking stubborn. Does Kurt know your full name? What about your birthday? Social Security number? Mother's maiden name? City you were born?" This was not asked in query. This was not asked gently. This was not asked to provoke thought—unless that thought was to point out that I was an idiot. And he wasn't done. "Considering *I* know the majority of those answers, I'm thinking your ex-*husband* has enough information to find you *anywhere*."

"Kurt is in jail!" I informed, and it was in a tone that said I thought *he* was the idiot.

"And he still found you!" he roared. "And put a gun to your head. And kidnapped your girl. And stole your fucking dog. And tried to shoot me. Maybe not Kurt himself. But one of his men. And if you think for one second that after you turned in seven hundred thousand dollars of his money that he's not going to use whatever means necessary to find you, then you are in for a rude awakening."

Pursing my lips, I glared. His attitude was shit. But his point was not.

"Fine. I'll go to a hotel," I suggested.

"Is the credit card going to be in your name?" he shot back.

I rolled my eyes. "I seriously doubt Kurt has any buddies who work for the bank."

"You willing to bet your life on that?"

"Maybe if it would get you to stop yelling at me."

With long strides, he closed the distance between us. "I'm only yelling at you because you are not using your head here."

My body came alive all over again. I couldn't breathe. Not with him that close. I couldn't imagine how torturous it would be to go home with him. I was barely standing after the two interactions we'd had. A couple of days with him would do me in. I didn't want to go to his house and see firsthand how beautiful it was. I didn't want to see pictures of his family hanging on the walls. I couldn't handle the reminder that losing me was the best thing that had ever happened to him.

Because losing him had been the worst.

I couldn't do it again.

Reality sliced through me, taking my desire to fight with it.

When my vision began to swim, I cut my gaze to the floor. "I don't know what to do, okay? I've never been in this situation before." I took a step away, desperate for space to breathe, but also to ease the sting his proximity was causing in my heart. "I'm not sure if you've noticed, but I'm kind of floundering here." I offered him a weak smile, but the act of trying to fake it only made my face crumble. "I didn't mean for any of this to happen." I choked and spun away. "I've been working my ass off to get my life back together, but it's always something else dragging me down. And yeah, before you even feel the need to say it, I know I did this to myself. I married Kurt. I stayed with Kurt. I lived his lies. And, God, it's been exhausting. So maybe I'm not using my head. But I just want to go *home*."

"Mira," he whispered.

Soft.

Sweet.

Tender.

Jeremy.

It made my tears fall harder. "I don't want you involved in this anymore. I was wrong to call you."

"But you did," he whispered. "And I'm here. *Trying* to help."

More soft.

More sweet.

More agony.

"Please. Please, I'm begging you, just....take me home."

I wasn't sure if I could survive Jonah or whatever else Kurt had planned for me, but I knew, deep down to the marrow of my bones and with an absolute certainty, I wouldn't survive even one night with Jeremy Lark.

CHAPTER ELEVEN

Lark

MY THROAT GOT THICK AS THE DARK-BROWN EYES THAT HAD dictated so much of my life stared up at me, pleading.

"Please. Please, I'm begging you, just…take me home."

She couldn't go home, but seeing her struggle gutted me. My mind told me to pull her into a hug and soothe her in any way I could. But it was my heart that kept my arms at my sides. I couldn't go back down that road with her. And I feared that anger and resolve were useless defenses if I had her soft body curved around mine.

Distance was my safest bet. Though, as tears fell from her eyes and dripped down her pink cheeks, and her arms folded over her chest as though she were trying to ward off a chill, distance felt like a cruel and unusual punishment to my soul.

This woman… Jesus. She didn't just fuck with my head. She fucked with my entire being.

It hadn't been twenty-four hours and I was crumbling at her feet all over again. It had been nothing more than wishful thinking from a delusional man when I'd told Leo that I was going to wash my hands of her. The truth was, if something happened to her…

A vise tightened in my chest.

Something *had* happened to her. Something that could have killed her.

That was on Kurt.

But this. Now that I was involved… If anything happened to her, that would be on me. And, no matter how deeply I'd convinced myself that I hated Mira York, the love I'd once held for her ran deeper.

"Please, Jeremy," she whispered.

God, I hated it when she called me Jeremy. I'd heard my name no less than a million times since she'd been gone from my life. But there was no substitute for the way she said it. That one word tumbling from her lips was enough to set me on fire with anger. And then, two sentences later, it was enough to bring me to my knees.

I pinched the bridge of my nose. "Mira…" I trailed off, unsure what else I could say to convince her. I couldn't exactly hold her hostage. "You seriously want to go home that bad?"

She cut her gaze down, her chin quivering as she stared at the floor. "Yeah. I do."

I groaned, that vise in my chest wrenching even tighter. "Fine. You can go home tomorrow, *after* I get someone out to your apartment to set up surveillance. I'll put you up in a hotel tonight. My credit card. My name."

"No," she replied just as I'd expected.

She was so fucking stubborn.

"No arguing," I growled.

She opened her mouth, probably to throw another snit fit, but I was done listening.

"This is not up for discussion, Mira."

She clamped her mouth shut, and as if right on cue, her tear-filled eyes narrowed to slits. I nearly laughed. I knew that look well. And it further proved my theory that some things never changed.

"You don't have to be a dick," she snapped.

"And you don't have to argue with every goddamn thing I say. Protecting people is what I do for a living. And, as a professional, I'm telling you I don't like this. I think it's stupid and irresponsible. But I can't stop you if that's what you want." I stabbed a finger in her direction. "I put my ass on the line for you today. So, if I can't convince you to come back to my place, where you'll be safe and we can both get some fucking rest, then you are going to play it my way. Tonight, you're going to a hotel. Tomorrow, you can go home."

She crossed her arms over her chest in an adorable and ridiculous display of attitude. "Can I pay you back?"

"For what?" I asked, exasperation making my tone rougher than I had planned.

She squared her shoulders and straightened her spine. "The hotel. The surveillance. Your time. All of it."

"Jesus." I rolled my eyes. Based on the shithole she'd been living in when I'd shown up that morning, she couldn't afford any of those things. But, if it would have gotten her to stop bickering with me any quicker, I'd have agreed to let her pay my fucking mortgage. "Sure. Whatever."

She nodded, keeping her chin high as she replied, "Okay. Then yes. I would very much appreciate you taking me to a hotel tonight."

I stared at her, incredulous.

She stared back at me, defiant.

One hundred percent classic Mira York.

It pissed me off almost as much as it turned me on.

Before I could acknowledge any of those feelings, I turned on a toe and marched out the door.

Not slowing, I made my way down the hall, her footsteps trailing behind me.

Rhion jumped to her feet when we made it to her living room. "Everything okay?"

"Fucking perfect," I smarted, going straight to the door.

"It's great, sweetie," Mira purred. "I really appreciate you letting me hang out here today. I'll shoot you a text and we can get together for that drink we talked about."

I silently decided that I didn't care what I had to do to stop it—that drink was not happening. Mira was leaving. She was going to a hotel. She was going home. And exiting my life forever—again.

And, for some fucking reason, that pissed me off all over again. The idea of her disappearing felt like a sledgehammer to the gut.

ALY MARTINEZ

Jude appeared at my side as the girls hugged and whispered their goodbyes. "You need anything?"

"Lobotomy and a gallon or two of tequila."

He chuckled. "Fresh out, my man."

"Of course you are. Given the way today has gone, I'm fully expecting prohibition to be reenacted tomorrow just to spite me."

"I don't know if that would be a bad thing." He tipped his chin at Rhion. "Take it from me: Alcohol and kryptonite don't mix."

I shook my head, frustrated that my fucked-up feelings for Mira were so transparent. "Yeah," I replied absently. "I'll keep that in mind."

When the women finally disengaged, I lifted my hand in a backward wave, and walked out the door with Mira trailing a safe distance behind me.

"Rhion says there's a hotel nearby," she said as we waited for the elevator to arrive.

"Yep." I popped the P. "I'll walk you over." *And then more than likely spend the night guarding the lobby. Fuck!*

"Sounds good," she whispered, nervously inspecting the ends of her hair.

I kept my head aimed straight ahead at the metal doors, all the while staring at her from the corner of my eye.

When the elevator arrived, I swept a hand out for her to enter first.

She moved to the back, while I damn near plastered myself to the number panel.

We rode down in silence.

She exited first, and I followed.

I held the door open for her as we left the building.

She offered me a courtesy smile and nod of thanks.

She carefully left several feet between us as we walked down the busy Chicago sidewalk, never so much as brushing against me as we sidestepped other people in groups. She'd occasionally steal a peek in my direction. I'd pretend not to notice and then returned the favor only when I was positive she wouldn't catch me.

It was all perfectly natural…if you were a death row inmate on your way to execution.

A suffocating weight hung in the air between us, each step more awkward and uncomfortable than the last. I told myself that I was grateful. Distance, right? But, as those feet between us became greater and greater, the dread in my stomach amplified.

I reminded myself that going to a hotel was what she wanted. It was better this way.

Fuck. No, it wasn't.

She was so desperate not to owe me anything that she was putting her own life at risk. And I was all but walking her to her grave.

I ground my teeth together and let out a groan. "Mira, wait—"

But that was all I got out. Out of nowhere, a man slammed into my side, his body colliding with my injured shoulder.

"Shit," I rumbled as he bounced off me and fell to the ground.

"Watch where you're going!" he yelled, pushing up onto his elbows.

"I was," I snapped back, rubbing my shoulder.

And I had been.

Eyes straight ahead.

Lost in thought.

The world passing me in a blur.

Everything I never did when I was with a client.

But she wasn't a client. She was…

"Mira!" I roared, spinning in a circle, the hairs on the back of my neck standing on end, my gut rotting with unease, telling me that something was seriously wrong.

She wasn't there.

Blood thundered in my ears as I scanned the busy sidewalk. I packed the panic down. It wouldn't have done either of us any good. I needed to keep my head and look at this logically without my connection to her shading the clues.

That shading turned black the minute I located her only yards away—a man's hand over her mouth, her arms flailing, her feet fighting for purchase on the sidewalk, an open car door waiting, her terror-filled eyes glued to mine and begging for help.

I felt every ounce of her fear as if she were carving into my soul with a dull knife.

A bomb detonated inside me, and raw fury I'd never experienced before shredded any ounce of humanity I possessed. I'd have set the city on fire and torn buildings to the ground before I'd ever let him escape with her. My heart slammed against my ribs and my vision tunneled as the crowded sidewalk disappeared. For those seconds in slow motion, all I could see were her frantic eyes and a dead man who was trying to take her from me.

The guy who had run into me lurched to his feet and attempted to grab me from behind, but it took exactly one swing of my arm to send him back down, his head giving a satisfying crack against the sidewalk.

All at once, my body exploded forward, every muscle straining to carry me faster.

Through it all, my gaze never left hers.

My resolve never faltered.

My rage never wavered.

My heart never slowed.

My lungs burned the closer he got to the car, but that pain only propelled me forward.

When I got close enough, she stopped fighting against him and reached for me, the tips of her fingers skimming mine. A blast of adrenaline and relief flooded my system when I caught her forearm. Her hand wrapped around my wrist, biting with the most euphoric pain I'd ever experienced. He dragged her off the curb and into the road, but my hand might as well have been fused to hers. Killing me wouldn't have been enough to make me release her.

Using her arm as an anchor, I slingshotted myself forward, my hand reared back and aimed at his face. It felt like an out-of-body experience, watching my fist sail through the air and land hard against his eye, blood erupting from his brow and spattering on the side of her terrified face.

Dazed, he stumbled, T-boning his back against the car door. His arms loosened for only the briefest of seconds, and I pounced, yanking Mira from his arms.

She flew forward, crashing into my chest, and I protectively curled her into my side before landing another punch against his face when he tried to regain his hold on her.

And that's when shots rang out from inside the car.

Mira's scream was barely audible over the deafening blasts, but it cut me deeper than any bullet ever could. Hooking her around the waist, I took us both to the ground. I crashed on top of her, desperate to get every inch of her under me. Her body trembled so violently it made collecting her an impossible task.

Tires squealed as the car peeled off. And then the whole world fell blessedly silent.

"Oh, God. Oh, God," Mira chanted.

I lifted my head and swept my gaze over the area for any lingering danger, but short of a few frightened pedestrians, it seemed clear. Turning my focus back to Mira, I witnessed her wide eyes fill with a magnitude of emotions.

"Are you hit?" I asked.

A piece of me died in the half of a second it took her to answer.

"I don't think so."

Pushing up to my knees, I patted her down and then flipped her over on the dirty road to check her back.

She didn't object, not even as I rubbed her ass and thighs down. There was nothing sexual about that moment, though there was no denying that my heart was involved.

Satisfied that she was unharmed, I blew out a ragged breath and rolled her back over. "You're okay," I announced—just as much for myself as for her.

Tears streamed down her cheeks as she croaked, "Are you?"

I wasn't. Not even close.

But not because I'd been hit.

Nodding, I reached down and cupped her face. Trailing my thumb back and forth across her cheek, I wiped away the drops of that asshole's blood and whispered, "Yeah, baby. I'm good."

"Oh, God," she gasped. "Jeremy?" she asked on a broken cry even though she was looking right at me.

I attempted the insurmountable task of willing my heart to slow. "Yeah, Mir. It's me."

Her breath caught and her eyes filled with a fresh round of tears, but as if the ground had suddenly been electrified, she flew up off of it and into my arms. Her face collided with my chest, rocking me back, but I quickly recovered and pulled her into a deep embrace.

"Shhh," I soothed into the top of her hair, tucking her face into my neck. I told myself the shake of my hands was because of the adrenaline.

It wasn't.

Mira was safe in my arms. And, as terrifying as that was, it was more terrifying to imagine her not being there.

Fisting the back of my shirt, she wedged her chest so tightly against my front I had no choice but to stand up or fall over.

Sirens screamed in the background and Good Samaritans made their way over to us, asking questions and offering help, but Mira never let go or even acknowledged that the world outside of my arms existed.

And, in those minutes, her heart pounding in rhythm with my own, her breaths coming fast and heavy, her small body flush head to toe with mine, I wasn't sure it existed, either.

Or if I ever wanted it to exist again.

CHAPTER TWELVE

Mira

"AND YOU HAVE NO IDEA WHO STEVE BROWEL IS?" DETECTIVE Jones asked, propping his chin on a densely tattooed forearm.

"No!" I swore, sliding my gaze to Jeremy, who was standing in the corner of the room, his arms crossed over his chest, his face the picture of contempt.

But, for the first time all day, it wasn't aimed at me.

"She already said she didn't fucking know him," he growled. "Ask a new goddamn question or let us leave."

The detective leaned back in his chair. "I like you, Lark, been friends for a long time, but you say one more fucking word, I'll cuff you myself."

"Then fucking cuff me already, Caleb." Jeremy kept his voice low, but he cocked his head to the side with attitude. "We've been sitting here for two hours, listening to you ask her the same questions over and over again." He swung his arm to the door. "And, for an hour before that, we were standing on the street, listening to you ask 'em. She doesn't know who he was. Maybe, instead of standing here, acting like she's a damn criminal rather than a victim, you'll get your ass down to the prison and ask Kurt Benton. Because I assure you: He knows who the fuck that was."

Yeah…my Jeremy had shown up big time. Temper and all.

I bit my lip to suppress a smile and looked back at the detective.

His mouth was hanging open as he watched Jeremy in what could only be described as awe.

Leo chimed in from the other side of his desk, humor thick in his voice. "I told you so."

Caleb shook his head and continued to stare at Jeremy, but his words were for Leo. "You were not wrong."

"Fucking schoolgirls," Jeremy grumbled.

I swept my gaze through each of them, silently questioning what they were talking about, but not a one of them offered me any enlightenment. This could have been because they were all involved in a broody bodyguard/boss/detective stare down and forgot that I was even in the room.

Clearing my throat, I broke the moment. "Listen, I've given you everything I have. I don't know anyone named Steve. I don't even know where he came from. I saw the guy bump into Jeremy and then a man grabbed me. It all happened so fast. I'm just glad someone thought to get the car's tag number." I peeked up at Jeremy to see that he had turned his death stare on the wall on the opposite side of the room, his jaw ticking to the point I feared for his teeth.

"Right," Detective Jones replied. "Okay, well, I'll be honest here. We have no idea if this was related to what happened at your apartment this morning. We've been interrogating Tony all day and haven't gotten anything out of him. But…I will say Jonah Sheehan has been on our radar for a while. He's small time. So, this?" He shook his head. "This doesn't feel like Jonah."

My head snapped back. "What? Then who do you think it was?"

He must have heard the panic in my voice, because his handsome face softened. "I don't know. We aren't ruling anything or anyone out. I'm just saying you need to be extra careful, because if this was Jonah, he's stepping up his game. After tonight, I'm going to recommend putting you into protective custody. It's—"

"She's coming home with me," Jeremy declared.

I swung my head toward him. "Jeremy, I—"

"End of discussion," he bit out, pinning me with a scary glower.

Jeesh. Not that I was going to argue. An attempted kidnapping and dodging bullets had definitely made me rethink my desire to be alone. And, while staying at Jeremy's house wasn't ideal for my heart, I figured that it was probably safest for the rest of the internal organs I needed to remain whole, and not filled with lead, in order to survive.

Flashing the detective a pair of wide eyes, I whispered, "I guess that's settled."

He shook his head and aimed more of his awe at Jeremy. "I guess it is."

"Good," Jeremy clipped, moving toward the door. "Now, can we fucking go?"

Caleb flicked his gaze to Leo—who, I'd like to note, was oddly grinning like a maniac—and shrugged. "Yeah. Sure. By all means." He rose to his feet and walked over to Jeremy. "As a cop, I'm telling you to keep your eyes open and call us if you see anything, or anyone, suspicious." He stepped closer and lowered his voice. "But, as your friend, I'm telling you, if you leave your house with her, I want you doing it armed for duty. Yeah?"

Jeremy stared back at him. His face was hard, but the most confusing flash of shame sifted through his features. "Way ahead of you." He jerked his chin at me. "Mira, let's go."

Leo stood at the same time I did. "Have a good night, babe. Stay safe."

I shot him a warm grin. "Thanks again."

He winked, his long, black lashes giving quite the show. "My pleasure. Let me know if this asshole gives you any trouble."

I giggled softly and nodded. On my way to Jeremy, I paused beside Caleb, my smile falling as I asked, "Any word on Whitney?"

He gave my arm a squeeze. "Not yet. But we're working on it. I promise."

I forced a sad smile, bile burning the back of my throat. "Thanks."

His mouth tipped up in a sexy smirk, which more than explained how he'd gotten that gold wedding band on his ring finger. "No problem, sweetheart."

With one last glance and nod to both of the men, I stopped in front of Jeremy, unsure of how close I could get without Mr. Hyde making another appearance for the day.

Out on the street, he'd held me in his arms long after the police had arrived. And, when they'd driven us back to the Guardian office, he'd slid in beside me, tight so our sides were flush, and slung his arm around my shoulders. I'd welcomed the comfort, relishing in the way my heart had slowed as the blanket of his warmth enveloped me. He'd released me the minute we got inside, and he'd stayed out of reach since.

Until now.

Sweeping a hand toward the door, he placed the other on my lower back and gave me a gentle push to get my feet moving.

My heart skipped at the contact, and I arched into his touch, the heat from his fingertips branding me through my T-shirt. I swallowed hard, doing my best not to read into it as he guided me through the vast office, his chest brushing against my back with every turn. As we exited the front door, the cool night air whipped around us and an unexplainable shiver traveled down my spine.

But it wasn't a good shiver, and it immediately set me on edge.

I was with Jeremy after what had felt like a million years, but as we waited for the elevator, the most familiar sensation of dread ignited inside me. I was no stranger to anxiety, and after the day I'd had, the only surprise should have been that it had taken so long to catch up to me.

In an effort to distract myself, I went for small talk. "So…how's your shoulder?"

"Fine."

Chewing on my bottom lip, I asked, "So…Detective Jones seems nice. Have you two known each other long?" I jumped when the ding of the elevator announced its arrival.

"Mmmhmm," he replied, using his hand on my back to guide me inside.

Two steps over that threshold and my pulse quickened and my

mouth dried.

Never leaving my side, he stabbed the button for the parking garage.

In an attempt to cut through the nervous energy ricocheting inside me, I rocked from my heels to my toes. "How long have you—"

He blew out a suffering sigh. "Can we cut the chitchat?"

My body tensed. Fantastic. I was about to jump out of my skin and the asshole was back.

"Is everything okay?" I asked, barely able to keep the shake out of my voice.

He angled his head down. "It's fine." The pressure of his hand on my back increased the tiniest fraction in what I assumed was supposed to be reassurance.

It gave me none.

Panic in the form of little pinpricks spread across my skin like a wildfire.

"I'm getting off first. Stay close," he ordered as the elevator came to a stop.

"W-why?" I stammered. "Are you, like, bodyguard spidey-sensing something right now?" I shuffled over until I was plastered to his side, Mr. Hyde be damned. "Maybe we should go back up. There were some really comfy-looking couches at your office. I wouldn't mind sleeping—Shit!" I screamed when the door cracked open, revealing the ominous shadow of a large man waiting for me on the other side.

Spinning, I tried to escape, but I crashed into Jeremy's chest. His thick arms protectively folded around me, and before I knew it, I was up off my feet.

My back hit the wall, and Jeremy filled my vision, which left him completely exposed.

"Get down!" I yelled, the idea of him getting shot more terrifying than taking the bullet myself.

"Mira, stop," he gritted out, resting one hand on my hip and the other on the wall beside my head to cage me in. "It's just Braydon. He's with us."

But I couldn't stop. It could have been Santa Claus and I still wouldn't have been able to get myself under control. That panic attack was about eighteen hours overdue.

My shoulders shook violently as I burst into tears.

"Jesus fuck," he cursed.

Embarrassment consumed me, and I buried my face in his chest so he wouldn't see my tears. "I'm…I'm…I'm sorry," I choked out between sobs into his shirt.

His body shifted closer to me, his powerful thigh wedging between my legs until he had me cocooned. "Look at me," he demanded.

I shook my head, and like pretty much everything else I'd done that day, it seemed to piss him off.

"Mira. Look. At. Me," he seethed through clenched teeth.

My frazzled mind could barely form thoughts, much less deal with his attitude. "Can you please not fucking yell at me for a minute?" I snapped at his chest. "I'm in the middle of a panic attack. I do not have it in me to argue with you right now." My hands shook wildly as I wedged them between us and did my best to dry my eyes.

"I'm not trying to argue with you. I'm trying to apologize."

My heart stopped, shock momentarily breaking through the panic.

"F-for what?" I stuttered.

He dropped his elbow to the elevator wall beside my head, bringing our mouths mere inches apart. "I fucked up," he stated, his breath whispering across my lips. "This morning, rushing in without considering who was on the other side. And then tonight, letting my guard down on the sidewalk. It shouldn't have happened."

Peering up at him through my lashes, I argued, "You didn't fuck up. We're both okay."

His hazel eyes flashed back and forth between mine, searching and imploring. "I *did*. Shit with us was personal and I…I wasn't thinking straight. But please hear me when I say: It will *not* happen again, Mira. That I can swear to you. If you are with me, you are safe. No matter what."

My stomach dipped. He thought I was freaking out because I didn't trust him.

It was a little sad, a lot sweet, and pure Jeremy.

My lungs ached for oxygen, but I couldn't force air into them. I'd missed him so damn much. All of these little glimpses of the man I'd lost were killing me. In a way, it had been easier when I'd thought he was gone forever. But there he stood, apologizing because he'd thought saving my life twice in one day hadn't been enough.

I stared up at him, selfishly attempting to memorize every curve of this new, older, but no-less-gorgeous version of him. From the slight lines around his eyes to the scar just below his bottom lip, I burned them all into my memory. Soon enough, they'd be all I'd have left of him.

Blinking back another round of tears, I whispered the absolute truth, "I trust you, Jeremy."

His body turned rock solid, but he didn't back away. He just stood there.

Staring.

Looming.

Shredding me.

Unable to take his scrutinizing gaze for a second longer, I cut my eyes to the ground. "I think I'm done freaking out for the moment. However, if any large men appear out of nowhere between here and your car, I'd like to reserve the right to have a minor snit fit. And that's not because I don't trust you, but rather because, as you so informed, snit fits are what I do."

He stayed close. "What happened to you now was not a snit fit, Mira. That was fear consuming you. Fear that, I'll repeat, you do *not* have to carry if I'm with you."

"And what about when you aren't with me anymore?" I hadn't intended to say those words out loud, but it felt as if they'd been poison my throat refused to swallow.

I waited for his answer, but there was none to be had. One day, when the immediate threat was gone, we'd go our own separate ways.

I couldn't afford to banish my fears. I'd need them to keep me alive in the not-so-distant future.

With tight lips, he continued to stare at me until he finally let out a resigned sigh and backed away.

And, just like that, the moment was over.

I told myself that it was for the best. But the chill that overtook me in his absence didn't feel like the best at all. It felt like the worst.

Sucking in a deep breath, I straightened my T-shirt, smoothed my hair down, and lifted my gaze to the tall man standing outside the elevator.

Jeremy waved a finger between us and introduced, "Braydon. Mira. Mira. Braydon."

"Hi," I whispered, my cheeks pinking with embarrassment—and because, well, he was ridiculously good-looking.

Dark hair, styled to be messy, brushed his forehead. He was long and lean, but defined muscles stretched the sleeves of his Guardian Protection polo shirt. One of his hands was propped on the door, preventing it from closing, the other gripping the back of his neck, apology heavy in his demeanor. "Leo sent me down to help escort you to the car. I didn't mean to scare you."

Feeling exceptionally vulnerable, I folded my arms over my chest as if he could see the cracks in my soul. "Please. Don't apologize because I'm a basket case."

He grinned, popping two mouthwatering dimples. "Basket case or not, I'm sorry."

Annnnd he was a nice kid. The women of Chicago were screwed. Probably both literally and figuratively.

"Well, I appreciate that, but—"

Jeremy cut me off. "We gonna go home or should I forward my mail to the damn elevator?"

I rolled my eyes and pasted on a smile. "It was lovely to meet you, Braydon."

He moved to the side, allowing me space to exit, and replied, "You too, Mira."

Fluid, and with a practiced ease that was almost as captivating as it was impressive, the two men fell into place on either side of me, Jeremy one step ahead of me on my left and Braydon one step behind me on my right. They guided me through the underground parking garage and then stopped at a gunmetal-gray SUV that made my eyebrows perk.

"You drive an Escalade?" I asked.

"What gave it away?" Jeremy deadpanned, wrapping his hand around my bicep and then leading me to the passenger's door. He didn't release me until I was fully inside and he had hit the lock before shutting the door.

Once alone, I fought the urge to dig through the center console and glove compartment to see what he had inside. The old Jeremy wouldn't have had more than a stick of gum and a few pennies. But this guy, the one they called Lark? I was dying to figure out who he was.

I settled for secretly glancing around as I anchored my seat belt. The floors had been vacuumed, the dash had been dusted, but an old paper coffee cup from a drive-through was crooked in the cupholder. I righted it, finding it empty, probably a leftover from that very morning.

So…he still liked to keep his car clean, and he still drank coffee. Not exactly the bounty of information I'd been hoping for, but I supposed it was a start.

I caught sight of the guys exchanging chin lifts, and then Jeremy opened the door and slid inside.

I picked at invisible lint on my jeans, lamenting that I hadn't grabbed any clothes before I'd left my apartment that morning. Though, if I was going to be wearing the same clothes for the foreseeable future, at least they were comfortable.

As we pulled out of the parking lot, my anxiety stirred to life all over again.

"Soo…" I drawled, crossing then recrossing my legs. He didn't reply. So I gave it another shot. "Soooo…"

"Spit it out, Mir," he told the windshield.

"Oh, nothing."

He slowed to a stop at a stoplight but never even glanced in my direction. "Woman, you have never in your life had nothing to say. So spit it out or stop trying to bait me."

I swung my head to face him. "I wasn't trying to bait you." I had been, but he wasn't supposed to know that. Or, if he did know that, he wasn't supposed to call me on it.

He chuffed. "Right."

I narrowed my eyes. "Do you have to be a jerk? Like, is there a quota you have to meet or something?"

"Not being a jerk. If you got something to say, spit it out. If you want to sit there and say 'sooooo' until you're blue in the face, by all means, go right ahead. Doesn't matter one way or the other. But don't expect me to break out a decoder and figure out what the hell you are or aren't trying to say."

"See! Like that!" I exclaimed, pivoting in my seat to face him.

He twisted his lips and furrowed his brow, or at least one side of his face did, because he *still* wouldn't look at me. "Like what?" he asked.

I drew a circle in the air, not that he could see it. "Like *this*. I distinctly remember you being able to carry on a conversation with complete sentences and courtesy."

Spoiler alert: It was the wrong thing to say.

His head swung my way so fast that I was shocked it didn't fly off his neck. "I'm *not* the man you remember! Stop fucking assuming you know me." He slammed the heel of his hand down on the steering wheel and then turned back to look at the road, his jaw ticking in time with my heart.

I blinked at him, reality icing my veins.

He was right. I'd told myself that I knew he was different. But I hadn't stopped looking, and hoping, for clues that he was still the same. Deep down, I'd still expected him to be the boy who would bicker with me for hours on end and then, one breath later, burst into laughter, wrap me in his arms, and kiss me breathless. It was one of the things I'd loved about him. I didn't have to filter myself with him. He knew when my anxiety would get the best of me. And he knew how to put me at ease.

But, now, I was his burden.

He was doing me a favor—or twelve—and *I* was the one acting like a jerk.

"I'm sorry," I whispered.

He scoffed. "You know, for someone who has repeatedly claimed that I've been yelling and arguing with her all day, you sure as hell seem to be giving your fair share."

Shit. He was right again. I turned away from him to stare out the window, repeating, "I know…and I'm sorry."

"For fuck's sake, Mira. This isn't easy on me, either. You're not exactly the girl I used to know, either, ya know?"

That didn't sound like a positive thing. I swallowed hard, my nose starting to sting. "I'm sorry."

He sighed. "Stop fucking apologizing."

I knotted my hands in my lap. "I'm sorry."

He groaned, and out of the corner of my eyes, I saw him drop his head back against the headrest. "Jesus, if you're just going to sit there and say sorry, I'd rather you go back to yelling."

I bit my lips closed to keep from apologizing again and nodded at my legs.

We sat in silence for the rest of the drive. Every so often, I felt his gaze brush over me, but I didn't dare look at him. I was scared of who I'd see, and not because I thought it would be the new Jeremy. I feared that it would be the old one.

Eventually, I leaned my head back, closed my eyes, and got lost in memories of truck beds, isolated woods, and country music.

CHAPTER THIRTEEN

Lark

HER DARK HAIR HUNG IN HER FACE, AND IT TOOK EVERY OUNCE OF self-restraint I possessed not to tuck it behind her ear. She was asleep, her head propped on her hand against the window, her lips parted, her breaths slow and steady.

I'd been sitting there, staring at her, for over thirty minutes. I'd thought she'd wake up when I cut the engine, but she hadn't budged, and I didn't have it in me to wake her. She was so damn beautiful.

I didn't want to admit it, not even to myself, but I'd fucking missed that woman something fierce. She pissed me off to no end, but I loved every second with her. She'd always been feisty, but much like it had tonight, it came from a vulnerable place. Mira was soft at the core. She was a chameleon who could adapt to any situation. But the one thing you could count on was she'd always break.

If I was being honest, those were the moments I loved most.

Because she gave them to me. The moments when she hadn't been able to breathe. The moments when she'd been completely overwhelmed. The moments when she'd let her walls down and allow someone to see the real woman struggling inside.

She hadn't chosen me when it'd mattered the most, but I knew for a fact I was the only person she'd chosen to show the real Mira York. I'd felt like the king of the world when she'd turn to me and silently ask for comfort only I could give her. I'd seen her with Kurt. She hadn't softened for him. But, then again, he'd never handled her with care. She had been forced to wear that façade of strength twenty-four-seven, to pretend to be who she'd thought she had to be in order to make someone care about her.

But that wasn't who she was. Mira was the crazy woman who could fight for hours, but with one touch, she'd curl into me like she'd finally come home.

She'd done it on the street after she'd almost been kidnapped. Long after her heart had slowed and her body had slacked, she'd clung to me as though not a minute had passed since she'd last been at my side.

And I'd let her. For as long as I could. Because there was a huge part of me that wanted to pretend we'd never been apart, either.

But we had. For too long.

And I was struggling to process that she was back.

However, she wasn't exactly back. I had not one doubt that Mira's stay was short. She'd take what she needed and then she'd be gone without as much as a backward glance.

And, every time a reminder of that slapped me in the face, my anger would get the best of me. She didn't deserve it. Mira could go toe-to-toe with the best of them, but it was wearing her down. And I hated that I was responsible for that. Kurt had been ruining her for the majority of her life. She didn't need me to follow suit.

I was still staring at her, drinking her in, and convincing myself not to steal a touch when she stirred.

"Mmm," she hummed, stretching her legs out in front of her. "Are we here?" she asked without opening her eyes.

"Yeah, Mir. We're here."

Like an adorable weirdo, she opened one eye and looked over at me. "Jesus. You're still there."

I chuckled. "You hoping I was going to fall out of the car while you were asleep?"

She sat up and twisted from side to side, stretching her back. "No... Well, maybe a little."

I laughed, and her gaze snapped to mine, those damn innocent eyes of hers blinking at me as if she'd seen a ghost.

But that wasn't the worst of it. She seemed excited about having seen that ghost. Her lips curled up, and her gaze dropped to my mouth, where it lingered for too long. But only too long because it allowed my gaze enough time to fall to *her* mouth.

I remembered how those lips felt when they'd moved with mine. The way her tongue twisted and teased. The way her soft moans tasted when I took it deep. The way her hands would slide into my hair as she…

My chest tightened, and suddenly, that SUV became suffocating.

"Don't move," I ordered, swinging the door open and angling out.

Quite possibly for the first time in her entire life, she obeyed and waited for me to round the hood and open her door.

Scanning the periphery, I led her up the sidewalk to my front door. She remained tight at my side as I ushered her inside and turned the beeping alarm off before resetting it.

Flipping the lights on, I walked into my living room, headed straight for my kitchen, assuming she'd follow. I stopped when I didn't hear her feet against the hardwood floors.

I turned, finding her still standing in the foyer, her wide eyes sweeping through the room, up, down, and back again.

"You coming in?" I asked.

She looked to me, her dark eyebrows drawn together. "This is your house?"

I glanced around the room. "Last I checked."

"It's so…empty."

I barked a laugh. She wasn't wrong. Short of three boxes that hadn't migrated up to my bedroom yet, a backpack I used to carry my laptop to and from work, and my overnight bag that was always locked and loaded next to the door, it was all pale-gray walls and wide, gray, planked hardwood.

I walked around the long, polished concrete-top bar that divided the living room from the kitchen and shrugged. "Thanks for noticing.

I was going for minimalist chic. But empty works too."

"Are you moving?" she asked, tipping her head to the boxes.

"In. Yeah."

"In?" she asked, thoroughly perplexed. Which only served to thoroughly perplex me.

"Um…yeah. Why do you seem surprised?"

She shook her head entirely too many times. "No reason. I just got the impression you'd lived here for a while." She waved me off and made her way over to the bar. Then she planted herself on one of the two barstools across from me. "Anyway…ignore me. It's been a long day."

I smiled, but something didn't sit right. I hadn't remembered talking about my house at all. "What gave you that impression?"

She smiled. Wide. White. Fake. "I don't know."

Christ, she was still shit for a liar.

"So, how long have you lived here?" she asked.

I propped my hip against the counter. "On and off for five years."

"On and off?"

"Lived here for a few years. Moved out for a few. Now, I'm moving back in. My wife and I bought the place a while ago." Yep. That was exactly what I'd said. And, when I'd said it, I'd kept my gaze on her, waiting for a reaction.

She looked down at the counter and gave nothing away. "Your wife?"

"Ex-wife," I clarified.

Her head came back up. "Oh. I'm sorry to hear that."

Another fucking lie. Only this one felt like I'd won the lottery.

I quickly reminded myself that I didn't even want a ticket to play the Mira York lottery.

"Don't be. It's been over for about two years. Hence why I moved out. She got the house in the divorce. My choice. I didn't like the idea of her uprooting the kids." Yep. I'd said that too. And I watched for that little news to sink in.

She fought a good fight, her face remaining unreadable for the most part. But I knew Mira well enough to see I'd gutted her.

"You always wanted kids," she whispered, her forehead crinkling as if it were taking a great deal of effort to keep her emotions locked away.

"Yep. Got two girls. Twins. Sophie and Amelia. My whole fucking world."

She smiled, and I swear to God it was genuine. *That* gutted *me*. She was happy for me. Happy I'd gotten something I'd always wanted. We'd talked about kids. Never specifically with each other, as that would have implied a level of commitment we'd never had. But I knew she wanted a family too.

"What about you? Kids?" I asked.

She shook her head. "No. Decided not to have any."

Fuck. Why did that feel like I'd been cut? I didn't have a lot of fond thoughts of her making babies with Kurt. But knowing she never got to...

"That a choice you made based on his career or a decision you and Kurt made together?" I asked more roughly than I had planned.

Her tired eyes softened. "It was a decision *I* made for *myself*, Jeremy."

At least there was that, but it still pained me.

I nodded and glanced at the clock on the wall; it was nearing midnight. "It's late. Let me show you to your room."

She rose to her feet, and I shoved off the counter before walking around to meet her. We were inside, the doors locked and the alarm on, so I didn't have to fall to her side for protection or keep her within arm's reach. I did it anyway. And, as I stepped in, confining her in the space between my body and the bar, I told myself that it wasn't because I loved the way she arched into my touch each time I rested my hand on the small of her back. I also told myself that it wasn't because I loved the way her breathing sped and her cheeks pinked when I got close. And I swore to myself that it wasn't because I loved the way her round ass felt as it brushed against me when I guided her from my right side to my left, yet...

"Other side, baby," I murmured, shifting her in front of me. I could have moved. I could have put her on my left from the start. But why take the easy route when I could torture myself?

I sucked in through my teeth as she sidestepped, stopping when her right shoulder brushed my left pec. Fuck, even that felt good.

"Stairs," I directed, applying pressure to her back.

She arched.

I bit back a curse.

And we moved together.

"Uhhh," she drawled when we stopped at the door to my bedroom.

The California king bed was unmade, and my workout clothes from that morning were strewn across the floor near the hamper, my hoops skills obviously not what they'd once been. However, the rest of the room was clean, the linens clean-ish, fresh towels in the master bathroom. She'd be comfortable there. I, on the other hand, would have to torch that damn mattress before I'd ever be able to sleep in it again.

Tipping her head back, she aimed pink cheeks up at me. "Is this *your* room?"

I ignored how breathy she sounded.

I also ignored the way she raked her teeth over her bottom lip.

And I definitely fucking ignored the way my cock stirred to life.

With the casual coolness of a man on fire, I hurried deeper into the room.

I kept my back to her as I went to my dresser and started pulling out clothes. "I'm gonna crash in the girls' room." I pulled the second drawer open. "T-shirts and shit you can sleep in are in here. Doubt any of my sweats will fit you." I pulled the third drawer open. "But they're in here if you wanna try. If you make me a list, tomorrow, I'll see about getting out to your old place and picking up some of your stuff."

"Jeremy," she whispered from somewhere close.

Too close.

I kept rambling, wondering if Guardian really had turned me into a babbling sorority girl. "I got a laundry room near the back door. Feel free to wash what you're wearing now so you have it for tomorrow. Soap's in the cabinet on the left."

"Jeremy." She was closer. So close that I felt her at my back.

I put my chin to my shoulder. "Yeah?"

"I'm not kicking you out of your own room. How about you point me to the couch?"

"You heard the part about how I was just moving in, right?"

"I did. But you're a man. I'm assuming you bought a massive sofa and a big TV before you bought shower curtains."

I grinned, the nerves I was also forcing myself to ignore ebbing. Pivoting on a toe, I faced her. "You'd assume right. I furnished the den in the basement first, but you're not allowed to go in there until I've had a chance to clean it up. I had my girls a couple nights ago. Swear to God, a Shopkins war broke out. It was a miracle I was able to get them out of there alive. I haven't been brave enough to open the door since. You go in there now, you're liable to lose a foot to a landmine."

"I'll take my chances." She giggled and snaked a hand out to touch my arm. There was no ignoring the bolt of electricity that traveled over my skin.

Yep. It was time for me to go. I needed to take a shower and fist my cock—first to make sure it was still there after all the bullshit that had been happening in my chest throughout the course of the day, second to wrestle that bastard into submission. I was a forty-year-old man—there was no fucking reason her hand on my arm should send sparks anywhere. And then, once that was done, I needed to crawl into one of the girls' tiny twin beds and spend the rest of my night replaying every single bruise she'd ever given me, all in an effort to keep my feet from carrying my ass back down the hall, into her room, and into her bed.

Not that I thought she'd want me there. Or maybe she would. Mira and I had always been spectacular together. My length buried to the hilt, her milking me through countless orgasms. It was all the other times, when I had been fully clothed and she'd been naked, in bed with my best friend, that had really seemed to be our problem.

And, just like that, the heat consuming me turned to ice.

"No," I clipped. Long strides carried me to the bathroom, where I collected toiletries like a tornado before heading straight for the door. "Make yourself comfortable. I'll see you in the morning."

"Jeremy," she objected.

But, much like I did with the stabbing pain in my chest, I ignored her.

It had taken forever for me to fall asleep that night. I'd tossed. I'd turned. I'd seen her face on the backs of my eyelids. Though that wasn't new. I'd felt her hand on my arm. My heart had raced as I'd remember that asshole trying to drag her into a car. My heart slowed when I remembered how right she felt pressed against me—safe and secure. My stomach ached as I thought of her losing it when Braydon scared her. My stomach rolled when I thought about the fact that I'd failed her, thus owning that fear. My skin tingled when I remembered how it felt to have her soft, naked body moving over mine. My skin burned when I reminded myself why I could never go back down that road.

And it had never even been my road to travel.

I woke when the sound of a glass breaking permeated my slumber. I was on my feet before my eyes opened.

"Mira!" I yelled, snatching the bedroom door open.

"I'm okay!" she yelled back. "Ouch. Shit. Fuck."

Jogging down the stairs, I repeated, "Mira?"

"Never mind. Not okay. Nooooot okay."

I rounded the corner and found her standing in the kitchen—or, more accurately, hopping in my kitchen.

"What are you doing?" I asked.

Her head snapped up and then her mouth fell open as her gaze landed on my bare chest. "Oh, wow," she breathed.

I ignored that too.

I only made it one step into the kitchen before she threw an arm up to stop me. "Don't come in here!"

She was wearing one of my plain, black tees, which damn near swallowed her, and a pair of gray sweats that somehow managed to mask even her roundest curves. She looked absolutely ridiculous and yet, somehow, absolutely gorgeous. She was holding her left foot. Blood was dripping onto the travertine, her every hop bringing her closer and closer to the broken remnants of what had to be the majority of my coffee cups.

"Shit. Stay still," I ordered, hurrying to the hall closet. After sliding a pair of running shoes on, I waded into the mess after her. "What the hell did you do?"

She draped her arm around my neck as I hooked her under the knees and swept her off the floor. "I was trying to get a mug, but I didn't realize I needed to be outfitted to climb Mount Everest to reach one."

I snagged a roll of paper towels off the counter and then carried her around to one of the barstools. "I'm not exactly short, Mira."

"No. But the top shelf? Assuming a person is not properly caffeinated, that is a highly dangerous location to store the coffee cups."

"I'm seeing this," I replied, crouching to get a better look at her foot.

She winced as I put pressure on it. "How bad is it?"

"Well...I don't think it needs to be amputated."

She glared and it stirred a smile to my lips.

"It's not too deep. Let me grab some Band-Aids." Still grinning, I stood from my crouch and walked to the first-floor bathroom to retrieve the first aid kit Melissa had purposely left behind when she and the girls had moved to be closer to her job. "All right. I've got My Little Pony or Dora. Pick your poison."

She laughed. "Definitely My Little Pony."

"Excellent choice," I replied. With the bleeding mostly stopped, I tore the plastic off the bandage and sealed it over her cut. "I personally have never been a fan of Dora's belly shirt. The child's, like, four, for God's sake. Put some damn clothes on her."

She rewarded me with a laugh that felt like the breath of life to a dying soul. Not even I, King of Denial City, could ignore the way my body came alive. And then I made the grave mistake of looking up at her. Her blinding, white smile was aimed down at me, the pure beauty radiating out of it enough to destroy a man's life and still leave him thanking her for it.

That was the exact moment I knew I was fucked.

Because I felt it—that magical spark that turned into a wildfire and melded people together. Time wasn't a factor. It didn't deteriorate or fade. Nor was it a physical thing you could break or a feeling you could get over. I'd found it—whatever the fuck it was—with Mira York when I was twenty-three years old. It didn't matter that our half-ass relationship had only lasted six months. It didn't even matter that she'd never felt that spark for me. It was still fucking inside me, taunting and tormenting me, craving her in any and every possible way I could have her.

And I didn't really want to ignore it at all.

"Are you okay?" she whispered, staring down at me.

"Not at all," I replied more honestly than I'd ever been even with myself.

Her smile fell and her face took on the most beautiful concern I'd ever seen. Inching forward on the stool, she reached out and rested her hand on my face. "How ya feeling? You're pale all of a sudden."

I gave it a seriously less-than-stellar attempt to stop my head from turning into her hand, absorbing her touch.

Her short nails bit into my neck as she flexed her fingers. "Jeremy, baby. You're bleeding through."

"What?" I breathed.

She slid off the stool and kneeled in front of me. "Let me change your bandage, and then maybe you need to go lay down for a while. You seem…off."

I was. But it was nothing a nap was going to fix.

Taking her to bed. Forcing her to stay. Living out my days at her side... Maybe. But not a nap.

Jesus. I needed some kind of intervention. This nonsense was ridiculous.

Drawing in a deep breath, I did my best to pull my shit together. Turning my gaze down to my chest, I saw the nancy bandage the doc had slapped on at the hospital had red seeping through. I snatched it off.

"Jesus, Jeremy! That is not a scratch! It's a gouge."

"It's fine," I assured, standing up, still trying to shake her spell off.

She caught my arm, that damn electrical charge from the night before humming inside me all over again. "It's going to leave a scar."

I shrugged. "Maybe. I'll talk to my plastic surgeon on Monday."

She blinked. "You have a plastic surgeon?"

Finally, a smile pulled at my lips, and I shook my head. "No, crazy. It was a joke. Besides, even if I did have a plastic surgeon, I sure as hell wouldn't be calling on him"—I leaned in close to whisper—"about a scratch on my shoulder."

Her sexy eyes narrowed. "Sit!" she ordered, snatching the first aid kit from my hand.

I held her challenging stare just for entertainment before giving up and sinking down onto the stool she had evacuated.

"Do you have any real bandages in here? I'm not thinking Dora and her offending belly shirt are going to cut it." She set the box on the counter before riffling through it.

I sighed, folding my hands in my lap. "Don't know. It's your turn to be the doctor. You tell me."

She flashed me a heart-stopping smile that radiated over my entire body. "I'd hardly call myself a doctor, but I have seen *Outlander*. So I guess that's close enough."

"I have no idea what you're talking about," I admitted, wincing as she dabbed a healthy layer of antibiotic ointment on the scratch, which she was right about. It wasn't a scratch at all. The bullet had taken a nice little chunk out of me. But it'd heal. Though, as her breasts brushed my arm, I wasn't sure I wanted it to.

She pressed a piece of gauze to my shoulder before tearing off a piece of tape with her teeth. "Of course you don't. You're a straight man. Starz hasn't been able to ensnare you with the fine specimen of a man that is Jamie Fraser. That man's ass is hypnotizing."

"Good to know," I replied absently, staring at her mouth and thinking that it had a few hypnotizing qualities of its own. "I'll be sure to pass that information along to Johnson."

Her hands stilled. "Johnson?" She gasped. "Oh my God, Sexy Guy is gay?"

I quirked an eyebrow and shot her a scowl. "You call him Sexy Guy?"

"Well, at first, he was Scary Guy, but then he smiled. After that, he was *definitely* Sexy Guy."

There was no way I could ignore the pang of jealousy that slammed into me. "What the fuck, Mira?"

Surprised, she looked at my shoulder. "Did I hurt you?"

Grinding my molars, I got my dumb ass back in check. "No. Forget it." I pushed off of the stool, desperate for space and possibly a brain transplant.

"I'm not done yet!"

"Yeah, you are," I said, heading around the bar. "I need to clean up the mountain of glass in the kitchen and then get some coffee."

"I'll clean up. Just let me grab my shoes."

I waved her off. "It's fine. I got it."

"Jeremy, seriously. I can do it. Are you hungry?" she asked. "I could make you something for breakfast."

My lips twitched. "I'm not thinking food poisoning is how I want to start this day." The mindfuck I was currently experiencing was more than enough.

"What's that supposed to mean?" she snipped.

I went to the pantry and retrieved the broom. "It means I remember your attempt at cooking at Kurt's birthday dinner. Two out of the three of us ended up hugging the toilet all night."

"That is not true!"

I shot her a challenging glare.

She crossed her arms and shot it right back.

Shaking my head, I got to work sweeping, grinning as I did it. "Mira, I've never been able to so much as look at pork since."

"Wow. Pigs around the world have probably hailed me a hero for that act of valor."

And, at that, my grin stretched into a full-blown smile. Christ, she was crazy.

I dumped the broken glass in the trash and then put the broom away. "Don't come in here without shoes. I need to vacuum to make sure I got it all, but I'd rather eat and drink coffee first. How about you park it on the stool and I'll cook us up some eggs."

"And you think your cooking is better than mine? I seem to remember you almost burning down the barracks while warming up leftover takeout in a microwave."

She settled on the stool and propped her elbows on the bar, her large boobs pressing together and drawing my eyes to them even through the baggy T-shirt. Shit. Was she wearing a bra?

"That was not my fault. Someone left a spoon in the container," I replied.

"That someone was you!"

And that's when I realized I was worse than fucked.

A loud laugh sprang from my throat. It was real in a way I'd only ever felt with her.

Her eyes lit as she watched me. It didn't take but a few seconds for her to join me. Her sarcastic comment wasn't that funny, but we both laughed long and hard.

And it felt fucking incredible. Like an integral piece of me had been missing and I hadn't even realized it until I got it back.

What Mira and I had was comfortable. Like hanging out with an old friend, not a long-lost love. Maybe we didn't need more than that. Maybe that was the solution to keeping the spark *and* protecting myself. Yes, I'd admit it. I was attracted to Mira in ways that did *not* say friendship. But I was a grown man. Surely I could find a way to lock that away. Sex had never been why I'd fallen in love with her. She got me. And, as I stared at her, her head thrown back in laughter, a far cry from the frightened woman in the elevator the day before, I knew I got her too.

It was going to suck. But it was best for both of us.

"We need to talk," I announced.

Her shoulders fell as she sobered. "Oh, God, not again."

I extended a hand across the bar. "I'm Jeremy Lark. Most of my friends call me Lark."

She flicked her gaze from my eyes to my hand and back again, but she eventually took it in a shake. "Mira York. Nobody calls me York."

I grinned.

She grinned back.

After giving her hand a squeeze, I released it and said, "I'd like to propose a truce."

A coy smile grew on her lips. "You have my attention, Jeremy Lark."

Using a single finger, I motioned between the two of us. "You and me. We've always been good at this. The talking and laughing. That was never our problem."

Her smile fell as she whispered, "No. It wasn't."

"So…let's stick to what we're good at. We got at least a few days before you can leave. Being at each other's throats isn't gonna make things any easier."

"I can do that," she replied. "The talking and the laughing, I mean." Grabbing the back of her hair, she pulled it over her shoulder and became enthralled with the ends.

Something I'd said had upset her. I didn't know what. And, if I knew Mira at all, she wasn't going to tell me—at least not yet. Eventually, it would eat her away until she couldn't hold it in any longer. She'd finally spit it out, probably on a yell. We'd fight about it. And then we'd make love until it was all forgotten.

Okay, so I was definitely going to have to figure out a better way to end that, but I could cross that bridge fully clothed when I got to it.

"No more arguing and yelling. Deal?" I offered.

She peeked up at me and faked a smile. "Deal."

"So, first order of this being-friends business: coffee. We might have to drink it out of bowls, but you think you can slip on some shoes and make it while I get busy on the grub?"

"Scrambled with—"

"Onions and cheese," I finished for her.

Her smile turned genuine and it made the left side of my chest squeeze.

"You remember," she breathed.

I half shrugged. "A lot of nights spent talking and laughing with you at the Waffle House."

She nodded and lifted her hand to her mouth, tears welling in her eyes. "A lot of *good* nights."

"A lot of *incredible* nights," I amended, that squeeze in my chest bearing down until I thought my ribs might crack.

Her chin quivered as she suddenly pushed to her feet. "I'll just go grab my shoes."

"Mira," I whispered, but I didn't follow it up with any other words. There was nothing left to say.

We'd agreed on talking and laughing.

Not holding and consoling.

"I'll be right back," she choked out before racing from the room.

I stood in the kitchen, staring at the stairs, thinking maybe talking and laughing wasn't such a great idea after all.

CHAPTER FOURTEEN

Mira

"A ND YOU ARE TELLING ME WHERE I CHOOSE TO PUT MY COCK just casually came up in conversation?" Johnson asked, arching an incredulous eyebrow.

"Well…yeah." I cut my gaze off to the side, stifling a laugh.

"Huh?" he said, kicking his feet up onto the coffee table and crossing them at the ankle. "You asking Jeremy about my cock?"

My gaze snapped back to his. "What? No!"

He stretched his arm across the back of Jeremy's long, black leather sectional and twisted to give me his full attention. "So it was Lark talking about my cock?"

I broke into a giggle. "No! Neither of us was talking about your… ya know."

"Cock?" He winked.

I rolled my eyes and laughed louder. "Yes. That. I simply mentioned Jamie Fraser and his magnificent ass. Jeremy didn't seem appreciative, but he agreed to pass along the info to you."

He playfully twisted his mouth. "You sure no one was talking about my cock?"

"Would you stop saying cock!"

He shook his head, and a rich, warm chuckle escaped his throat.

I'd been wrong. Sexy Guy wasn't sexy at all.

He was *extraordinary.*

After breakfast that morning, Jeremy had called Johnson to come over and babysit me while he drove back to my place to pick up a few of my things. I'd begged him to let me go with him. I didn't much like the idea of him going through my panty drawer, mainly because I hadn't been with a man in forever. Therefore, my panties were seriously sucking in the sexy department. But also because *anyone* going through your panty drawer who wasn't intimately acquainted with what you looked like outside of said panties was just plain weird.

My begging was met with a firm no and a you've-lost-your-damn-mind glare.

That was met with a firm yes and a you-don't-have-to-be-such-a-bossy-asshole glare from me.

We stared, but in a true show of maturity, neither of us yelled. No insults were hurled. And I didn't even burst into tears. (Seriously, I had to get a handle on that shit. It was out of control.)

And, within minutes, I relented to his declarations that it wasn't safe for me to go with him. Though secretly that surrender had only come because I'd remembered that the majority of my clothes had already been packed—including my panties.

Johnson showed up right before Jeremy left. And it was a good thing because he was there to talk me off the ledge of insanity when I caught sight of the gun on Jeremy's hip as he headed for the door.

He pulled me into a hug that was only slightly less consuming than Jeremy's and whispered, "He knows how to handle himself. You losing your shit is only going to get in his head and distract him when he needs to be out there with his head clear, eyes open, and focused on handling himself."

It made sense. Even if I hated it.

And then he released me, stepped away, and said, "You know how to cook? I'm starved."

For the next hour, I made Johnson a meal fit for a king. Pan-fried ham, onions, and green peppers, homemade mac and cheese, and a lovely green salad that went untouched. The ham and mac and cheese did not. It was safe to say I'd picked up some culinary skills over the years. Kurt had loved to eat, and I'd loved to get the hell away from him, so I'd spent most of my time in the beginning of our marriage hiding in the kitchen, learning my way around.

After we ate, I carried all the dishes over to the sink and promptly burst into tears. Whitney always did the dishes. She was worthless in a kitchen unless she was warming up a can of soup or a frozen dinner. I'd cook. She'd clean. Together, we made the perfect team. And, now, my girl, my partner, my best friend, was out there lost, frightened, wrapped in Kurt's filth because of me. I couldn't breathe, but as I sank to the floor, rivers of salt dripping off my chin, all I could do was pray that she still could.

I didn't hear it when he approached me, nor did I open my eyes when I sensed rather than felt Johnson lower his bulky body to the floor beside me. Then his strong arm curled around my shoulders.

"She's going to be okay," he rasped, reading my mind. "A lot of good men are out looking for her. Men I trust. You don't know this about Leo, but someone taking a woman, any woman, whether he knows her or not, it becomes a priority. He'll play it cool. Act like he's calling in a few favors just to help Lark. But I swear to God, Mira, he's got everyone including the hounds of Hell out looking for your girl right now. She *will* be found. And Guardian will bring her home."

I opened my eyes and peered up at him, firm resolve laced with kindness showed on his handsome face. My heart told me to believe him. What choice did I have? But the anxiety spiraling inside me, winding me higher with every slam of my heart, sabotaged my attempts to collect myself.

For such a gruff-looking man, Aidan Johnson had the patience of a saint. He sat there on the floor with me, allowing me to soak the front of his shirt with overwhelming doubt for who knows how long. When my tears finally dried and my heart slowed, he shot me a beautiful wink and rose to his feet, pulling me up with him.

"We're done with that," he announced. "You get one crying jag a day." After glancing down at the wet spot on his shoulder, he rubbed it with his palm. "And I'm officially assigning Lark to take the next shift."

I smiled, the moment of levity doing wonders to soothe my exposed nerves.

And then he walked away with heavy, purely masculine steps, heading straight to the TV in the basement. I watched as he disappeared, and then I sucked in a deep breath, sent up one last prayer for Whitney's safe return, and got busy doing the dishes.

Over the next half hour, Johnson came up periodically to check on me, acting like he was just grabbing a soda or using the restroom. But his sodas went untouched and I never heard the toilet flush.

When I finished in the kitchen, I decided to go upstairs and look around. Okay. Fine. I was snooping. It wasn't my proudest moment, but I was going stir-crazy and it helped me pass the time. It didn't give me many clues about Jeremy because he was, in fact, just moving in and most of his things were still in boxes.

I recognized the outside of the house from pictures I'd seen on Facebook, but the inside was a different story. On my way around, searching just enough to ease my curiosity but not enough to be intrusive, I stopped at the girls' bedroom. With pale-pink walls, white wicker furniture, and princess bedding, it was the only room in the house that was fully decorated. There were two twin beds on opposite sides of the room that simultaneously made my heart smile and my chest ache. I could imagine their sweet little faces as their father tucked them in at night. Jeremy had said that the girls were his whole world, and I didn't doubt it for a second. And, if I'd been a betting woman, I'd have put my money on the fact that he was their entire world too. He could be a real dick; he'd proved that. But I knew all too well how soft, warm, and comforting he could be too. This memory caused another smile—and another ache.

When I ran out of things to keep me busy, I decided to go down to the basement and make myself useful. Jeremy had not been lying when he'd said that a war had broken out down there. Toys were *everywhere*. I burst into laughter when I saw big, tough Johnson sitting on the couch, ESPN blaring on the TV, his biker boots propped on the table, a mountain of Barbies, ponies, and baby dolls surrounding him.

After I finished organizing, dusting, sweeping, and mopping, I begged Johnson to take me to the grocery store. He said no.

Then I begged him to take me to the mall so I could buy a change of clothes until Jeremy got back. He said fuck no.

Then I begged him to take me to Bed, Bath, and Beyond so I could at least buy Jeremy a small housewarming gift. He glared at me.

Eventually, I'd settled beside him on the couch and forced him to entertain me. We'd talked. We'd laughed. It hadn't been nearly as fun as it was when Jeremy and I did it, but it was a welcomed distraction. I'd told myself that distraction was the real reason Johnson had agreed to come over while Jeremy was gone rather than facing the fact that I was in imminent danger that required me to have a buff, bodyguard babysitter. And Johnson was such a good guy. He'd smiled and chatted, allowing me a few hours of comfort to pretend that my world hadn't imploded overnight.

And that was how Sexy Guy became extraordinary.

"Mira!" Jeremy called, interrupting my conversation with Johnson, thankfully before he had the chance to say *cock* again.

"Down here!" I yelled.

I heard his feet on the basement stairs as he jogged down.

I rose to greet him. "Hey."

"What are you doing down here?" he asked, scanning the now spotless room.

Johnson stood up. "We were just talking about my cock."

I couldn't stop the laugh when Jeremy's eyebrows shot up so high they nearly hit his hairline.

"Come again?"

Johnson meandered around the couch, a smirk playing on his lips. "Yeah. It seems everyone's talking about it these days."

Jeremy curled his lip and planted his hands on his hips, which only made me laugh harder. "The fuck are you talking about?"

"I'm talking about the fact that Mira has known me for less than twenty-four hours and already knows where I like to put my cock. I did not realize my sexuality was such a hot topic."

I leaned forward and whispered to Jeremy, "He won't stop saying cock. Don't bother trying to make him."

Johnson ignored me. "Now, I mean, I get the obsession. It's a nice fucking cock." He stopped in front of Jeremy and stabbed a finger in his chest. "But, the way I see it, the only reason it could have come up is because you were either interested in experiencing it for yourself…"

Jeremy's face snapped back in horror.

Yeah. I laughed again.

Johnson continued. "Orrrr you wanted to make sure Mira knew she wasn't my type so she didn't get the idea of trying to experience it for herself."

My laughter abruptly stopped. I hadn't considered this theory, but the idea of Jeremy being jealous did some seriously warm things inside my chest—okay, and some hot things to a few other places farther south.

Jeremy's face got hard as he tipped his head to the side, holding Johnson's gaze out of the corner of his eyes. "Orrrr she was talking about some man's ass and you are *literally* the only man I know who would be interested in that crap."

Okay. That was another possibility I *had* considered, but it wasn't nearly as exciting as Johnson's theory.

My head swung back to Johnson as he retorted, "Then you won't mind that she knows I love women too, and after spending the day kicking back and getting to know her, it has not escaped me that she's a good one."

"Aww." I reached out and gave Johnson's arm a squeeze. "Thanks. That was—"

Static filled the air, and I swung my gaze to Jeremy in time to see his face flash murderous.

A scary vein danced on his forehead as he seethed, "Get the fuck out of my house."

Uh-oh was my first thought.

My second was: *Oh my fucking God, he is jealous!*

Unsure of what to do with that little tidbit of information other than break into song and dance, I decided to slip into the middle of the hot-guy stare-off.

Wedging myself between the men, I said, "Okay, well, as very awkward as this has been, maybe it's best if Johnson retires for the evening. Less the excessive use of the word...um, well, *cock*. It has been a nice day, and I'd hate to ruin that with a fistfight in the middle of the freshly cleaned basement."

Johnson leaned around me and dropped his voice to a low rumble. "Would you look at that. She's funny, sexy, *and* smart." When he turned his dark gaze on me, I couldn't exactly see Jeremy, but the air became suffocating and I thought there was a good chance that that dancing vein was about to rupture.

My first thought again: *Uh-oh!*

And then I felt Jeremy's hand snake around me from behind and land on my hip.

My first thought after that was: *Oh my fucking god, he is totally jealous!*

"Not going to say it again," Jeremy snarled, shifting me against his chest.

I bit my lip to keep the smile from splitting my face.

Johnson did *not* miss Jeremy's hand *or* my smile. Shaking his head, he backed away. "Relax, my man. I'm just fucking with you. Leo has strictly forbidden me from making any godchildren with Mira."

"What?" I laughed...and kind of accused at the same time.

Jeremy muttered, "Fucking schoolgirls."

Johnson shot me a wink and a one-sided smile, and before I could ask him about making godchildren, he disappeared up the stairs.

I braced for another flare-up of my leprosy, but Jeremy kept his front flush with my back and his hand anchored at my hip.

My breath caught in my throat when his head dipped, the short stubble on his jaw grazing my temple as he stated, "You've been busy today."

Drawing in a deep breath, I closed my eyes. Then I stammered, "W-what do you mean?"

He swayed me closer, my ass hitting his hips, and it was all I could do not to moan.

"Making Johnson fall in love with you *and* cleaning my basement," he rasped.

My skin came alive with tingles, his heat at my back igniting a fire inside me. Keeping my eyes closed, I arched my back, pressing into him, and murmured, "He's harmless."

His breath teased my neck as his hand slid around to my stomach, where he used it to rock me deeper into his curve. "Who, Sexy Guy?" he asked, his lips so close that I could feel every syllable. "That's what you call him, right?"

I gasped as his hand glided up, his thumb stopping so close to the bottom of my breast it caused an ache between my legs.

"He's just Johnson," I whispered.

His other hand landed on my hip, and his tall body curled forward until I was forced to curl with him. "You sure about that?"

I turned my head toward him and his nose brushed my cheek. "Yes," I breathed.

"He won't be coming back," he announced as though I should care.

"Okay."

I heard him lick his lips at my ear, and as chills shattered across my skin, nerve endings I'd long since forgotten about roared to life. One caress of his tongue at my neck or sweep of his thumb at my breast and I would have fallen apart.

It had been too long.

Too long since any kind of desire had found me.

Too long since I'd longed for a man's touch.

Too long without him.

"It's not a problem if you don't see him again, right?" he pushed.

The ache between my legs intensified, devastating my senses. Reaching over my shoulder, I slid my hand into the short hairs at the nape of his neck. "Jeremy," I moaned.

"Asked you a question, Mir. Answer it."

I swallowed hard, a sensual smile curling my lips. "No, baby. It's not a problem if I don't see him again."

"Good," he snapped.

And then, all at once, he was gone.

My eyes flew open as I glanced around the room, unsure of what the hell had just happened.

"You didn't have to clean, but I do appreciate it," he said from at least ten feet away, cool and casual like I hadn't just almost orgasmed in his arms.

Slowly, I swiveled around to face him, my mouth hanging open, sexual tension and confusion muddling my brain. "It was...no problem."

Stoic, he gave me a quick head-to-toe, not even a twinkle of heat lingering in his eyes. "How's your foot?"

"My foot?" I asked.

He pointed to the floor. "Your cut from this morning."

I blinked and then repeated, "My foot?"

He frowned. "Never mind. Forget I asked. Look, I got your things. I found your purse, no problem, but I couldn't find some of the shoes you asked for. The rest should be there though. I was thinking we could order in for dinner. You good with that?"

"Uh, yeah. Fine... That's... Jesus." I shook my head, trying to get rid of the fog, all the while wondering if I'd imagined that entire interaction.

Nope. My fevered skin and peaked nipples indicated that it had been one hundred percent real. Even if I was the only one who seemed remotely affected.

He started up the stairs. "I'll grab your stuff out of the car."

When I was sure he was out of earshot, I whispered, "What just happened?" Touching the spot his whiskers had scrubbed my face, I repeated, "What the fucking hell just happened?"

Not surprisingly, no one answered.

Well, that is if you don't count Johnson's voice playing in my head. *"Orrrr you wanted to make sure Mira knew she wasn't my type so she didn't get the idea of trying to experience it for herself."*

A sly smile lifted my lips as Jeremy's voice in my head answered the question.

"It's not a problem if you don't see him again, right?"

Hope burst like a dam inside me.

Oh, yes. Jeremy Lark was jealous.

I could soooooo work with that.

CHAPTER FIFTEEN

Lark

"WE GONNA EAT SOMETIME THIS CENTURY?" I YELLED UP THE stairs.

"I'm coming!" she called back.

I assumed that meant she was on her way down, but my mind drifted back to the way her breathing had shuddered when I'd guided that sweet ass of hers into the bend of my hips. Jesus, the way she fit against me was nothing short of perfection. And then, when her hand had snaked up to my neck, my mouth mere inches away from hers… I was fucked. Again.

It had taken a massive show of self-restraint not to take her to the couch and literally fuck us both.

I reminded myself that it was just supposed to be talking, laughing, and friendship.

Bullshit. Bullshit. Bullshit.

I'd thought I could handle it.

In the span of twelve hours, it had become abundantly clear that I could *not*.

Over onion-and-cheese scrambled eggs, she'd given me back Mira.

And, in turn, I'd given her back Jeremy.

With Mira, gravity seemed lighter. Smiles came faster. Every breath was easier than the last.

And the hardest part of experiencing all of that was that I hadn't realized before that morning with her that gravity had been weighing me down. Or that smiles were formed through conscious effort. Or that my lungs hadn't fully expanded in seventeen years.

I should have kept up the asshole gig. At least then she wasn't showing me the sweet.

But, then again, Bitchy Mira had never fazed me much.

A world of hurt was rolling in on me in waves. And, because it was her, my heart was all but volunteering for me to drown.

Going out to her house and picking up her things hadn't helped, either. My resolve was rapidly crumbling, and my anger had once again bubbled to the surface. I wanted answers. Who she was? What had she been doing for all those years? But, mainly, why had it taken fourteen years and his going to prison before she'd left Kurt?

I'd been greeted at her house by two women who Mira had told me were Sherri and Tammy. She'd mentioned that they were strippers, though after one glance, I'd have emptied a mutual fund to pay them to keep their clothes *on*. They were nice enough. Chatting with me about Mira and asking a million questions about Whitney. They were the same questions Mira had asked me with tears in her eyes before I'd left. I gave them the same answers I'd given her. None. I'd called Leo and Caleb, but there was still nothing on Jonah, Whitney, or how Steve Browel and the attempted kidnapping was linked to any of it.

As soon as Sherri and Tammy wandered back to their bedrooms, I got to work searching Mira's room. It was wrong on basically every level, but I couldn't stop myself. I needed to know what I was getting myself into. Or, as I kept swearing to myself, *not* getting myself into.

Top to bottom, leaving no surface untouched, I combed her room. I prayed that I'd find the hidden dregs of her life. Instead, I got slashed to the bone by the knife of reality.

That. Fucking. Woman. She hadn't changed at all.

Her nightstand was overflowing with a mixture of old pay stubs and notebooks bursting at the seams with photos of lavish bars it looked like she'd printed off the internet. In the back of the folder was a handwritten ledger of what appeared to be money she'd been saving, and based on those pitiful pay stubs, it was the majority of what she brought home.

In a box marked *pictures*, I steeled myself for an onslaught of Kurt Benton and their life together. Of course she would have held on to that shit. Probably crying herself to sleep, wishing she could have him back, no matter how fucked up it had been.

But, much to my elation, all I found was Mira.

Mira with a tiny puppy curled into her arms. Mira with a gorgeous brunette, who I knew was Whitney Sloan, tucked into her side. Mira alone, standing on the beach, her arms thrown out to her sides, her eyes aimed at the camera.

Mira smiling. Mira laughing. Mira slaying my resolve from the other side of a fucking photograph.

Before I left, I did a quick search through her car. The damn thing was only slightly nicer than the piece-of-shit house, but it was clean and smelled like her. In the center console, I found a volunteer badge from the Humane Society. Because, seriously, it wasn't fucking bad enough that I knew she was living life tight, saving up all of her money to finally open the bar she'd been dreaming of since her teen years, and that she filled her walls with pictures of her friends and her favorite pet. No…I just had to fucking know that Mira York spent what little free time she had after work at the animal shelter tending to homeless dogs.

Fuck. Me.

And then I'd gotten back and seen her with Johnson, talking about his cock like she was his goddamn urologist. I never should have called that prick, but with all the other guys at work or off on assignments, he'd been the only man I trusted to keep her safe. I hadn't been thinking straight when I'd pulled her into my arms and essentially pissed a circle around her. Or maybe I had been thinking, because in that second, there had been nothing in the world that could have stopped me from claiming her.

But that was the thing. Mira had never been mine.

I needed to remind myself of that.

Silently cursing, I made my way back to the kitchen and got busy organizing dinner. For a broke girl from Alabama, she'd always ordered a small feast when we'd gotten Chinese. Sweet and sour chicken, salt and pepper shrimp, crab ragoon, spring roll (not to be confused with an eggroll), and egg drop soup. I only remembered because I'd fucking loved all of it and it had taken me years to be able to stomach any of it again.

My phone rang on the counter, my girls' gorgeous faces glowing on the screen. I instantly picked it up. "Well, hello, sweeties," I cooed, aiming the camera at my face.

"Daddy!" they squealed in unison.

I missed my babies. It was supposed to be my weekend with them, but after bringing Mira home, I'd had to call Melissa and switch. She'd assumed it was because of the half-ass bullet through my shoulder, and I had not corrected her. My ability to argue with a woman had been depleted thanks to the one upstairs, taking her sweet time to get ready. No way I was getting into shit with Mel over another woman. She had a boyfriend, so she probably wouldn't have lost her mind like she would have a few months earlier, but it was not a risk I was willing to take. Especially considering that she knew all about Mira.

"What are you crazies doing tonight?" I asked my babies.

Sophie's face nearly vibrated as she exclaimed, "Brent is taking us to da toy store! He said we can pick out anything we want."

Amelia's face popped on to the screen, shoving her sister out of the way. "Anything!"

I turned my head to the side so the girls couldn't see me roll my eyes. Of course he was. He'd been laying down a shit-ton of cash, trying to buy his way in with the girls since Mel had introduced them to him almost a month ago. We'd talked about it first. I'd met him. He seemed like a decent guy. Not exactly the definition of masculinity I wanted watching over my girls, but he paid for Wednesday night dinner with a black American Express card that told me he could at least afford a top-notch alarm system if and when he ever moved Mel in with him. I supposed spoiling my girls wasn't the worst flaw a stepfather could have.

I mocked excitement. "Anything?"

"Yes!" They giggled.

I shook my head and barked a laugh at their excitement. "He taking you to dinner too?"

They nodded eagerly.

I moved the phone closer to my face and whispered, "Order the lobster."

They looked at each other. "What's that?"

Smirking, I continued to whisper, "Only the most delicious—"

"Okay, that's enough," Melissa interrupted. "Tell Daddy you love him," she said, taking the phone from the twins.

"Love you!" they called unison.

"Love you too!" I called back.

Melissa's deep-green eyes appeared on the screen, a scowl covering her face. "Lobster, Jeremy. Really?"

I laughed. "What? It's good for them to experiment with new foods."

The background was a blur as she moved through the house, her red hair brushing the top of her shoulders. "I'll be sure to remind you of that next time you're footing the bill."

I grinned. "No way. I'm still working on carrot sticks and broccoli while I've got 'em. I think we should let our good pal Brent handle the surf and turf."

She let out a tiny laugh and then narrowed her eyes on the screen. "How's your shoulder?"

"It's good." I nabbed my beer off the counter and tipped it to my lips.

"Oh my god. Are you supposed to be drinking? You know mixing painkillers and—"

"Mel, it's a scratch. I'm not on any painkillers. Leave it alone. I promise I'm okay."

She sighed. "Yeah, and you promised me before we got married when I begged you to come work for my dad that you'd never get shot."

I shrugged. "Still haven't broken that promise."

She scoffed. "Whatever." Suddenly, her eyes narrowed and her face twisted. Mel's being a bitch wasn't something new, but it still shocked the shit out of me when she said, "I'll let you go. Tell the trollop of the week that it's safe to come out now. The mean old wife is gone."

"Trollop?" I repeated in confusion, but she'd already hit the end button.

"Shit," Mira whispered from behind me.

I spun and found her standing at the base of the stairs, embarrassment pinking her cheeks.

"I'm sorry. I wasn't trying to eavesdrop. I promise. I just didn't want to interrupt."

I opened my mouth to let her off the hook and apologize for Melissa, but the words died on my tongue the minute I raked my gaze down her body.

Ho. Lee. Shit.

My body locked up tight, and I immediately regretted going to her apartment to get her stuff. I could deal with Mira in jeans and a long-sleeved T-shirt. I could even deal with her prancing around in my clothes while hers were being washed.

I could *not* deal with this though. Hell, a room full of celibate monks couldn't deal with this.

Her straight hair was now hanging in thick, chunky curls, and her makeup was subtle, more of a highlight to her beauty rather than a mask. She was wearing a pair of dark washed jeans that sat low on her hips, which were capped off by a pair of black patent leather heels that made her already long legs somehow longer. And the farther up her body I got, the worse—and better—the Mira York package became. Her bright-pink top was made of some type of silky material that looked freaking incredible in contrast to her dark hair and her tan skin, but what really pushed me over the edge was the way it dipped into a deep V in the front and exposed a generous—and entirely dangerous—line of cleavage. On any other woman, it would have been sexy. On Mira? It was mouthwatering.

I gave her my back and tilted my beer high for a long draw that ended entirely too quickly.

"Everything okay?" she asked, sauntering into the kitchen.

No, it fucking wasn't.

"Yeah," I replied, snatching the fridge open. I went for another beer, wishing that it were a pint of tequila instead. "You want a beer?" I asked roughly.

Out of the corner of my eye, I saw her lean her spectacular ass against the counter and cross her legs at the ankle.

"That'd be great, *Jeremy*." Smooth. Soft. Seductive.

Shoot me!

I bit the inside of my cheek and bent to retrieve a bottle of beer off the bottom shelf. After twisting off the top, I passed it her way. "Why'd you get all dressed up? I told you we're staying in."

"So?" she replied, tipping the beer to her lips but keeping her gaze leveled on me.

Fuck. That was sexy too.

"So...we're staying in?" I said.

She offered the beer back to me. "And?"

Without thinking, I swiped it from her hand and took another long, deep draw, desperate for the alcohol to numb the voice in my head that was screaming for me to take her in my arms—and then plant myself between her legs.

Tears filled her eyes even as she smiled impossibly wide.

I passed the beer back. "What?"

"Nothing," she whispered, shaking her head.

She took another sip and passed it back.

We stared at each other for several seconds.

She blinked, her long, black lashes torturing me.

I blinked, trying to get a read on her.

This went on for a while.

Suddenly, she became unstuck from the counter and moved to the food. "Jesus, are you feeding the whole street?" Her hair curtained her face off, blocking my view as she asked, "Is that egg drop soup?"

"You still like that, right?"

She twisted her lips, but it still showed in her smile. "I never liked it."

My chin jerked to the side. "What? Yes you did."

She laughed and started opening containers. "Nope. Or sweet and sour chicken. Or salt and pepper shrimp." She bit her bottom lip and winked. "Though that's a nice-looking spring roll."

"What the hell are you talking about? This was exactly what you used to order when we went out to dinner."

"Yeah. But I didn't eat any of it. I don't even like Chinese." She took a big bite out of the spring roll and then motioned for me to pass the beer.

I held the bottom and offered her the neck. "You are so full of shit. We used to go all the time."

She drained the rest of the beer and set the empty on the counter. "Because *you* loved Chinese, especially that little place next to post."

"No. You're not remembering right. *You* loved that restaurant more than I did. You even paid most of the time." I didn't delay in retrieving another brew from the fridge, twisting the top, and passing it her way.

She barked a laugh and then did that weird, nostalgic teary-eyed smile thing again as she took it from my hand. "I'm absolutely remembering correctly. It used to take you two hours to eat all that food because you refused to waste any of it."

I chuffed. "Yeah, because you ordered enough to feed four, and it's not like you helped much, barely picking—" I abruptly stopped talking.

"Bingo!" she replied, tapping the end of her nose.

My back shot straight as realization dawned on me. "Holy shit."

"Told ya." She grinned with pride and took another bite of the spring roll.

"Fuck...that's crazy. I would have sworn this was your favorite."

"Well, it's not like I ever told you or anything." She shrugged and plopped two of the crab-and-cream-cheese puffs onto a plate. "It's okay. You remembered the important stuff. Spring rolls and crab ragoon for the win." With the beer dangling between her fingers, she started past me when a thought hit me.

I snaked a hand out and caught her elbow. "So, why did we go there so often?"

She angled her head back to look up at me, her cheeks flashing to the most amazing shade of pink as she whispered, "Because sometimes it rained."

"What?"

She kept her gaze locked on mine. "We didn't go to the woods when it rained. And... I missed you. So I'd call and offer to buy you Chinese food I knew you loved and couldn't refuse. I ordered a ton because, let's be honest, back then, you didn't even chew as much as you inhaled food. But, for however long it took you to finish, just so nothing would go to waste, I got you on a night when I otherwise wouldn't have."

My stomach sank. Jesus. Christ. If I'd thought knowing she was saving up for a bar and volunteering at an animal shelter was bad, this shit blew it out of the water. I didn't need to know she'd ever missed me. I didn't need to know she'd faked reasons to spend time with me. And I sure as fuck didn't need to know that talking about it now put that sparkle of regret in her eyes.

I needed to keep things in perspective.

I needed to keep my head together.

I needed to...

"C'mere," I urged. With one hand, I took the plate from her hands and caught the neck of the beer between two fingers. Then I folded the other arm around her shoulders and pulled her against my chest.

She came all too willingly.

"I'm sorry..." There should have been a million words to finish that thought, but I wasn't ready to say any of them. So, instead, I finished with, "That I got Chinese."

She laughed, but it broke when her arms encircled my hips. "Don't be. It may not be raining, but I'll still eat Chinese any day of the week if it buys me time with you."

I *really* didn't need to know that, either.

Closing my eyes, I did the best I could to ignore the burning in my chest.

But it was too strong.

Too intense.

Too…Mira.

I let out a heavy sigh and gathered her closer. It was exhausting to pretend not to feel things for her.

"You're killing me with the sweet, Mir." Sliding my hand down to the small of her back, I dipped under the flowing material of her shirt and allowed my fingers to splay over her bare skin.

She gasped and arched into my touch, pressing her breasts against me.

I smiled to myself and whispered, "And that's not helping, either."

"Huh?" she asked, tilting her head back but keeping her cheek to my chest.

Tucking a stray hair behind her ear, I stared down at her and allowed myself to fully absorb the moment.

It was so surreal to have her there.

In my house.

In my arms.

In my life.

But was she back?

I'd barely come out of the other end of losing her once. But that had been a different time. A different place. And, for the way my heart was slamming around in my chest, I hoped like hell that it had been a different Mira. There was only one way to find out.

"What happened after you told me to leave that day?" I asked.

Her body went stiff, and she flicked her gaze off to the side. "A lot happened, Jeremy."

"Then I want to hear it all. You and Kurt. Kurt and the drugs.

You after Kurt. I need to know. And I need you to give that to me, baby."

Her eyes came back to mine, and they were so bright it would have melted any kind of resolve I'd still had left. If I'd had any.

"Anything," she breathed.

CHAPTER SIXTEEN

Mira

"THAT DUMB FUCK!" JEREMY BOOMED, PASSING THE BEER TO ME. I had a nice little buzz, but I was far from the lightweight I'd once been. We'd polished off a six-pack over dinner with no signs of slowing.

God, I'd missed the fine art of doing absolutely nothing with someone else and enjoying every single second of it.

After we'd eaten, we'd both kicked our shoes off and settled on opposite ends of his couch in the basement. After several trips to retrieve more beer from the mini fridge, the space between us was growing smaller and smaller.

And, with every inch that disappeared, my pulse raced faster and faster.

"Well…yes, he was. But you haven't even been gone from the story for twenty minutes yet."

"And he's already a dumb fuck!" He blew out an exasperated huff and flopped back against the couch, snapping his fingers for me to hurry up and give him the beer.

I giggled, tipped it up for a short sip, and then sent it his way.

I hadn't exactly been thrilled at the idea of telling Jeremy all about my past with Kurt. I felt like we were finally making headway between the two of us. And, while I had no idea what direction that headway was taking us, it was a hell of a lot better than where we'd been.

He kicked his feet up on the coffee table and pointed his gaze to the ceiling. "Okay, so you help him back inside, he calls you a whore, and then what happened?"

"I slapped him." I grinned as Jeremy's head jerked to mine.

"For real?"

I laughed. "He called me a *whore*."

Chuckling, he looked back up at the ceiling. "What next?"

"I got in his face, told him that, if there was a whore in our relationship, it was him."

"That's the damn truth." He passed me the beer.

"We got to arguing and the craziest thing happened. He stopped acting like I was the one in the wrong. He was more adamant on covering his own lies than he was about coming down on me for having an affair with you. I kept bringing up women that I knew he'd been with and he kept denying it or overexplaining, talking in circles." I pursed my lips and turned my gaze on Jeremy, regret clouding my vision. That one day defined my entire life.

And I'd paid for it, hand over fist, for almost half of my life.

Now, there I was, sitting on Jeremy Lark's couch, passing beers back and forth, wishing that I could turn back the hands of time so I could have been doing *this* for almost half of my life instead.

Deciding to live in the here and now, I scooted another inch toward him. "Anyway. His reaction enraged me. We'd always argued about his suspected cheating in the past. But he always had some kind of stupid excuse. And, honestly, back then, I had you, so I didn't really care what he was doing. But, in that moment, with you gone, while I was rattling off a laundry list of women that I knew he'd been with, the reality of it all came crashing down on me."

He took the beer from my hand and polished it off in one long pull. Then, without a word, he stood up, went to the mini fridge in the corner, and was back in less than a minute, a fresh beer in hand.

I smiled weakly as he twisted the top off and offered it to me.

And then he sat down.

Right next to me.

As in *directly* next to me.

Shoulder to shoulder.

Arm to arm.

Thigh to thigh.

Calf to Calf.

The side of his foot even pressed against mine.

It was exactly how we'd always sat on the back of his truck. And it hurt almost as much as it healed the gaping wound in my chest. My throat got thick with emotion, but I forced myself to take a sip of the beer before passing it.

I nearly choked when his large hand landed just above my knee.

Another familiar gesture.

Another pang of regret.

The tiniest morsel of hope igniting inside me.

"Keep talking," he gently ordered.

His proximity was stifling, because I couldn't think about anything but him. Short of crawling into his lap, I couldn't get much closer, but that didn't stop me from wanting it. Every inch of his body touching every inch of mine. And none of that was sexual. Not that I wouldn't have minded his warm, wet mouth, his hard length driving inside me, or losing myself in an orgasm that I knew would be spectacular because they always had been with him. But all of that was second to how much I wanted to feel his arms around me. Too many nights, I'd imagined he was there. Holding me. Whispering his hopes and dreams into the top of my hair. His heart beating in time with mine.

Safe.

Secure.

Comfortable.

Three things I only ever felt with him.

Those memories had gotten me through a lot of hard times. No matter how many shadows had been hanging over me. With the lights off, my eyes closed, a pillow held to my chest, Jeremy had always been just a dream away.

Taking the risk, I leaned against him and continued talking. "I stormed to our bedroom and started throwing shit in a bag. Kurt lost his mind. I'd never seen him like that. He dropped to his knees. Begged me to stay. Told me how sorry he was. Swore that it would never happen again." My lips got tight. "I was utterly shocked."

"He was probably afraid you'd go back to me," he said.

I bit my lip and tried not to focus on the sharp sting in my chest. God, had I wanted to do that. I'd stood in that room, a tote bag filled with everything I'd ever need, and contemplated calling Jeremy and begging him to come back for me. I had not one doubt that he would have come, but it would have only been out of spite. He had been pissed that Kurt had ruined his career, so I couldn't blame him. But I hadn't been real excited to be used as his tool for revenge.

Jeremy had cared about me. I knew that. But it was never the way I wanted him to.

We were friends who hung out and had sex. I made it all too convenient for him. But I wasn't the woman who stopped his heart or filled his lungs. Nor was I the woman who consumed his thoughts or owned his soul.

Despite that, he'd always been that man for me.

And, that day, as I'd stared down at my bag, tears rolling down my face, no place to go, no money, no car, nothing that wasn't connected to Kurt fucking Benton, I'd accepted that it was easier to stay with a man who claimed he loved me with words, but not with actions, rather than to love a man with my entire being when he didn't love me with either.

Swallowing hard, I replied, "Yeah. He couldn't stand the idea of you besting him."

"That man had more pride than anyone I'd ever met. The minute I told you to get in my truck, it became about me taking something from him. In Kurt's world, he was the king and I was nothing more than his loyal subject who was challenging him. It was the same bullshit with him putting the ammunition in my wall locker. He'd cottoned on that we were too close, but judging by the look on his face when I told him we were sleeping together, he had no clue it had gotten that far." His hand spasmed on my leg, and his eyes filled with apology.

A pressure I didn't immediately recognize filled in my chest, and I dropped my head onto his shoulder. "Yeah…that day. You showing up drunk. It didn't quite work out for any of us."

"I know," he whispered before clearing his throat. "So, you stayed?"

"I didn't really have anywhere else to go. Though the street corner might have been a better option. But you know how I am. Change gets me all worked up until I just want to shut down. So that's exactly what I did. I locked myself in our bedroom for two full weeks, only leaving to work. Kurt and I didn't speak, but for those fourteen days, he didn't go out with the guys. He came home after work. Cooked dinner. Left it in the microwave for me. And then took up residence on the couch for the rest of the night."

"So, he finally pulled his head out of his ass?"

"That would be a big, fat no."

He gave my leg another squeeze. "Shit."

"For the first few months after you left, I convinced myself that he was a changed man. He'd seen the light. The error of his ways. Learned his lesson. All that crap. And, for a while, we actually stopped fighting all the time." I lowered my voice to a whisper. "He proposed that first Christmas."

Jeremy's body sagged, and then chills scattered across my skin when I felt his lips on the top of my hair as he said, "I heard. Mutual friend called to ask me if I was going to be at the wedding. I thought about showing up with two engagement rings. Pushing my luck one last time."

My head snapped up, nearly knocking him in the mouth. "What?"

He chuckled, but it was sad. "Then I remembered I couldn't even afford gas to get there, much less two engagement rings. And *then* I remembered that was exactly why you picked him to begin with. So I got drunk instead."

He tried to pass me the beer, but I couldn't do anything but stare.

"You thought about showing up with two engagement rings?"

He shrugged, his lips twitching with humor. But I found not one thing humorous about what he was saying.

Oh. My. God.

"Seriously?" I croaked.

"I assumed he'd only given you one. I figured two would sway the odds in my favor."

I battled for oxygen while what was left of my heart shattered into a million jagged pieces, each one slicing me to the bone as it crashed to the ground at my feet.

His whole handsome face softened, the most unlikely of smiles curling his kissable lips. "Don't look at me like that. I know it sounds pitiful, but back then, I was a wreck."

I blinked back tears, my stomach twisting into a rope of knots. "It doesn't sound pitiful," I whispered.

He chuffed. "Right."

Chancing the rejection, I reached down and covered his hand on my thigh with my own. "I'm serious. It doesn't sound sad at all, because all dolled up in an expensive wedding dress that had been custom made for me and a pair of heels that cost more than I made in month, I stared at the door of that church, wishing and praying with my entire being that you'd suddenly appear and whisk me away to the woods."

It was his turn to be shocked. "What?"

My nose started stinging, so I forced a laugh to keep the tears at bay. "Turns out, it's really hard to marry a man when a part of you belongs to someone else."

He moved fast, yanking his hand out from under mine as he slid across the couch, leaving several feet between us. "What?" he repeated, his eyes wild.

My face flashed with embarrassment. "I...um..."

After setting the beer on the end table, he pushed to his feet and raked a hand through the top of his hair. "You expected for me to show up at your wedding and whisk you into the woods?"

I shook my head rapidly, panic building within me. "No. That's not what I meant."

"That's what you just fucking said."

I knotted my hands in my lap. "I said, I wished and prayed you would. Not that I *expected* you to."

"Right. Because *you* sent me away." He took a step forward and stabbed a finger down at me. "*You* were the one who told me to go. And *you* were the one who chose him."

Confused, I peered up at his irate face. His breathing was labored, and his jaw had turned to stone.

Mr. Hyde had arrived.

Unable to look at him any longer, I cut my gaze to the wall and confirmed the biggest regret of my life. "Yeah. I did that."

"You did what?" he asked, but it was more of a demand than a question.

Tears filling my eyes, I gave him my gaze back and softly replied, "I sent you away and picked Kurt."

I waited for the onslaught of anger. The fighting, the yelling, the rehashing.

But the strangest thing happened. The angry man in front of me disappeared.

His shoulders sagged, and he blew out a hard breath. His brutal stare gentled, and with one slash of his hand, he grabbed the beer off the end table, pivoted on a toe, and then parked himself on the couch.

Shoulder to shoulder.

Arm to arm.

Thigh to thigh.

Calf to Calf.

Poof, like a magic trick only missing the cloud of smoke, my Jeremy reappeared.

I had no idea what the hell had set him off. He'd confessed that he'd thought about showing up with two rings, but it had enraged him for me to say that I'd dreamed he'd followed through. It made no sense.

And my confusion only intensified when he pushed the beer in my direction and casually prompted, "So, what happened after you got married?"

I stole a glance at him as I took the drink, and then I did a double take to make sure my eyes weren't deceiving me.

Nope. Definitely my Jeremy.

I took a long sip, hoping to buy myself enough time to tamp my emotions down and also reflect on my years of watching *Criminal Minds* in hopes that I could remember the best way to handle someone with split personalities. But the beer was empty long before I came up with any answers.

I hadn't set the bottle on the coffee table before Jeremy made a trip to the mini fridge and came back with *two* beers in his hand.

For some insane reason, two beers felt like more space than he could ever put between us with distance.

Disappointment churned in my stomach when he stopped in front of me, twisted the top off, and placed the drink in my outstretched hand.

"You drink faster than you used to," he muttered. "We're never going to get through seventeen years if I keep having to get up for another."

And then he set the other unopened on the end table.

My cheeks heated as a genuine smile split my face.

He resumed his place at my side.

Shoulder to shoulder.

Arm to arm.

Thigh to thigh.

Calf to Calf.

And, this time, he threw his arm around my shoulders and pulled me against him.

I wanted to relish in his affection and crawl in closer, but I'd been starved for his arms for too long. However, I'd be damned if I once again allowed Kurt to taint it.

"Can I have some space?" I whispered.

His arm fell immediately and he started to slide away, but I slapped a hand down on his muscular thigh to stop him.

Licking my lips, I peeked up through my lashes. "But not too much."

His gaze dipped to my mouth, and then his chin gave the tiniest of jerks. "Whatever you need, Mir."

I passed him the beer, dread filling my veins because I had so much left of the grand, fucked-up story that was Kurt and me.

But Jeremy had asked me to tell him all of it.

And there was nothing I wouldn't do for him.

"So, Kurt and I got married. He really had cleaned up his act. No more clubs. No more women. I thought I was happy."

"You thought?" he asked softly.

I shrugged. "From the outside, everything was good. We bought a little starter house. I had a home for the first time in my entire life. I quit my job at the bar when Kurt was promoted and I became the consummate NCO wife. But none of that was real. His parents owned the house. Not even the power bill was in my name. And it turned out the consummate NCO wife doesn't do a whole lot besides pack her husband's lunch, fold his laundry, and show up with a bright smile to FRG meetings. I was just a girl playing house with a man who had built an illusion in order to keep her caged." I shot him a smile and motioned for the beer. "Time marched on. On my twenty-first birthday, he was away in California for a month-long field exercise when I got a call that he'd been arrested for possession of steroids."

He cleared his throat to cover what had sounded like a muffled curse. But there wasn't a name I hadn't called Kurt left in the book.

I continued. "His dad hired a big-time attorney and managed to get him off without jail time. But he got kicked out of the Army and had to do a boatload of community service. So we moved back to Driverton."

His hazel eyes came to mine, a knowing twitch flickering at the corner of his mouth. "You lose your shit about moving?"

I laughed and gave him the bottle. "That snit fit was epic."

"Figures." He tipped the beer back, but his smile showed around it.

I rolled my eyes, but I was smiling too. "I have to say, I have no idea how Max and Terry Benton spawned a child like Kurt."

Jeremy barked a laugh. "I've wondered that myself many times."

I turned on the couch and propped my back against the armrest so I was facing him. "When we got to Driverton, the Bentons welcomed us with open arms and never brought up Kurt's arrest again. But they never stopped asking about you."

This was not an exaggeration. At first, it had nearly destroyed me to go to the Bentons' house. There were as many photos of Jeremy on the wall as there were of their son. Kurt had never told them about me and Jeremy or why their surrogate son wouldn't be coming back. But, every year, Terry had made Kurt promise to call Jeremy and invite him over for Christmas dinner. And, every year, she'd looked crestfallen when his seat at the table had remained empty.

Jeremy shifted uncomfortably and then crossed his legs ankle to knee. "I don't want to talk about the Bentons."

I reached out and rested my hand on his forearm. "I still talk to Terry a good bit. We had lunch while she was in the city a few weeks back. I'm sure she would love to hear from you."

He snatched his arm away. "I said, I'm not fucking talking about the Bentons. Move on. What happened after you got back to Driverton?"

"Jeremy," I whispered.

"Driverton, Mira. Start there or we're done talking."

I frowned, promising myself to revisit the topic of the Bentons at a later date, when Mr. Hyde wasn't perilously close to the surface.

"Fine," I huffed. "After we got back to Driverton, Kurt lost his mind."

"He still had a mind to lose at that point?" He winked and took a long pull off the beer.

Annnd…he was back to teasing. Christ, I couldn't keep up. Though I wasn't about to complain that my Jeremy had returned.

I smiled. "After that, he started working for his dad. And, God, did they fight. Eventually, those fights came home with him. And we started fighting. It wasn't long before he started storming out and not coming home until two or three in the morning. And, after *that*, it wasn't long before I found some texts from a woman in his cell phone. I confronted him. He denied it. I left."

His eyebrows shot up. "You left?"

"He cheated on me. Of course I left."

"Mira, he cheated on you at least a dozen times in the first six months you two were dating."

I shot him a glare. "Yeah. But I was nineteen, dumb, and sleeping with his best friend. I didn't exactly have a moral leg to stand on."

"But you married him," he half laughed, half accused.

My imaginary hackles stood on end. I knew I had been an idiot, but knowing it and hearing someone you care about practically say it to your face were two totally different things.

"And I divorced him!" I defended.

He removed his hand from my thigh, scooted to the end of the couch, propped his back against the armrest, locked his fingers, rested them on the back of his head, and kicked his long legs up onto the couch, stretching them all the way down to my end so I was forced to shift to one side to make room for them. And he did all of this while laughing at me.

He also did all of this while pissing me off.

"What the hell is so funny?"

"Babe," he stated. And I knew from having spent the day with Johnson that that one word was his answer, not a term of endearment.

Cocking my head to the side, I mocked, "Yes, *babe.*"

His laugh got louder. "Mira, seriously."

My anger got angrier. I shoved his legs off the couch and once again mocked him. "Jeremy, seriously."

He eyed me skeptically, but I should note he was still smiling. "Are you about to have a snit fit?"

I was *not* smiling when I retorted, "I wasn't planning on it until you started laughing at me."

"I'm not laughing at *you*. I'm laughing at your rationale. You dated a man who cheated on you damn near weekly. He swore he was a changed man, so you married him. Then he got strapped with an arrest, moved you back to his hometown, and then cheated on you again, what, four years after you got married? So *then* you left. But, seeing as to how Caleb told me you were married the day he got arrested, I'm assuming you went back and stayed with him for another decade. Baby, please tell me your head is not still so fucked up with his shit that you can't see the absurdity in that. I get it. It's in the past, but—"

"You get nothing!" I yelled.

His whole body jerked at my outburst.

I didn't have it in me to care if he thought I was having a snit fit or if I looked like a madwoman as I scrambled off the couch, walked over to him, leaned down, and stabbed a finger in his face. "You think you've heard the whole story? You've barely dipped your toe in the quicksand that has been my life."

His jaw went hard, and he pointedly looked at my finger. "We're having a good night, Mir. I highly suggest you find a way to reel in the bitch before shit gets ugly."

"You going to reel in Mr. Hyde?" I snapped back. But I said it seriously bitchily even to my own ears, so I decided not to have a snit fit about his calling me out on being the aforementioned bitch.

He scowled at me.

I glared at him.

Ultimately, it was Jeremy who put an end to it. And he did it in a way that didn't just make me reel in the bitch. It exorcised her from my body altogether.

"For fuck's sake," he growled. Snaking his hand up, he caught my wrist and gave me a hard pull.

I flew forward and crashed down on top of him. One of us could have been seriously injured if, at some point in the one-point-four seconds it took me to fall, he hadn't shifted to the edge of the couch, leaving a nice little Mira-sized spot between his body and the back of the couch. And like magic—again missing the cloud of smoke, but including a little bit of him juggling me—I miraculously became wedged in it.

My shoulder tucked under his shoulder, his arm wrapping around me and resting on the curve at my waist.

My breasts smooshed between us, which made them alarmingly close to popping out of the front of my shirt.

My stomach plastered to his side.

My other arm resting across a gloriously hard set of abs that felt even better than they had looked when I'd seen them that morning.

And then, because all of that wasn't enough, he reached down, caught my leg at the back of the knee, and lifted until my thigh draped over his hips.

And it all happened so fast that I didn't have the chance to make up my mind about whether I wanted to burst off the couch and sprint from the house like I was on fire or sink in deep, curl in tight, and live out the rest of my days on that couch with him. It was simultaneously the most uncomfortable and comfortable I had ever been in my life.

"Uh…" I drawled.

His voice was low and husky as he said, "Yeah, Mira. I can reel in Mr. Hyde. Though I'm thinking he might have a thing for your bitch."

This statement only made me more uncomfortable—my body went stiff.

But also more comfortable—my nipples started to tingle at the idea of his having a thing for any part of me, including my bitch.

"Well, then…" I stated for no real purpose except that I was seriously struggling to form a coherent thought.

His chest shook, and then it rumbled when he ordered, "Relax."

"I'm not…unrelaxed," I stated ridiculously, because—again—coherent thoughts and the lack thereof.

"Baby, you look like rigor mortis has just set in." Using his free arm, he guided my head down to his shoulder. Then he pressed on my stiff arm until it curled around his stomach, making contact from my elbow to the tips of my fingers, and after that he rubbed his hand over my thigh until it slacked and I gave him some of my weight. "There ya go," he praised, folding his arm behind his head. "Much better."

I had to admit that he wasn't wrong. My heart was still racing and my mind was a swirling mess, but this definitely was better.

When I tilted my head back, he tilted his down to catch my gaze.

Not surprisingly, he was grinning. And it was huge. And beautiful. And content. And full of life. And that one tooth that turned in just the tiniest bit was showing, so I knew it was real. And it was a gift no one could ever take away from me.

And that was when it happened.

After seventeen long years, I finally relaxed.

"Is this what always happens when shit gets ugly?" I asked softly.

"With you? Yeah." His grin stretched. "It's shockingly similar to what happens when shit gets fucking perfect."

My heart stopped, and based on the way his grin turned into a megawatt smile, I was relatively sure my cheeks went up in flames.

"Jeremy," I whispered, squeezing him tight.

He squeezed me back, but his smile faded. "Look, you want space while we finish this conversation, I'll give it to you. But talking about you being married to Kurt for fourteen years is not my idea of a good time. It was mildly manageable when I was listening to it while passing beers back and forth and a little more manageable when you leaned into me sweet and soft. But this—holding you, feeling you, knowing you're here and not a fucking ghost from the past come to haunt me— might make it significantly more tolerable."

I liked that he thought this, because despite my pleas for space earlier, his holding *me*, feeling *him*, and knowing *he* was there and not a ghost from the past come to haunt *me* would absolutely make the next part of my story significantly more tolerable.

Holding his gaze, I announced, "Two weeks after I left Kurt, I found out I was pregnant."

His eyebrows snapped together. "I thought you said—"

"I had a miscarriage. But not before he'd convinced me to give our marriage another try and I'd moved back in. In hindsight, it was for the best. A baby in the middle of his bullshit would have been a mess. But it still hurt…a lot."

His lips found my forehead, where he mumbled, "Jesus Christ. Mira, I'm sorry."

"It's okay. I rebounded. I got busy trying to distract myself and decided to get off my ass and finally open that bar I always dreamed of. Kurt was still in kiss-my-ass mode, so he told me he'd help. Which you know Kurt, so you know that help usually means he goes to his parents and *they* help. But I was sick and tired of mooching off Max and Terry. They'd already given us so much. So I made Kurt swear not to ask them for anything. So Kurt, still in kiss-my-ass mode, took out a small personal loan the next day.

"I found a building. Kurt bought the building. I needed a business license. Kurt got it. I was on my hands and knees in there every day, scrubbing the floors, painting the walls, tearing shit down, and building it back up. I did the work and Kurt financed it all. Seriously, Jeremy, it took me months to convert that piece-of-shit old laundromat into a bar. By the time the Sip and Sud opened, I'd never been more exhausted in my life. The idea of a laundromat bar was unconventional, but I think that was exactly why it worked. And, God, did it work."

With a bright smile, he tucked a hair behind my ear, pride beaming in his eyes. And not pride because he was proud of me.

Pride because he knew I'd gotten something I'd always wanted.

Pride a person could never understand unless they, too, had been on the losing end in life.

Pride Kurt had never felt for me.

Pride that coming from Jeremy was another gift. And one that was even bigger than the smile.

I kept talking. "A year later, we opened two more locations. Same concept. Same success. I swear I worked damn near eighteen hours a day for those first two years, but I was happy. And not because I *thought* I was happy. I just…was." After rolling so half of my body was on top of him, I propped myself up on his chest. I was so caught up in the story that I almost missed it when the hand he'd had in the curve of my waist turned with me so it was now resting on my ass.

Jeremy did not miss that I'd almost missed this movement; he also did not delay in testing the waters by giving it a generous squeeze.

And, because it had been a really fucking long time since a man, any man, had touched me like that, and factor in that said man was Jeremy, I gasped and rocked in deep with my hips, searching for friction in places that had no business in a conversation about Kurt.

"Jesus, fuck, baby," he rasped. Hooking me around the waist, he dragged me the rest of the way on top of him.

My breasts pillowed against his chest, and he immediately dropped his heated gaze to them while licking his lips.

Oh, yes. I knew that look. I'd envisioned it late at night as I'd touched myself too many times.

"How much story you got left?" he asked my chest.

"About eleven years," I breathed.

Closing his eyes, he sucked in a sharp breath and released it on a tortured, "Fuck me."

Which was appropriate because that was exactly what I was hoping to do.

CHAPTER SEVENTEEN

Lark

"**M**AYBE WE CAN PRESS PAUSE ON THE PAST FOR A LITTLE WHILE," she purred, her sweet ass rolling in my hand, her sweeter pussy rolling on my thigh.

Fucking.

Fuck.

Fuck.

Fuck.

I'd have pressed pause on the entire world if it would have gotten me more of her. The ability to finally take her mouth, taste more than the lip of a beer bottle we'd shared. Her tongue tangling with mine, hunger and desperation fueling us both. My hands in her thick hair, holding her against my mouth as if oxygen were a secondary need.

And then I'd be peeling off that flimsy shirt she had been torturing me with all damn night. Each time she moved, I waited with bated breath for her breasts to pop free. Despite a tremendous effort on my part, it seemed God didn't answer nip slip prayers. He probably knew what he was doing, because if I got her shirt off, one perfect fucking tit filling my hand, the other pink nipple between my lips, her frenzied moans serenading me, there was going to be nothing God could do for either one of us.

Out of all the times we'd been together, I'd never *fucked* Mira York. We'd had sex—fun and fast.

I'd made love to her—slow and tender.

She'd ridden me—hard and long.

But I knew with an absolute certainty that, if I ever got inside her again, it wasn't going to be any of that.

I'd longed for that woman too many years for it to be anything but feral.

And not with need.

But with punishment.

She'd wasted my entire fucking life. And I knew this because she'd been back not *two days* and that was all it had taken to realize that, for the last seventeen years, I hadn't been living.

And I fucking hated her for that.

Because I loved her so goddamn much that it had only been *two fucking days* and I was already scrambling trying to figure out how I was ever going to let her go.

So, no.

If I got her pants off, I was going to fuck Mira York with every ounce of hate I'd ever felt for her.

Raw.

Brutal.

Savage.

Her breasts would be covered with bruises.

Her neck with my teeth marks

She'd scream my name until they became the only three syllables her mouth knew how to produce.

She'd come, I'd make sure of it—not stopping until that fucking wet silk of hers covered my hands. And then my mouth. And, finally, my cock.

And then, when it was all said and done, she'd beg me for more.

Day after day.

Night after night.

And I'd give it to her.

Any way she wanted it.

A willing victim.

Because, unlike the last time, I knew what I was signing up for.

She'd come.

She'd go.

Only, this time, she wasn't taking my entire fucking life with her.

"You want to pause the talk?" I asked, grazing my finger over the swell of her chest.

Her mouth fell open, and her lids fluttered closed. "Jeremy."

Dipping my finger inside the front of her shirt, I only needed one sweep to find her pebbled nipple. "Not an answer, Mir."

Her answer was a moan as she threw her head back and offered more access. But it wasn't enough. She still had that fucking shirt on. Those fucking tight-ass jeans. And God only knew what beneath.

Knifing up, I took her with me. Her legs opened to straddle me, her knees to the cushion, her heat rocking over my thickening cock, her body swayed back, her breasts thrust toward me, her hand at my neck, her fingers in my hair, her eyes dark with desire, and her cheeks pink with anticipation.

Fuck. That was beautiful. All of it. And I felt every point of connection like an electric current.

I ignored the stabbing in my chest. The one that told me to kiss her. The one that told me to give rather than take. The one that told me that fucking would never be *fucking* with Mira. The one that screamed that she had always been a part of me. The one that had caused me to wither. The one that had been reborn the moment my eyes had landed on hers. The one that made no fucking sense because it had never stopped loving her no matter the time or distance.

I ignored all of that completely. It had no business in this moment.

Pushing that shit out of my head, I latched my mouth on her delicate neck, working my way up with long strokes of my tongue.

Every swipe was followed by a nip.

Every nip was followed by her gasp.

Every gasp was followed by a roll of her hips over my painfully hard length.

And every roll forced a symphony of groans from both of our mouths.

Continuing my assault on her neck, I asked, "You gonna let me fuck you, baby?"

"Please," she panted, circling her hips to grind down on my denim-covered shaft.

Moving her hand up the back of my neck, she attempted to angle my head and take my mouth. Her lips skimmed mine, but that was all she got before I dipped low and snatched the front of her shirt down, her two perfect fucking tits pouring out of the worthless, black bra pressing them together. I wasted exactly zero seconds before sealing my mouth over one, my hand going to the other, eager to explore.

I kissed and sucked my way over both of her breasts, losing myself in the swells and the valley. Teasing and plucking her nipples with my fingers while my tongue swirled and soothed. She cried out when my teeth grazed her sensitive flesh, but she followed me forward, asking for more each time I tried to pull away for a breath of air.

"God, Jeremy," she cried, threading her fingers into the top of my hair. "I need more."

She was not alone in that. My body was buzzing like a broken streetlight, her body being the only repair.

Moving fast, I laid her down on the couch, rose to my feet, and peeled my shirt over my head. Then I started on her: first her shirt, then her bra. And then...I stalled.

"Jesus, woman," I breathed, taking in the sight of her lying on my couch.

Heavy, full breasts, honey-tanned skin, deep dips and curves in all the right places, her hair cascading over her shoulders, and those rich, brown eyes peering up at me, worry shining bright as if she had no idea that she possessed the power to bring a man to his knees with a single blink.

And then she blinked.

And, just as I'd suspected I would, I landed on my knees.

Frantic and fevered, I shot my hands straight to her jeans, where

I snatched the button open, gripped the denim on either side, and roughly tore the zipper down in the same fluid movement I stripped them down her legs. I was sure there were panties involved, but I hadn't known when or how they hit the floor, because with one look at her, all conscious thought had tumbled into extinction.

My vision tunneled, and my mind swirled in a heady combination of anger and desperation.

Need and longing.

Possession and defeat.

I slid a finger through her slick heat seconds before I found her clit, and then seconds after that, my tongue found it too.

"Oh, God," she choked.

Her body arched off the couch and a melody of blessed curse words tumbled from her lips as I ate at her wildly, recklessly, and relentlessly. I was a man on a mission. Bitter and hungry, determined to simultaneously punish and worship her.

"Jeremy!" she cried, her hands flying into my hair.

Using both of my hands on her ass, I lifted her up to my mouth, twisting and turning her to devour her from every angle with a fierce possession I had no right to feel.

But this was primal. Born in the depths of a man who needed his woman to know who she belonged to—even when she didn't.

Hooking my arms under her legs, I dug my fingertips into her soft flesh, and I bit the inside of her thighs, branding what was mine.

Her cries, reverent and pleading, were music to my ears. Her writhing body was damn near folded in half, only her back still resting on the leather. Her legs were draped over my shoulders, shaking as though she were being splintered in two, lost somewhere between ecstasy and oblivion.

And I…did…not…slow.

I sucked.

And licked.

Savoring and coaxing.

"Jeremy," she chanted, my name slicing through me almost as

much as it sent me soaring.

"Say it again," I growled, punctuating it with a firm flick of my tongue over her clit.

But she didn't say it. She didn't say anything. Her whole body tensed, the muscles in her legs flexing as she bared down, her heels digging into my back as her release roared to the edge.

Screwing her eyes shut, she slapped her hands down on the couch and fisted invisible sheets. "Oh, God."

And like a ton of bricks, panic I'd never felt before crashed over me. My vision flashed red, and my pulse thundered in my ears.

Her eyes were closed.

Her fucking eyes were closed.

She could have been anywhere.

With anyone.

But she wasn't.

She was with *me*.

She was mine.

She needed to know that.

"Noooo," she cried as my head snapped up and I suddenly released her legs.

With frenzied hands, I took approximately three seconds to undo my pants and free my cock. I didn't get them over my ass before I drove inside her, hard and rough, planting myself at the hilt.

A strangled cry tore from her throat, and her hand flew up to my chest, her nails raking down my pecs as if she were searching for purchase.

Only she wasn't trying to get closer—she was trying to get away.

"Fuck," I rumbled as her body took the slow path to stretching around my length. Jesus, she was tight.

"Don't...move," she panted—and not in a good way.

Instinctively, I drew out.

Her hand slapped on my forearm. "I said don't move!"

I froze and stared down at her, rational thought finally breaching through the madness in my head.

As my tunnel vision expanded, the red faded, which allowed the woman in front of me to return to focus. She was naked, hanging half off the couch in an awkward position that couldn't possibly have been comfortable. Her legs were wide, my fingerprints welted on her inner thighs, and her breasts were red and raw from my attention. Her neck was covered in hickeys and bites, her eyes wrenched shut and her face twisted in pain.

And *I* had done every bit of it on some fucked-up rampage to finally possess her.

"Oh, fuck," I breathed, shoving off of her. Scrambling away, I fell to my ass and slammed my back into the coffee table.

"Shit!" she exclaimed. "What part of don't move did you miss?"

My hands shook as I watched her sit up. When she winced, my gut soured. What the fuck was wrong with me? I'd lost it. In some crazed attempt to soothe the conflicting need to both claim her and protect myself, I'd lost control.

Scrubbing my palms over my face, I boomed, "Fuck!"

"Jeremy?" she whispered, concern thick in her voice.

I barked a humorless laugh. I'd manhandled her like a whore and she was concerned about me.

"Jesus Christ," I cursed, pinching the bridge of my nose, trying to forge my way through yet another Mira York–induced nervous breakdown.

"Baby," she whispered from somewhere close.

When her hands landed on my thighs, my whole body jerked and my lids flew open. Those big, brown eyes were staring at me with the most heartbreaking mixture of fear and embarrassment.

I pulled her against my chest and tucked her face into my neck—probably too roughly, given the marks I'd already left on her. "I'm so fucking sorry."

"For what?" she asked timidly.

Leaning us both forward, I snatched a throw blanket off the corner of the sofa and wrapped it around her nudity. My chest heaving with labored breaths, I kissed the side of her face and replied, "For coming at you like that." I paused and smoothed down the back of her hair, pressing another kiss to her temple.

She tipped her head back, and I braced for another slash of guilt her innocent eyes would surely inflict before meeting her gaze.

An unlikely smile tipped her lips. "Are you freaking out because you think you hurt me?"

I palmed both sides of her face. "No. I'm freaking out because I *did* hurt you. Your neck looks like you were mauled by a fucking animal."

Resting her forehead on mine, she murmured, "Best mauling of my life."

I closed my eyes and shook my head. "Don't do that. That shit just now did not come from a good place."

She traced a finger down my chest and it felt like a hot knife carving into me. "Then where'd it come from, Jeremy?"

Grabbing her wrist to stop her descent, I lied. "I don't know."

"Then how do you know it wasn't a good place?"

"Because you're gonna be covered in bruises tomorrow."

"Look at me," she ordered, her voice quiet but demanding.

My eyes opened immediately.

Both of her hands came up to frame my face, another goddamn smile pulling at her lips. "Baby, I've been covered in bruises for a lot of years. They were just on the inside, and most of them were self-inflicted, but they still hurt." She took my hand and intertwined our fingers before resting them on her breast. "These bruises will be gone in a few days, nothing but a memory. But tonight, being with you, feeling you, being in your arms." She paused, her mouth curling playfully. "Passing beers, talking, and laughing. Baby, those bruises inside me finally started to fade."

The stabbing in my chest returned as she moved our joined hands to rest over my heart.

"But, now, I'm starting to see that I'm not the only one who still carries the wounds of the past. Maybe I should be the one apologizing."

My stomach twisted as I confessed, "I'm not sure I want to be the man to make those bruises on the inside of you fade."

Her body jolted as if I'd slapped her, but I gripped her hips to prevent her from moving off me.

Anger building inside me all over again, I cut my gaze away. "I'm really struggling with all of this. I have hated you for so long. For choosing him. For breaking me. For taking away my family."

"Your family?" she breathed, trying to shift off me, but like everything else with Mira, my need to keep her close overrode any desire I had for space.

"Mira, I can't talk about the Bentons because I lost them the same day I lost you."

"What the hell are you talking about?" she snapped, shoving on my chest, but I tightened my grip on her hips. Fuck, probably leaving more marks.

"Clean break. It was the only way I could move on. Growing up, the Bentons were more like parents to me than my own. I probably could have dealt with the fallout of losing Kurt. They wouldn't have cared if he and I hated each other. Hell, his dad probably would have been on my side. But, dammit, knowing you were a Benton. It was too much. So I stayed away. Swear to God, Terry practically stalked me for a few years, calling so often I had to change my number. Few years later, Max tracked me down at a strip club I was bouncing at downtown and beat the shit out of me." I laughed at the memory. "I looked like such a bitch, but it wasn't like I was going to fight back against the old man. He made me swear I'd come home. I quit my job and moved the next day."

Her mouth fell open, and tears filled her eyes. "You avoided them because of me?"

I shrugged. "Sitting around a Thanksgiving table, you wearing Kurt's wedding ring, possibly one day carrying his baby, smiling and laughing without me, was *not* something I could handle."

Her beautiful face got hard, and her eyes narrowed. Then, suddenly, the air between us changed in a way that made my lips twitch when it should have been impossible. She was naked, wrapped in a blanket, and cuddled close in my lap, but a snit fit was coming. And it might have made me an asshole but I waited with humor-filled, rapt attention.

"I haven't been at the Bentons' Thanksgiving table in eleven years, Jeremy. And Kurt hasn't been there for at least six," she declared.

My twitching lips suddenly stopped. "Eleven years?"

She swayed away and crossed her arms over her chest, lifting her boobs in such a sexy way that had I not been absolutely stupefied, my cock would have probably stirred back to life.

"Yes. *Eleven* years. And I remember the day Max found you because he walked into *my* bar, jotted your phone number and address in Chicago down on a cocktail napkin, slid it across to me, and said, 'Baby doll, I highly suggest you use that. Seriously doubt my boy's going to like the idea of you living under Kurt's thumb.'"

I blinked, the oxygen in the room disappearing.

Too much had been said in those few sentences, and I couldn't decide which part to focus on first.

Eleven years and Mira hadn't sat at the Bentons' table. No fucking way Terry would have let her daughter-in-law be anywhere else on a holiday. That woman made Martha Stewart look like a novice when it came to a celebration.

And then Max had called me his boy and Kurt just fucking Kurt. It didn't matter that I was forty years old. That shit hit me deep, right in the heart of the kid who'd never had a real family, and knowing that, even when I'd turned my back on them, they still considered me a son.

And lastly, and most importantly...

"You were living under Kurt's thumb?" I asked gruffly.

She quirked an incredulous eyebrow. "Yep. Right up until the day I turned him over to the cops."

I thought there was a solid chance my eyes were actually going to bulge from my head for as wide as they flared.

Caleb had briefed me about Kurt while I'd been at the hospital. But never had he mentioned Mira's being the one to turn him in. And, quite honestly, I wasn't sure how I felt about this little revelation.

However, the stirring in my chest seemed a whole hell of a lot like relief—and elation.

"*You* turned him in?" I accused in the best way possible.

She swayed her head from side to side. "Well, yes. But that stays between me and you. Technically, it was one of the waitresses at the bar, who I paid six hundred bucks to call and turn him in. But I damn sure made it happen."

The smile that split my face was unrivaled. I didn't know why I found this so humorous. Kurt was a fucking idiot. Proof being that he'd had a woman like Mira and he'd cheated on her rather than selling his soul to the devil to convince her to make beautiful brown-eyed babies with him. If that wasn't dumb enough, he'd managed to get himself locked away instead of spending the rest of his life on his knees, praising the Lord that she had miraculously seen enough in his stupid ass to have allowed him to slide his ring on her finger.

"You turned your own husband in to the cops?" I laughed.

She shot me a glare. "Hey, don't you dare get all judgy. He wasn't my husband and he hit me."

And that felt like *she* had hit *me*. My chin jerked to the side, and my laughter abruptly died. My voice dropped low and ominous as I leaned into her face and seethed, "He what?"

She pressed a hand in my chest. "Relax. First and last time. I was done taking his shit. He'd been harassing me, controlling me, and being an all-around dick for too long. So, the minute his hand hit my face, I decided I was done. I knew where he stashed his supply." She cut her gaze over my shoulder, lifting one of her own. "Or at least I thought I did. I paid Wendy six hundred bucks so I didn't have to risk my neck. She made an anonymous call and Kurt was arrested the next day."

I squinted, the gears in my head turning every which way as I tried to make sense of the timeline. "What do you mean he wasn't your husband when you called the cops?"

She curled her lip. "I told you I left him."

"And you also told me you went back."

"Yeah, for, like, two years while I was building up the Sip and Sud and avoiding him at all costs. We were far from married during that time. The final straw came when I found out he was using steroids again. He was always so damn superficial. He said he couldn't stand the way his body was changing as he got older. But let's be real here. He didn't like the way women didn't fall at his feet anymore. We got into a huge fight about it. He lied. I left."

No less confused than the first time, I said, "But you went back, right?"

"Hell no, I didn't go back. I moved out the next day. I gave him chance after chance. I figured seventy-seven strikes were enough."

I blinked, still lacking the ability to follow the bouncing ball. "But you were still married until he went to jail."

"Only on paper," she explained. "After I moved out, I filed for divorce. But, like the master manipulator he had always been, he pulled out his ace of spades. Turned out, he owned my bars. They were mine, but his name was on everything. And, Jeremy, I mean everything. The loans, the building, the licenses, *everything*. He threatened to take them from me in court, and despite the fact that he was a giant asshole, his parents had the money to back him if he tried. I didn't know if they would or wouldn't, but those were *my* bars. My sweat and tears. My dreams. I'd be damned if he was taking that away from me. So I caved. Our personal relationship ended, thankfully, but we were still partners. He helped me run things, we split the profits, he got to keep me under his thumb, and I got a new address way the hell away from him. It wasn't exactly a win, but it was far from a loss."

"Business," I muttered, nodding. "Melissa and I do that with the kids. No fighting. No bickering. Just doing our jobs as parents. Or, in your case, owners."

"Pretty much. And, really, I don't know why I was surprised when he wouldn't let me go. From day one, he'd done everything in his power to keep me dependent on him. It was like he knew that, if I ever got my feet under me, I'd hit the door running. He isolated me. My family was shit, but I wasn't even allowed to go back to Alabama to visit.

You know me and my mom didn't get along well. But she was still my mom. And friends? Forget about it. He didn't even like it when I hung out with Terry. I was his. No one else's."

Suddenly, a light bulb in my head illuminated the past. I'd always thought the reason Kurt had gone to such great lengths to get me kicked out of the Army was because he'd cottoned on to my feelings for Mira and he had been pissed that I would dare try to take something of his. But the truth was he had been livid that something of his had wanted *me*. He never had cared that she and I spent so much time together. It wasn't like I'd ever been good at hiding my feelings for her. Hell, he'd probably adored the fact that I was in love with her. Knowing she was his and I couldn't touch her.

But I could.

And I had.

And he'd spent the rest of his free life making sure she could never stray again.

Grinding my teeth, I swept my gaze off to the side. "You were always mine. And he knew it."

Her breath hitched so violently that it made her body buck. I swung my head back to face her.

A plethora of emotions danced in her eyes, the worst of all being shock. "I was?" she asked.

I twisted my lips. "Of course you were."

She pressed her lips together like she was fighting back tears, and it caused that stabbing pain to return to my chest.

After brushing her dark hair over her shoulder, I cupped the curve of her jaw and stared deep into her eyes. "Baby, I withered for you. I burned at the stake day after day, knowing he didn't love you. Knowing you'd chosen him. Knowing there was not one goddamn thing I could do to make you change your mind. Hating you was the only way I survived."

"I didn't know," she whispered, a single tear rolling down her cheek.

Using my thumb, I caught it before it reached her chin. I allowed my gaze to roam her face, the truth blazing from within. It boggled my mind. I loved that woman down to my bones, maybe deeper. How the hell did she not know that she'd been mine? But there it was, shining in her eyes, dripping down her cheek, rising and falling with her heaving chest. She had no fucking clue what she'd meant to me.

And the first chance I'd gotten with her again, I'd taken her body, hard and punishing. Brutal for no other reason than I'd been scared.

Scared she was back.

Scared she was going to leave.

And, most frightening of all, scared she was going to stay, which would force me to deal with the knowledge that she had never chosen me but that I would *always* choose her.

My gaze fell to her mouth. Perfect. Pink. Unmarred. The complete opposite of the rest of her body.

It was a good thing I was already on my ass, because regret and remorse tore through me, leveling me in their wake.

This woman. The one who I claimed was mine. The one who was as much a part of me as gravity and air. The one I'd been starving for most of my life.

And her lips…were utterly untouched.

"Christ. I didn't even kiss you," I whispered before dipping low and pressing my lips to hers. It was chaste, packed with apology on both sides.

Her blanket fell away as she lifted her arms to circle my neck. Her mouth opened, and mine followed, slanting until her warm tongue brushed mine, the hum of desire engulfing us both.

It was new and different, yet the most familiar kiss of my life.

Our mouths moved with a practiced ease while every rolling wave of our tongues was in exploration. I folded my arms around her hips, guiding one hand into the back of her hair, holding her impossibly tight, as though I could anchor her to me for…well, forever.

I kissed her long and hard. Deep and wet. Hungry and carnal.

I kissed her freely, like we were kids again and the bruises didn't exist inside either one of us.

And, when I finally tore my mouth away, my heart racing, my breathing ragged, my head spinning, my limbs boneless, I realized that every kiss I'd ever given or received after her had been a fraud.

"Please tell me you feel that between us?" she whispered almost painfully.

"I feel it," I assured her.

Still holding her back, I pushed up to my knees and then to my feet. Her mouth came back to mine, peppering kisses over my lips as I lowered her to the couch.

"You going to let me back in you, baby?" I asked, following her down, supporting my weight on an elbow at either side of her head. "Easy this time. I won't hurt you again."

Her legs fell open, inviting me home. "You didn't hurt me. It's just...been a while since I've been with a man."

My chest warmed. "How long?" I pushed before taking her mouth again.

Her hips circled off the cushion, searching for my length. "Don't make me answer that."

After skimming a hand down her side and then in over her hip, I found her heat.

Her head flew back against the couch, a breathy moan flowing from between her swollen lips. She'd told me how long it had been since she and Kurt had been anything but business partners and that was a long...fucking...time...ago. Mira was a beautiful woman, but I suspected that running three bars and living under her ex's thumb hadn't left her much time to sample the male population, an assumption I liked a fuck of a lot.

I amended my question. "Anyone since him?"

She met my gaze, her dark lashes blinking rapidly as she gave me the most arousing reply of my life. "No."

"Oh, baby," I rumbled with apology, nuzzling her cheek with mine.

Her breathing stuttered as I slid two fingers inside her, curling and coaxing, stoking her fire.

And she lit for me, fast and hot.

She writhed beneath me, her breasts swaying with her every movement.

"Oh, God," she cried, clinging to my shoulder while her other hand gripped my bicep, her face contorted in beautiful ecstasy.

And, as she came, her eyes closed, her body tense, jagged waves of her climax consuming her, it was my name that fell from her lips.

She was still soaring high when I withdrew my fingers and guided my length to her entrance.

"Mira, baby," I breathed, and her eyes fluttered open, that stabbing in my chest so intense that there was no way to ignore it. So, I didn't.

I finally let it shred me.

Hate melted.

Anger erased.

Self-preservation abandoned.

Sealing my mouth over hers, I slid into her tight heat with a devastating control.

I swallowed her cry, and she devoured my groan. Our tongues danced as I gave her time to stretch around me. And, when her body had relaxed, her legs drawing up to fold around my hips, I took that as my cue.

With long strokes followed by deep glides, I did anything but *fuck* Mira York.

In the end, we were both panting and covered in a sheen of sweat, her languid and sated body sagging beneath me, my release dripping from between her legs, and I felt my very first bruise fade in seventeen years.

CHAPTER EIGHTEEN

Mira

I WOKE UP SMILING BEFORE I'D EVEN OPENED MY EYES. STRETCHING like a cat, I reached a hand out to the side and patted the cool, empty bed where Jeremy had spent the night with his hard front flush with my back, his arms wrapped around my chest, holding me safe and secure.

My body ached from head to toe in the most glorious way, and my heart skipped as I allowed the memories of the night before to flood my mind.

After he'd taken me on the couch with a breathtaking reverence, he'd cradled me and carried me upstairs, peppering kisses over my face with every step. We'd showered together, alternating between kissing and washing each other as the water had rained down over us. Jeremy was gorgeous. But fully naked Jeremy was a sight to behold. And I took my time getting reacquainted with every inch of him. Defined muscles showed beneath a thin smattering of reddish-brown hair on his chest. Six perfect ridges textured his stomach, and a moan-inducing V at his hips guided my hands down to his long, thick cock, which hung sated between his legs. With soapy hands, I catalogued the muscles on his powerful thighs before sliding them around to his firm ass, which was the cherry on top of the entire mouth-watering package.

He was eager to return the favor, and to say that it was intimidating was a massive understatement. I'd been young the last time he'd truly seen me naked, at least when a sexual fog hadn't been clouding our vision. At thirty-six, everything that had once been sculpted and taut was now soft and curvy. The years had changed us both, but mine were far more noticeable. However, as his heated gaze followed his sensual hands while they roamed over me with a gentle dominance, I'd never felt more beautiful in my life.

He stared at me as we got out of his shower. Shame and apology were dense in his gaze as he silently inspected the numerous bites and bruises on my neck and breasts. Luckily for us both, I had a vast scarf collection in one of the boxes he'd picked up from my house. It was going to be at least a week before the dark purple faded and I was able to wear anything else.

Wrapping me in his arms from behind and resting his chin on the top of my head, he said, "I'm sorry."

I wasn't. Not at all. I'd bear his marks with pride for the rest of my life if it got me that moment with him. Yes, he'd been rough. But he hadn't hurt me. Not in any way that I didn't enjoy.

Kurt had never brought me to life like that. And, after we'd been separated, he'd taken it upon himself to make it known to every man I could possibly come into contact with that I was off-limits. I'd eventually given up on the idea of sex and love altogether. But, with one touch, Jeremy had ignited a blistering lust, years of dormant desire engulfing me in a sea of his flames. Pain and pleasure had mingled in the most intoxicating combination, leaving me drunk and at his tortured mercy.

After the shower, he guided me to bed, tucked me into his side, and, without a word spoken, fell asleep.

I woke him twice throughout the night. Once with my ass rocking against him until he slid inside me from behind with the same quiet gentleness as he'd shown me on the couch.

And then, some hours later, just as the sun had started to peek into the room, I'd climbed on top of him and taken him with fierce desperation that'd left a few bruises and bite marks on *him*.

So, as I rolled out of bed that morning, a satisfied smile curling my lips, my body screaming with sweet objections, my heart full, and my lips swollen, I did it without the weight of regret for the first time in seventeen years.

And I did it with a hope for a future swirling in my veins.

After nabbing Jeremy's T-shirt off the floor, I dragged it on and then padded to the door.

I froze when the deep rumble of his laughter hit me.

"So, was it good?" he asked.

The angelic voice of a little girl replied, "Ew, no. Lobster is bisgusting."

He laughed again, and I couldn't help but smile. He was talking to his babies. Jealousy reared its ugly head inside me, but I'd become all too skilled at keeping it hidden over the years. That wasn't my life. It had been a sacrifice I'd inadvertently made the day I'd married Kurt Benton. I'd accepted it over the years, but that didn't mean the ugly green monster didn't sneak up on me every now and again.

Rather than chancing being caught eavesdropping again, I went back into the bedroom and quietly closed the door. I went straight to my phone on the nightstand, the picture of Whitney and me holding Bitsy on my home screen slaying me like the sharpest knife. My stomach twisted as I sank down on the bed. It had been taken Christmas morning after Whitney had given me a teeny tiny doggy raincoat and booties she'd scored at Goodwill for a dollar. We'd laughed for hours as poor Bitsy had trotted around the house like she were walking on hot coals. It was crazy to think how happy we'd been that day. We'd been too broke to buy a tree, and Christmas dinner had consisted of baked chicken and sweet potatoes we'd pooled our money to afford. Yet, I couldn't remember being happier.

And, now, they were both gone.

As I dropped my chin to my chest, guilt seeped from my eyes.

"Mir?" he called, cracking the door open.

I kept my head low and hurried to wipe away the dampness on my cheeks. "Hey," I croaked.

"What's going on?" he asked cautiously.

I did another sweep under my eyes. "Nothing. I just woke up and heard you talking to your girls. So I decided to wait up here." Without giving him my eyes, I lifted my phone in the air. "Play some Candy Crush or something."

His bare feet appeared in my line of sight, his hands landed on my knees, easing them apart, and then his whole handsome face appeared as he dropped into a squat in front of me. His palms curved around my neck and tilted my head so he could see me.

My heart swelled when he offered me a warm smile.

"You losing that bad?"

I laughed, but it only made a fresh tear spill out.

His grip on the back of my neck tensed as he ordered, "Talk to me. Whatever it is. I'll fix it."

And then I really lost it.

God, it had been so fucking long since I'd had anyone to lean on. I'd been on my own for so damn long. I'd had Kurt, but asking for help had come with a price tag. He didn't do anything for me out of the kindness of his heart. I had no fucking idea what was going to happen with me and Jeremy after the night before.

I knew what I wanted.

I knew what I hoped.

I knew what I read in the depths of his kisses.

I knew that he'd said that I'd always been his.

But the past was the past, and losing yourself in a person physically did not equal starting a relationship.

Regardless, Jeremy Lark had just given me another gift. For however long it lasted, I wasn't alone.

"I woke up smiling," I confessed.

His lips tipped up. "Good."

Shaking my head, I rested my hand on his forearms and inched closer to the edge of the bed. "No. It's not good. Whitney's still missing and I woke up smiling."

Understanding hit his face. "You think she'd rather you wake up crying?"

"Well, no, but—"

"She your best friend?"

I nodded matter-of-factly. "Like a sister."

He skimmed a hand up the outside of my thigh up to my stomach where he gave me a gentle shove. As I fell back on the bed, he followed me forward. Horizontal across the bed, he settled on his hip and propped his head in his hand. His front was plastered to my side, his palm resting on my stomach, and his warm eyes were aimed down at me. My belly did a little flip. There was nothing sexual about that position. It was pure casual comfort, something Jeremy and I had always had together. Something I'd missed to the point of distraction.

"She feel the same?" he asked.

Whitney did. Despite our age gap, we were inseparable in that way that we both knew, no matter what life threw at us, our friendship would weather any storm.

"Yeah," I replied.

He dipped and pressed an all-too-brief kiss to my lips. "Then I'm guessing that, wherever she is right now, if she saw that smile on your face this morning, she'd be smiling too."

She totally would. She was amazing like that.

A God's-honest giggle sprang from my throat. "She'd probably be happier to know I finally got laid."

He winked. "Couple times."

With a single finger, I traced the outline of his pecs through his white T-shirt. "She's been hounding me for years to start dating. She went so far as to set me up with one of her college professors. It didn't go so well. We had a lovely dinner. Went back to his place for drinks, where he proceeded to tell me he peed sitting down, and then, when I rejected his advances, he asked if it would be okay if he masturbated in front of me."

His mouth fell open before a loud laugh bellowed out. "No fucking way."

"Unfortunately...way. I attract all the crazies. Hence why I've given up on men."

He slipped his hand up my stomach and stroked his thumb at the bottom curve of my breast. "You attract me."

"Exactly my point. You have split personalities."

His smile transformed into a scowl, but it held no heat.

I leaned up and kissed the tip of his nose. Then I got serious again. "So I'm guessing this pep talk doesn't end with news that Whitney has been rescued from a lavish resort where she's been vacationing in the lap of luxury?"

Using my hip, he rolled me to my side. "Sorry, babe."

Never one to pass up a Jeremy Lark cuddle, I tucked my arms between us and nestled into his front. "Yeah, I didn't think so."

"Though we do got a few things to talk about, and I hate to do this, seeing as you are currently laying on my bed and not wearing panties."

My cheeks heated because that was all very true. And then my face paled because whatever those few things he wanted to talk about were did not sound good. "Do we have to do the talking thing?"

"I'll make it fast. Then it will be over and I'll take you to breakfast."

I groaned but quickly relented. Getting out of the house did sound good. And doing it with my Jeremy while Mr. Hyde seemed to have been banished—at least temporarily—sounded amazing.

Craning my head back, I rested my chin on his chest and said, "Okay, fine. Lay it on me."

He tucked a stray hair behind my ear and then set about laying it on me. "Caleb called a little while ago. He finally got in a room with Kurt last night. He's claiming he has no involvement in any of Jonah's activities. Caleb pushed, told him everything that happened at your place, exaggerating in a few places. Kurt exploded the minute he heard Jonah put a gun to your head. They had to bring in three officers to subdue him."

I blinked, a sick feeling churning inside me. "Kurt's a good liar, Jeremy."

"I know that, Mir. Warned Caleb about that too. But he thinks the surprise was genuine."

I gaped at him. "So this wasn't Kurt?"

"Now, I didn't say all that. I just said Kurt was surprised and pissed. He's agreed to work with the cops on finding Jonah. They haven't been in contact since he was locked away, but they were tight before, so Caleb thought he might be of some use."

I sat up suddenly, crisscrossing my legs in front of me, and began worrying the ends of my hair. "Jonah said it was Kurt who sent him, helped him get the gun and everything. And that Kurt was still working on the inside." I paused, so much more information sitting on the tip of my tongue—but I wasn't sure I wanted to utter any of it.

Jeremy had made it known that he thought I was an idiot for having chosen Kurt, and I had been. And then I knew how stupid he thought it was that I'd stayed with him for so many years, even when we weren't together. And it was going to hurt like hell to validate those assumptions, but I had a feeling my next statement was going to do just that.

"But...it's never sat right with me that Kurt would send Jonah after me. Even when he showed up at my house, I told him that Kurt would put a bullet in his head before allowing him to put his hands on me."

Jeremy twisted his lips, his face getting hard, and his voice dripped with absurdity when he said, "You yourself admitted that Kurt hit you."

See? Further proof he thought I was a fool.

And maybe I was—but I'd spent almost two decades playing the fool. And, in that time, even when he hadn't been my husband in the biblical sense, I'd gotten to know Kurt Benton really fucking well. He was an asshole who'd controlled me and run all over me. He hadn't cared that I only got one life to live or that he was ruining it. He was selfish—his wants and desires were always more important than anyone else's. Especially mine. But the one thing Kurt Benton lived by was the if-I-can't-have-you-no-one-can mindset.

"I think he might be telling the truth, Jeremy, because I really don't think Kurt would ever hurt me."

He eyed me warily, but I ignored it and kept talking.

"There was this beer distributor who used to deliver to the Sip and Sud a few times a week," I announced. "Justin seemed nice, but he made it no secret that he was interested in me. Kurt made it no secret that, if he ever touched me, he'd rip his head off. I wasn't interested anyway, so for once, Kurt's being a dick actually worked in my favor. Well, one morning, Justin called and asked if he could deliver on Sunday because he was heading out of town and didn't want to turn the Sip and Sud over to the new guy covering his route. Begrudgingly, I got dressed and hauled my ass up to the bar to meet him. And that's when everything went wrong."

Jeremy's eyes turned dark, but I kept talking.

"Justin had me alone and took his shot. He cornered me and tried to kiss me. When I rejected him, he got pissed, decided no was not an answer he intended to take. He ripped my shirt off and snatched my bra down."

"Jesus, Fuck!" Jeremy boomed, suddenly sitting up. "Do not tell me this bullshit, Mira."

I patted his thigh. "Relax. Nothing else happened. He groped me a little, tried to get my pants off, but I fought back. I cracked him in the nose with the back of my head, broke it good. Blood was everywhere. All over me. All over him. He finally pinned me on the floor and had his hands around my throat, choking the life out of me, when Kurt appeared out of nowhere. The second he saw me, paralyzing fear and rage filled his eyes. I'd never seen him look like that. I actually had a moment where I feared for Justin's life. He was a shitbag who deserved to rot in jail, but I knew for certain he wasn't making it out of the bar that day. Kurt snatched him off me and set forth in making that assumption a reality. He beat the shit out of that guy. When Justin started fighting back, Kurt stood off of him, reached into the back of his pants, and pulled out a gun."

Jeremy sucked in through clenched teeth and then growled, "Please, God, tell me he put a bullet in his head."

"Christ. Testosterone must be a hell of a drug." I rolled my eyes.

"No. He didn't put a bullet in his head. I dove between them before he had the chance. Kurt was livid, but I wasn't letting him commit murder on my behalf." I swayed my head from side to side. "Or in the back of my bar, where I'd probably have to shut down for a few days, considering it'd be a crime scene and all. Anyway, Kurt and I started fighting about it. I'd never seen him so mad, but a lot of that was driven by fear. He said he thought I was dead when he'd first walked in and saw me covered in blood, Justin on top of me. We fought and we fought. But it ended with Kurt backhanding me across the face before storming off. A few of his guys came in, got Justin's unconscious but still very-much-alive body, and threw him into the front of his truck in the parking lot. An hour or two later, after he came around, I watched Justin drive away. An hour after that, I paid Wendy six hundred bucks to call the cops and tell them where Kurt kept his stash of steroids."

Jeremy's face remained covered in a whole lot of pissed off, but his brow crinkled in confusion. "Now, hear me when I say this… I'd like nothing more than to personally kill Kurt Benton after hearing this, but I really fucking wish you would have let him finish the job on that asshole."

I smiled. "I know. But I know you, Jeremy. And, when you say you want to kill someone, you mean beat the shit out of them until they are only breaths away from meeting their maker—but then you'd stop and call the cops. Because that's the right thing to do. But Kurt was legitimately going to kill him. And it was the first time in my entire life that I was scared of him. He'd been spiraling down into violence for a long time. He'd always been a dick, talked a big game. But, on the inside, he was harmless. But, that day, I saw it in his eyes. He'd changed. He'd hit me because he was mad…and scared. But, while it was the first time he'd ever laid a hand on me, I can assure you it wouldn't have been the last. I'd been a fool for a lot of years. I admit that. I'd put up with a lot because I was too afraid to take the risk on myself and take on the world on my own. But him hitting me? Even him threatening to hit me again? I was done."

His hard expression melted, and I'll be damned if that flicker of pride didn't spark in his eyes. His palm came to my face, and his thumb stroked across my cheek. "You did the right thing, baby."

"I know," I stated with my shoulders back and my head held high. And then they both fell. "It bit me in the ass though. Cops showed up. Apparently, the product Kurt had stashed at his house was only the tip of the iceberg. Hundreds of thousands of dollars in drugs, cash, and weapons were recovered from all of the Sip and Suds. Feds seized everything, and since my entire life was tied up with Kurt's, they took it as well. There was a big investigation into my possible involvement before I was finally cleared. But, before it was all said and done, I'd lost everything I had to show for my life."

He inched closer. "Jesus, baby. So that's why you're living cheap and saving so much money? To start another bar?"

My gaze snapped to his. "How do you know that?"

He grinned sheepishly. "I may have gone through your night-stand when I went to pick up your things."

"Seriously?" I whined, doing a mental inventory of everything that was in that nightstand. Relief struck me when I remembered a few specific items I'd packed with my panties to prepare for the move.

He cocked his head to the side, and his smile transformed into a smirk. "And, before you fly into bitch mode, don't think I didn't notice that you did a little snooping of your own the other day. All the boxes in my office were out of order when I went in there this morning."

Okay, so I had done that. But I hadn't found anything good, so I reserved the right to be annoyed. "Yeah, but yours was just a bunch of framed pictures of your kids and random paperwork. That's hardly fair."

Chuckling, he wrapped me in a bear hug and dragged me down onto the bed. "I also went through your car and found out you volunteer at the animal shelter. Gotta say, Mir. This shit is sweet."

"You know what's not sweet?" I said, one level below bitch mode. "Invading someone's privacy."

He laughed, rich and hearty. Rolling on top of me, he pinned me to the bed.

I turned my head like I was mad, but really, it was because I wasn't wearing panties and his hips had fallen through my legs, putting pressure in all the right places.

Clearly, Jeremy was not buying my attitude façade, because he rolled his hips, adding glorious friction to that pressure in all the right places. "Can we get back to the main topic, or are you going to have a snit fit over me looking through your stuff and finding shit I liked? The same shit that made me soften to you despite the fact that I was trying like hell to remain hard. And shit that told me, even though you've been given a crap hand, you still have a good heart and are fighting like hell to turn that shit into something you can be proud of."

God, how did he make that feel so good? My stomach dipped, and I gave him my gaze back when I whispered, "I think perhaps I'll take a temporary stay from the snit fit."

Smiling, he met my lips with his, and then his smile disappeared as he opened his mouth and kissed me long and wet.

My hands twisted in the back of his shirt as his tongue plundered my mouth with a dizzying effect.

He stopped all too soon, his chest heaving, giving me hope that the dizzying effect wasn't limited to me.

"And that's another thing we need to talk about," he stated. "You on birth control?"

My body got stiff. "Um…"

I wasn't. Inadvertent born-again virgins rarely found themselves in need of such protection. That is unless said person's walking, talking dream man suddenly reentered their life and they found themselves naked beneath—and on top—of him in a mere matter of days. Then yes, that inadvertent born-again virgin, i.e. me, should have definitely been on birth control or at the very least suggested the use of a condom.

But I'd been too wrapped up in the fantasy of having him back for any of that to cross my mind.

"Shit," I breathed.

"Right," he grumbled. "So I'm assuming you know your cycle

then…what's the likelihood we made a baby one of the three times I came inside you last night?"

I swallowed hard. "Um…well, I'm thirty six, so…I'm not thinking likely."

He arched an incredulous eyebrow. "Last time I came inside a thirty-six-year-old woman, Mira, I made a set of twins. I'm asking if you think we need to worry about this based on your body, not your age."

Pangs of jealousy and disappointment hit me at the same time, stealing my breath.

It wasn't right that I felt jealous of his ex-wife because she'd gotten that from him. Two beautiful babies with his beautiful smile. That woman had no idea how lucky she truly was.

And it definitely wasn't right that I felt a twinge of disappointment by the fact that I should have been starting my period any day, thus more than likely putting us in the clear as far as baby-making went. We weren't together. Hell, in a few weeks, we probably wouldn't even be speaking. I should have been relieved.

Yet it still hurt as I whispered, "I think we're good. I'm due to start this week."

His eyes narrowed as he searched my face. It was as if he could read the conflicting emotions warring inside me. "You sure about that?" he asked.

"Positive. No babies." I smiled—weak and sad on the inside, bright and cheery on the outside.

Thankfully, he seemed to buy it. "Okay, then. While we're out, I'll pick up some condoms for tonight."

"Okay."

With sex off the table until we got condoms, he shifted off of me. "Right. Now, again, I hate to do this, but we gotta get back to Kurt."

God, I was so sick and tired of everything going back to Kurt. But such was my life.

I huffed. "I'm starving. Any chance we can snatch this Band-Aid off? You tell me whatever you need to tell me so we can get that breakfast you promised me?"

Blessedly, he obliged. "Just to recap, you locked Kurt away because you thought he was getting violent, but you don't think he would hurt you?"

"Wait, that's not exactly what I said. I wasn't willing to risk that Kurt would turn that violence that was so obviously growing inside him on me. *That* is why I called the cops. But, *really*, I don't think he would ever allow anyone *else* to hurt me. I was very much Kurt's property."

Jeremy's face took on a steely edge. His lips thinned and his gaze intensified almost as though he were bracing himself.

Oh, God. Given that look, whatever he had to say did not bode well for me.

After licking his lips, he unleashed his burden like a curse. "Then you might like to know that Kurt's asking to see you."

My tense body sagged as I blinked up at him. "That's it?"

His eyes grew darker. "Depends. You gonna go?"

I blinked up at him again, and this time, I saw something else. Nerves were contorting his face. Maybe a little anxiety and apprehension thrown in there, too. That steely edge was born out of jealousy, and the intensity was as if he were trying to get inside my head in order to force me to make the right decision.

I smiled, feeling happiness radiate through my body. Even after everything I'd told him about my wasted life spent married to Kurt. Even after we'd spent the night together, reuniting in ways that included multiple orgasms and falling asleep in each other's arms. Even after he'd told me he was going to pick up some condoms, which I assumed meant we were going to spend another night in much the same fashion. He was worried I was going to rush back to Kurt.

I would have been insulted if I hadn't been ecstatic.

"*Hell no*, I'm not going to see him. I appreciate his concern for my safety. I would also appreciate any information he could give to aid in Whitney's return. But that gratitude will not be shown by dragging my ass up to the prison to give reassurance to the asshole who manipulated and tormented me for the majority of my adult life. So the only way he is ever going to see me again is if he uses his imagination to draw up the memories of those years because I am done being a part of his games. I officially resign as his queen."

There was no way to adequately describe the sheer beauty that lit his eyes and split his mouth as he stared down at me and said, "You mind if I go see him, then?"

"You going to tell him how you only fucked me three times last night and still managed to give me more orgasms than he ever did in our entire marriage?"

That impossibly beautiful smile grew. "It might come up."

Looping my arms around his neck, I swung myself up until I was only inches from his mouth and whispered, "Then by all means, baby. Have at it."

CHAPTER NINETEEN

Mira

"THIS IS YOURS?" I ASKED IN AWE, TRAILING MY FINGERS OVER the shiny, black hood of a newer-model Ford pickup truck.

He'd lifted it and put huge tires on it, and while the top was spotless, there was a thin layer of mud covering the running boards, letting me know that it didn't stay locked away in his garage waiting for a Chicago snow. It actually got used—and in places that weren't covered in asphalt. My Southern heart, which had been relocated to the Midwest all those years ago, quaked in its stunning presence.

He stared at me, his arms crossed over his chest, the muscles of his neck straining beneath a gray henley, but not because he was stressed or upset, but rather because his muscles were so thick and defined that they were always straining.

He answered with a simple, "Babe."

I swung my hand to the Escalade parked in the driveway. "What about the SUV?"

Twirling the keys on his finger, he walked over to me. "It's not a crime for a man to own two vehicles." Gripping my hip, he swayed me toward him. "If I have the kids, I drive the Caddy. If I'm by myself and the Caddy isn't blocking the garage, I'll take the truck." He grinned, dipped low, brushed his lips to mine, and whispered, "If I'm with Mira, I take the truck even if the Caddy *is* blocking the garage and I have to move it so it's not."

My stomach performed gold-medal-worthy somersaults as I pushed up onto my toes and gave him far more than a lip brush.

His mouth opened, inviting me in. His warm tongue rolled with mine, acting as the welcoming committee. My head became light and I fisted my hands in the front of his shirt for balance. The moan that slipped from my throat made his tantalizing lips curve up in a smile before he pulled away.

Resting his forehead to mine, he rumbled, "Breakfast and condoms, baby. We can't do anything without them."

"Not completely true," I murmured. "I saw a loaf of bread in your kitchen. Toast will serve as sustenance, and you can eat while I do other things with my mouth that don't require condoms."

His hand slipped down to my ass. "I've missed your mouth, Mira. But not a chance in hell you start things on your knees and I don't end them inside you. And, for that, I'm gonna need more than toast. So it looks like we're back to breakfast and condoms." He gripped my ass, rocking me against him. "But we're going to take the truck so you can slide in real close. And, on the off chance you feel like getting handsy while I drive, I won't object."

That had happened a lot when we were younger. The minute my ass had hit his seat, he'd lift his arm in invitation and I'd slid all the way over, as close as I could get without being in his lap. And then he'd drive. Windows down, the world passing us in a blur, him being the only thing in focus.

Inside that truck, I had been free to be Mira.

And, the idea of having that now, after seventeen years of feeling like someone else, I became giddy with excitement.

"You have a bench seat?" I gasped, staring up at him with a megawatt smile.

Smirking, he released me and opened the passenger's door. "When I lift the armrest, I do."

I giggled. "Jesus, it's like you knew I'd be coming back."

His shoulders jerked, and his jaw turned to granite. And then Jeremy Lark slayed me, brought me back to life, and then ruined me once and for all. "No. Because if I'd thought there was any chance of you *ever* coming back, I'd probably still be sitting on the tailgate of that clunker in the woods, waiting."

Oh. Yes. He'd said that. And, as much as it hurt, it was the sweetest thing anyone had uttered to me.

My throat got thick with emotion. "Baby," I whispered.

His Adam's apple bobbed, but his voice was jagged as he ordered, "Get in the truck, Mira."

I stared up at him, his words from the night before echoing in my ear. *"You were always mine."* My heart broke, but those bruises inside me faded a little more.

"I didn't know," I told him in apology.

"Get in the truck, Mira."

I scooted in closer, wrapping my arms around his hips and pressing my chest against his as if my racing pulse could somehow convey my truth. "I swear. I didn't know. I always thought—"

"Mira," he snapped, strategically avoiding my gaze while removing my arms. "Truck. Now."

He didn't want to talk about the past, and giving him that was the very least I could do after all he'd done for me.

So, after kissing the underside of his jaw, I climbed into his truck, pushed the cup-holder-armrest thingy up, and waited for him to join me in my own personal version of heaven.

"As far as bouncing went, this place was the cream of the crop," he said as we sat in a little diner located in a strip mall. It had candy-cane-striped booths and rude waitresses who acted like coffee and tap water were an inconvenience. But the man across from me made it the most amazing breakfast of my life.

Adjusting the infinity scarf I'd been forced to wear to cover the marks on my neck, I clarified, "For a strip club, you mean."

He smirked. "You can't call Lux a strip club. If you didn't make seven figures a year, this place did not exist. Everything was super secret. Private rooms. Private entrances. Membership and background checks were required. I had to sign an NDA before they'd even give me the address for the interview. Pay was incredible."

"Really," I drawled. Leaning forward, I slid my empty coffee out of the way and rested my elbows on the table. "You think they're hiring?"

"Fuck no," he growled. Leaning forward, he mirrored my position and kept his voice low. "Though, you put on those fucking heels and dance naked in my bedroom tonight, I'll pay better."

I laughed. "I meant as a bartender. Though, depending on your body guarding price per hour, rent for putting me up at your house, and feeding me the last couple of days, I might need to take you up on that to work off my debt."

"Not planning to take your money, baby. However, that is one repayment I will gladly accept."

I narrowed my eyes. "You promised you'd let me pay you back."

He stretched his arm across the back of the booth, his eyes taking on a heat that made me squirm as he said, "I woke up this morning to you riding my cock. You want to talk nickels and dimes, I'd say, after that, I'm the one in the red."

I glowered, ignoring the spark that ignited between my legs. "You promised."

Reaching across the table, he took my hand. "You gonna let me finish my story, or am I going to have to sit here while you have a snit fit about money?"

I scowled.

He winked.

I let it go. "Fine. Finish your story."

"So there I was. Best job a man like me could have hoped for. I'd been working there about a month. With clientele like that, nothing ever happened. Until one night it did. Big fight broke out at the door. Guns were drawn."

I cringed, but he grinned.

"I got in the middle, unarmed one of the men, pinned him to the floor until a different man hit me from behind like a battering ram."

I'd never understand what it was with men that made them enjoy fighting like a sport. But there it was, written all over Jeremy's face: forty years old and nostalgic about brawling.

He continued. "We rolled around on that floor for at least five minutes, exchanging punches and chokeholds. The other bouncers tried to separate us, but neither of us had been willing to accept defeat. Finally, the original guy with the gun was able to drag me off his buddy. Damn near broke my arm to do it though." He laughed. "While I was down, those two assholes unloaded on management, demanding I be fired. I was so clueless as to what the hell was going on, but I lost my job before I even got back to my feet."

"Jesus," I breathed. "Wasn't that the whole point of you being there? To break up fights."

"Yeah, but I took down the wrong men. The guy who had started the shit took off while I went to war with the innocent guy's personal security."

"Oh, shit." I laughed. I'd have felt bad if he hadn't been laughing, too.

"Ten minutes later, I walked out to my truck officially unemployed, and found both of the assholes I'd fought leaning against it, waiting on me. I mentally prepared for another round, and I was just pissed off enough to do some serious damage, but when I got close, my whole life changed. Leo James pushed off the truck, extended a Guardian Protection Agency business card my way, and said, 'I hear you might be looking for a job, son.'"

I gasped, covering my mouth with my hand. "No way."

With a cocky grin, he replied, "Yep. Best fucking mistake of my life. Johnson was the other guy, and they hired me on the spot. I had to do a few months of training, but Leo more than tripled my salary. Been there ever since."

"Holy shit, that's crazy." I giggled, and I could feel it—that pride that I so often saw in Jeremy's eyes, I was aiming it right back at him. And, when his face softened and his hand clutched mine even tighter,

I knew he felt it just as deep as I did.

We silently stared at each other for few seconds.

His gaze locked on mine.

That casual unspoken comfort lulling us both.

Perfection unlike I'd ever experienced before.

We were older. We were different.

But, right then, while holding hands in a shitty diner after we'd eaten cheap greasy food, talking and laughing long after the bill had been paid, we were still us.

"You ready to go, baby?" he whispered.

"Not really," I confessed.

His thumb stroked the back of my hand, and he amended his question. "Okay. You ready to go *together*, baby?"

My cheeks heated, and my lips curled. Oh, yeah. Jeremy was totally feeling it too.

Without verbally answering his question, I gathered my Gucci, slid out of the booth, and waited for him to throw his arm around my shoulders and curl me into his chest.

He did not disappoint.

When we exited through the restaurant door, his hand fell to my lower back. We hadn't made it off the sidewalk when a deep, masculine voice caught my attention.

"Mira?"

I turned, but Jeremy turned faster, shoving half of my body behind his as we came face-to-face with the brightest green eyes I had ever seen.

A smile broke across my face and I tried unsuccessfully to step back around Jeremy as I replied, "Walter?"

Shoving his hands into the pockets of a tailored, black suit, he strolled our way. "Mira Benton, I swear you get more beautiful—"

"York," Jeremy corrected on a growl.

Walter's ridiculously handsome face never left mine as he replied, "Yes. I heard you finally shook yourself free of Kurt. We were all heartbroken about the Sip and Sud closing."

I sighed, again trying to move around Jeremy. Again failing. "Yeah. It was a mess. I'm working on opening another one though."

He arched a dark eyebrow. "Oh, you are?"

"Yeah, but it'll be a few months before I can get it up and running. Any chance I'm going to find you parked at my bar again?"

"Chicago is a long way from Atlanta. But for you…" He raked his teeth over his bottom lip as he leaned around Jeremy to give me a head-to-toe.

Jeremy's body went stiff and it almost made me laugh. Walter was harmless. He traveled to Chicago for business a lot. And, for some reason, which I was thankful for considering he tipped fifty bucks a drink, he'd made his home away from home at the Sip and Sud. He loved to flirt any time he came in, but not even overprotective Kurt thought anything of it. And I knew, if he took his hands out of his pockets, he was wearing a shiny, gold wedding band. I'd once met his wife, Clare, and there was no denying given the way he watched her every move that he was head-over-heels in love with her.

"Well, okay, then," I said. "Keep an eye out for the grand opening and tell all your friends. A girl can use all the business she can get."

"Of course," Walter murmured. His emerald gaze jumped to Jeremy's golden one before coming back to mine. "It was so lovely to see you again, Mira." He lifted a finger in the air as though he were hailing a cab in the middle of the parking lot, and sure as shit, a black town car pulled up to the curb. "Do take care of yourself." He smiled, tipped his chin at Jeremy, and then prowled the few steps to the car, unbuttoning his suit coat on the way.

"You too!" I yelled as we watched him gracefully fold inside before shutting the door.

Jeremy's taut body slacked as the car pulled away. He blew out a hard breath, saying, "Who the fuck was that?"

He finally allowed me to slide around to his front, his hand returning to my lower back.

I placed a hand on his chest and smiled up at him. "Walter Noir. He was a regular at—"

That was all I got out before Jeremy's hand at my back flew around to my stomach and knocked the breath out of me as he lifted me off my feet and spun us both. I felt his body jerk, and then I went down hard, my palms skinning on the concrete as I tried to break my fall.

"Motherfucker!" Jeremy boomed above me. He was still on his feet.

I rolled to my back, my pulse racing and my mind swirling as I tried to figure out what the hell was going on. But, just as quickly as I had fallen, a large, bald man with pale, white skin landed face-first on the concrete beside me.

"Get back!" Jeremy barked at me, still in movement as his knee came down in the middle of the man's back, his upper body bending over him, and his palm landing on the man's wrist, pinning it to the sidewalk.

My mouth fell open, my heart stopped, and bile clawed up the back of my throat as I saw a large metal blade in the man's hand.

"Drop it!" Jeremy growled, pure fury making his voice almost un-recognizable. Using his wrist, Jeremy again slammed the guy's hand down on the concrete, the sound of his knuckles cracking making my skin crawl.

He howled in pain, but finally, after the second slam, the knife skittered free.

"Oh, God," I cried, scrambling away on my ass.

"Nine-one-one, Mira. Now," Jeremy growled.

He did not have to tell me twice. With shaking hands, I dove for my purse, which had sailed across the sidewalk when I'd fallen, and then dug my phone out.

I dialed those three numbers in record time.

CHAPTER TWENTY

Lark

"**E**ASY. YOU'RE GOING TO START A FIRE," I TEASED IN A WHISPER, my hand landing on her knee, which was anxiously bobbing up and down at a million miles a minute.

It was a poor attempt at levity, but it was all I had in me. Beneath the façade, my blood was boiling. However, every time I got loud, her anxiety spiraled higher like some fucked-up chain reaction. I'd tried to pack it down, and holding her was helping, but it was taking sheer force of will to keep my ass planted in that chair and not up pacing the room.

She turned her overwhelmed eyes up to me and asked, "What the hell is going on?"

I didn't have an answer.

After pressing my lips to her forehead, I turned my gaze back on the rest of the room.

Leo was leaning on the corner of his desk, watching Mira with the quiet brutality of a hurricane. It wasn't aimed at her. That hurricane had been cultivated on her behalf, and I had not one doubt that his wrath would be exorcised on the men who had dared to touch her.

We'd spent much of the day at the police station. A parade of cops and DEA agents had interviewed Mira. Leo had been kind enough to send in Guardian's attorneys to ensure that their questioning had remained on the up-and-up. Not that she'd had anything to hide. She'd been just as dumbfounded as the rest of us.

We were now back at Guardian and it was well after five. Caleb was thundering around the room, his phone held to his ear. Johnson was standing in the corner, his agitated eyes trained on Apollo, who was sitting behind Leo's panel of computers, doing God knew what, probably all of which was illegal. However, considering we'd been informed that Mira's old pal Walter Noir was actually one of the most powerful and dangerous men in the country, we were all willing to turn a blind eye.

To hear the DEA tell it, Noir's name had been inked at the top of those most wanted lists for some years. He was deep in everything from drugs and money laundering, all the way up to murder and organized crime. In certain parts of the country, he was the king of the underworld, but it was becoming clear that his army stretched far and wide.

So yeah...while Apollo banged away on that keyboard, doing what he did best, trying to catch a lead on any of Noir's known associates, none of us asked questions.

Caleb hung up and looked to Leo, a grim shake of his head doing nothing to quell the rage burning inside me.

"What's going on?" I questioned.

He blew out a ragged breath and crossed his thick, tattooed arms over his chest. "Noir's already back in Atlanta. Private plane. I'm not going to waste time trying to dig up flight records. They won't exist."

"Fuck!" I growled, causing Mira's body to go stiff at my outburst. I gathered her closer, pulling her from the chair beside me and into my lap.

Leo and Caleb exchanged a knowing glance that seriously pissed me off, but given that Mira was in deeper shit than any of us could have imagined, my mind was focused on things other than office gossip.

I leveled them both with a scowl. "You two gonna braid each other's hair now or finish telling me about the man I took down outside the restaurant?'

Caleb smirked. "The guy you caught was a known associate of Noir, but the dumbass has lawyered up. Claiming you attacked him."

"Of course he did," I muttered.

"It's only a matter of time before Noir's legal team gets him out."

My jaw turned to granite. I should have killed the fucker when I'd had the chance.

Mira's head tipped up and she flashed her frightened gaze around the room. "He was always so nice. I…don't understand."

Leo piped up before I had the chance to answer. "You got played, babe. I'm guessing your ex was into some dirtier shit than just steroids and Noir was a part of that. But don't worry—"

He was suddenly interrupted by Zach, Guardian's nighttime security officer, calling over the intercom from the surveillance room. "We got a problem."

My back shot straight and I moved Mira to her chair as I pushed to my feet.

"What's going on?" Leo called back, moving briskly to his computer. Johnson was doing the same.

Apollo was already on it, and as he pulled up the camera to the parking garage, it was clear we did in fact have a serious fucking problem. Eight men looking like the Secret Service in dark suits encircled a tall, lanky, well-dressed man. He appeared to be in his late thirties and was wearing black slacks, his hands casually shoved into his pockets. A white, tailored button-down covered his shoulders, the top two buttons open, his sleeves rolled up to his elbows. For the way he looked, he easily could have been one of Leo's A-list clients. But the commanding power in his unyielding stare as he glared up at the hidden camera beside the elevator, all but challenging the doors not to open, spiked my pulse.

"Motherfucker," Leo whispered low and ominously.

"Weapons up, boys," Johnson replied, moving toward the safe Leo kept in the corner.

I caught his elbow and forced him to face me. "Who the fuck is that?"

He cracked his neck and then snatched his arm from my grip. "Your worst nightmare or your sweetest dream. It all just depends on the day."

I stepped toward him and seethed, "And what about today?"

His gaze flicked over my shoulder to Mira, and then he shrugged. "We're about to find out."

"Zach," Leo called to the ceiling. "Get Jude up here and lock down Rhion's apartment."

"Braydon's down there watching the game," Zach replied.

"Good. Get his ass up here too." He marched to the safe and re-trieved a forty-five, checking the magazine before tucking it into the back of his pants. "Don't open that elevator until I give the word, you got it?"

"On it," he replied.

Leo turned to his brother-in-law. "You need to get the fuck out of here."

Caleb's eyes flashed wide. "Please fucking tell me that is not who I think it is."

Leo moved to the office door and yanked it open. "You want to keep that badge on your hip, I highly suggest you leave. Take the stairs. Go out the front. I'll call you later."

Silently, I watched the men go back and forth like a Ping-Pong match, a vile sense of unease settling in my gut.

"Are you fucking insane?" Caleb questioned, fisting his hands on his hips.

"Now!" Leo boomed.

I jerked when I felt Mira's heat at my back.

"What's happening?" she asked, fear thick in her voice.

I had no answers. I was as clueless as she was, but one thing I was sure of: I didn't want her to have any part of whatever the hell was about to go down. Sliding an arm around her shoulders, I shifted her around to my front and then into my chest where I whispered in her hair. "Go down to Rhion's, baby. I'll come get you in a—"

"No," Johnson and Leo bit out in unison.

Shocked, I flicked my gaze between the two of them. "The fuck? She's not staying here."

Johnson shrugged on a shoulder holster and replied, "Yeah. She is. That man is here not eight hours after Walter Noir tries to put a knife in your woman. I promise you he's not here for tea and fucking biscuits. This is not Rhion's bullshit, and we sure as fuck are not leading this man to her front door. Mira stays. We'll keep her safe. But, if he's here for her, you could send her to the fucking moon and it wouldn't help."

Suddenly, that vile sense of unease turned to acid devouring me from the inside out. My throat constricted, and I peered down into her terrified, brown eyes.

"Jeremy," she whispered, her body trembling against me.

I'd just fucking gotten her back. I'd be damned if I was going to let anything happen to her.

I forced a smile. "Everything's going to be fine. I swear."

Her breathing shuddered, but she nodded, trust I wasn't sure I deserved blazing from her eyes.

Less than two minutes later, Caleb was gone. Leo, Johnson, Jude, Braydon, and I all stood in a semi circle around the front door. Mira and Apollo were locked in the security room with Zach. And, while I thought she'd be safe with them, I felt like I was going to have a god-damn nervous breakdown from not having her within reach. Nobody could protect her like I could. I still had no idea what the fuck was going on, but as we waited by the door, Johnson gave me the basic rundown. And, when I say basic, I mean bare fucking bones. I believe his exact words were, "Mateo Rodriguez. Bad man. He and Leo have a history. Stay sharp."

That. Was. It.

Without a knock, the front door swung open, and then the entire room filled with static as the well-dressed man came sauntering in. He left the door open, but his entourage stayed on the other side of the threshold.

My body went solid as he swept his gaze over each of us. His lips turned up in a slow smile as he lifted his chin to Johnson, and then his gaze landed on Leo. A thick Spanish accent curled around his words as he asked, "Where is she?"

Leo gave him no reaction as he said, "Good to see you too, Mateo."

He took a challenging step forward. "Mira Benton. Give her to me."

My body jerked, and I instinctively moved my hand to the gun on my hip.

His gaze slashed through the room before landing on mine. "You'll be dead before you ever pull that trigger."

Leo took a step forward, strategically moving in front of me, his hands lifted in surrender. "Mateo. Please. Mira is—"

I didn't think. I didn't consider if it was a truth or a lie. I didn't weigh my options. My mind didn't actually have any part of my decision at all. The word just tore out of me as if it had been poised on my tongue for my entire life, waiting for its chance to fly free. "Mine," I declared, my shoulders rolling back as I stood impossibly taller. Holding his icy stare over Leo's shoulder, I added, "And *you'll* be dead before you ever lay one fucking finger on her."

His body went taut, the air around him becoming toxic.

Braydon and Jude slid in close to me, flanking each side, while Johnson shuffled forward to have Leo's right.

"What he means is, " Leo started, and then I lost the conversation completely.

The two men broke into Spanish. Mateo spoke; Leo fluidly replied. This went on for several minutes. Their tone never rose, but the tension between them never ebbed.

Based on all two years of high school Spanish, I was able to catch a few words. Mira, Lark, Benton, bitch, and that was about it.

I glanced to Braydon, who was staring out the door at the huddle of *Men In Black* agents A through H. Jude was stoic as ever, his eyes fixed on Leo. And Johnson stood stock-still, boring a hole in Mateo.

Finally, Leo switched back to English. "Zach," he called. "Send Mira out."

All at once, my blood ignited in a wildfire. "No fucking way," I barked, my body exploding forward.

Leo's hand came up, slamming into my sternum to stop me. And then he smiled. Like an honest-to-God shit-eating grin. "Relax," he ordered.

He turned his head back to Mateo, who was surprisingly smiling too.

"See? I told you," Leo said, his voice filled with humor.

What...the...fuck?

The bad dude, who Johnson had so eloquently warned me about, gave me a quick head-to-toe and replied, "I can see."

And then the entire room broke into chaos.

Happy, gleeful, long-lost-friends-finally-reuniting-for-the-first-time-in-a-century kind of chaos.

I seriously thought that my head was going to turn into a geyser when I watched Johnson extend a shake to Mateo before pulling him in for a chest bump and a back pat. "Good to see you again, my man," he said.

"You as well," Mateo replied. Cheerful. *Fucking cheerful.*

When he snapped his fingers, his goons filed in through the door before carefully shutting it behind them. For the record, they did not look happy or gleeful, but they seemed relaxed and quite honestly bored.

"Can I get you something to drink?" Leo offered.

I blinked, more puzzled than ever. Jesus Christ. Clearly Johnson had been wrong. Maybe they had shown up for tea and biscuits.

"I wouldn't turn down a scotch," Mateo replied.

Leo headed for the kitchen, calling out, "Coming up."

I was perilously close to losing my goddamn mind when I heard her voice.

"Mateo?" she whispered.

We all turned at the same time, my heart lurching when I saw her standing in the hallway, her dark hair cascading over her shoulders, her red-rimmed eyes now lit with an even more confusing mixture of anxiety and relief.

With long strides, I descended upon her. Leo's tea and fucking biscuits aside, she was still my woman and Johnson's brief to stay sharp still rang in my ears. Protectively, I tucked her into my side.

Then, swear to God, shit got weirder.

Her eyes remained on the man across the room as she timidly asked, "Are you a drug lord too?"

He stared at her for several beats before erupting into a fit of laughter.

What in the fucking hell was going on?

When the man finally sobered, he strolled toward us.

I tensed, ready for war.

Thankfully, he stopped an acceptable distance away, and then rolled every R as he said, "Yes, *Preciosa*, I am what *you* would call a drug lord. However, I'm here to help." He waved a hand at me like he was one of Barker's Beauties on *The* fucking *Price Is Right* and said, "Introduce me to your new man, and then we'll all get down to business."

And that was the exact moment I decided I was quitting my job, getting my girls, chaining Mira to my bed, and then spending the rest of our natural lives in an underground bunker.

Have no fear. A self-proclaimed drug lord was there to help.

Fuck.

My.

Life.

CHAPTER TWENTY-ONE

Mira

I F WALTER NOIR HAD BEEN ONE OF MY BEST CUSTOMERS AT THE SIP and Sud, Mateo Rodriguez had been the *absolute* best. He was a gorgeous Hispanic man from Miami. Who, much like Walter, had only come through a few times a month when he'd been in town on business. He'd tipped well, but that wasn't why I'd been excited each time I'd seen him across the bar. Truth be told, beneath that arrogant exterior, the man was hilarious. He'd always come at random times when the place was dead, and he'd sit there for hours, trying to teach me Spanish. It was a hopeless cause. I didn't have much of my Southern accent left after having lived in Chicago for so long, but my tongue was physically unable to make the sounds required to pronounce words like *correr* or *rápido*.

For a while, I'd thought Mateo was interested in me. And, for a while, given the way Kurt had tiptoed around him, I'd hoped he was.

Like everyone else in my life, I'd lost Mateo when the Sip and Sud had closed. And, as fucked up as it was, even knowing he was a drug dealer of the worst kind, I felt a certain happiness about seeing him again.

We were sitting on the long, chocolate-leather couches in the Guardian living area. Leo was sprawled out on one end like he owned the place. Which, technically, he did, but Johnson had had to pull up a chair and Braydon was forced to remain on his feet to be a part of the conversation, so it seemed odd.

I was curled into Jeremy's side—or as curled as a person could get while cuddling a slab of granite. It was safe to say my guy did not share my enthusiasm to be hanging out with my old friend.

Mateo had settled into one of the overstuffed recliners. He didn't kick it back and get comfortable. He sat straight up, an inch of scotch in a highball glass, swirling it and looking every bit as regal as the king of crime I was learning he was. His men had scattered to various points around the open room, all of their backs to the wall and all of their eyes leveled on their fearless leader.

In hindsight, this could maybe...possibly... Fine, it definitely was why Jeremy was so uptight.

"So, this man put a gun to your head?" Mateo looked to Leo. "Jonah Sheehan, is it?"

Leo nodded.

"I know the name," Mateo told me. "Small time. I feel certain he was acting alone, approaching you after being fed incorrect information about the Sip and Sud. I'll see what I can do about your friend." Mateo's gaze snapped to one of his men.

Silently, something was communicated. Something I pretended not to see, considering I was pretty sure that communication had been Jonah's death sentence. Though, if it got me Whitney back, I'd have been willing to personally attend his execution.

Mateo turned his attention back to me and asked, "Then Steve Browel sent someone to abduct you?"

I leaned toward him, but Jeremy's hand got painfully tight on my thigh, so I leaned back before whispering, "Yeah. Do you know who that is?"

He chuckled like I was a silly child, but it wasn't insulting. "Mira, love, do you remember the bald guy who always brought in his laundry? No shirts. No pants. Just seventy-five pair of men's underwear. And he only showed when you had the boys working? He'd never drink. He just stared, his hand every so often disappearing under the table."

My mouth fell open. "Oh my God! Stevie the perv?"

He winked. "Also known as Steven Browel."

Appalled, I scooted to the edge of the cushion and was promptly pulled back by Jeremy. "What the hell would he want to kidnap me for?"

He looked back to Leo and then awkwardly took a sip of his scotch.

"Mateo?" I prompted.

When I tried to rise from the couch, Jeremy once again prevented me by hooking his arm around my shoulders and dragging me back down.

Frustrated, I craned my head back and snipped, "Would you stop?"

Mr. Hyde got in my face, his eyes dark, his face hard, his jaw clenched. Then he said, "No." Only he didn't just say no. He enunciated it slowly and drew it out like I had suddenly gone deaf and needed to read his lips.

I twisted my mouth. "You cannot be serious right now?"

He did this crazy thing with his eyes where they somehow bulged and narrowed at the exact same time. And it told me that he was more than just serious; he was one blink away from becoming an X-Man.

"Sit," he demanded, forcefully shifting me deeper into his side.

I groaned, not having the energy to argue with him *and* get the deets from a drug lord/good friend about why people were trying to kidnap me. (Jeez, my life was weird.)

When I gave Mateo my eyes back, he was chuckling. "I already like him better than the last one. He at least *tries* to keep you safe."

"Yeah, but you hated Kurt," I replied flippantly.

Since I was pinned to Jeremy, Mateo leaned forward, lifted his glass in the air in a show of cheers, and whispered, "Mira, everyone hated Kurt. Including you."

"Touché." I giggled.

He smiled, the white of his teeth flashing like a ray of light against his dark complexion, and then he leaned back in his chair. Crossing his legs at the knee, he looked Jeremy straight in the eye and ordered, "Hold her tight. This is going to hurt."

Jeremy was already holding me tight, and I didn't figure he could...

"Hey!" I objected as his arms anchored around me, not as much painful as they were uncomfortably restraining.

Discarding his drink to the end table, Mateo locked his gaze on mine and then ruined my entire dirty, filthy, garbage-filled, already-ruined life.

"The reason all of these men have come after you is because word is out that you are starting a new Sip and Sud. *Preciosa*, I know you believe that your bar was clean, but the Sip and Sud was one of the largest money laundering operations in the country."

I scoffed. "Pssh. Please. The Feds told me Kurt ran a couple thousand dollars through my books when they seized the place. But that was it."

Mateo's face got soft, and so did his voice, "No. That's all they *found*. Kurt made sure of that."

I blinked, chills pebbling my skin. "W-what are you talking about?"

He cleared his throat. "I'm not privy to how it started for Kurt, but by the time I became involved, the Sip and Sud was a well-oiled machine. Our men would deliver him cash, he'd log them as sales, clean and clear, and then he would pay it back to us, less his cut through business accounts set up to appear as subcontractors. Do you happen to remember Scott's Lighting?"

My stomach dropped. "They... That was who he insisted we hired to do the custom lighting on all the dryers." My nose started to sting, and my throat got thick. "They strobed in time with the music."

He nodded. "That was one of my accounts. It cost me seven grand to have the lights installed. Kurt paid me two hundred and eighty thousand dollars."

"Jesus, fuck," Jeremy muttered.

Breath flew from my lungs as if I'd been punched in the stomach, reality scorching my throat on its way out.

But he wasn't done gutting me yet. "After he maxed out the books at your first bar, he did the same with the next two. And, when those became so successful he was unable to make the influx of money seem plausible, he branched out. He recruited other businesses and eventually became one of the highest-paid middlemen in the business, collecting a percentage of money he never even touched. As much as it pains me to admit, Kurt Benton was far from an idiot. And the fact that he went down for distribution of anabolic steroids, something that was a hobby of his, *not* his career, all without a single of his real clients catching any heat, proves it."

"No," I said, shaking my head. "You're wrong. My bar stayed packed. We got shut down by the fire marshal on Halloween one year."

He uncrossed his legs and folded forward. "Because Kurt was *smart*. You can hardly run a bar making that kind of cash without a single customer walking through the door. People would notice. And, Mira, I say this with love, but it was a laundromat *bar*. That kind of business does not make that kind of cash *period*. A crazy idea like that goes bankrupt before the doors open."

Blood thundered in my ears. I was vaguely aware of Jeremy whispering something to me, but I couldn't take my eyes off Mateo long enough to focus on what it was.

Kurt had always lied to me. He'd controlled me mentally, physically, and emotionally. He'd manipulated me to stay in a marriage I'd desperately wanted to escape and forced me to live under the cold chill of his shadow. I couldn't have a family or friends. Forget about children. But the Sip and Sud... It was my light.

I loved that bar. I loved that it was unique. I loved that I had created it from nothing. And I loved that it had been successful because that meant, no matter how shitty and miserable my life had been, I was successful too.

It had given me a purpose. A reason to wake up in the morning. I had finally been good at something. And I'd made a substantial living doing it. As silly as it sounded, for a girl who had grown up with nothing, the ability to buy myself a wildly expensive designer hand-bag had meant more to me than the dozens Kurt had spoiled me with using his parents' credit cards. When the Feds had seized all of my belongings because they were covered in Kurt's filth, I'd felt like I'd lost a part of myself. And not because I needed a closet full of Manolo or Louis Vuitton. But rather because it'd made me feel like a fraud. Like nothing I had worked my ass off for had ever truly been mine.

And there I was, finding out that those feelings might have been valid.

"How much?" I asked in a broken whisper.

Mateo cocked his head like he didn't understand the question, so I expounded.

"How much of the money I made was real?"

His eyes dimmed as he quasi lied. "It was all real, *Preciosa*."

Not even Jeremy Lark was strong enough to hold me down as I exploded to my feet, dove at Mateo, and screamed into his face with life-shattering devastation. "How much of it was mine!"

Every man in the room moved. The army at the wall lurched forward, eight guns appearing from under their coats. Johnson sprang from his chair, and Leo came up off the couch, more guns raised high. Jeremy hooked me around the waist, lifting me off my feet, my arms and my legs swinging wildly as he cocooned me with his upper body. But it was Braydon, who appeared behind Mateo, pressing the tip of his gun to the back of his head, who halted the chaos.

Through it all, Mateo's gaze never left mine. He didn't have to answer. Pity was written all over his face.

I'd experienced that look from a lot of people in my life. Growing up the way I had with a drunk for a mother, who paraded one abusive man through the trailer door after another. Then again when I'd made the astronomically stupid decision to marry a man whose only positive quality was that he'd *told* me he loved me, regardless that he'd proved with his every action that he hadn't. Hell, Kurt's own parents had looked at me with that same pity as I'd spent countless years letting him dictate my every move just so I could cling to a stupid fucking bar that had always been my dream.

And there it was—more pity—staring back at me in the eyes of a drug lord who had drawn the short straw when it came to finally telling me the truth because I had been too big of a fool to ever see for myself.

My whole life had been a lie.

"No!" I screamed with everything I had left in me—which, admittedly, wasn't much.

CHAPTER TWENTY-TWO

Lark

THE BUZZ OF ADRENALINE COURSING THROUGH MY VEINS WAS deafening. There were too many guns, too many threats, too much going on with my fucking woman in the middle of it, especially while she was fighting against me as if I were the enemy.

"Mira, stop," I snarled.

"Rodriguez?" Leo called. It might have only been one word, but it was the most important question in all of our lives.

My heart slammed into my ribs with an alarming velocity as an eerie calm-before-the-storm feeling filled the room.

But, finally, in a deep, malevolent growl, Mateo ordered, "Down."

Relief surged through me.

That was the right fucking answer.

All at once, his men tucked their guns away, and then Johnson and Leo followed suit.

Lastly, and only after Leo had clipped, "Bray," did Braydon lower his gun as well.

The change in the room could be felt physically. The relief on all sides was tangible.

"Everybody out," Mateo demanded, his men moving before the T had cleared his lips.

Turning Mira in my arms, I hugged her to my chest. "I'm not fucking leaving."

"You stay. Leo too. The rest of you. Out. *Now.*"

Johnson arched a questioning eyebrow at Leo, who nodded in response. And then he and Braydon disappeared down the hallway while the rest of the men filed out the door much the way they had entered.

And, when the door had closed behind them, a blessed calm washed over the room. Or at least it washed over most of us. Mira was a different story.

The second I put her back on her feet, she stormed toward Mateo, yelling, "You son of a bitch!"

"*Preciosa*, we all thought you knew," he purred, rising to his full height.

"You thought I fucking knew?" she yelled, a sob catching in her throat. "Like I was some scum-of-the-earth criminal laundering *drug money?*"

His face got hard, and I protectively dragged her back, her heels sliding against the wood floor until she hit my front.

My chest ached for her. It really did. She loved that bar. Anyone could see it etched in her face when she talked about it. The night before, when she'd told me how Kurt had used it to keep her in his reach, had been bad enough. But this? She had every right to be livid.

However, I really fucking wished she'd unleash that anger on someone who didn't have a squad of men ready to wage war for someone so much as raising their voice at him.

My body remained coiled tight as I watched him retrieve his drink off the end table.

Lifting it to his lips, he paused before taking a sip to say, "This became clear when I heard you were starting a new Sip and Sud."

Fisting her hands at her sides, she hissed, "It's not *that* kind of Sip and Sud."

"Perhaps not. But the men Kurt stole three point four million from believe otherwise."

My back shot straight and Mira went solid, but it was Leo who found his words first.

"I'm sorry. I'm going to need you to repeat that."

Mateo's lips thinned as he set his drink down again. "When Kurt went to jail, he had millions of dollars that had not yet been fully cleaned in his possession. This money has never been recovered. The government doesn't know it exists, and despite our attempts on the inside, Kurt isn't talking. Honestly, I'm surprised the man has lived this long. He left a lot of angry customers when he went down. People who could have easily turned their anger on Kurt's family." Mateo kept his eyes on Mira but spoke to Leo. "I've had Mira under my protection since her divorce. However, the moment word got out that she was opening a new Sip and Sud, those men were willing to risk my wrath at the shot of getting that money back."

"I don't have it!" Mira cried. "I was trying to get a loan from the bank. I've got, like, twenty-five thousand dollars squirreled away. But that's it."

My stomach rolled. The severity of the situation fell over me like a million rusty razor blades. "That's why Noir was here?" I breathed, the acrid taste in the back of my mouth stifling my voice.

"No," he replied firmly. "Noir was here because he didn't like the idea of someone treading on his territory. He took over Kurt's accounts and has been running them for years. But with news hitting of Mira opening another Sip and Sud? To him, that was a challenge." He swayed his head from side to side. "While I have every intention of making Noir pay for going against my orders, I can't blame him for his reaction. There was no mistaking Mira's play as anything but competition."

"It was a fucking bar!" Mira yelled. "T.G.I.Fridays is my competition. Not whatever the hell illegal operation Walter Noir is running."

Mateo grinned, cunning and sharp. "And, if you had been trying to open a T.G.I.Fridays, none of this would have been an issue. But you didn't. You decided to open another Sip and Sud—a laundromat bar, which I will repeat with love"—he lifted his hand to cover his heart—"is a silly concept that could not possibly be a successful business endeavor." He paused and lowered his voice to a whisper.

"Unless, say, you were laundering money."

Mira stared at him for several beats, her chest heaving.

And I stood there, holding her, helpless to do one damn thing to fix any of it for her. Suddenly, I was a twenty-something kid again, watching Kurt ruin her all over again.

"*Preciosa*," Mateo said softly, lifting his hand toward her face. His dark eyes flashed to mine for what I told myself was his way of asking for permission—though it came across as a warning.

Unwilling to provoke him, I allowed it. Though I did readjust my hold on her, just in case.

Cupping her jaw, he said, "I'll take care of Noir. He is not an unreasonable man. But my reach is only so wide. These other men, the masses, they aren't going to back down. Not all of them. Before now, my word was enough to keep them away from you. But the idiots like Steven Browel will always find you. Now…if you want to come with me back to Miami, I give you my word to personally keep you safe for the rest of your life."

"The fuck you will," I snapped. Muscles I didn't know I possessed strained inside me, the sound of a time bomb ticking in my ears.

Luckily, before I had the chance to detonate, he released her, linked his hands behind his back, and sauntered away. "But I do believe your affections for me would suffer when I am forced to bury your man here."

I jolted toward him. "You mother—"

"Stop!" Mira demanded. "Jesus Christ. Fucking stop. Both of you. The testosterone in here is suffocating. I can't even think." Peering up over her shoulder, she demanded, "Let me go."

A vise clamped down on my chest. I prayed she was asking for me to release her physically, but the words were too familiar to a choice she'd made in the past to offer me any comfort.

"Mira," I rumbled.

"Oh, for fuck's sake. He's not going to hurt me. He just said he's been protecting me for the last three years. So, unless you're worried about Kurt owing Leo over there three point four million dollars, I think this might be the only fucking room in the entire continental United States where you can safely let me out of arm's reach." She drew in a deep breath and then continued her rant. "And I would highly suggest you take advantage of this moment, because if everything Mateo says is true—and let's face it, it's fucking Kurt, so of course it's true—then after tonight, if you are still hell-bent on keeping me alive, you are going to have to have me surgically attached to your side. So here it is, your last moment of freedom. Don't waste it."

And, with that, the vise in my chest disappeared. I couldn't even fight it. A grin broke across my face. Relief was so thick in my veins that the tension of the entire day was momentarily forgotten. "Baby, if I'm getting you surgically attached to me, it's not going to be at my side."

Pushing out of my arms, she snipped, "By all means. Feel free to get creative." After marching straight to Mateo, she stopped a few inches away from him and said, "Not to sound ungrateful or anything, but seeing as to how I divorced one criminal not too long ago and his shit is still stuck to my shoes, I'm going to have to take a pass on your invitation to join your harem in Miami."

Mateo wasn't immune to the ridiculous charm of a Mira York snit fit. He, too, grinned. "No harem, Mira. I haven't had time in my life for one woman, much less twelve."

"Then you are missing a great opportunity. Because I know there are a lot of women who would seriously get off on the whole arrogant-bad-boy-with-a-good-heart thing you have going on. I, however, am *not* one of them."

When she gave him an attaboy punch to the shoulder, I couldn't decide if I wanted to burst into laughter or tackle her to the floor before eight gun-wielding men had the chance to storm back into the room because she'd touched him.

As he shook his head, his grin stretched. "I'll keep that in mind."

"You do that." She nodded curtly.

And then all of our smiles fell as the snit fit faded and an unmistakable desperation filled her voice.

"Now, what if I can get the money back? I'll go visit Kurt, explain the situation to him. I'm sure he'll tell me where it is."

"Baby," I whispered, advancing on her from behind.

She frantically swung her gaze to mine. "We can just give the money back to whoever Kurt owes it to. No harm no foul, right? He'll tell me, Jeremy. I know he will."

A knife twisted in my gut. "Mira, Kurt got you into this mess. What makes you think he's going to do you any favors to get you out of it?"

She stared at me for several seconds, her face growing tighter with every blink. "Because he will."

I shook my head. "He won't, baby."

"He will," she chirped.

"Sweetheart, he's never done one selfless thing in his entire goddamn life. If he knows where this money is, he's had three years to turn it over, knowing good and damn well that you could be at risk. Why would he do it now?"

And then, right in front of my eyes, I watched Kurt Benton finally succeed at destroying her once and for all.

"Because he has to!" she screamed, the sound slicing through the room, cutting us all. "Because he fucking has to!"

With two strides, I closed the distance between us and turned her into my chest. No sooner than she was in my arms, her knees buckled and tears flooded her eyes.

"That fucking man," she cried. "Was it not enough that he stole almost twenty years of my life? Now, he's going to get me killed and steal the rest of it?" Her hands fisted the front of my shirt, her body shaking as she screamed, "What the fuck did I ever do to deserve this shit? I wanted to open a bar! Something that I could call my own! And truly my own, not something he lorded over me. I..." She trailed off, breaking down all over again. "He stole it from me. He stole *everything* from me. Jesus Christ. I have nothing left."

"You have me," I swore, smoothing the back of her hair.

She writhed against me, the emotional pain becoming physical.

"No, I don't! He made sure of that too. Yes, I made the choice all those years ago, Jeremy. But it was always one big fucking game for Kurt. He laid the groundwork, making me dependent on him so I could never leave, and I fell for it. So goddamn dumb and desperate, I would have done anything to escape that life. But, somehow, I ended up running away with the devil himself. I'm so sick and tired of paying for that mistake. I made the wrong choice. I admit it. I take full responsibility for everything that happened after that. But he won't let me go."

Fuck. She was slaying me. Never had I felt a pain that dense before. Her every word was twisting me, wringing me out, snapping my bones one at a time.

And I could do nothing but hold her.

I glanced up at Mateo and Leo, who were watching us both and looking equally as shattered.

But we were all helpless.

"I'll do what I can on my end," Mateo announced.

"Me too," Leo added.

I dipped my head in gratitude to both of them. Holding her tighter than ever before, I whispered, "See, baby? You got people at your back."

She sucked in a shaky breath. "Which means it's only a matter of time before he takes all of you from me too. I'll never be free, Jeremy."

But she was wrong. Because, even if it took my entire life, I'd make her free. And, in the process of doing that, I would make her mine once and for all.

CHAPTER TWENTY-THREE

Mira

FOR OVER AN HOUR, LEO, MATEO, AND JEREMY STOOD IN A HUDDLE, watching me warily out of the corner of their eyes, whispering God only knew what to each other as I sat on the couch and stared into space, lost in a worthless black hole of regret.

Eventually, Mateo broke away, pausing only briefly to press a kiss to the top of my head—one I was positive Jeremy hated—before he left.

Johnson and Braydon emerged within seconds and joined the huddle. The whispers never grew louder, the lingering stares never grew shorter, and the pity in all of their eyes was more prominent than ever.

I had no idea what time it was when Jeremy guided me out the door of Guardian. Braydon, Johnson, and even Leo escorted us to the truck in the parking garage. I forced a smile and thanked them all. They returned those thanks with tight grins and chin jerks. Braydon threw in a gorgeous wink for good measure, but the pity still showed like a beacon of light in his baby blues.

As we drove back to Jeremy's house, I stared out the window and retreated into my head again. It was safer there. It was the only place Kurt had never been able to reach me.

When we arrived, Jeremy came around the car and did the body-guard bit, ushering me through the door of his house, locking it, and setting the alarm before releasing me.

He started toward the stairs, but I stood frozen, so lost that I didn't even know how to put one foot in front of the other.

"Mira, come on. Let's go to bed, baby."

Glancing around his empty living room, I dropped my Gucci on the floor at my feet. It really was a beautiful house. A place any woman would be lucky to call home. Granted it needed furniture, maybe a few pictures on the walls, but all of that was easy enough. Though earning a place in a home like that... Now, that was a different story.

"What are we doing here?" I asked, defeat making my tone rough.

He turned to look at me, confusion pinching his eyes. "We're going to bed."

"Why?"

"Uhhh... Because, after the day we've had, I'm in the mood to lock the doors, crawl into bed, and shut out the rest of the world for, oh, about eight to ten hours."

God, that did sound fabulous. But that wasn't my life. Hell, I didn't even know what my life was anymore. But I knew with an absolute certainty that it was not with Jeremy Lark.

"I think it's time you finally took me to that hotel," I announced, my voice steady and filled with resolve.

His eyes narrowed, the barest hint of Mr. Hyde peeking out. "A hotel?"

Confused, I confirmed, the barest hint of my bitch peeking out too. "A hotel."

He stared at me, his mouth hanging open like I'd grown a second head. "You're kidding me, right?"

I'd just found out that my entire life was a lie. It was safe to assume jokes were off the table for the night—and possibly the next century.

"Nope." I sucked in a deep breath, refusing to acknowledge the agony in my chest, and stated as calmly as I could muster, "It's been a few days. And you've been more than a gracious host, but I think, at this juncture, we should go our separate ways. You have a family to get back to. I..." I paused and beat the tears back. "Well, I have to figure out what the hell I'm going to do with the rest of my life and do it in a way that won't get me kidnapped or killed. So I'm thinking maybe a convent. Perhaps I could talk to Caleb about me doing a stint in the Witness Protection Program. But, whichever way I end up going with that, you don't have to worry, okay? I'm a big girl. I always bounce back."

"Ah. Okay. This makes more sense," he said, nodding. After walking over to the bar, he retrieved a barstool and carried it back over and placed it on the floor a few feet in front of me. He settled on the edge, kicked his legs out in front of him, crossed his arms over his chest, and asked, "Have you considered Mexico? I hear it's gorgeous this time of year."

I blinked. Not what I'd expected him to say, though not a terrible idea.

Rolling my shoulders back, I replied, "I…don't…um, have a valid passport."

"That's probably for the best. No one knows where to find you, it's hard to get yourself kidnapped or killed."

I pursed my lips. "Excellent point."

"Though." He raked his gaze over me from head to toe before coming back to my eyes. "A woman like you wanders into the wrong parts of Mexico, you might find trouble of a different nature. How do you feel about shaving your head?"

I gasped, dragging my hair over my shoulder as if to apologize to it for his offensive suggestion. "Have you lost your mind?"

And that was when Jeremy proved he had.

Exploding up off the stool, he stormed toward me, heavy footsteps closing the distance between us.

My eyes flashed wide as I scrambled away. I wasn't afraid of him—well, not exactly. I was more concerned he wouldn't be able to stop fast enough to keep from plowing me over.

He followed me forward until my back hit the wall. His muscular chest collided with mine while his hands landed beside my head. "Yes!" he roared into my face.

My heart pounded in my chest as I searched his face, pure confusion ricocheting inside me.

"Yes...what?" I asked timidly.

His face got closer, and his tone took on a malevolent edge. "Yes, I've fucking lost my mind. And it happened the first time Mira fucking York walked into my room at the barracks on another man's arm. I spent half of my life withering, telling myself I was better off without her. Went so far as to marry another woman who could never live up to the standard she'd left behind."

My heart stopped. Oh my God.

Oh. My. *God.*

"She couldn't live up to my standard?" I whispered in disbelief.

He laughed, but it held no humor. "You have no fucking idea the wasteland you left inside me when you chose him. My whole fucking life, I convinced myself I hated you. But you were always there, baby. Under my skin. In my head. In my veins. Refusing to let me go... Even after you actually...fucking...let me...*go.*"

My mouth dried, shock combining with an emotion I couldn't quite put my finger on, making my head spin. I rested my hands on his sides and twisted them in his shirt. "But I never let you go," I admitted.

"You did," he shot back. "You fucking chose him, and you broke me. You destroyed me, Mira. I had nothing to offer you, but if you had just gotten in my fucking truck that day, I would have had every fucking thing that mattered."

Like someone had flicked a cigarette onto a trail of gasoline, I ignited into a blazing fury. A million emotions I'd stowed in the recesses of my mind for seventeen years all joined in a conflagration that held the power to burn me to the ground. Wanting the answer almost as much as I feared it, I yelled at the top of my lungs, "Then why didn't you fight for me!"

And then Jeremy's fiery rage tore from his soul as well. "Why did I have to!"

Our chests moved together, rising and falling, silently colliding against each other with labored breaths.

He slapped his palm against the wall by my face. "Jesus, fuck, woman. All I ever wanted was to be enough for you."

I stared at him, and for the first time, I saw a poor, broken kid who had never had anything of his own staring back at me. I'd always known that Jeremy and I shared a lot of demons, but this... That... It was as though I were looking in a mirror. My stomach rolled, tears springing to my eyes. The burden of the truth in that moment was too heavy to bear.

I wasn't the only one Kurt had played. Jeremy had been his pawn long before I'd entered the picture.

Tears rolled down my cheeks as I confessed, "I know I made the choice that day. But every day that we were together for the six months before that, I needed you to choose me over Kurt. And not because you were mad or drunk or bored. I wanted you to choose me because you loved me. Because I loved you so damn much that I couldn't deal with knowing you didn't."

He shifted deeper against me, one of his hands moving from the wall to the back of my neck, his fingers sifting up into my hair. "I did love you. Jesus, Mira. I've always loved you. You've been back in my life three fucking days now. We're goddamn strangers. I am not positive I'll even like you two weeks from now. But I know with every fiber of my being that I *love* you, Mira York. Because it never died. Not for me."

I couldn't breathe. I couldn't think. I wasn't even sure my heart was still beating, because Jeremy had said that he loved me past and present and it felt a whole lot like I had died and gone to heaven.

"I used to pretend you'd come back for me," I confessed. "For years, I used to hold my breath and stare at my bedroom door, waiting for you to storm through and rescue me from the flames of hell."

He closed his eyes and shook his head. "Jesus. I would have. In a heartbeat."

Encircling him with my arms, hugging him tight, I half laughed, half sobbed, "God, I hate Kurt even more now. And, thirty minutes ago, I didn't know that was possible."

A beautiful smile broke across his face. "Does that mean you aren't joining a convent?"

I sniffled. "Oh, please. I'd be kicked out after my first snit fit."

He chuckled. "This is probably true." Lowering his mouth, he brushed a kiss across my lips. "I'm not letting you go, Mira. We'll take some time, get to know each other again. But, if you think for one second that I'm letting you go again, *you* are the one who has lost your fucking mind."

I dropped my head to his shoulder and whispered, "How is this my life?"

"Don't worry about Kurt's bullshit. Leo and I—"

I cut him off with a kiss, soft and sensual, wishing I could convey how much everything he'd not only said but also done for me had meant. Jeremy had done more for me in three days, emotionally and physically, than everyone in my entire life combined.

"I don't mean Kurt's shit. I mean being here with you. After all this time. Finding out that a part of you always belonged to me." I kissed him again. Deeper and filled with reverence. "It never died for me, either, Jeremy. I've always loved you." My voice cracked at the end, the sheer elation too much for my exhaustion to handle.

He backed away only far enough to slide his arm between me and the wall. Then he shifted me into his curve until we were flush head to toe. Closing his eyes, he nuzzled his nose with mine. God, I loved how gentle he could be.

"Christ, Mira. Seventeen years… Seventeen fucking years I could have been loving you. Holding you. Making a life with you."

"But then you wouldn't have gotten all this. Look around you, Jeremy. Everything we talked about. Everything we dreamed about. You got it all."

Pain was carved in his face as he argued, "But I didn't get you."

"You got Sophie and Amelia," I retorted.

His lips went thin. Yeah. He loved his kids.

I carried on. "And your career. And this house. It's not the mountains. But it's still gorgeous. And a new truck…*and* an Escalade."

"But I didn't get *you*," he repeated more firmly.

"But you got—"

"My girls. That is your only valid argument. I wouldn't trade them for the world. Not even for seventeen years with you. But, if you think for one second that I wouldn't give up every possession I got to go back in time and rescue you from the flames of hell, selfishly saving myself from them as well, then you are fucking delusional."

I opened my mouth to argue, but he didn't give me a chance to speak.

"But I don't have a time machine. All I have is the future. So, right now, before you have the chance to go off about joining convents or the Witness Protection Program again, I'm going to need you to shut up, follow me up the stairs, get naked, let me make you come, you return the favor, then go to sleep in my bed so we can both wake up in the morning, smiles on our faces, drive out and get the rest of your shit from that goddamn piece-of-shit house you lived in, potentially set your car on fire, then set up your shit here, and set forth about starting said future together."

I blinked. And not because that was a really freaking long sentence and he never stopped for air, but rather because he had just declared that we were setting my shit up in his house. It wasn't a sentiment that insinuated hearts and flowers, but it was the most romantic thing anyone had ever said to me.

He didn't have a time machine—but he had the future.

A future with me.

A future he wanted to start on immediately.

And that's when I finally realized I didn't hate change at all.

Through the years, I'd started my life over at least a dozen times. The day Jeremy had left. The day I'd married Kurt. The day Kurt and I had moved to Illinois. The day I'd left. The day I'd found out I was pregnant. The day I'd gone back. I'd sworn to myself over and over that each and every time was going to be different, but deep down, I'd known that it was always going to be the same.

The same struggle. The same lies. The same regret.

I had been terrified that *nothing* was going to change. And, for almost twenty years, that had been the case.

But not this time.

Not with Jeremy.

Therefore, as I stared up into his hazel eyes, a future was finally within my reach. And it was a future with a good man. A kind man. A man who would look out for me and let me look out for him. A man who believed in following his dreams, so I knew he wouldn't try to stop me from following my own. A man who could ignite me with a single touch and soothe my darkest demons. A man who never made me feel bad for being myself. A man who had always owned my heart from the time I was nineteen years old. The same man who'd told me that his love for me had never died. And that man was offering me a future?

The answer flew from my tongue faster than a lightning bolt. "Okay."

His eyes flared. "Okay?"

"Jeremy, if you want me to build a future with you, I'll move to Mars."

He smiled, that poor and broken kid who had only ever wanted to be enough staring back at me. "Mars is a long way away, baby."

"I don't care. Say the word and I'm there, Jeremy. Wherever you are, I want to go."

I didn't even have time to gasp before his mouth was on mine, and then I was up off the floor not a second later.

Looping my legs around his hips, I slanted my head to take the kiss deeper.

"Fuck, Mir," he groaned into my mouth.

"Upstairs," I murmured, shifting my attention to his neck.

Palming my ass, he strode to the stairs and then up them faster than I thought possible.

"You gonna move in with me?" he asked, kicking the door to his room shut.

I stopped my assault on his neck long enough to reply, "Is that where you are?"

"Fuck." He deposited me on the bed, immediately prowling up after me. His mouth hit mine again and I could taste the desperation as his tongue swirled with mine. But that wasn't why I smiled.

Breaking the kiss, I asked, "You thought I was going to freak out about moving in with you?"

Stretching his hand over his shoulder, he tugged his henley off and then threw it into the darkness. "It's been three days, Mira. If we had half a brain between the two of us, we wouldn't do this." Gently, he untwisted the scarf over my head, and then, with one swift movement, he tore my shirt off.

I kept right on smiling, but I did it while undoing the clasp on the back of my bra while he went to work on the button of his jeans. "Second thoughts?" I teased.

After getting off the bed, he slid off his jeans, saying, "Not at the moment. But ask me again in six months, when I discover that you snore and you won't stop bitching at me about leaving the toilet seat up." Looming at the edge of the bed, he started on my jeans, peeling them down my legs.

"I don't snore," I informed him on a giggle.

My breath caught in my throat when his sensual fingertips grazed my thighs as he dragged my panties off.

Once I was fully naked, he finally looked up and quirked an eyebrow. "I notice you didn't mention anything about not bitching about leaving the toilet seat up."

I smiled. "It's a safety hazard."

One foot still on the floor, he put his knee to the bed and bent until our faces were mere inches apart. "Mira, shut up."

"I'm serious, Jeremy. In the middle of the night—" I lost all train of thought as his hand dipped between my legs, one finger sliding up my opening until he found my clit.

My mouth fell open as every nerve in my body roared to life. I arched off the bed, my breasts pressing up, an offer he did not refuse. His warm mouth sealed over my nipple, teasing in time with the movement of his hand.

"Oh, God," I breathed, threading my fingers into the top of his hair.

Just as he had the night before, he played my body with bold caresses. I became lost in him, equally focused on the sensation and the man giving it to me.

An orgasm in and of itself was a spectacular event.

An orgasm given to you by a man who owned your heart was glorious.

An orgasm given to you by a man who owned your heart and had just declared that you were building a future together... Well, that was life altering in every sense of the word.

And, as a shattering climax crashed into me, his head popped up from my breast. Resting his forehead on mine, he opened his mouth, consuming my release in the sound of his name.

"Fuck, baby. You can bitch about the hazards of me leaving the toilet seat up one second and then the next come on my hand like that... I'm thinking we are going to be just fine living together."

With all of my energy spent on passion, I didn't have it in me to fire off a witty response, but a smile still cracked my face.

"There she is," he rumbled, brushing the hair out of my face. "My Mira."

Sated and spent, I pried an eye open and found him staring at me, his gaze so heated it sent a shiver down my spine.

He kissed me, allowing his lips to linger long after our puckers had disappeared. And he continued to hold my mouth, his exhales filling my lungs as we shared the same air. When he finally climbed on top of me, his heavy weight feeling like everything I'd been missing in my life, I opened my legs wide, pleading without words for what I knew he had every intention of giving me. And, as he slipped a hand between us, guiding himself home, his length stretching and filling me until the love had no choice but to spill from my eyes, I realized that maybe, just maybe, change was really a fucking good thing.

CHAPTER TWENTY-FOUR

Lark

THE ROOM WAS BRIGHT WHEN I WOKE UP AND SENSED THAT MIRA was no longer in the bed beside me. The clock read eight, but it was still too early. It had been one hell of a night; we both should have been sound asleep until the morning hit double digits. But neither of us had been able to find any rest that night. Or, more specifically, Mira hadn't been able to sleep, so she'd tossed and turned all night, making it so *I* was unable to sleep.

That shit with Kurt was heavy. It was going to settle deep in her chest and weigh her down for a good long while. And, until I could figure out how to make her safe once and for all, it was going to weigh me down too. Though that wasn't why I'd asked her to move in with me.

Christ. I'd *actually* asked her to live with me.

The night before, I'd spent the majority of our ride home from Guardian prepping for when she told me no about moving in. I'd had no less than twelve different reasons for why it was best we live together locked and loaded on the tip of my tongue. Her one simple "okay" had rendered them all useless. Okay had officially become my favorite word in the English language, though the way she moaned my name as I slid inside her was a close second.

I had no regrets about taking this next step in our relationship. In a lot of ways, it felt like we were picking up where we'd left off. If she'd gotten into my truck that day and chosen me over Kurt, we wouldn't have driven off into the sunset to get separate apartments. She had been *it* for me back then. I didn't need weeks or months of living apart to recognize that she was still *it* for me. I hadn't been able to wipe the smile off my face since she'd agreed. Every time I thought about waking up with her, bickering over who got to watch what on TV, and arguing over who had to do the dishes, my stomach would pitch like I was riding the highest roller coaster, laughing and loving every second of it. I hadn't enjoyed any of that shit with Melissa. Not even in the beginning, when I was supposed to enjoy those things.

But this was Mira. And she was finally back. Yes, living together after only a few days of reuniting was probably crazy and rash, but I wasn't letting her get away again. She'd asked me why I hadn't fought for her. If a fight was what she'd wanted, I'd battle to the ends of the earth.

After knifing up, I put my feet to the floor and set about finding her, pausing only long enough to snag a pair of sweats and tug them on.

Knowing my girl, she was probably downstairs, her knees pulled to her chest, a cup of steaming coffee in her hand, her gaze aimed at a wall while panic and anxiety devoured her.

I didn't make it to the bottom of the stairs before the smell of pancakes and sausage hit my nose. This would have been fucking incredible except I hadn't been to the store in a week, so the contents of my fridge and my pantry were seriously lacking. I was sure there was no pancake mix or sausage to be found.

The alarm bells in my head started ringing.

Picking up the pace, I jogged down the last few stairs and rounded the corner to the kitchen. Sure as shit, there she was, standing over the stove, spatula in hand, flipping fucking pancakes. But the worst of it was she was fully dressed. Tight jeans, a pink, long-sleeved top that should have been conservative had it not clung to her breasts and her flat stomach, and another one of her scarfs wrapped around her neck to keep people from seeing the bites on her neck.

People.

As in *other* people.

It was eight o'clock in the fucking morning. She should have still been bra-and-panty less in my black T-shirt she'd fallen asleep in.

Those alarm bells in my head switched to screaming.

"What the hell are you doing?" I growled.

"Shit!" she squeaked, spinning to face me. "Jesus, Jeremy. You scared the hell out of me."

I glanced to the front door and saw her purse on the floor in the same place she'd dropped it the night before, but a pair of black ballet flats were now beside it. The alarm was still armed, but I'd given her my code, so that didn't mean much. As I was turning my attention back to her, all the puzzle pieces snapped together when I saw the Caddy keys, which usually hung on a small hook in the pantry, sitting on the edge of the bar.

Panic hit me like a freight train. "Did you fucking go somewhere?"

She frowned and shot me a glare. "And good morning to you too, sunshine."

I thundered toward her, snatching the keys off the bar and thrusting them in her direction as I repeated, "Did you fucking go somewhere?"

Curling her lip, she replied, "Just to the grocery store, and before you get all Mr. Hyde about me driving your precious Escalade, I was going to take the truck, but I couldn't find the keys."

The panic inside me twisted into a vortex of fury. "Have you lost your fucking mind!"

Her head snapped back, and her glare became incredulous. "I believe we covered that topic last night. Yes. We have both lost our minds. No use in harping on it." Her lips turned up into a grin. "At least not when there are hot, fresh chocolate chip pancakes to be consumed."

She turned back toward the pan, but I caught her arm. "Mira. I'm fucking serious here."

She pointedly looked at my hold on her arm and retorted, "I can see this, Jeremy. What I'm not following is *why* you would be serious right now. I'm making pancakes. It's hardly an offense."

"You cannot leave this house by yourself. Jesus, woman. Were you not there last night when Mateo said there are some seriously bad fucking men after you?"

Snatching her arm from my grasp, she shoved the pan off the burner and discarded the spatula to the counter with a clatter. "Oh, I was there." Tipping her head back, she closed the inches between us. Her chest bumped mine, but it wasn't because she was trying to hug me or seeking out affection. She was pissed to the highest power. *Fucking phenomenal.* "Were *you* there when I found out my entire life has been a lie? And the nothing I thought I had before was actually negative nothing because my ex played me so hard that I deserve a championship ring?"

I gritted my teeth. "This did not escape me, Mira. But that doesn't mean you can go gallivanting around town unprotected."

She rolled her eyes. "I'd hardly call hitting the grocery store gallivanting."

I glared.

She returned it, matching my frustrations pound for pound.

Her death glare faded first. "I'm not living in another prison, Jeremy."

"Not asking you to, but you—"

"The rug was yanked out from under me last night," she announced. "My life, my career, my dreams were all lies. I should have been crushed. I should still be in bed, lights off, covers drawn up over my head, and toeing the line of being catatonic. But I couldn't sleep last night. I couldn't get comfortable. My mind wouldn't shut off." Resting her hands on my chest, she shot me a warm, content smile. "Because of you."

I pressed my lips together and felt my forehead crinkle. "Because of me?"

She pushed up onto her toes and nuzzled her cheek with mine. "I'm happy," she whispered. "I haven't had a lot of this in life. I wasn't sure what to do with it. It scared me. Feeling that kind of perfection made me panic. Not the fact that I've almost been killed *three* separate times in so many days. Nor because there are men who are still intent on doing just that. No. I panicked because laying next to you—the man that I had fallen in love with as a teenager, the one I'd never let go? Well, he asked me to move in with him. And he asked me to move in with him because he'd always loved me too." Her voice cracked, and it cracked my heart too.

"Jesus, baby," I breathed, folding her into a hug.

She kept talking. "I couldn't sleep because I was afraid, if I did, I'd wake up and it all would have been a dream. I couldn't risk that." She sucked in a ragged breath and forced a smile. "So yeah, Jeremy, I got out of bed early this morning, went to the grocery store because your fridge was empty, and now we are eating homemade chocolate chip pancakes and sausage because, if and when this all disappears, this time with you might be all I have to take with me."

"Fuck," I rumbled, tucking her face into my neck. "It's not going to disappear, Mira."

"Hopefully not," she murmured. "But, if does, I won't be blindsided."

Using her shoulders, I shifted her away from me so I could see her face. "Mira, baby. It's *not* going to disappear. We were dumb kids the first time. We both fucked that up and Kurt, being Kurt, he capitalized on it. But look at us now? One weekend and the fire between us is roaring out of control. An inferno like that doesn't burn out in time. Not seventeen years. Not fucking ever. I'm in this, Mira. So I need you to settle in, get comfortable, be happy, and be in it too. Because it's not always going to be this easy, baby. No matter how much we say the past is in the past, there are going to be times when resentment claws its way through our flames. And it's going to take both of us, together, working as a team to fight that back." I tucked a stray hair behind her ear and allowed my gaze to roam her beautiful face. Fuck, this woman owned me. She always had. Always would. "I'm committing to do that with you, Mira. I'm committing to fight harder than I've ever fought for anything in my life. Because we're fucking worth it."

She blinked up at me as if she couldn't believe her own eyes. "Jeremy."

Dipping low, I brushed my nose with hers and reiterated, "I'm *not* going to disappear. And right now would be a really good time for you to promise that too."

"I promise." Her chin quivered, and tears finally slid down her pink cheeks. And then Mira said the only words I'd ever wanted to hear her say. "I choose us. Now and forever. I swear to you I'll always, for the rest of my life, choose us."

Relief tore out of me in a way that made me rethink the reasons I hadn't slept well the night before. Maybe I had been waiting for her to disappear. Waiting for her to find a better offer and take it, leaving me to wither all over again.

"You sure?" I asked, my voice thick with emotion.

She smiled. "Positive."

I nodded at least a dozen times, my chest puffing as my lungs inflated with enough air to last me a lifetime strictly because it had once been hers. And then I gave it back to her. "I love you."

Her face got all squishy in a way that couldn't possibly be construed as attractive. But it was Mira, and she said, "I love you too." So it was the most beautiful face I'd ever seen.

I hugged her tight, regretting the moment I had to let her go.

But that was the sweetest part about it. I didn't have to.

I did, however, have to set her straight about something.

After clearing my throat, I said, "Now, we need to get back to you going to the store alone this morning."

Her lips pursed and her face unscrunched and it did it morphing into a scowl.

"Jesus, Jeremy. You really know how to ruin a moment." She tried to step away.

Chuckling, I anchored her around the waist. "See, I disagree. I'm trying to enhance those moments. By making sure you stay alive so we can have more of them together. As the man who has always loved you, has asked you to move in with me, and is planning to start a future with you, I'm kind of hoping that future lasts more than one night."

With her attitude still on full display, she twisted her lips. "I've been trapped in Kurt's prison for a long time, Jeremy. I'll be damned if I volunteer to stay in it any longer. He doesn't get to dictate my life anymore. So, if I want to go to the grocery store to make my man breakfast, then that's what I'm doing."

I groaned. She had a point. Just not a point I wanted her to make.

I kissed her, short and chaste. "I'm not saying you *can't* go to the grocery store, Mira. I'm saying I was right upstairs. You could have woken me up to go with you."

"Then it wouldn't have been a surprise," she argued.

"No, but it would have been a huge fucking surprise if I got a call that you were dead in a ditch."

Her body jerked, and she opened her mouth, but I didn't let her get a word in.

"I know this sucks, baby. Trust me, I don't want you living in his prison, either. But, until we can figure out how to get you in the clear, I need you to play it safe. We have the rest of our lives for you to surprise me with breakfasts. But I only have one of you. And, if something happens to you, knowing I could have prevented it, I'll be stuck living in that prison *forever*."

Sheepishly, she looked away.

Yeah. She saw my point too.

Wiggling in close, she asked, "So, if I promise to do everything in my power to keep myself alive and out of a ditch, you think you can park your sexy ass down on a stool and eat this delicious breakfast I risked my life to provide for you?"

I smirked. "Depends. Am I going to risk my life by eating that sausage? We all know what you did with pork last time."

"Hey! I can cook."

From the way the kitchen smelled, she was not lying. But it was more fun to pick on her than tell her that. "So you keep telling me."

"I can!" She glowered and it made me chuckle.

Yeah. Definitely more fun.

Smiling, I kissed her again, this time slowly and tenderly until whatever attitude she had been gearing up to sling at me melted away. Leaving her cheeks pink and breaths labored, I sauntered around to the barstool and sat my ass down. "Then feed me, woman."

And feed me she did.

Opening the microwave, she produced the largest stack of pancakes I had ever seen. It was as if she had unearthed the holy grail of breakfasts. My mouth watered. I fully expected her to fork off a few onto a separate plate for me, but she didn't. She just sat the whole damn plate in front of me and grinned.

"Sweets still your weakness?"

My stomach rumbled, answering her question, as I blinked at the heavenly, chocolate-speckled, pan-fried imitation of Mount Everest.

As a general, self-imposed punishment—er...I mean rule—I only ate junk on Fridays, when Rhion brought in muffins and all that other shit for us at the office. I was forty and my career required me to stay in shape. I did not have enough time in the day to work off the amount of crap I would have liked to eat.

However, it had been a few years since I'd had a woman to make me chocolate chip pancakes.

Without tearing my eyes off the pancakes, I asked, "You gonna help me work off the seven thousand calories it would cost me to eat all of these?"

She giggled. "By running beside you at the gym? No. By getting naked and letting you have your wicked way with me? Absolutely."

My head popped up, a grin splitting my face. "Judging by the height of this stack, that's going to be a lot of wicked ways, Mir. You sure you're ready for that?"

Her grin grew to match mine as she placed a bottle of syrup on the bar in front of me. "I think I can manage."

God, I loved that woman.

I didn't get the first bite to my mouth before a knock at the door stole my attention.

Rising off the stool, I lifted a hand in Mira's direction and whispered, "Don't move."

"Are you expecting someone?" she asked, anxiety rising in her tone at the end.

"It's fine," I lied.

People did not just show up at my door at eight thirty in the morning. People didn't show up at my door period.

Cautiously, I went to the window that overlooked my driveway, and then my lungs deflated on a rush. Melissa's Acura MDX was parked directly behind my SUV.

"Shit," I mumbled.

Melissa didn't just randomly show up at my house, either. Especially not an hour after I knew she dropped the girls off at daycare halfway across town.

She'd been a bitch when she'd seen Mira in the background of our video chat. I could only imagine she was there to spew more of that shit on me. But I had no intention of taking it. Not with pancakes and a woman eager to help me burn them off waiting.

I yanked open the door. "What are you doing—"

"Daddy!" they squealed, crashing into my legs.

Oh, shit.

Shoving past me, Melissa walked inside, her heels, which probably cost a fortune, clipping on the hardwood. "Good lord, Jeremy. Could you at least put on a shirt?"

"Didn't know I'd be receiving company," I replied. Scooping the girls up into my arms, I planted one on each hip and cooed, "Hey, babies."

"We're not babies!" they giggled in unison.

"Where the hell have you been?" Melissa snapped. "I've called you at least a dozen times. I finally broke down and called Guardian. Sarah said you had the day off. Thank God."

I flicked my eyes over Mel's shoulder to Mira, who was standing stiff as a statue in the kitchen, her eyes wide and her face red. Jesus, fuck. Not exactly the ideal way to introduce her to my ex and my kids. But there was nothing I could do about it now.

"Melissa, this is—"

"Listen, I need you to keep the girls. Amelia was running a fever when we got to the daycare today, so she couldn't stay. I have a huge meeting this morning that I can't miss."

I looked to my daughter on my left hip and asked, "You feeling okay, sweetie?"

"I'm Sophie," she replied.

Christ, they looked so much alike.

I winked. "Of course you are." Then I looked to Amelia on my right and repeated the question. "You feeling okay, sweetie?"

"No," she croaked, resting her head on my shoulder.

Melissa put her hand to Amelia's forehead. "I gave her medicine before we headed this way. Her fever should break soon." She flipped her hand to Sophie's forehead. "This is the one you need to keep an eye on. She's fine right now, but you know they pass this stuff back and forth. It's only a matter of time before—" She slapped her hand to her chest when her gaze finally landed on Mira. "Oh, God."

And here we go!

Silently, Mira lifted her hand in an awkward wave. It would have made me laugh if I hadn't felt Melissa swing a pair of green laser beams on me.

Bracing, I glanced back at her.

"Is she seriously *still* here?" she seethed, her face so tight that it was a wonder it didn't shatter.

I shrugged, the girls' red curls jostling with the movement of my shoulders. "Well, she kinda lives here now."

Yeah. I could have been gentler while dropping that bomb, but it didn't matter when or how I'd dropped it. To Melissa, it was always going to be a bomb. It also didn't matter that we were divorced. Or that she was with Brent. She'd find a reason to be pissed off no matter what. But, with the girls in my arms, I knew she'd at least keep it together long enough to get them—and hopefully Mira—out of earshot.

Her mouth fell open, and her narrowed, green eyes filled with disgust. "She *lives* here? *She*"—she pointed a perfectly manicured red fingernail toward Mira—"*lives*"—she pointed to the floor—"*here.*"

I gave her a side-eye and warned, "Watch it."

"Watch it," she repeated, incredulous. "There is a woman living in my house and you want *me* to watch it?"

My body tensed as I fired back as calm as I could manage, "One, not your house anymore. I bought it outright when you decided to move. Two, not another word in front of the girls."

Her eyes bulged. "Of course. Not in front of the girls. *Our* girls. Our children, whose home you moved your little plaything into without talking to me first."

The muscles in my neck strained, but I dropped into a squat, placing the twins on their feet. And then I performed the miracle of keeping my voice low and even as I said, "Sophie, Amelia, go play in your room for a minute."

Melissa barked a laugh. "Ohhhh, no, you don't. They aren't staying. No way in hell I'm leaving my kids with some woman I've never met before." Grabbing both of their hands, she started to the door, continuing to rant. "You all but ran a security clearance on Brent before he was allowed to meet the girls, and here you are just up and moving a woman into our house. No discussion. No notice. No…" She snatched the front door open. "No nothing."

My blood was boiling. Pissed was one thing. Acting a fool in front of the kids was totally different.

"Mel," I growled.

And, because things were already going so smashingly, Mira decided that this was the perfect moment to wade into the chaos. "No, wait. Please. It just kinda happened yesterday. We weren't planning it or anything. We've only officially been together a few days, I'm positive he was going to talk to you before we got my things today."

Dear. God. Shoot. Me.

Melissa's mouth fell open, and she did a slow blink at Mira.

I dropped my head back between my shoulders, stared up at the ceiling, and called out, "Not helping, baby."

Melissa ominously whispered, "A few days?"

Mira tried to defend me again. "Well, I mean—"

"A few days!" Melissa screeched—fucking *screeched*—right there in front of my kids. One of whom was sick. Both of whom were too damn young for this bullshit.

"Enough," I snarled. Striding toward the door, I hooked an arm around Sophie first, easing her back on my hip, before doing the same with Amelia on my other side. Then, leaning toward their mother, I ordered, "Outside. Now." Firm, but at least a dozen octaves below the shout I wanted to use.

I flashed a smile to each of the girls as I carried them back to their mother's car. I hadn't seen them in a few days and I wouldn't have minded making up for lost time even if it was nursing them back to health. But, if that meant having a yelling match with Melissa in front of them, I could wait until the following weekend.

After I got to the car, I opened the back door and deposited Amelia into her car seat. I kissed her on her forehead, finding it still hot, therefore immediately feeling guilty that my sick baby had to get back in the car instead of curling into my lap on the couch to watch her favorite cartoon until she was feeling better.

As I rounded the hood to put Sophie in her seat, Melissa moved in to buckle up Amelia. Once both girls were situated, I leaned into the backseat, blew countless kisses, promised I'd see them soon, and then shut the door.

And then, and only then, did I turn back to face my ex-wife. She was still pissed as all hell, leaning against the door, her arms crossed over her chest.

"What the fuck was that?" I whispered.

"You tell me," she whispered back.

"Fine. That was you showing your ass in front of our kids the way we swore to each other we would never do when we separated."

"You know what else we said we wouldn't do? Randomly move people into a home where our children sleep."

She was not wrong about that, and guilt momentarily curbed my anger.

Melissa was a good woman. Strong. Borderline bitchy. Fiercely independent. Short tempered, but she had a good heart. Everything I'd told myself I'd needed after Mira had wrecked me. By the time Mel and I had met, I'd been in my late thirties and traveling through life, bouncing from woman to woman, trying to replace the one who got away. Honestly, as fucked up as it was, part of the reason Melissa and I had worked was because she was the first woman who had not one single thing in common with Mira York. She wasn't soft or gentle. I didn't have to take care of her or wonder what was going on in her head. If Melissa had a problem, I knew it immediately. There was no guessing or playing games. If she thought it, she said it. Good, bad, or ugly. Sure, we had good times together. She made me laugh, but it was on a surface level. It made my lips pull back and a deep sound vibrate from my throat, but the sensation of happiness didn't travel through my entire body down to the marrow in my bones. There was only one woman who had ever given that to me.

Then again, my marriage to Melissa had been born out of a mutual convenience, not all-consuming love, lust, or even desire. When we'd met, we were both getting older, reaching that point in our lives when you either made a family or gave up on the dream.

Melissa had told me on our very first date that she was looking to settle down. She'd had it all planned out. Big house. Two kids. Her career. Her husband working for her dad. Summers spent in the Hamptons. Winters spent in the Keys. Eventually retiring somewhere on the beach.

I'd also told her on our first date that all I had to offer her was the kids part.

Apparently, that had been enough for her.

We had great sex, became good friends, but not surprisingly, if you didn't love someone, it was really fucking hard to commit your life to them.

Though, short of the two angelic faces peering out at us from the backseat of her car, I hadn't been able to commit my life to anyone since I'd been twenty-three years old.

And she had known this. I'd told her. But she'd married me anyway.

She'd come to regret it too.

At some point during our three-year marriage, Melissa had fallen in love with me. Real love. True love. The kind you don't move on from. The kind I could never return.

The kind I had with Mira.

So, rather than pretending for any longer or hurting her any deeper, I left. I wasn't a dick about it. We sat down and talked. She didn't like it, but she couldn't argue that it wasn't for the best.

It was still for the best, and deep down, she knew it just as well as I did. We needed to move on, and while she'd shown that her jealous streak didn't always stay hidden, she was at least rational about it.

"I'm sorry," I said sans all anger.

She accepted my apology with a nod, keeping her gaze trained on the driveway. "So she seriously lives here?" Her words were no longer packed the anger, but the hurt was evident. "After knowing her for a few days?"

I sighed and gripped the back of my neck, suddenly very aware that I was standing in my driveway shirtless while about to drop a bomb that I knew was going to wreck my ex-wife. But it had to be done.

"It's Mira," I informed.

Her head snapped up as she sucked in a sharp breath. "W-what?"

"She called me on Friday. She and her ex... Well, shit went down and it was bad. She came back here for a few nights, some things happened, and here we are."

"Just like that," she whispered, incredulous. "She just walks back into your life after all this time and you're standing there with open arms, ready to take her back?"

Yes. Basically. That was exactly what'd happened.

"No, Mel. We've talked. There was a lot of miscommunication

back in the day. She's been living with bruises. I've been living with bruises. We've talked through them and—"

"In a weekend?" She pushed off the car and stopped directly in front of me. "I spent three years of my life trying to make you love me. And this woman…who you spent, what? A few months with forever ago? She comes back and, one weekend later, you're starting a life together? How convenient." She laughed quietly and really fucking sadly. "Next weekend, you two getting married? Starting on kids the following?"

I stared at her. It was rare she broke down. She was always such a rock. I hated this part of my life. There was nothing I wouldn't do for my children. But staying with their mother only to repeatedly break her heart was not one of those things. She deserved the truth no matter how much it hurt.

"No. Mel. That's not what's going to happen next weekend or the next. But you need to be ready for all of those things to happen *eventually*. Look, I'm happy for you and Brent. He seems like a nice guy, and he loves you. You can see it in his eyes every time he looks at you. But that was never the way *I* looked at you. And I told you that would never be the case from the day we met." I waved a hand out to indicate the back of her car, where our twins were sitting inside, probably arguing with each other. "We made beautiful babies. That was all I ever promised you. You knew that going in. This is not, and has never been, a you-versus-Mira thing. What she and I have is different. I don't know why. And don't know how. But, yeah, it only took a few months when we were younger and then this past weekend to know that she's the woman I'm meant to spend the rest of my life with."

She blanched, her face paling as she cut her gaze away.

God, it fucking sucked. But I was telling her the truth. Something we'd vowed to always give each other. But, when she looked back in my direction, the tears rolling down her cheeks gutted me.

Catching her at the back of her neck, I pulled her into a hug. "I'm sorry. I swear to God I am. But I can't change it, Mel. She's a part of me."

She stood in my arms for a few beats, sniffling and doing her best to hide her face, and then, in true Melissa fashion, she stepped out of my arms, rolled her shoulders back, and took the world on with her chin held high. "I think we should sit down with the girls together before they officially meet her and explain things. Perhaps over family dinner on Wednesday. I'd also like to schedule some time to talk to her. If she's going to be involved in the girls' life, I'd like to lay out a few ground rules with her woman to woman."

I nodded. It made sense. It was going to be awkward as fuck, but I had faith Mira could handle it. "Fair enough."

"I'll find someone else to keep the kids today. Since you're..." She pursed her lips and disapprovingly raked her gaze over my chest. "Busy."

I shoved my hands in my pockets and rocked up onto my toes. "I'll be sure to put on a shirt next time you show up at my house... unannounced...on my day off."

She rolled her eyes and it made me chuckle.

"Hey, why don't you give Rhion a call? I'm sure she'd love to keep the girls. I'll throw on some clothes and head that way. Mira can stay down at Guardian while I spend time with the kids."

She arched an eyebrow. "What? You don't trust her to stay home alone?"

I clamped my mouth shut. Nope. Nope. Nope.

No way in hell was I getting into *that* conversation with Melissa.

"She likes to hang with Johnson," I blurted.

A huge Cheshire-cat smile split her face. "Don't we all."

I chuckled. "I'm learning that this is true. You call him Sexy Guy too?"

She shrugged. "I'll call him whatever he wants me to. You might want to make sure your beloved Mira doesn't though."

I glowered, but it only made her smile grow.

Turning on a toe, she tugged the car door open. Pausing halfway in, halfway out, she gave me a tight smile. "I'm sorry, too, by the way."

"I know," I murmured.

"You've never lied to me, Jeremy. Not even when I'd wished you would."

Jesus.

I didn't know how to reply to something like that, but thankfully, she let me off the hook before I had to try.

"I'll call Rhion and text you with what she says." She turned, put her chin to her shoulder, and said, "Tell Daddy bye."

"Bye!" they parroted.

"Bye, sweeties. Hopefully I'll see you in a few."

They both smiled, wide and toothy.

I gave Melissa one last chin jerk, and then she closed the door. I stood on the driveway, watching one half of my heart leaving.

And then I put one foot in front of the other and went back inside—to the other half.

CHAPTER TWENTY-FIVE

Mira

"**A**RE YOU OKAY?" JEREMY ASKED FOR APPROXIMATELY THE twentieth time.

I was sitting on the big, overstuffed couch at Guardian. The massive TV mounted over the double-sided fireplace was playing The Food Channel, but Jeremy had muted it the moment he'd sat beside me. He'd spent the last few hours down at Rhion's, hanging out with his daughters. Meanwhile, I'd been stuck at Guardian with nothing but my thoughts to keep me company. And, given my mindset, time alone in my head was a dangerous thing.

After Jeremy had dealt with Melissa back at his house, he'd come back inside, wrapped me in a hug from behind, apologized for his ex, kissed my neck, felt me up, and then told me he loved me. All of this, I had immensely enjoyed.

Meeting Melissa—assuming you could consider her yelling and being appalled "meeting"—had been exactly one level of discomfort above having a tooth pulled. But it was what it was. She was going to be part of Jeremy's life for forever, and it appeared as though I was too.

While Jeremy had waited for his pancakes to warm in the microwave, he'd given me the rundown of what they'd talked about in the driveway. I'd been shocked—okay, fine, and ecstatic—to learn that she knew who I was. This meant he'd talked about me at least once over the years. (Yay!) This also meant that I'd caused him so much heartbreak that he'd been unable to find any kind of happiness with another woman. (Not so yay.)

Then, between heaving forkfuls of pancake, he informed me that Melissa wanted to have a one-on-one with me. Yeah, okay, fine. Whatever. I was good with people. Even, and maybe especially, the bitchy ones.

But then, just as his fork clattered on his empty plate, he mentioned that the aforementioned one-on-one was because Melissa wanted to discuss things because I was going to be part of the girls' lives from there on out. As in their children. Their innocent, beautiful children.

I smiled, excused myself, trotted up the stairs, locked myself in the bathroom, and then had the panic attack of all panic attacks.

Jeremy was an incredible man. I'd loved him with my entire heart for half of my life. It hadn't worked out for us in the past, but over the last few days, I'd dared to hope that it could be different for us in the present. And then, just that morning, only hours earlier, that hope had transformed into a reality as Jeremy had declared that he was committing to making us work and I'd sworn to always choose us.

It had felt like a dream.

But, with one simple realization, I'd been forced to wake up.

Back to the nightmare.

Jeremy and I had no future.

Kurt had made sure of that—again.

Which was exactly why I was sitting on the couch at Guardian, my head a jumbled mess, my lungs aching with every breath, and my soul shriveling with the prospect of a life without him.

"I'm fine," I lied, finishing with a smile to really sell it.

He blew out an exasperated breath and mumbled a not-so-stealthy, "Bullshit."

"Stop. Seriously. I'm fine. Go take the girls to Melissa's. I'll be here when you get back."

He eyed me warily. "Is this about Melissa?"

I laughed, but it never made it to my heart. "No! Good lord, stop asking. I'm not upset about your ex. I'm fine. Everything's fine."

He scooted over until our thighs became flush. "Mira, you are *not* fine. You weren't fine at the house. You weren't fine on the way over. And you sure as fuck are not fine now."

He was absolutely right.

I rolled my eyes anyway. "I'm just tired. You know I didn't sleep last night."

His lips thinned. "You sure?"

I pointed to my eyes. "Have you seen the bags under my eyes?"

He smiled—so damn beautifully that it hurt. "Now that you mention it, you do look like hell."

I gaped at him. "What is wrong with you? You don't say that to a woman. The appropriate response when a woman criticizes herself is always, 'Oh, please, you're beautiful, blank.'"

His lips twitched. "Blank?"

"That is where you add the term of endearment. *Always* add a term of endearment. Gorgeous, sexy, love, or whatever tickles your fancy."

He scooped a hand behind my knees and twisted me on the couch so that my legs draped over his lap. Using the back of his hand, he brushed my hair over my shoulder and murmured, "You tickle my fancy."

I turned, putting my feet back on the floor and adding a much-needed few inches between us. "Your cheesiness knows no bounds."

He grinned, his eyes getting dark as he whispered to no one, "She's going to make us work for it."

Disbelieving, I glanced around the room. "Who are you talking to?"

He nodded, held my gaze, and then answered his own damn question. "That she is, Hyde. That she is."

My head jerked back. "Are you seriously having a conversation with your alter ego right now?"

He didn't answer—either of them.

But, suddenly, I was in his arms, up off the couch, and then back down on the couch. My shoulder blades were to the cushion I'd just been sitting on, my legs stretching the length, and the solid wall of muscle that was Jeremy Lark came crashing down on top of me. He landed on me hard but gently, his hand going over my head to the armrest to support some of his weight. But his hips landed on mine, zipper to zipper, lining us up in the most spectacular fashion.

"Jesus," I breathed, cutting my gaze off to the side, lamenting how incredibly perfectly we fit together.

"Talk," he demanded.

I swallowed hard and forced a smile. "You're so crazy. Nothing is wrong."

He cupped my chin, squishing my lips together as he turned my head back to face him. "You know you are going to have to tell me eventually."

"Aren't you supposed to be taking your daughters home?" I mumbled, refusing to meet his gaze.

"I am. And the sooner you tell me what the hell is going on in your head, I can do just that. Then I can come back here, take you home, and spend the rest of the night soothing, arguing, or fucking whatever demon has taken hold of your head out of you." He leaned in close, still holding my face, his lips almost touching mine. "I'll even let you choose."

I swatted his hand away from my face and bucked beneath him. "If you don't get off me, you aren't going to be fucking anything for a long while."

He laughed. "You know what the bitch does to me, baby. I'm not going to be able to hold Hyde back much longer with you slinging an attitude like that."

I rolled my eyes so hard that it felt as though they did a full rotation. Shoving at his chest and bucking beneath him, I ordered, "Jesus Christ, go take your kids home. I'll be fine when you get back."

He didn't budge, and his already firm body turned to stone. "You got a problem with my girls?" he asked roughly.

My eyes snapped to his. "What? No! Why would you even think that?"

His forehead crinkled as his eyes turned to slits. "'Cause you're acting fucking weird and you won't tell me why, but you seem to think you'll be fine after I drop my girls off."

I sighed. "Jeremy, I have no problem with your children. They are dolls. Amelia and her crooked smile, and Sophie with her penchant for dresses and tiaras. I mean, really—what's not to love?"

His slitted eyes somehow became slittier. "How do you know about Sophie and her dresses? Or Amelia's smile?"

Oh, fuckity fuck fuck fuck. I did not think that one through.

Somehow, I guessed *"Because I've been stalking you and your family on Facebook for the last few years"* wasn't going to be a turn-on, so I attempted to squirm out from under him and lied. "I saw them today."

His weight got heavier on top of me. "For two seconds. And Amelia was sick, so she wasn't smiling, and Sophie was wearing leggings and a sweater."

Shit! Why had I never perfected the art of lying over the last thirty-six years?

I still gave it another try. "I used to be a little girl, Jeremy. And all girls like dresses and tiaras. It was just a guess, but not exactly a longshot."

He continued with his disbelieving, slitted stare. "And the smile?"

Now, this wasn't a lie, so I grinned. "Have you looked in the mirror?"

"Right," he clipped, but thankfully, his body slacked.

Relief blasted through me.

That is until he stated, "You always wanted babies."

It was my turn to go stiff.

He continued talking. "You used to ramble for fucking ever about how you'd be a better mom than the one you had. You wanted three by the time you were thirty so you could be a young mom who would still be young when they had kids of their own. Nineteen years old and you were already planning for grandkids."

My stomach twisted, and my chest ached. Why did he have to remember everything I'd ever said? Normally, this would have been a great trait when trying to rekindle a relationship from seventeen years ago, but this... This I could have really benefited from him forgetting.

Because I wanted to forget too.

His hand once again landed on my face, but this time, it was gentle and consoling. "You wanted a big family, Mira. Everything we never had growing up. What happened to that?"

Emotion thickened my voice as I replied, "I changed my mind."

"Why?" he asked, but it was more like a prompt than a question.

"Because."

"Because *why*?" He dipped low and kissed me, and he did it softly and slowly. It was a kiss filled with an apology as if he'd already worked out the answer.

And it was Jeremy—so he probably had.

Therefore, there was no use lying anymore, and the truth tumbled out along with a few tears. "Because, on the back of the truck when we talked about all of those things, I was imagining that I'd be making and raising those babies with you."

"Jesus, I wanted that too." He inhaled, long and deep, but his dark gaze never left mine. "So seeing my girls, it's hard for you. A reminder of something you never got."

I shook my head adamantly. "No. I mean...yes, I'm jealous sometimes. But I swear I don't have a problem with your kids. I would have loved to get to know them and spent time with you, watching you be a dad. You were so happy today when you saw them. It was like you were pissed off but, the minute you heard them say, 'Daddy,' this monstrous smile covered your face. I don't think you even realized it. It was beautiful, and seeing you so happy made me happy. And it's killing me, knowing that I can't be a part of that."

His chin jerked to the side. "And why can't you be a part of that? Just because we didn't officially introduce you to them today—"

"Because it's not safe," I blurted. "Jeremy, there are people trying to kill me. No way am I bringing that to those sweet little girls' doorstep. What if something happened to them? For fuck's sake, Jonah kidnapped my best friend. She is twenty-three. Imagine what he would do to your girls?"

His face was hard as he suddenly sat up, taking me with him, but he allowed me no space. Holding me securely on his lap, he grumbled, "First of all, no one is going to touch my girls."

"No. Because I'm going to a hotel," I stated.

And just like those were the magical words to summon him, Mr. Hyde appeared. "Stop fucking saying you're going to a hotel! You're not going to a goddamn hotel. Ever. Never." He leaned in closer to my face with every word, where he finished with, "Fucking ever."

Finally able to free myself from his lap, I stood, crossed my arms over my chest, and started to pace the floor, all the while mumbling under my breath, "Well, then, that is going to make vacationing difficult in the future."

His chest heaved as he rose to his feet. "Jesus Christ, woman. Stop trying to get away from me."

I stopped and looked to him. "I'm not trying to get away! Don't you see? I'm trying to keep you. Your kids are important to you, Jeremy."

"Yes. More than anything in the world. But *you* are important to me too. Have a little faith that I know what I'm doing here. You don't think I've considered that Kurt's bullshit—"

I opened my mouth to interject, but he stabbed a finger in my direction and snarled, "And don't fucking try to tell me this is *your* bullshit. This is all on Kurt. Every fucking bit of it. And I'm taking care of it."

"How? As of this morning, I'm not even allowed to go to the grocery store by myself. And yet you're going to let me play Suzie stepmother to your girls?"

He planted his hands on his hips. "No, Mir. That was not part of the plan. I don't want you *playing* shit. I want you to *be* their stepmother. I want to marry you and make those babies with you that we never got to have. But, most of all, I want you to stop keeping this shit to yourself, open your goddamn mouth, and talk to me before you build it up in your head to something it is *not*."

Spoiler alert part two: This is the scene where the heroine dies.

Dead.

Croaked.

Kicked the bucket.

Flatlined.

The whole shebang.

"W-what?" my corpse, who could surprisingly still talk even though I was D-E-A-D dead, stammered.

"For fuck's sake. That whole goddamn not-talking-to-each-other thing is how I lost you the first time. I'm done with it." He took a scary step toward me, but I was still dead, so I couldn't back away. "You got something to say? Fucking say it." Another step. "Something is bothering you? Fucking *tell* me." Another step. "You're worried about something. Fucking *say it*!" He stopped directly in front of me. Snaking his arm around my back, he tugged me against his chest and lowered his voice to say, "But you get those crazy-ass ideas about going to a hotel again? You keep that shit to yourself."

I just stood there, staring up at him, wondering how I was still on my feet at all.

And he just stood there, staring down at me, his twinkling hazel eyes searching my face.

"Say it, baby," he prompted. "Whatever you are thinking right now. Give it to me."

I swallowed hard and blinked back tears. And then I told him exactly what was on my mind. "I think I'm dead."

His brows pinched, but his lips twitched. Slipping two fingers beneath my scarf, he pressed them to my neck. "Nope. Still got a pulse."

Well, that was good news.

"You want to marry me?" I whispered, not trusting my voice.

He shrugged. "I'm not saying today. But that's kinda the goal when you're in love with someone."

My vision started to swim as I croaked out, "And have babies?"

"If you still want 'em. I love being a dad, and I love my girls. I'll love our kids too."

God, the pain in my chest was agonizing. But it was the most beautiful pain of my entire life. "I'm creeping up on thirty-seven, Jeremy."

"Okay, so this time, we won't wait seventeen years to have them. We can wait a few months, make sure we still like each other." He winked. "In that time, we can take care of making you a Lark and then get down to the baby-making, hopefully getting number one out before you turn thirty-eight."

I choked, coughing right in his face. "Number one?"

He arched an incredulous eyebrow at me. "Kids is still plural, right? I don't know about three, but we should have time for two before you turn forty. We'll see how it goes. Play it by ear."

I blinked.

Then blinked again.

And then I died all over again.

Slapping a hand over my mouth, I said, "You've thought this out."

He grinned, sliding a hand between my shoulder blades, up my neck, and into my hair. "Yeah, Mir. When you were tossing and turning last night, worrying that I was gonna disappear...I was busy planning a life where you didn't."

I felt it long before I could identify it.

It was somewhere deep inside me.

And it hurt. So fucking badly. Like I was being stabbed with a million fiery knives while simultaneously being run over by a stampede of horses.

I'd never felt it before. I'd never even known that place inside me existed.

Once, when I was a kid, I'd gotten tonsillitis. I remembered asking the doctor how that was possible because I didn't have tonsils. He'd assured me I did and that they'd always been a part of me. It just wasn't until they'd started hurting that I'd become aware of them.

I'd always known I had bruises inside me.

They, too, were a part of me. Every day. For my entire life.

But, if you've never felt relief, you can't recognize pain.

In that moment, with Jeremy staring down at me, offering me everything I'd ever wanted—including a life with him—I realized just how dark and diseased those bruises truly were.

Because I finally felt them disappear.

Circling my arms around his waist, I hugged him tighter than ever before. "I love you," I whispered. It wasn't enough, but I'd pay him back for what he had just given me over time—a lifetime. I decided to start with, "I'll stop talking about going to a hotel."

"Love you too, baby," he rasped before kissing the top of my head. "And I'd appreciate that."

I sucked in a deep breath, keeping my arms locked around him, and swayed my upper body away. "But what are we going to do about the girls? I'd never be able to live with myself if something happened to them."

"Trust me. That's not going to happen. Leo, Mateo, and I are working on some things. Caleb is trying to get me a sit down with Kurt. He might be a cop, but he's a good guy who has no problems turning a blind eye in order to do what's right."

I frowned. "I don't know that you meeting with Kurt is a good idea, Jeremy. If you're expecting him to turn over the whereabouts of this money, you should probably not mention that we're together."

He squeezed me. "I know that, baby. I don't want you stressing about this. We're going into this smart. And I don't want you worrying about the girls, either. The minute Mateo dropped that shit on us last night, they were at the forefront of my mind. They're covered. Johnson cut the central power to Melissa's house last night. It's going to take the repair man—a.k.a. our camera guy, Zach—a few days to get it fixed, so she and the girls are currently staying at Brent's."

My mouth fell open in a mixture of shock and amusement. "He cut the power?"

"Yep."

"And Zach is going to repair it?"

"No. Zach just answered the call Apollo rerouted from her phone. We'll wait a few days until all of this dies down and then send the power company to fix it. I'll foot the bill and no one is the wiser."

My already gaping mouth stretched wider. "Apollo rerouted her call?"

He shook his head. "Apollo can do a lot of things that I promise you do not want to know about. Now…are we done? Any chance I can take my girls back to Melissa now?"

"Depends. Am I going to learn at year six of our marriage that Guardian Protection Agency is a super-secret division of the CIA?"

I was only half kidding.

He smiled. "First thing tomorrow, me, my former-DEA-agent boss, a cop with a keen sense for justice, and a drug lord who is quite possibly in love with you are going to figure out how to end Kurt's bullshit for you once and for all. Trust me: The CIA doesn't want any part of this."

A laugh sprang from my throat. "That sounds like quite the team."

He bent low, brushed his lips with mine, and then whispered, "Let's hope."

CHAPTER TWENTY-SIX

Mira

"**D**O YOU HAVE A GIRLFRIEND?" I ASKED FROM THE SAME SPOT on the Guardian couch I'd been sitting in the majority of the day. I was pretty sure it would have a permanent imprint of my ass on it by the time I left.

Jeremy had gone to drop his girls off. After that, he was coming back for me and then we were going to walk across the street to the bar Apollo owned (seriously, that man was intriguing) called Murphy's with Jude, Rhion, Johnson, and Braydon. I'd convinced myself that we were all just hanging out and I didn't need a team of bodyguards in order to have a beer with my boyfriend. But whatever. I was happy.

Braydon arched his sculpted, brown eyebrow. But not sculpted in the feminine way. Sculpted like he took pride in his appearance and had probably learned his way around a set of tweezers over the years. And, given that his nails were all filed to a short, even length, his cuticles were spotless, his white button-down shirt was pressed, and his jeans were tastefully tattered, I figured he'd learned his way around a nail salon, a dry cleaner, and the mall too.

"Not at the moment. You offering?" He smiled, popping those delicious dimples.

"Nah…I kind of got pre-engaged and pre-pregnant today. It's best if I stick with the man I got."

His brows shot up. "Pre-engaged and pre-pregnant?"

I smiled huge and nodded. "Two kids before I turn forty. But only after I become a Lark."

His dimples danced as his lips twitched. "Well…congratulations?"

"Thanks. I'll be sure to let you know when I'm post-engaged and post-pregnant."

He chuckled and went back to watching TV, which was no longer on The Food Channel, but ESPN.

I'd also convinced myself that he was just chilling, waiting to walk over to the bar with us, rather than babysitting. But, again, whatever. I was happy.

The highlight reel was looping around for the third time when my phone started ringing. I didn't recognize the number, but I lifted it to my ear anyway.

"Hello?"

"When I first saw you, I thought you were the most beautiful woman I'd ever seen."

His accent was unmistakable. "Mateo?"

Braydon's gaze flew to mine, his eyes wide with alert. He rose from the couch and prowled toward me, snapping his fingers before holding his hand palm up, asking for the phone.

I waved him off as Mateo kept talking in my ear.

"Your Spanish was terrible, but your laugh could breathe life into dying men. And for a while there that was exactly what I was."

Okay, so Jeremy had been right. Mateo was definitely in love with me. Seeing as he was a powerful drug lord from Miami with a good heart who had decided to plod into the mess that was my life, the least I could do was let him down easy.

"Um…thanks." I dodged Braydon's attempt to take my phone. "You're really sweet—"

"But you didn't belong in my world. Living with Kurt, you were already a caged bird who had forgotten how to sing. I couldn't bear to watch you suffer trying to fit into my lifestyle. But, Mira, please know, that should you ever be lost, I will always be the one to find you."

My body jolted. What the hell did that even mean?

It sounded like a compliment, so I went with that.

"Mateo, I—"

"Never forget that," he carried on. "But that is not the reason for my call, *Preciosa*. I believe I have something of yours." His voice became muffled as he moved his mouth away from the phone to ask someone else, "Her name is Bitsy, right?"

The hairs on the back of my neck stood on end.

I loved my dog. She'd held me together when I'd thought all had been lost in life. She'd warmed me when everything outside had seemed too cold. And she'd made me smile when I'd thought it was impossible. Bitsy meant the world to me.

But that wasn't why tears exploded from my eyes or adrenaline surged like a tidal wave through my veins.

With a huge smile on my face, I listened to Whitney reply, "Yeah. Bitsy's her name."

Lark

"Love you too, sweetie." I smiled, backing out of Brent's door.

Sophie ran toward me with one of the new Barbies she'd just unboxed. "Daddy, look what Brent got us!"

"Wow, sweetie." I feigned excitement. "That is *so* cool."

"Look at mine!" Amelia squealed, bouncing into the foyer.

"Wow, sweetie," I repeated. "That is *so* cool."

Christ, he was going to spoil the hell out of my kids.

"Girls!" Melissa called. "Come eat your dinner and let Daddy go."

Mel had been icy with me since I'd arrived to drop the girls off. She'd offered the mandatory courtesy greeting and forced a smile, but after that, she'd retreated to the kitchen, leaving me to say goodbye to the girls while Brent stood at the door. She'd get over that shit eventually, but I hadn't spent three years married to the woman without learning she was going to put me through the wringer first.

I watched with a warm chest as my girls scurried away.

I looked to Brent. "Thanks for letting them stay here."

He smiled like a fucking goof. "Happy to have them." He paused. "Listen, I've been wanting to talk to you for a few weeks now, but I haven't found the right moment." He shoved a hand into his pocket and then rocked from his heels to his toes. "Melissa told me you moved a woman into your house today…and, um, I was thinking maybe you'd be okay with me asking her and the girls to move in here—permanently."

Jesus. This guy, with all his ums and Barbie dolls, was not who I'd thought would be helping to raise my daughters. But, then again, I'd never thought Mira would be helping, either. A smile grew on my face.

"I'm good with that," I replied. "I'm sure Apollo and Johnson would be happy to check out your security system."

I'd be damned if the motherfucker's cheeks didn't pink like I'd just awarded him the highest acclaim. "Yeah. Send them over. Whatever the price. I'll make it happen."

Yeah. There were definitely worse stepdads out there than good old Brent, who just wanted to spoil my kids and live with their mother under his roof.

I extended a hand his way. "You convince Melissa to talk to me again without the guilt trip over not telling her in advance about Mira, I'll have them hook you up free of charge."

He grinned, clasping my hand in a surprisingly firm shake. "Yeah. I don't know that I can work that kind of magic. Just have them send the bill to my office."

I chuckled. "Fair enough."

"Have a good night, Jeremy."

"Take care of my girls, Brent."

He nodded, his chest puffed out like a blowfish. "Always."

I jogged back to my car, happier than I'd been in years.

That should have been my first warning. Happiness came at a price.

After I climbed into the Escalade, I grabbed my phone off the dash in order to shoot Mira a text letting her know I was on my way back.

Seven missed calls. Three from Braydon. Four from Mira.

The vise in my chest cranked down as I immediately clicked Mira's number and lifted the phone to my ear.

A sliver of relief eased the vise when she answered. At least she was okay. Whatever else was wrong, I could fix it.

"Thank God, finally!" she rushed out.

"What's going on?" I asked, backing out of the driveway.

Braydon's voice boomed through the line. "Oh, hell no. You are not allowed phone privileges anymore!"

"Hey!" Mira objected.

But it was Braydon's voice who came on the line. "We got a serious problem, Lark."

My pulse sped. "Then fucking tell me."

"One, I would highly suggest you get un-engaged and un-pregnant. Because your woman is a fucking nutjob."

"Hey!" Mira objected again. "Screw you too!"

I ground my teeth. "What the fuck is going on, Bray?"

"Mateo Rodriguez called Mira's phone about twenty minutes ago. He's got Whitney and the dog."

My whole body jerked in surprise. This should have been good news—except for the fact that it was Mateo Rodriguez. I did not trust that man one fucking bit. While he'd pledged his allegiance to Mira's cause, he was still a dangerous and unpredictable *criminal*. Only hours earlier, Caleb had texted me that Steve Browel, along with three of the men suspected in Mira's attempted kidnapping, had all been found dead in their apartments overnight. Mateo's retribution, no doubt. And, while I wasn't exactly crying over the loss of scum like that, I wasn't sure how I felt about mass murder as punishment, either.

Mateo and Leo were "friends," yet the minute Mateo had shown up at Guardian, Leo had acted as though he'd been going to war. For fuck's sake, when your buddy comes over, you don't greet him with guns locked and loaded. Mira was in trouble, so I had been more than willing to accept whatever help Mateo could offer. But that didn't mean I wanted him anywhere near her. And I sure as fuck didn't want him calling her phone with bullshit he should have run past me or Leo first—like, say, rescuing her best friend and her dog.

I white-knuckled the steering wheel and stepped on the accelerator. "Where?"

"Nine seventy-one Tarapin Court. Some fancy-ass neighborhood south of the city. While I was on the phone, trying to call Leo to see what he wanted me to do, your nutjob of a woman hauled ass out the front door and hailed a fucking cab."

Mira argued, "You were taking too long!"

"I was making a goddamn plan," Braydon shot back.

I wanted to be surprised. I really did. But come on. It was Mira. Nothing surprised me anymore.

"Hey, hey, hey! Chill. Just take her back inside. I'll hit Mateo's and get Whitney and the dog and meet you at the office."

"Inside?" Braydon laughed. "Lark, I'm standing in the fucking driveway of nine seventy-one Tarapin Court, physically restraining your woman to keep her from storming into Rodriguez's castle."

Okay. I had been wrong. There were some things with Mira that still surprised me.

"What?" I growled, my throat burning like I'd swallowed a drum of acid.

"Did you miss the part where she caught a fucking cab? It was a miracle I got here in time to stop her. She was trying to scale a gate, Lark. Legit. No man at her back. Completely unprotected. And she was trying to scale Mateo fucking Rodriguez's gate in a pair of heels, with a goddamn Gucci purse slung over her shoulder."

Mira snapped snottily, "The gate was shut. What would you have preferred I do?"

"Not fucking turn into King Kong in drag!" he retorted. "Do you see what I'm dealing with here, Lark?"

"Put her on the phone," I ordered, slamming my hand down on

the steering wheel and stepping down harder on the gas pedal.

"Snitch," Mira seethed before her voice transformed into a sugary-sweet tone and she chirped, "Hey, baby."

My blood thundered in my ears, and I gripped the phone so tight that it was a wonder I didn't crush it. "Mira," I rumbled, doing my best to keep the anger out of my tone. I did not have time to venture into the middle of one of her snit fits.

Calm. Cool. Collected. That was the only way I was going to get through to her.

"Get in Braydon's car. *Now.*"

"No," she replied in the next beat.

"Get in his fucking car!" I yelled so loudly that it rattled the windows.

Yeah. That was as long as the whole calm-cool-and collected thing had lasted.

"Whitney is in there, Jeremy. I'm not leaving her."

I bit the inside of my cheek so hard that I tasted the metallic tinge of blood. "Yes. And she will still be there when I arrive in about fifteen minutes."

"I'm not leaving."

Weaving through traffic, I declared, "Well, you're not fucking going inside, either."

"Jesus, Jeremy. It's just Mateo!"

I swung a hard right onto the interstate. "Yeah, baby. That's exactly the problem. It's just *Mateo*. Do not forget who that man is. Remember what we talked about this morning? A future. A family. A forever."

Her voice gentled. "Of course I remember."

"Okay," I breathed, my anxiety starting to fade. "Then I'm asking you to please get in the car with Braydon. Go back to Guardian, where I know you'll be safe. Let *me* get your girl. And then, as soon as I get back, we can start on all of those things."

"Jeremy—"

"Mira, *please*. That's all I'm asking here. Fifteen minutes and I'll have her back to you."

The line went silent.

"Mira?" I prompted.

She huffed, but I knew I'd won. "Fine. But hurry up. I'm going crazy over here."

I blew out a ragged breath, victory singing in my veins.

Little did I know, the battle was just getting started.

Mira

I glared at Braydon as I hung up the phone.

He was returning the glare from less than a foot away.

"You're an asshole," I declared, tucking the phone into the back of my jeans.

"You're a nutjob," he declared, his tall, muscular body not moving an inch.

I rolled my eyes. "Jeremy says you're supposed to take me back to Guardian."

He smiled, and even if he was being an asshole, it was still gorgeous. "Did he now?"

I rolled my eyes again, making sure he saw it before I marched to the door of his tiny, royal-blue convertible Mercedes sports car. It was a miracle his long legs fit inside. No way it could be comfortable for him to drive something that small.

Opening the door, I glanced back at Mateo's mansion. Yes, *mansion*. For a man who lived in Miami and only visited Chicago a few times a month, it seemed like overkill. But I guessed that drug lords didn't worry about the minor details of practicality. Jeremy had made it clear he didn't trust Mateo, but I did. He'd been nothing but nice to me since the day we'd met. He'd take care of Whitney until Jeremy could get there. And only that knowledge allowed me to put my ass to Braydon's leather passenger's seat.

The minute the door clicked behind me, Braydon became unstuck and started toward the driver's side.

Abruptly, he stopped at the front of the car and turned his head to look at something over his shoulder.

I followed his gaze and saw the big iron gate at the front of the house sliding open.

At the exact same time, my phone started ringing in my pocket. I quickly dug it out and saw the same number from before flashing on the screen.

"Mateo?" I answered.

"Leaving so soon? Aren't you forgetting something?"

"See...Jeremy's on his way. He kinda wanted to be..." I trailed off when, out of the corner of my eye, I saw Braydon turn all the way around, and then his body locked up tight.

His palpable panic slammed into me. My pulse skyrocketed despite the fact that I had no idea what I was afraid of yet.

I could only see the side of his face, but the most unforgettable combination of confusion and horror twisted his handsome features.

I slung my head back toward the massive house, this time finding Whitney standing on the front porch. She was wearing a filthy men's white button-down shirt, her curly, black locks were matted to her head, and her left eye was swollen and black. She was barefoot, barely able to balance on her shaking legs, with Bitsy tucked into the crook of one of her trembling arms.

My heart stopped as I flung the car door open and took in the sight of Mateo at her side, the phone still held to his ear, his malevolent gaze locked on mine, six of his suited bodyguards standing in a perfect line behind them.

My scalp prickled, and the chill of unease traveled down my spine.

The man staring back at me wasn't the Mateo I knew.

He wasn't the man from my bar.

He wasn't even the man from Guardian.

He was the man Jeremy had warned me about.

And, suddenly, everything got a hell of a lot worse.

All at once, Braydon exploded forward, Whitney's middle name—Dawn—tearing from his lips—and, from the way it sounded, his soul as well.

One of Mateo's men stepped out from behind him, pulled a gun, and trained it on Braydon, forcing him to a stop.

"No!" I yelled, sprinting toward them.

As I ran, Whitney's scream pierced through me. "Dimples!" she cried.

Even more puzzled, I watched her launch herself in Braydon's direction, but Mateo caught her at the back of her shirt, roughly pulling her up short.

"You know him?" he asked her.

Tears fell from her eyes as she nodded repeatedly.

"Interesting," he mumbled.

Yes, it was *very* interesting, but that would have to wait for another day. A day when funerals weren't only a trigger away.

"Let her go!" I shouted without a single shred of concern for my own safety.

Mateo's lips tipped up into a sinister smile. "Mira, we need to talk."

I blinked, panic spiraling higher than ever. Whitney's dark eyes finally flittered to mine, her face crumbling all over again.

"Mir," she choked out through a sob.

My heart physically ached as I imagined what she'd been through, but I pushed the pain aside and tried my best to steady my voice. "It's going to be okay now, Whit. I promise."

Another sob shook her shoulders, but she turned her gaze back to Braydon. He was watching her with his hands in the air, a gun aimed at his chest, and paralyzing terror carved into his face.

But that terror was not because he feared for his life.

It was all for her.

I needed him to get her out of there, and fast, ending this nightmare for her once and for all.

Even if it meant walking into my own.

Straightening my shoulders, I took a step forward. "Let them go and we can have whatever conversation you'd like."

Mateo's smile stretched, and a twinkle hit his dark eyes. "That, my love, is the right answer."

Lark

According to the GPS, I was only a few miles away. Leo hadn't answered any of my calls, and it was starting to unnerve me. I had no fucking idea what to expect when I got to Mateo's. It didn't sit right with me that he'd taken Whitney back to his place and then called Mira to come get her. If he had no motives, he could have dropped her off at Guardian. Or called Leo or me to meet him somewhere.

But he'd called Mira.

He was definitely up to something, I just couldn't figure out what. My only peace came in the knowledge that Braydon had taken Mira back to Guardian.

My phone started ringing in my lap. When Braydon's number flashed on the screen, I did not delay in putting it to my ear. "What's up?"

"She went inside with him," he stated, his voice gritty and raw, barely recognizable. "He had guys guarding the door. I couldn't get back in there. I know Leo said no cops. But we need to call Caleb or whoever."

The oxygen in my car suddenly disappeared, and my gut rotted. I knew the answer before I even asked the question. I just didn't want to believe it. "Who?"

"Mira," he replied, ending my life as I knew it.

He continued to talk, but the phone fell into my lap as the most staggering pain I had ever felt sliced through me. My vision tunneled, and adrenaline hit me so hard that it jolted my body.

No fucking way.

This was not happening. This was *not* happening.

This…was…*not* happening.

Not to Mira. Not to me. Not to us.

No one. Not Kurt Benton. Not even fucking Mateo Rodriguez could take her away from me. Not after she'd promised me forever. Not after we'd made a plan. Not after I'd fucking finally gotten her back.

Suddenly, an unnatural calm washed over me.

I should have been frazzled, with desperation and fear clouding my thoughts.

But I wasn't. I was going to get her back. And whoever dared to touch her would pay.

With their lives.

I don't remember driving the last few minutes to Mateo's house, but when I arrived, Braydon's car was nowhere in sight. The gate was open, inviting me inside. I didn't hesitate as I flew all the way up the brick horseshoe driveway, and then I came to a screeching stop just inches from the porch, taking out what I was sure was a strategically planted rose garden by the front steps. After palming the forty-five I'd retrieved from the glove box, I folded out in record time, not bothering to turn the engine off. I wouldn't be there long anyway.

My heart thundered with every step toward that door. I didn't give the first fuck who was on the other side. All I knew was that Mira was somewhere in that house. And it didn't matter if I had to tear the whole goddamn thing to the ground in order to find her.

That is until a man came out of nowhere, hitting me like a battering ram from the side as he tackled me to the ground—in the most familiar way.

Mira

I was lying on a king-size four-poster bed that, on any other day, would have made me salivate. But, that day, lying in only a pair of jeans and a bra, with one of my hands tied above me, while a man I didn't know was diligently working on securing the other, I had other things to think about.

"Jeremy is going to kill you," I told Mateo as he paced the foot of the bed.

He barked a laugh and then swept his furious gaze over my chest and my neck. "Not before I kill him. You look like you were fucking beaten."

"They're hickeys!"

He stopped and glared at me. "Perfect. Then that is what I'll call the black-and-blue bruises my fists cover him in before putting a bullet in his head."

"Stop," I whispered before sucking in sharply as the rope cinched painfully tight around my wrist.

"Easy," Mateo growled at the man. "You leave one goddamn mark on her, I will feed your carcass to the rats."

"Ew!" I whined.

"Shut up, Mira. I am not in the mood to deal with that fucking mouth of yours. If I had known what was beneath that scarf last night..." He trailed off, his jaw ticking as he resumed his pacing.

For fuck's sake, how was this my life?

Oh, right.

Kurt.

I startled when the flash of a Polaroid camera nearly blinded me.

Mateo shook the image for a second before throwing it onto the bed beside me. "Fucking disgusting, a man leaves marks like that."

"Says the man tying me to a fucking bed!" I fired off.

Ignoring me, he continued to rant to himself. "Her ass? Maybe. I've left more than a few palm prints in the heat of passion. But for fuck's sake, I could inspect the man's dental work from the bites he left on your chest."

A guy I didn't recognize poked his head into the room. "Her man just pulled up."

My stomach fluttered at the thought of Jeremy being there, but then, just as quickly, it dropped when Mateo's eyes flared wide and his lip curled into a snarl.

"That motherfucker," he breathed, marching to the door.

Oh, shit. Oh, shit. Oh, shit.

Jeremy was there, probably pissed off to the ends of the earth that I'd gone inside the house, and Mateo wanted to kill him for having put hickeys on me. Both of them were probably armed. And…well, testosterone and all. This was not going to end well.

"Mateo!" I screamed as he disappeared through the door. "Oh, God! Please don't kill him!"

"No promises!" he called through the open door.

My heart pounded against my ribs, regret suddenly engulfing me. "Please!" I cried. "I got pre-pregnant today! Don't take that away from me!"

The deep, masculine chuckle from the chair in the corner caught my attention, reminding me he was in the room.

I cut my gaze to him and hysterically asked, "He won't really kill him, will he?"

Leo smirked, his humor-filled chocolaty-brown eyes meeting mine. "No, babe. He won't kill him."

Lark

"How ya holding up?" Caleb asked, walking into the prison's private visitation room and patting my shoulder before giving it a squeeze.

I turned a murderous glower his way. "How the fuck do you think I'm doing?"

His brows shot up in surprise as he set a manila file folder on the table. "Normally, I'd tell you to chill the hell out, but given our current situation, feel free to keep that up."

I pushed to my feet and the metal folding chair tipped over backward, making a deafening crack as it hit the tile and then echoed around the small room. I moved to what I knew was a two-way mirror and inspected my face. My lip was split, there was a huge gash in my hairline that probably needed stitches, and the road rash that spread temple to chin from Mateo's sidewalk made me look like Two-Face.

The list of people I needed to kill was growing longer by the minute, and as much as I loved the woman, Mira had managed to brand her name at the very top.

"He'll be here in two," he said, casually settling in the chair and crossing his legs ankle to knee.

I looked at the mirror and replied, "This is fucking insane." But I wasn't talking to Caleb.

"You are not wrong," Caleb replied. "I lose my job over this shit, my wife will slaughter me. But she'll do it real slow and sweet, so you know it's torture but you can't complain about it. First, she'll stop cooking, acting like she's tired from work and the kids, when in reality she knows I hate ham sandwiches, but I can't bitch because she's tired. Then she'll start sleeping naked but telling me she's not in the mood. I mean, she always eventually gives in, but Christ, she makes me work for it. Then she'll start talking about having more kids, which she knows I would fucking love but wouldn't be able to afford because, ya know, unemployed and all. Seriously, Lark. The woman is a domestic terrorist."

I continued to stare at the mirror, ignoring his absurd tangent about his wife. My heart was pounding, my chest was heaving, and I'd been on the brink of explosion since I had been hauled into Mateo's house to find Mira in a fucking bra, covered in bruises, and tied to a bed. There was a part of me that I knew would never recover from that. I only thought I'd withered the day she'd left seventeen years ago. But, when I'd seen her like that, the fear I'd felt corroding my insides guaranteed that I'd never be the same.

It was the exact moment I knew that it had to end.

The door to the room buzzed, signaling his entry, but I kept my eyes on the mirror and looked through my reflection.

"Ho. Lee. Shit," Kurt drawled as he was escorted into the room. His voice was exactly the same as it had been the last time I'd heard it, and just like that day all those years ago, the nonchalance in his tone caused my blood to boil over.

It took every ounce of restraint I could muster, and there was very little left at this point, but I managed not to turn. I listened as the guard anchored his cuffs to the table before the sound of chair legs scraped the floor.

But still I didn't turn. I didn't trust myself to see him. Not yet.

"You need me to stay?" someone, who I assumed was a corrections officer asked Caleb.

"Nah," he replied. "I got it from here. I'll let you know when we're done."

"Jeremy fucking Lark," Kurt laughed. "Christ. To what do I owe this unfortunate pleasure?" The familiarity in his laugh made my skin crawl. It had once been followed by my own laugh as we'd talked about anything and everything under the sun.

I continued to stare at the mirror. My hazel eyes stared back at me.

My girls had their mother's greens. Her red hair. Her fair complexion.

What would Mira's and my kids look like? Would they get her deep-brown eyes surrounded by dark lashes, all innocent and angelic? Would they get her thick brown hair or honey-tanned skin? What about her smile and the way it could light even the darkest night?

I blinked at the mirror, a battered and beaten man blinking back at me, and wondered, *Will I ever get to have those children at all?*

And then a smile tipped the corners of my battered mouth.

I would have that. I knew it to the marrow of my bones.

I would have *her*, and I would give her the *babies*, and then Mira and I would finally be able to live the life we were always meant to have.

For seventeen years, he'd played us both.

Today, we turned the tables.

I was walking out of that prison with everything I'd ever wanted. And I'd leave behind the man who had stolen it from me—from her—to rot and wither until his dying breath.

Only then did I turn around.

He barked a laugh and reclined in his chair as far as his cuffs would allow him. "Fuck, man, what happened to your face?"

Silently, I walked to the chair and lowered myself into it, allowing myself a minute to take him in. Time had not been kind to Kurt Benton. His face was round, his frame was carrying at least an extra forty pounds, and none of it was muscle. His belly protruded beneath the gray prison-issued sweatshirt. His blond hair had been buzzed, but there was no missing the receding hairline that was only inches from disappearing completely.

Jesus, he was six months younger than I was, but he looked like he was at least a decade older.

"What the fuck happened to *your* face? You look like you haven't slept in a year. What's a matter? Your cellmate not sharing the covers?" It was a cheap shot, but I didn't waste a second taking it.

His eyes flashed dark, but he smirked. "You know, you're looking a little tired yourself there, asshole. You still crying yourself to sleep over my wife?"

"Ex-wife," I corrected through clenched teeth. I had to fight the urge to dive across the table and let him know just whose wife she was—or was going to be. But I'd promised Caleb I'd keep it together.

I had to.

For Mira.

"She'll always be mine, Jeremy. But I'm taking that you are still crying over her. I don't blame you. She's always had the sweetest ass. And that mouth?" The bastard winked.

I had to give it to him—he still had some balls.

I shrugged. "What the hell would I be crying about? I've had Mira's sweet ass pressed up against me and her mouth moaning my name. Nah, man. No tears here."

His smile instantly fell. Putting his forearms on the edge of the table, he angled his upper body toward me and hissed, "Bullshit. You were never man enough to take her from me. You might have gotten between her legs a time or two, but even Mira knew you were too big of a fucking pussy to ever take care of her."

"Take care of her?" I whispered ominously. "Take. Fucking. *Care* of her?" My blood ran cold, but my anger became volcanic. "Is that what you think you've done for all these years? You think *you've* taken care of her?" I pushed to my feet slowly and controlled for fear of erupting. "Is that why, not four fucking days ago, your fucked-up friend put a gun to her head?"

"I had nothing to do with that!" he snarled.

My face vibrated as I yelled, "You put her in that life! You had everything to do with that!"

He clamped his mouth shut.

"Mira is not like you, Kurt. She didn't have the taste for trouble. She just wanted to make a life for herself. And you...you fucking piece of shit, you dragged her down so goddamn low she could never claw her way back up." I sucked in a deep breath through my nose and shook my head. "And now. Those fucking men you stole all that money from? When they couldn't get to you, you knew they'd come for her. Fucking ruining her life wasn't enough for you. You had to throw her to the goddamn wolves, too?"

Nervously, he flicked his gaze to where Caleb was looming in the corner before looking back to me. "I...I don't know what you're talking about. I didn't steal any money."

I slammed my fists down on the table and roared, "Liar! You fucking killed her."

His whole body jerked, and panic flashed in his eyes. "What the hell are you talking about?"

I grabbed the top file Caleb had set on the table and flipped it open. "I can't get her out of this one, Kurt. This is not my world." I peeled the top picture off and slid it his way. I didn't need to look at it. I'd been there when it had been staged, and even though I'd known that it was fake, seeing her like that had damn near caused me to have a nervous breakdown. I'd had to be dragged from the room when Mateo put that gun to her head.

Johnson had already fucked my face up when he'd tackled me outside the door. But I'd gotten the gash and split lip thanks to Leo as he'd tried to restrain me. Those fucking bastards. They had known I'd never go for that bullshit. No fucking way I'd risk putting Mira in the middle of this shit with Mateo.

But he'd lured her to his house and given her the choice, and she'd agreed.

Behind my fucking back. Without discussing it with me first.

I didn't think I'd ever been so pissed at a woman in my life as I'd been when Mira had filled me in on their little plan.

The one thing we all knew about Kurt was that he loved Mira. It was sick and twisted and controlling and ugly.

But, to Kurt, that was love.

"See, that's the thing about the world, baby," Mira had whispered. "Life is not black and white. There is an entire spectrum of grays that we forget about. Good guys aren't always good. And bad guys aren't always bad. We know all too well that choices define a person. Choices we make with our heads. But even the darkest souls still have a heart. He manipulated me for years. It's time we return the favor."

That fucking woman.

As soon as I got her home, slid a ring on her finger, and put a baby in her belly, I was going to unleash immortal hell on her. Though seeing her wearing my ring and carrying my baby would probably turn that hell into a seriously lackluster tongue-lashing.

I had been the one who'd insisted on being there when Caleb broke the news to Kurt. I wanted to witness firsthand as the agony slashed through him when he found out what Mateo had done to her. I wanted to feed off his pain when he realized she was as good as dead because of him. I wanted to relish in the moment when he was forced to make a decision—him or her. And I wanted to bask in the glory of ruining him while freeing her.

So there I was, standing over him, watching the blood drain from his face as he stared at a polaroid of Mira in a bra, covered in bruises and bite marks, her head turned away from the camera, Mateo kneeling on the bed with one hand at her throat and the other holding a gun to her head.

"I have two hours to get this motherfucker his money," I rumbled. After grabbing the rest of the pictures of Mira in various tortured poses—all of which I was going to have to have burned from my retinas when this was all over—I fanned them out in front of him. "You know Mateo. You know what he's capable of. Where is it, Kurt? Just tell me where the money is and let me get her back."

His fingers shook as he tenderly touched her face in one of the pictures.

He was still sitting in the chair, but I could see it.

The man was on his knees.

And, after everything he'd done, I fucking loved it.

"I..." He flipped his gaze to Caleb again and then back to the pictures. "He won't give her back. He's always had a thing for her. It's not even his money."

Oh, fuck!

My heart stopped. I did not need Kurt to be logical about this. It was the only hole any of us had been able to see in the deception. We'd hoped that showing him Mira like that would be enough to keep him emotional and irrational.

"He..." I started with no real explanation in mind.

Thankfully, Caleb did. Sauntering over to the table, he said, "Mateo paid off your debts. He's been protecting Mira from the shit you left behind for years. Problem came when she hooked up with Lark. It did not make him happy to see her moving on with someone who was not him. He made a decision, and it's come down to either her or the money." Caleb sat on the edge of the table and picked a picture up. "Now. What's your decision? Her"—he blindly stabbed a finger at one of the pictures, never breaking eye contact—"or the money?"

Kurt swallowed hard and tilted his head back until his gaze met mine. "I'd have turned it over years ago, but they never got me on the money laundering. If I cop to this now, I'm never getting out of here.

They'll add time to my sentence and I will *die* in this prison, Jeremy."

The despair that laced his voice gave me pause, and for a brief moment, I *thought* about feeling guilty. I swear there was *almost* a pang of guilt in my gut.

But then I remembered when Mira had been shaking in my arms when she'd realized that her life had been a lie. And I remembered when Mira had clung to me on the street after Steve Browel had tried to kidnap her. And then I remembered the way the tears had pooled in her eyes when I'd told her that I wanted a future with her.

And then I remembered that, while Mateo Rodriguez had not in fact kidnapped Mira, the threat that someone would was very real. If we couldn't find that money and publicly break her ties with Kurt, there was good chance I really would lose her one day.

And that alone made it all too easy to stare my ex–best friend directly in the eye and tell him the God's honest truth. "And she will die if you don't."

CHAPTER TWENTY-SEVEN

Mira

Two hours later...

NEVER IN MY LIFE HAD I WANTED KURT BENTON TO PICK ME.

Jeremy, yes. Always and forever.

But...Kurt?

Yet, as I'd stood at the mirror, waiting to see if my ex-husband loved me as much as he'd always claimed, I'd never wanted something more.

I'd burst into tears the moment he'd asked for a piece of paper to write down the location of the money. Leo had pulled me into a hug, but it was Jeremy's hazel eyes, which flew to mine from the other side of the mirror, that had given me the most comfort. He couldn't see me, but he knew exactly where I was.

We couldn't be sure if Kurt had lied about the money or not, so despite my pleadings, no one had been willing to let him know that I was safe and sound.

I'd have given anything to see his face when he realized he'd been played.

But I'd have given more to finally be free of his shit and able to live the rest of my life with Jeremy, his kids, and hopefully *our* kids one day without fear.

We were now sitting at Guardian, waiting for word from Caleb.

I was in Jeremy's lap, trailing my finger up and down Bitsy's back, while he bitched at me for having agreed to Mateo's plan without discussing it first. I was ignoring him for the most part. And it was obvious that he knew, because every so often, he'd sigh and order, "Say you understand me, Mira!"

I'd hum my agreement and then go right back to loving on my dog while nestled against the man who loved me.

On our way back from the prison, Jeremy had stopped at the hospital so I could see Whitney. I hadn't been able to get her in my arms fast enough. We were both sobbing as I'd hugged her harder and tighter than ever before. She hadn't been forthcoming about what exactly Jonah had done to her over the last few days, but she assured me that she was fine. And, with her clean bill of heath, I knew she was—at least physically. Her hollow eyes as she stared back at me said otherwise.

They were keeping her overnight for observation, but I offered for her to stay with me and Jeremy indefinitely upon her release. She refused. Which was probably a good thing, considering that an angry vein on Braydon's head started dancing the minute I made the suggestion.

Why he called her Dawn, I had no idea, but there was no doubt he was the mysterious Dimples she'd been dating until recently. I couldn't say that I wasn't happy about this. His calling me King Kong in drag aside, I liked him for her. And, as he'd lounged in the bed beside her, his big body wedged in the small space, his arm curled around her shoulders, her hand resting on his thigh, I'd assumed they were picking things back up.

"Say you understand me, Mira!" Jeremy demanded once more.

"Mmmhmm," I replied, dipping my lips to kiss Bitsy on the top of her head.

"She's not fucking listening," he mumbled.

I grinned and looked up at him. "No, Hyde. I'm not. You give me back my man and that might change."

"So you missed the part about us going ring shopping tomorrow?"

My back shot straight, and I climbed off his lap so I could see him better. "Seriously?"

He glowered. "No, Mira. I didn't say that at all."

I slapped him on the chest, but I did it gently so as not to jostle my snoozing Bitsy too much. "You're a jerk."

He grinned. "I am? So I guess, now that I have your attention, I shouldn't ask if you maybe want to go ring shopping tomorrow?"

My whole face smiled. "Seriously?"

"No." He laughed.

I slapped him again on the chest, harder this time. "Stop doing that!"

He laughed and came to me in order to press a kiss on my lips. "Tomorrow, we are going to get the rest of your shit from your house. Assuming Mateo and Caleb give us the all clear on the heat being off your back, I have to get Melissa's power turned back on, and then you two need to schedule a face-to-face to discuss when and how you are going to meet Sophie and Amelia."

I grinned. I liked all of that. A lot.

"You know, after today, I think I can handle your ex-wife."

He blew out a ragged breath. "I'm glad one of us can. Because I'm going to walk into the line of fire and tell her that, the day *after* tomorrow, I'm taking you ring shopping and then making you a Lark by the end of the week."

My straight back shot even straighter, and I bit my bottom lip. "Seriously?"

He laughed, deep and rich. "Yeah, baby. Seriously."

Careful not to crush Bitsy, I giggled and launched myself into his arms.

Yes, I might have been a thirty-six—creeping up on thirty-seven—year-old woman, but when the man of your dreams says he's going to take you ring shopping and then make you his wife by the end of the week, you are still allowed to giggle and launch yourself into his arms.

I was still in the middle of my impending-engagement celebration when Leo came into the room and announced, "We're good."

The air rushed from my lungs as Jeremy rushed to his feet and took me with him. He gently placed me beside him and asked, "As in good, good?"

Leo nodded. "Caleb found the cash, along with all of Kurt's books hidden behind a bunch of shit in an old storage unit registered to Jonah Sheehan. Bad news is he turned his back and I'll be damned if that shit didn't just run away."

I gasped. "What?"

"Yeah. It was the craziest thing." Leo smiled huge, scratching the back of his head. "I mean, luckily, Caleb got enough in the books and records to make a shit-ton of arrests. And keep Kurt locked up for the rest of his life. All good things for the city. But the cash just vanished. It was like a known drug lord, as you call him, Mira, just drove up in a U-Haul, had five guys load up three million dollars, and then drove off."

I blinked, utterly confused. "It was *like* that happened…or that *did* happen?"

He exaggerated a shrug. "I don't know. But, hypothetically, if that really did happen, I'm assuming word would be out on the streets that someone else besides Mira York has possession of that money now. And again…*hypothetically*, I wouldn't suggest opening another Sip and Sud any time soon." He paused as my face fell, but he held a hand up, stopping me from speaking. "But I hear Apollo might be looking for someone to take Murphy's off his hands now that he's working for me full time."

My nose started to sting, and my throat got thick. Covering my mouth with my hand, I asked a muffled, "It's over? Like really over? I don't have to be his queen anymore?"

Jeremy hooked me at my hips, and pulled me into his side, kissing the top of my head. "It's over, baby. It's just me and you from here on out."

That warmth inside me spread, filling me in unimaginable ways. "And your girls," I whispered.

I could feel it as his lips formed a wide smile. "And my girls," he confirmed.

"And our babies," I squeaked, my free hand spreading across my belly.

With his lips against my ear, he agreed. "And as many as you want."

Bitsy wiggled in my arm, as if reminding me that she was still there.

"And Bitsy."

Jeremy didn't speak again, but he pressed another kiss into my head.

But it was Leo who had the last word.

"Babe. Everyone knows that the queen is the most powerful piece on the board." He walked over, offered Jeremy one of his hands in a shake, and then patted my back with his other. "Welcome to Guardian, Mira."

EPILOGUE

Mira

One week later...

THE SOUND OF HIS ALARM BLASTED THROUGH OUR BEDROOM. Okay, so maybe blasted was a bit of an exaggeration, but that was the way it felt when it jarred me from sleep.

"Snooze," I croaked.

He chuckled. "I think hitting snooze four times is enough."

I stretched out, my front flush with his side. "Noooo. Just one more time. Everyone knows five is the magical number."

He transferred Bitsy from his chest—her new favorite spot to sleep—to mine and whispered, "Okay, you go for magic with number five while I take a shower."

I smiled and cuddled her in close, the sounds of Jeremy starting the shower quickly lulling me back to sleep.

The day after the men of Guardian (and Mateo) had freed me of Kurt's mess, Jeremy had taken me back to my old house to pick up the rest of my things. But the moment we'd walked into my bedroom, his hand tightly wrapped around mine, I knew there was only one thing I wanted to take with me.

Jeremy.

That house had never been my home. It had been my refuge from my life with Kurt. I had a shitty bed, an ancient dresser, a wobbly nightstand, and that fucking coffee table I'd bought after my divorce had been finalized.

I didn't want those things.

And more, I didn't want those memories following me into my new life with Jeremy.

I was grateful I'd had those possessions when I'd needed them. But someone else could have them now.

I just wanted Jeremy.

I didn't care where we went or how we got there. As long as I had him, the rest didn't matter.

Sherri and Tammy were more than happy to keep my things. With the room being furnished, it would be easier for them to rent it out.

So, after hugs and murmured goodbyes, I'd ridden away, the armrest up, Jeremy pressed close to my side, and I'd watched a life of fear and regret disappear in the rearview mirror.

His deep, rasping voice woke me again. "Time to get up, crazy. Apollo's expecting you to sign the papers to Murphy's at ten."

"I'm not signing those papers," I grumbled, using my left hand to sweep my hair out of my face.

A giant, white smile curled his mouth as he stared down at me, the most amazing twinkle shining in his eyes.

"What?" I asked.

He continued to stare—and smile—as he tightened the towel around his hips. "Nothing." He flipped the lamp on.

My lids slammed shut, my eyes objecting to the sudden brightness. "Jesus, a little warning."

He chuckled. "Get up. You're signing those papers."

When I pushed up onto my elbows, Bitsy jumped off me and trotted to the end of the bed. "No, I'm not," I replied. "He wants ten thousand dollars, Jeremy. *Ten thousand dollars.*"

He dipped low and kissed me. It was chaste, but he was still smiling like a maniac.

I narrowed my eyes on him. "Why are you so chipper this morning?"

He shook his head, and that damn smile grew. "No reason."

He was so full of shit. While he wasn't exactly a bear in the mornings, he wasn't known to be Mary Sunshine, either.

I rolled my eyes and tried to flip over, but he caught my hip. He sank down to the mattress. Even cranky and half asleep, I was unable to resist the opportunity to curl around him.

Gliding his hand up my neck to cup my jaw, he ordered, "You're signing those papers, Mira."

"Ten thousand dollars, Jeremy," I repeated.

"How much you got left of your Sip and Sud savings?"

Ten thousand, three hundred, nine dollars, and twenty-nine cents.

Of the original twenty-five grand I'd saved, I'd spent a large chunk of money over the last week. The first thing I had done was cut a check to Whitney for a year's worth of rent. She was wearing a brave face and seemed to be doing better after the whole Jonah ordeal, but it would catch up to her eventually. Guilt consumed me every time I saw her dim eyes, where a spark had once been. She was staying at Braydon's place in the short term. But I knew Whitney too well to assume she was moving in with him permanently. And, now that I was living with Jeremy, she wasn't going to be able to afford a place on her own. I wished like hell I could have done more for her, but it had been a miracle that she'd even accepted that check from me at all.

After that, I'd spent a little bit of my remaining savings on new furniture for Jeremy's living room. It probably wasn't my smartest splurge, considering I didn't have a job yet. But he'd furnished the rest of the house. One room seemed like the least I could do.

I stared up at him defiantly. "That's not the point."

He grinned again. "You need to borrow some money?"

"No. I have ten grand," I huffed. "You know that. And, somehow, Apollo magically knows that too. Which is why I'm not signing those papers. That building alone is worth a cool million. It's in a prime location in the middle of Chicago. Ten thousand dollars wouldn't cover the cost of buying the barstools."

He caught my arm at the wrist and rested my hand on his thigh.

"Then it sounds like a good deal, Mira."

"It sounds like charity."

His smile somehow got wider. "He's keeping fifty percent. That's hardly charity. He needs someone to run it. Someone with experience. Hell, you'll be helping him out. The man is worth a fortune. But, if it will ease your conscience, just remember you'll still be putting money in his pocket every month while he does his thing for Leo."

He had a point. Ten thousand dollars was a steal. But I hated the idea that he was offering me that bar out of pity. I'd had enough of that in my life. I didn't need more.

"Baby," he whispered. Soft. Sweet. Gentle. Jeremy. "I have to get to work. Promise me you'll sign the papers. This is a really good opportunity for you." He kissed me again and rested our joined hands on my stomach. "For *us*."

Us. God, I loved the sound of that. I wasn't pregnant yet. But, each time he talked about it, a bubble of excitement swelled inside me.

I did need a job. And having one that enabled me to do something I loved, make my own schedule, and earn more than just tips sounded like the pot of gold at the end of a rainbow.

Sucking in a breath, I relented. "Fiiiine. I'll sign the damn papers."

He winked. "Good. Now, I need to get to work because I just took a chunk out of my savings account that's going to need to be replaced sooner rather than later." He smiled so big that I thought his face was going to split in half as he gave the ring on my finger a pointed wiggle.

My entire body locked up tight, and my heart stopped.

Oh. My. *God*.

It was a ring that had *not* been there when I'd fallen asleep the night before.

A ring that had *not* been there when he'd woken me up in the middle of the night by sliding in deep from behind.

A ring that had *not* been there when I'd drifted off to sleep in his arms, naked and sated.

But it was a ring that completely and totally explained the shit-eating grin he'd been wearing all morning.

"What did you do?" I hissed.

True to his word, Jeremy had taken me ring shopping.

It hadn't gone well. Like, at all.

And it was precisely the reason why I still hadn't become a Lark yet.

Two hours into our shopping excursion, Hyde and my bitchy attitude had had an all-out brawl.

For too long, I'd had a man who'd bought me things and then treated me like shit. Now, I had a man who treated me like his most prized possession. I didn't need *things* from Jeremy to feel loved. So I'd picked out something small and tasteful. (Read: cheap.) Then I'd attempted to explain to Jeremy that we were just starting our lives together. There was no point spending a small fortune on a ring I didn't need.

He had promptly lost his mind.

"Seventeen years and you think I'm gonna buy you that piece of shit?" he'd said, swinging an angry arm toward the jewelry case.

I'd swung my angry arm out to the jewelry case he was standing next to, all of the price tags containing at least one extra zero than the rings in mine. "Seventeen years and you think I want to start our marriage out with that kind of debt?"

"I got fucking money, Mira," he'd growled, thoroughly offended.

"Fan-fucking-tastic. Let's keep it that way," I'd retorted snottily.

He'd glowered.

I'd scowled.

We'd continued to argue—less than quietly.

Then we'd been asked to leave.

Without a ring.

For five days, we hadn't been able to broach the ring topic without an argument.

Long story short, this was why waking up with what felt like a very large diamond on my finger had made my heart stop—and my blood boil.

He quirked an eyebrow at me. "How is it possible that I somehow got the only woman on the planet who wants to bitch about her man buying her an engagement ring that didn't come out of a gumball machine?" He stood up and sauntered to his closet while continuing to mutter, "It was bad enough I had to sneak the damn thing on your finger in the middle of the night like a goddamn ninja just to dodge a fucking snit fit."

"Who says you dodged it?" I snapped, but it held no heat. Probably because I was too busy inspecting the cushion-cut diamond surrounded by a halo of diamonds with even more freaking diamonds set into the band.

To say it was gorgeous did it no justice.

The ring was spectacular.

And completely unnecessary.

But still so ridiculously stunning that it made tears pool in my eyes.

"We talked about this," I whispered, petting the center stone as though it could feel the affection something that beautiful so obviously deserved.

He tugged a pair of black boxer briefs on. "No. *You* talked about this. I pretended to listen and then did whatever the hell I wanted." He flashed me a smile over his shoulder. "A trick I learned from you."

My mouth fell open. "I don't do that!"

"Oh, no?" He stepped into a pair of charcoal-gray slacks and turned to face me. "Then explain to me how I came home two days ago to a fucking couch and loveseat complete with yellow throw pillows and coordinating wall art?"

I pressed my lips together. Yeah, okay. I'd done that.

"We needed furniture," I argued, but I did it while once again stroking my ring.

He smirked. "And you needed a ring."

"No, I really—"

"Stop," he ordered gruffly.

Surprised by his sudden attitude, I tore my gaze off my finger and found him prowling in my direction. His body was taut, the muscles in his neck straining, and the ridges on his stomach rippling. And yes, while still pissed off, I took the time to appreciate all of those things.

Bending over, he caught the back of my neck and lifted me to meet him halfway. "Do you have any idea how long I've waited to see my ring on your finger?"

My mouth dried as guilt washed over me. Yeah. I definitely shouldn't have fought him on the ring.

"Baby, I—"

His blazing gaze flicked to my hand. "To know that I gave you that? To know that I could finally *afford* to give you that? To see it while you sleep in my bed, under my roof, living a life *I* provided for us?"

Chills pebbled my skin as I reached up with my right hand and cupped his cheek. "Jeremy, I—"

His feet remained on the floor, but he bent lower and rested his forehead on mine. Using his thumb, he twisted my ring back and forth. "To see it when I make love to you, knowing I get to spend the rest of my life with you?"

My chest ached, but not from pain. Something only weeks earlier I'd thought was impossible.

"Baby," I breathed, brushing my lips with his.

His lids fluttered closed. "Jesus, Mira. That ring. It's not about money. It's about us. You do not get to give me shit about this. You do not get to have a snit fit. You get to say yes or no. That's all."

It was a miracle my heart was still beating. That was my man: bossy, demanding, and still breathtakingly romantic at the same time.

I nodded and then slipped the ring off my finger.

He must have felt the movement, because his eyes popped open, a storm brewing within them.

"Mira," he warned.

I pressed a kiss to his lips to silence him while dragging his hand off my neck. Blindly, I placed the ring in his palm and then closed his fingers around it.

Only then did I whisper, "Yes." I lifted my left hand between us and wiggled my ring finger at him. "If it's so important to you that I wear what could be our future children's college tuition around on my finger, I'll be more than happy to oblige you. *But*, it's important to *me* that *you* know I would still say yes with no ring. I love you. I'd marry you, Jeremy Lark, barefoot in the middle of the woods without a dollar to either of our names. Just like I should have all those years ago."

His face softened, and his eyes lit. "I know. And I love you too. Which is exactly why I want you to have this. You may not need it. But I've spent seventeen years of my life wanting to buy it for you. Let me have this moment, Mira."

I smiled, the tears finally rolling down my cheeks. I could do that. It wasn't like wearing an unbelievably gorgeous ring was going to be a hardship. I'd spent seventeen years of my life wanting him to have bought it for me. Maybe something a little smaller and more cost effective. But who was I to argue?

"It's beautiful, Jeremy."

Putting his knee to the mattress, he tore the covers back. Poor Bitsy barely made it out of the way in time before he climbed back into the bed. "*You're* beautiful, Mira."

His heavy weight came down on top of me, and then his mouth sealed over mine in a toe-curling kiss.

In that moment, with his tongue swirling with mine, our hearts beating in harmony, and a future greater than I could have ever dreamed of laid out in front of us, it was easy to forget that the bruises inside us had ever existed.

And the very next day, when we said, "I do," at the courthouse, my engagement ring blinding everyone in the room, our hearts full, unexplainable happiness intoxicating us both, it was easy to see that those bruises were gone for good.

One week later...

The house was quiet. I was sitting on the couch in the basement, my feet curled under me, a mug of coffee in my hand, my phone in the other. That once torturous Facebook app was open, my husband's profile pulled up and a picture on the screen.

Me and my girls.

That was what the caption read.

Short. Simple. To the point.

Yet they were the most magical, glorious, beautiful, life-altering words that had ever been spoken—or, in this case, typed.

The picture was stunning. Well, actually, it was horrible. My hair was plastered to my face with sweat, and my makeup had started to run after a day spent playing chase at the park. But Jeremy was beside me, Amelia on his lap and Sophie on mine, and all of our smiles were aimed at the camera. Yeah. That was what made the picture so stunning.

When I heard Jeremy's heavy footfalls upstairs, I pressed the little "like" button and then opened my text messages to send him a quick note to let him know I was in the basement.

It was our first weekend with his daughters, and I'd been working myself into a frenzy while trying to make a good impression. This had included a homemade picnic at the park, cooking breakfast for dinner, and then letting them stay up late to eat ice cream and watch a movie. They'd passed out about halfway through, when the sugar rush had worn off, but I'd sat there on the couch, Jeremy's arm slung around my shoulders, our legs tangled together on the ottoman, and watched them sleep for over an hour.

God, those little girls were beautiful. Being with them had been so surreal. I'd expected to feel that familiar pang of jealousy I'd experienced when I'd seen their pictures, but the minute they'd walked through the front door, Jeremy acting as a pack mule for the massive bags of toys and clothes they hadn't needed to bring with them, I'd fallen head-over-heels in love with them. How could I not? They were a part of him.

But, as the day had worn on, I'd fallen in love with them because they were the sweetest, most precious girls I'd ever met.

Amelia was a daddy's girl through and through, so she spent most of our first night together in his lap, talking incessantly about whatever flittered through her mind. Sophie, on the other hand, was all too interested in me. Or rather my makeup, my jewelry, my heels, and, last but not least, my perfume. We were all going to be in trouble when she hit her teen years.

Teen years I was going to get to be a part of.

A few days earlier, Melissa and I'd had our little chat about my involvement in the girls' lives. She wasn't a bitch about it. She definitely wasn't warm and welcoming, either, though. I couldn't blame her. Those were her babies. It was her job to protect them, even when she didn't need to. I left that day knowing she and I were never going to be friends, but it meant the world to me that she was willing to allow me to be a part of their family at all. She could have made it hell on all of us—especially Jeremy. But she didn't. She might not have liked how quickly our relationship had progressed. Hell, she might not have liked me at all. But she loved her kids, so she put her own feelings aside and did what was best for them. I respected the hell out of her for that.

The basement door creaked as Jeremy opened it. He quietly shut it before padding down the stairs. "What are you doing down here?"

"I didn't want to wake up the girls."

He smirked as he made his way to me with a steaming mug. "Baby, you sipping your coffee in the kitchen isn't going to wake them up. As late as they stayed up last night, I'm not sure a marching band in their room could wake them."

I laughed and then set my cup on the end table. "Better safe than sorry. I'm exhausted. I'll need at least one refill to keep up with them today."

"It's probably best you make that two. They turn into gremlins on Saturdays."

I giggled. "Good to know."

Smiling, he sat down, slid his arm around the back of the couch, and turned to face me. "Hey, you know those pictures of the girls you hung upstairs? The one on the left is uneven. We should fix that today."

I jerked my head back. "What? No, it's not. I used a level."

He leaned over me and set his coffee beside mine. Staying close, he intently held my gaze. "Yeah, it is."

I twisted my lips. "Are you talking about the one to the left of the couch or the one to the left of the chair?"

"The one to the right of the chair. To the left of the couch."

Thoroughly confused about what picture he was talking about, I asked, "Wait, you mean the picture of Amelia on the slide?"

His eyes narrowed on me. "I thought that was Sophie."

Rolling my eyes, I replied arrogantly, "Trust me. It's Amelia."

Spoiler alert part three: This is the scene where the Zombie Mira, who had been parading around in my already dead body, finally dies—from embarrassment.

He sucked in a sharp breath and then ominously whispered, "I fucking knew it."

I swayed away from him, but it was worthless because he had me caged into the corner of the sofa. "You knew what?"

He laughed. "Jesus Christ. Are you shitting me here?"

"Um," I drawled, shifting my eyes from side to side before giving them back to him. "It's hard to say because I have no clue what you are talking about."

"Oh my sweet, sweet lying wife," he murmured, chuckling to himself. "I thought I was going crazy. But you got me good. I had no fucking idea you could lie like that."

I stared up at him in bewilderment. "What are you talking about? I haven't lied about anything."

Hooking his arm at the back of my legs, he dragged me down the couch until I was flat on my back. He settled on his side beside me, resting his head in his palm, and stared down while his lips twitched with amusement. "The day the girls were born, we had to paint Sophie's nails pink so we didn't switch them. I still struggle with telling them apart if they aren't talking or looking straight at me. But you, Pinocchio, can tell them apart with no problems despite that you've only spent one day with them."

Oh, shit.

I cut my gaze away, mumbling, "They don't look that much alike."

He barked a laugh. "Baby, their daycare teachers get confused when they wear different shoes to school. They *do* look that much alike."

Sucking in a deep breath, I gave him my eyes back. "Maybe I'm just good at stuff like that."

He nodded, completely unconvinced. "I considered that yesterday when you corrected me *twice* when I called them the wrong names. But then I remembered how you mysteriously knew where I worked the day you called me and that, the first time I brought you here, you'd thought I'd been living in my house for a while. *And* how you knew Sophie, not Amelia, liked dresses and tiaras. So I got to thinking."

Oh, shit. Oh, shit. Oh, shit.

My stomach knotted as I tried to squirm out from under him. "I should probably start breakfast. The girls will be up soon."

He held me tight to prevent my escape and dipped low, nuzzling his nose with mine while whispering, "You've been stalking me, baby."

My heart slammed in my chest, panic and embarrassment heating my cheeks. "We're married and live together. It's hard *not* to stalk you."

He chuckled and then swept his lips across mine. "No, baby. You've been stalking me for *years*."

I scoffed. "You're crazy."

"Oh, I'm crazy?" he asked, incredulous. "Mira, a few minutes ago, I got a notification on my phone that my high school English teacher liked my picture of us on Facebook."

Oh, shit. Damn. Fuck.

But that wasn't even the worst part.

He finished with, "Which is really extraordinary if you think about it, considering I heard she died two years ago."

My entire face went up in flames. "Wow, that's..." Silently cursing that beautiful picture for making me forget that I was still signed in as Mary Collier, I once again tried to make a break for it.

Not shockingly, Jeremy stopped me. "Oh, no, you don't. I believe it's time we had a talk about how much you seem to know about me."

Shit. I was cornered. Literally and figuratively. I could have gone on with the lies, but it was useless. Honestly, it was a miracle in and of itself that I'd been able to keep the ruse up for as long as I had. My ability to lie had not improved with age.

Unable to get away from him, I did the only thing I could do and screwed my eyes shut so I didn't have to face him when I finally admitted, "It was a…um…difficult stage in my life."

"The kind of difficult that makes you start a fake Facebook profile pretending to be a seventy-year-old high school English teacher to stalk your ex-boyfriend?" he teased.

Prying one eye open, I snapped, "I am one step away from dying of embarrassment and you're enjoying this?"

He grinned and brushed his nose with mine again. His warm breath tickled my skin as he whispered, "Immensely."

"Any chance you could stop enjoying it and start forgetting about it?"

He nipped at my bottom lip. "Probably not." He rolled onto me, his thick thigh falling between my legs, the other supporting the majority of his weight against the cushion. "But, if you happen to have the urge to take your pants off and ride me hard and fast before my girls wake up, I'd be willing to forget about it for about fifteen minutes or so."

"Shit," I groaned. Mainly because I knew he was going to make me actually explain before letting it go. But also because he moved his hand to my breast and used his thumb to circle my nipple.

"Your call, baby," he murmured.

So, yes. I was embarrassed about having been caught.

I was also newly married to an extremely sexy man who did the most incredible things to my nipples when I was on top. And, while I was a woman who was madly in love with the aforementioned sexy man and could pretty much have him whenever I wanted, I also had a day to spend chasing two divas in my future, which would surely end with me falling asleep before my head even hit the pillow. So I bit the bullet.

Shimmying out of my pajama pants, I huffed. "Fine. Yes. I made a fake profile. I found Kurt's high school yearbook one night. Made a few fake profiles of your old classmates. You accepted none of the friend requests. I waited another week. Made one for your high school English teacher, you accepted, and then boom, I was in dirty-little-secret heaven. Yes, I stalked you. Yes, I used to torture myself with pictures of your beautiful daughters. No, I swear it was not as creepy as it sounds." I swung a leg over his hips. "No, I shouldn't have lied to you about it. But knowing you were happy and seeing pictures of you and your family got me through a lot of rough times. So I won't apologize for doing it."

His smile suddenly faded, and his eyes filled with more love than I'd thought would ever be aimed at me. "I don't want you to apologize," he rasped. "Baby, I'm not upset. I'm fucking thrilled." He slipped his sweats down low enough to free his length, but his piercing eyes never left mine. "I don't want to even think about what would have happened if you hadn't made that account. That's how you knew where to find me." Using my hips, he guided me down and sank into me. "It's the reason we're here."

My head fell back and a gasp slipped from my throat.

His hand moved to my breast, and I circled my arms around his neck to balance.

Our hips rolled together like a tender assault.

"One phone call, Mir," he murmured against my neck, kissing his way up to my ear, "brought you back to me."

My heart skipped, warmth and love washing through me with a slow current.

I hadn't known it when I'd dialed his number, but that one phone call had changed my entire life.

Bigger and better than my wildest dreams.

A small smile pulled at my lips as I remembered the first time I'd kissed him on the back of his truck in the woods. I had already been irrevocably in love with him.

I'd known it then; I'd just been too scared to admit it.

I knew it now, and I was never letting it go.

Stilling on his lap, I cupped either side of his face and whispered the words I'd said to him all those years earlier. "In another life, we could be soul mates."

His hands at my breasts spasmed, and his back shot straight, his eyes darkening as the memory hit him.

And then, just before I kissed him, effectively losing myself in him for all of eternity, I breathed, "This is that life, baby."

Lark

Two years later…

A flash of heat lightning illuminated her smiling face while the hum of classic country poured through the speakers. My wife was on her side, facing me, one hand tucked under her head, the other resting on my cheek.

"My mom's still a bitch," she whispered.

"That she is," I agreed, placing my hand in the deep curve of her hip and giving her a squeeze.

The distant thunder rolled in with a peaceful rumble, echoing off the trees surrounding us.

Her thumb ever-so-gently stroked over my lips as she said, "I'm still glad we came. Thank you for bringing me here."

I smiled and kissed the pad of her finger. "Don't thank me. It's your family."

Another flash from the sky gave me a brief glance at her dark-brown eyes. She'd just turned thirty-nine, but in the back of that truck, we were kids again.

It was the wrong woods. Turned out our secret little hideaway was now the parking lot of a strip mall. But that hadn't stopped us. We'd driven around for over an hour, searching for a secluded spot where we could park and stare up at the sky. Judging by the private property signs I'd driven past on the way in, we were breaking more than a few laws. But it was worth it to have that moment back with her.

We didn't have a cooler full of beer this time. Nor did we have Kurt Benton dividing us.

But it was Mira and me.

The way it always should have been.

"Hey, baby," I murmured. "I've got an idea."

"Oh, yeah?" she replied, sliding her hand down to my neck. "Do tell."

I pushed up onto an elbow and smiled down at her silhouette. "What if we drive down to the beach?"

She giggled just like she had so many times as a girl in the back of my truck. "Tonight?"

"Yeah, tonight. Destin is only a few hours away, remember?"

"Are you serious?"

I leaned forward and kissed her forehead. "Completely."

"We're supposed to meet the Bentons at the house in the mountains in two days. That's a lot of driving."

After a lot of discussion and more than a little hesitation on my part, Mira had convinced me to have dinner with Terry and Max Benton. What the hell was I supposed to say to them after I'd essentially gotten their son locked away for life and then married his ex-wife? I knew they'd loved me like a son once, but that should have been enough to sever any kind of lingering feelings. Though I should have known better when it came to the Bentons.

It had been years since I'd seen them, but they'd welcomed me home with open arms. Well, that's not completely true. Terry had slapped me the second she'd opened the front door. She'd spent the next hour scolding me for having stayed gone for so many years. And then she'd scolded me for not having come back for Mira sooner. And then she'd scolded me for having Sophie and Amelia and not bringing them to see her. And then, when she had finally finished with all of that, she'd thrown her arms around my neck, burst into tears, and welcomed me back home.

We didn't see them much, but Terry and Mira talked on the phone a good bit. And, every month or so, they would come over to the house on a weekend when we had the girls and spoil them rotten with a toy store worth of gifts. They were good people. Regardless that their only child had turned out to be such worthless scum.

A few months earlier, we'd invited them to spend a few days with us in the little cabin we'd bought in the mountains of North Carolina. They'd eagerly agreed, and Mira had been bouncing off the walls about it ever since.

"Come on," I pleaded. "We can stop at the gas station, pick up some sandwiches and drinks, and drive through the night to the beach like old times."

Another flash of lightning revealed her lip curled in disgust. "Gas station sandwiches might not be your most effective selling point anymore." She paused. "Especially since I can't eat them anymore."

I arched an incredulous eyebrow. "Since when is a gas station ham and cheese too good for you, fancy pants?"

"Since I'm pregnant."

My entire body went rigid as a blast of adrenaline shot through me. "What? How?"

She laughed. "Well, when two people love each other..."

I slid my hand to cover her belly. "I know that, smartass. I mean... so soon?"

"We both know you don't get to time these things," she replied, stroking the dark hairs on the top of our son's head as he slept snuggled in a blanket between us.

Avery Christopher Lark had entered the world at a healthy eight pounds, two ounces only twelve weeks earlier. With chocolate-brown eyes and thick, dark lashes, he looked just like his mother—perfect in every way. I'd never seen Mira happier than when they'd laid that screaming, bloody newborn on her chest. And, as she'd aimed her tear-filled eyes, blazing with pure love, up at me, that happiness had radiated through me as well.

We'd worked hard for that little boy, and given that it had taken us well over twelve months to conceive him, we'd both resigned ourselves to the possibility that having another child might not be in our future.

But God had always had other plans for the two of us.

A loud laugh rumbled from my throat, excitement coursing through my veins. "Are you sure?"

She lifted our son to her chest with the practiced ease of a doting mother and then sat up. I followed her as she inched down until we were sitting side by side on the tailgate, our legs dangling over the edge.

"I haven't been to the doctor or anything, but the small fortune I spent on pregnancy tests this morning when I lied about going out to get breakfast confirmed it."

"Jesus," I breathed, slinging my arm around her shoulders and pulling her into my side, careful not to squish Avery.

"Not to count our chickens before they hatch or anything, but that would be two before I'm forty."

My throat was thick with emotion and my chest tightened, but I managed to sound quasi masculine when I said, "Did you just call my baby a chicken?"

Her shoulders shook with laughter, and she craned her head back to look up at me. "Thank you," she whispered.

I blinked. "For what?" No way I'd heard her correctly. Not after what she'd just given me. Another baby? I should have been the one thanking her.

"For loving me. For taking care of me. For understanding me." She kissed the top of Avery's head. "And, most of all, for giving me a beautiful life."

Jesus. This. Fucking. Woman.

After tucking a stray hair behind her ear, I moved my hand down to rest on our son's back. "You don't have to thank me. Loving you, taking care of you, understanding you. Those aren't favors I've done for you. I give you those things because that is what you deserve. I know it's still hard for you to see sometimes because you spent a lot of years withering. But from here on out"—I kissed her—"as long as we're together…we thrive."

THE END

ACKNOWLEDGMENTS

I'm going to keep this short and sweet…

Every book I write is the hardest thing I've ever done. From number one to number fifteen, (Holy wow, FIFTEEN!) it never gets easier. Before I even dream of hitting the magical publish button, I lean on a team of amazing woman to help me through the process. THRIVE wouldn't be the same without them.

To my husband for talking me off the ledge.

To A.S. Teague for talking me off the ledge.

To Mo Mabie, Meghan March, and Erin Noelle for talking me off the ledge. #JJL4Life

To Amie Knight, Miranda Arnold, Megan Cooke, Kelly Markham, and Lana Kart for talking me off the ledge.

(Anyone noticing a pattern here?)

To Lisa Paul for talking me off the ledge.

To Mickey Reed for talking me off the ledge.

To Julie Deaton for talking me off the ledge.

To Stacey Blake for talking me off the ledge.

To my kids…well, they just gave me a reason to drink more wine and yell, "STOP FIGHTING!" all the time. But I love them and couldn't have written this book without them.

MORE BOOKS BY
ALY MARTINEZ

Guardian Protection Series
Singe
Thrive

The Wrecked and Ruined Series
Changing Course
Stolen Course
Among The Echoes
Broken Course

On The Ropes Series
Fighting Silence
Fighting Shadows
Fighting Solitude

The Fall Up Series
The Fall Up
The Spiral Down

The Retrieval Duet
Retrieval
Transfer

The Darkest Sunrise Duet
The Darkest Sunrise
The Brightest Sunrise

ABOUT THE AUTHOR

Originally from Savannah, Georgia, *USA Today* bestselling author Aly Martinez now lives in South Carolina with her husband and four young children.

Never one to take herself too seriously, she enjoys cheap wine, mystery leggings, and baked feta. It should be known, however, that she hates pizza and ice cream, almost as much as writing her bio in the third person.

She passes what little free time she has reading anything and everything she can get her hands on, preferably with a super-sized tumbler of wine by her side.

Stay Connected

Facebook: AuthorAlyMartinez

Twitter @ AlyMartinezAuth

Goodreads: AlyMartinez

www.alymartinez.com

www.bookbub.com/authors/aly-martinez

www.facebook.com/groups/TheWinery

67336657R00182

Made in the USA
San Bernardino, CA
21 January 2018